NEW YORK TIMES BEST

JANELLE TAYLOR

CAN FORBIDDEN LOVE SURVIVE BETRAYAL?

MOONDUST SERIES ~ BOOK FOUR

MOONBEAMS
AND
MAGIC

Originally published by PINNACLE BOOKS, a division of

Kensington Publishing Corp.
850 Third Avenue
New York, NY 10022

First Printing: October, 1995

ISBN: 9781092639330

GGP

MOONBEAMS
AND
MAGIC

Moondust Series – Book Four

JANELLE TAYLOR

GGP
GEORGIA GIRL PRESS

Table of Contents

SHE WAS AS INTOXICATING AS A DRUG ...

Yana was half relieved and half disappointed that the handsome space pirate was departing without attempting to seduce her. She walked him to the door, but he turned before he pressed the open button.

Dagan gazed into her rich blue eyes and scanned her faint blue skin and blond hair with the same blue tinge. "You're a beautiful and desirable woman, Yana; I hope we'll see a lot of each other before you're gone."

"That will please me," she responded. But that was not totally true. Not in her shapeshifted form as Asisan Yana. And not as the wanted criminal Starla Vedris, her alleged identity. She craved him as Bree-Kayah Saar. That wasn't possible as long as she was on a crucial Elite Squad mission for the UFG, and the infamous Dagan Latu was one of her targets. Be he bad to the core or half-good, the virile Kalfan was out of her reach as anything more than a teammate. At least she had her android Cypher and a cloaked ship nearby...

To my Family, Friends, and Fans who have supported and encouraged me when writing the original series long ago and while revising and reediting these four new editions recently. I want to give a special thanks to Kat Eickhoff (AKA super talented author Ashley Fontainne) for the extraordinary new covers and interior designs for the print, ebook, and audio versions.

Chapter One

"Moig, I have a big problem down here," Starla told her teammate on the transporter's upper deck via a wrist communicator. Winded from a struggle with a tall and muscular man, she explained between gasps for air, "There was an intruder in the last bay. He's human. I subdued him, so he's still stoked from his fierce glare. Do I leave him unconscious or take him with us?"

"No, Vedris, kill him!"

To prevent a surprise attack, Starla remained on alert at a safe distance, a laser weapon aimed at the center of the auslander's broad chest. She was dismayed by her companion's swift and deadly response, as they tried to avoid trouble during their criminal raids on other spaceships. Her heart pounded in dread and from physical exertions, though she kept her expression impassive. She gazed at the man on his knees, his palms resting on sleek thighs and still breathing hard. A look of astonishment in his dark-blue eyes at being bested in a fight by a female who now had him groveling before her changed to one of anger as he overheard the icy extermination order. The woman known as Starla Vedris lifted her arm and spoke into her communication device. "Moig, did you say, 'kill him'?"

"Yes, we can't leave an open mouth to speak into the wrong ears about us. He's seen your face and knows our names, so get rid of him. We were told one android would be aboard this vessel, but our talker was wrong. Somebody's going to catch *Karlee* for this mistake."

"We shouldn't make this crucial decision on our own. You know the penalty for life-taking during a raid: disintegration in an annihilator unit."

"Do it, Vedris, or I'll come down there to send him into oblivion myself! If I have to do your job for you, that'll prove you aren't as brave and loyal as our leader thinks. You'll be out of Tochar's hire in a blink. Blast him to *Karlee* or he could be the death of us later. Don't forget, I'm in charge. Zap him, Vedris, now!"

Starla took a deep breath and scowled. "Don't zone out, Moig. I'll get rid of him, but this is the only time I'm taking such an order from anybody. I didn't agree to have life-taking charges added to my I-GAF record, which is already too long and grim for comfort."

"It's for self-defense to save all of our skins!"

"I said I will do it. Vedris out," she told Moig, ending their talk. She said to her android, who was aboard her ship nearby, "Cypher-T, I'm fine. Thanks for the warning and keep alert for more trouble. No reply needed."

The man stared at the armed and beautiful space pirate who was clad in a snug bronze jumpsuit that covered a shapely figure from slender neck to small wrists and blackbooted feet. Long and lustrous brown tresses tumbled over her shoulders in thick waves. Green eyes examined him with what appeared to be a mixture of professional and personal interest. Her tawny complexion was flawless and glowed with good health. Her features were perfect, exquisite, arousing even now in this vexing situation. Her stance and posture exhibited confidence, and implied a dash of arrogance. The way she held her weapon told him she knew how to use it. She had proven she was skilled in hand-to-hand combat. He was amazed—under those grim circumstances and following an embarrassing defeat—that he noticed so much about her, but his perceptions came easily and from an instinct borne of necessity. Was she a hazard, even if her lovely features were set in resignation of obedience? Yes, he decided, but he had gotten out of

2

worse predicaments, so he watched for an opening. Why was she indesisive?

Starla knew if she refused to kill him, Moig would do so without remorse, and she would be ejected from Tochar's nefarious band. She realized there was only one thing she could do to protect herself and her plans. She gave a loud sigh and shrugged. "Sorry, handsome, but you're in the wrong place at the wrong time. You've made your last error in this life phase."

As he started to rise and argue, Starla warned, "Don't be reckless; this weapon isn't set on *Stun*. I can put you down forever before you get to your feet, much less reach me. You may be the most irresistible and best-looking specimen I've ever seen, but I still have my wits and orders. You won't suffer."

"You don't want to do this, Vedris. If you obey him, you'll be in deep trouble. Killing me isn't worth a visit to a disintegration unit or permanent habitation on a penal colony on some barren planetoid. That's no place for a beautiful woman. If you'll spare my life, I'll—"

"Silence!" she ordered as he fingered his mussed black hair. *Don't let him distract or sway you.* "To fail my leader offers more of a threat than your words coming true. If I betray him, there will be no place for me to hide in the entire Microcosm. Too bad, handsome; you would've made a valuable captive on the slave market if I had time to be troubled with you. With your looks and spirit, I bet you'd be an excellent breeder, highly skilled on a *sleeper.*" Time was limited, but her plan was made. Starla's finger pressed a button on her weapon to fire a beam into his broad chest before the grinning male could respond. A buzzing sound filled the area and a dazzling shaft of light illuminated it. The stranger fell backward and didn't move again.

She lifted her left arm and said, "It's done, Moig. Let's get this cargo loaded and blast off before any parsec jumpers show their unwanted faces. I'm not in a mood to challenge an *I-GAFer.*" The last thing she needed was to be confronted by anyone from the Inter-Galactic Alliance Force. Each of those space rangers was extremely hazardous, and facing more than one meant certain capture or death to *villites.* She knew that *I-GAF*ers—often called "parsec jumpers"—were almost a law unto themselves, elite agents who roamed the united federation of five galaxies-the *UFG*-investigating and solving multijurisdictional crimes. She didn't want to be thrust into conflict with men of such awesome power and authority; that would ruin or imperil everything she had worked for since leaving her world of Maffei. Thankfully, the Free-Zone was beyond *I-GAF and UFG* reach so its members couldn't interfere with the completion of her crucial goal—if she could make it back there alive. Starla frowned, as the sly auslander's intrusion struck her as being a bad omen.

"Do you need any help down there?" Moig asked.

"I'll be up in *a preon;* I'm finished. Vedris out." She used her alleged last name as was Moig's custom.

Starla switched off the communication link to Moig to finish her task in a rush, but the one with Cypher—her android—always remained open. She took a quick last look at the attractive male. She grabbed a tan sack of thin material, dumped its contents, and covered his face before giving him a necessary injection from a phial in her belt holder. She gathered the items she had been sent after and headed for the passageway.

Before she reached the exit, the door swished open and Moig entered the vessel's smallest compartment. "Why did you come down?" Starla asked. "I said I was on my way up. I took care of the problem, and I have the sunbursts. We need to shove off; we've taken too long. Even if *I-GAF*ers aren't in this quadrant, *Sekis* might be; this is Kalfan space."

"This won't delay us much, and your android will warn us if any space rangers appear on his sensors." Moig walked past his vexed companion to where the male was lying as he must have fallen, almost on his stomach. He noticed the sack on the man's head and assumed she hadn't wanted to look her victim in the eye while slaying him. Wisely, he did not tease her about that action. Moig squatted and placed several fingers on the man's jugular vein, waited a few moments, then pressed his ear to the center of the man's back. He felt no pulse and heard no heartbeat and was pleased.

"Your actions imply you don't trust me," Starla accused in a chilly tone.

Moig looked at the brown-haired beauty with the annoyed gleam in her green eyes and he grinned. "Just being sure you didn't make a mistake that can endanger us later. You're tougher and stronger than I imagined. Good work, Vedris. Tochar will be pleased with your obedience and with these weapons. We're in for a nice cut of this deal. Let's finish loading our haul and blast off. I'm ready to spend a lot of time at the drinker."

The sooner we get out of this sector, the better, you reality-impaired Icarian! "Let's do it."

As the last crate of weapons was passed through the *jerri* hatch to Starla's ship and the two pirates went aboard, Moig asked, "Why are you so stoked? Your jaw is clenched and your eyes are stormy."

The woman stood after securing the hatch and looked at the man with small dark eyes and a short golden beard, as all Icarians had various shades of blond hair and black eyes. "Blast it all, Moig! I'm tired of being tested! Surely by now, you and Tochar and the others

5

know I can be trusted without me having to prove it again and again. I'm beginning to think I shouldn't close my eyes or turn my back if I ever make a mistake. That puts me on edge, and distraction in dangerous."

"We trust you, Vedris, or you wouldn't be working with us and for Tochar."

"If that's true, why am I never told where we're heading or when we'll depart until the last *preon?* Our destination is kept secret until we take off, and so is our target until after we reach its location. Since we use my ship part of the time, I need those facts to make certain I have enough energy for my warp drive and enough supplies for the trek. I need to plan the best and easiest way to reach our destination, and plot escape paths in case of trouble. If I'm trusted, why the secrecy?"

The burly man shrugged. "Tochar don't trust nobody with such facts except me, Auken, and Sach. That way, there's no problem with loose lips."

Starla knew the names of Tochar's top hirelings and friends, Icarians like himself. "I've never suffered from that condition, by accident or intention. I'm loyal to whoever hires me. My record speaks for itself, and Tochar checked me out in every way, including the use of truth serum."

"Be patient, Vedris, and you'll eventually enter the upper ranks with us. Now, let's blast off. I won't relax until we're on the other side of that stargate, out of this parsec, and back in Tochara."

"Cypher-T knows to get us under way as soon as the *jerri* hatch is sealed. He's already disengaged our connection, cloaked the *Liska,* and we're leaving this vector before another ship can reach it. Did you set the transporter's auto-pilot for the opposite direction?"

"Yes," Moig confirmed, "but I don't want to be near that vessel when it's sighted, boarded, and checked, and that body is found. I wonder who he was?"

"Since he was hiding below, probably a free-rider on the run. I didn't ask him any questions and he didn't volunteer any information."

"You don't think he was a *Seki* or cargo protector or ranger, do you?"

"No, his hand didn't bear any of those authority symbols and he wasn't in a uniform, just an ordinary jumpsuit. He didn't seem to be there to trap any raiders. He wasn't even armed. I doubt he realized he was traveling on a ship transporting weapons or he would have broken into one of those crates earlier and been able to defend himself against me."

"That's *crazimous* after being aboard so long."

"Not if he was on the run," Starla explained. "Any tampering with those crates would have exposed him to the android pilot/guard when it patrolled the ship."

Moig continued to dissect the bug. "He could have disabled the robot and got his hands on a weapon."

"Then, who would have piloted the vessel to its next port? If he lacked the skill to take over, he would have drifted in space until he died or the ship was tracked and boarded and he was captured." She saw Moig shrug and frown, for not reasoning out those points himself. The crud could be witless at times.

"How did you overpower a big, strong male?"

Since her ship was cloaked and was en route to their base, they both relaxed; and in the process, she might learn something valuable. "Since the transporter is piloted by an android, there probably isn't any food or drink aboard, so he must have been weakened from a lack of them. Like most men, he no doubt assumed a female wasn't a serious threat or any real competition in

7

a hand-to-hand fight. I tricked him and, as you noticed, I won."

Moig chuckled and stroked his fuzzy beard. "Perhaps Tochar should keep a sharp eye and ear on you. With your skills and intelligence, you could replace him as our leader if you had a mind to challenge him."

"I have no interest in becoming a leader. Serving Tochar suits me just fine. He doesn't have to worry about a challenge from me, as if a takeover were possible by anyone."

"That's good, Vedris, because Auken and Sach would slay anybody who harmed him."

"Do *you* envy or covet Tochar's rank?"

"No, he's my friend and he pays us all well."

"True. I'm tense and sweaty after my struggle with that intruder. I'm going to refresh myself, then I'll join you and Cypher-T on the bridge." She did not have to worry about Moig following her to her quarters and trying to seduce her. Although she perceived his lust for her, the alien lacked the courage to do anything to displease Tochar or to provoke his leader's wrath. She detested the man and his presence on her ship, her home when away from her galaxy, but she had to pretend to like and accept him.

"You talk to and about your android as if he's alive," Moig teased.

"To me, he is. He's my best friend, my family. We've been together for *yings.* He's saved my life and gotten me out of danger countless times."

"Is that why you keep communications open when we use your ship, so he can warn and protect you?"

"Yes, and that's why I'm sometimes nervous when we're using Auken's ship and Cypher-T isn't around to guard me or alert me to danger. I don't understand why we can't use my ship during every raid. It's faster, better equipped, and my cloaking device is newer. Some forces have the capability of penetrating Auken's old style, so we could be detected and attacked."

"Auken won't raid using any ship except his. If you're worried about our safety, loan him your cloaking unit until they learn how to attach a *Destructoid* to his ship like Tochar uses to protect Tochara. Of course, after his *Adika* is armed with one of those new beamers, we can attack and destroy any vessel and location; they'll be helpless against us."

Moig had spoken a horrifying fact she and her superiors realized all too well, as the *villites* had stolen the only three *Destructoids* in existence, weapons with formidable capabilities and near-impossible to replace. "Auken's ship lacks the power to operate and the means to install my type of cloaker. We've been fortunate to come and go undetected, Moig, but our luck could jettison any *preon* with galactic leaders weary of our costly raids, especially the Kalfans and Serians. I don't even want to imagine what would happen to us if *Sekis* or *I-GAF*ers got their eager hands on us."

"Tochar agrees to Auken's wishes, so we have to obey their orders. Don't worry, Vedris," Moig soothed, "we won't get caught; Tochar knows many secrets."

There must be a special reason for using Auken's ship when we raid for moonbeams, our most dangerous and profitable treks. If not, we'd use Liska. I need that answer fast. "I know, but if the *Adika*'s cloak is penetrated, we'll be tracked to Noy; and Tochar tries to appear innocent of our daring raids." *The arrogant evil monster even named his settlement after himself!*

"Wouldn't matter none if we're tracked; Noy's in the Free-Zone. It's closer to Thracian and Ceyxan galaxies than to the Federation. The *UFG*'s *I-GAF*ers and Kalfan rangers don't have any authority beyond the boundary.

Besides, nobody can invade Tochara, not with our defense system."

Starla knew that the Thracian—of which Icaria was a planet—and the Ceyxan galaxies had tolerated the *villite* strongholds on Noy and several other small planets in the Free-Zone because the pirates provided them with things they wanted and because the *villites* wisely did not operate in their sectors. Yet, if those empires changed their minds, the stronghold of Tochara was impregnable, even by starships. But *I-GAF* teams from the United Federation of Galaxies—made up of Maffei, Seri, Kalfa, Androas, and Pyropea—could decide to challenge the *nefariants* who preyed on their solar systems. A bold course of action could not be undertaken, however, until matching weapons were built, which could not happen until more large white crystals of the same size and power were found either in Seri or Kalfa. "For now, we seem to be safe, but who can say what the future holds?"

"Tochar's too smart to endanger himself, his stronghold, and men." Moig's strong tone reflected his confidence and admiration in the leader.

Not his hirelings, you brain-lacking yema; he sends us into great peril on every raid! He can replace us in a deega! "That's why I hired on with him: he's the most powerful leader beyond the *UFG* boundary."

Four days later as Starla and Moig sat chatting while eating a meal, she received a message from her android on the bridge. "What is it, Cypher-T?"

"We are approaching Stargate Portal. We will enter Free-Zone in twenty *preons.* No interceptor registers on rear sensors. There are no instrument malfunctions. There are no obstacles in forward view."

"That's good news, Cypher-T; continue on course. We'll join you soon." Starla looked at her repulsive companion. "Well, Moig, we'll reach Noy in three *deegas* and complete another successful trek. Tochar should be pleased with us." *Three more days with him.*

Starla remained quiet and alert as she listened to Moig's report to their leader, an attractive male with nape-length blond hair and piercing black eyes. Tochar was four *hapaxs*--what would be a little more than an *inch* in her mother's language--taller than Starla's own height of sixty-nine *hapaxs.* His lean, sleek body and commanding aura implied virility and power, but an evil and avaricious air exuded the alien male. She knew it was dangerous to cross or challenge him, as some men had learned the hard way before their painful deaths, but she was willing to take that risk in order to defeat him. With his band of thirty Enforcers, he ruled and controlled this settlement. It was one of several on the planet, but none other had his impenetrable defense system. He existed in luxury in a large and magnificent abode on the side of a low mountain; yet, despite his power and wealth, he could not live or travel where he willed because of his past criminal activities. He was forced to habitate in the Free-Zone, a man who sat atop the worst pile of *villite* debris in the Universe. Starla had a healthy fear of him, but she would work for him until she achieved her goal for coming to Tochara and hiring on to his nefarious band.

Tochar smiled and said, "A superior job as usual, Starla. You continue to impress and please me. I was smart to take a chance on you."

11

Starla forced a smile in return. "Thank you, Tochar, but I would like to settle one matter now: no more killing unless our lives are in jeopardy."

"Leaving a witness behind does place us in jeopardy, Starla. You and Moig acted wisely to eliminate any possible threat to us. As a reward for your extra task, please select any four weapons you desire from those you delivered to me. This," he said, as he handed her payment for her job, "should be an ample cut for your services this time."

Starla accepted the bag of *crozes* and thanked him again. It wasn't necessary to count or examine the gems, as they were spendable anywhere she traveled. "You are most generous, Tochar, and I appreciate your faith in me. If that's all for now, I'll take my leave and get needed rest."

"I will summon you again when your services are required. It will be soon, Starla. At that time, your cut will be even larger."

"I stay ready to comply." Starla nodded farewell and, after selecting the four weapons she wanted from several open crates nearby, departed.

She stepped from the *trans-to* at the base of the high ridge and headed toward the grid where her shuttlecraft had landed—a *ten-preon* walk away—leaving a landrover for Moig's use for transportation into the settlement. En route, Starla scanned the area below her still-elevated position where Tochara stretched out for a long distance in the canyon.

Since her arrival, she had learned that Noy was a world of semi-desert to arid desert terrain in various shades of red. Nature had sculpted many rocks, cliffs, ridges, and knobs into rugged and unusual formations. The oppressive red cloak was rent only by an occasional splotch of light or dark gray rock, so hard it rarely crumbled enough to add its shade to the fiery-colored soil whose dust was a nuisance. According to the weather or the time of *deega,* even the sky was a pale to vivid red. In every direction, mountain ranges—whose odd configurations seemed to have ruptured the ground almost violently during an upheaval eons ago— provided boundary markers. Thick-walled structures with formidable defense weapons sat on two flat-topped bluffs. Starla glanced at those sites with a feeling of hopelessness before returning her thoughts to a study of the locale.

Due to a lack of fertile soil in this wilderness, some food plants and fruit bushes were grown in containers inside enclosed domes and were watered by a crude system of pipes and pumps from sources owned and controlled by Tochar. However, the majority of supplies was imported, usually after being stolen by bands of *nefariants* who either lived or traded there, which created a steady flux of space traffic. Caves found inside three ridges possessed springs and pools of fresh water; they were guarded and their valuable resources dispensed by Tochar's thirty Enforcers, as were the two defense sites. Though rains were infrequent, when a deluge came, it sent torrents of water gushing down the upheavals and washes, and was absorbed by dried mudflats and hardy red plants.

Tochara was one of many colonies on the secluded planet and, from what she had been told, was the best and safest place in the notorious Free-Zone; it was a vivid contrast to the mutant-roaming wastelands and other crude villages and harsh landscape where even the plants and animals were hazardous. Though noisy, the area was unlike the profound and eerie silence beyond it where only the wind was heard.

The story—she had learned--was that Tochar had arrived with his large band of *villites* two *yings* ago and conquered the lesser armed and unskilled inhabitants who had created the colony after fleeing oppression in an alien world. The original occupants who were not slain were sold into slavery on other planets which still allowed the barbaric practice.

Starla was glad there were no children here, as birth control with *Liex* was an easy task and these were not family people. There were few pets and none were permitted to roam free. Abode builders were wealthy because materials were imported and expensive. Still, in many areas where the unkempt and less successful raiders dwelled, it was smelly and dirty and cluttered. They lived in huts and shacks made of discarded scrap materials such as metal and wood. Lacking advanced technology, fuel for cooking sent gray and pungent smoke drifting upward where it was devoured quickly by a hungry red atmosphere, as were the fumes from generator-created electricity from stolen fuel.

Most of the inhabitants were rough and lawless men— dregs of the Universe, people from many planets and galaxies, pirates, smugglers, traitors, adventurers, *bijonis,* and those males and females who earned their subsistence by satisfying the *villites*'s carnal and servile needs. Most clustered and worked in groups for defense and profit during raiding treks, though all were ruled and levied by Tochar and kept regulated by his mighty band of Enforcers. The inhabitants' goals appeared to be eating, drinking, partaking in risky deeds, fulfilling sexual desires, and having a safe haven. All facets of life and the inhabitants were primitive and coarse when compared to the people and places Starla loved and missed. An odd camaraderie flourished among them—a respect, affection, and loyalty to each other, and unflinchingly to their leader. That same type of bonding was true for carnivorous desert mutants—*Skalds*—and for colony fringe scavengers. It was fortunate for all UFG aliens that aural language translators were implanted in everyone's ear canals at birth. Those devices converted any language into their own, except for slang and words that existed in only their world. An hour, day, week, month, year, inch, mile, etc. did not change since those measurements were not the same on all planets. Also, mouths did not move in unison when words were vastly different. She was using an intergalactic language to prevent exposing her Maffei origin.

While waiting for the shuttle door to open and the steps to extend, she glanced at Tochar's abode, which overlooked the leader's domain. The rectangular, bilevel structure had been built on a wide rock shelf and nestled against a lofty peak high off the ground for defense and for observing his stronghold. Most of its many chambers had views of three directions through floor-to-ceiling *transascreens* made from a material visually impenetrable from the exterior, even when the interior was illuminated at night. A generator-operated *trans-to* carried the owner and his visitors to and from the remarkable location.

As she loaded the weapons and closed the door, Starla recalled other things she had learned. One alien slave and several robots tended to Tochar's dwelling and needs. A well-endowed and sultry creature named Palesa sated his carnal cravings. A forceful and wicked alien from the planet of Icaria in the Thracian Empire, Tochar fed his lusts on riches and power, and within Palesa's sensuous body. He seemed to care nothing for politics elsewhere or conquest of any planet, but Starla feared that *deega* would come. His sole deprivation lay in being unable to enjoy freedom and safety anywhere he

15

yearned to travel, at least until he obtained the capability of mounting a moonbeam laser weapon on his ship. She knew from the *fiendal's* record and from her observations that Tochar Glaic was clever, careful, greedy, and dangerous. He stayed in Tochara—beyond any galaxy's boundary and authority and attack ability—while his small band of *spacekis* foraged the nearest sectors for goods he sold at high prices. He remained safe—his life and possessions protected—and seemingly innocent of those raids.

Discovering Tochar was indeed her target had been a quick and simple task. Uncovering his distant partners and capturing him or luring him away and into a trap would be difficult but heady challenges.

Starla prepared the shuttle for lift-off to return to *Liska*. She hated Tochara and those who lived there. She could hardly wait to be gone. At least she had her ship—clean, safe, comfortable. She couldn't imagine having to quarter herself in the crude settlement and was relieved the head *fiendal* had not insisted she do so.

She landed the shuttle in the docking bay and joined her companion on the ship's bridge. She ordered a drink from a *servo* unit and sat near the control panel. She looked at Cypher and took a deep breath.

"You are tired and your spirits are low, Bree-Kayah," the android noted, having been programmed to communicate as a person. "Explain."

"After spending three *malees* under Tochar's probing gaze, I know he's responsible for the pirating of moonbeams we were sent to investigate. Yet I still don't know how he obtains facts about their transport schedules and routes. Having hirelings or partners in Seri and Kalfa is the only way he can know when and where to strike at those secret cargoes. Only men in power have access to those facts and to untraceable communications;

yet, no one in either of those locations has fallen under suspicion or been caught sending word to him. Until I earn these *villites'* complete trust and acceptance and gather those facts, we can't finish our mission and leave."

The young woman almost leapt to her feet to pace the deck, an unusual action for her, and one the android grasped and evaluated.

"This assignment is crucial, Cypher; moonbeams are too powerful to fall into enemy hands. Their many uses in weapons, medicine, and defense are awesome. Researchers find more uses for them during every *malee* that passes. That is why Thracians and Ceyxans and other galaxies will pay or do anything to get their hands on as many as possible. Once those crystals' full potential is known and put to use by those who aren't in the *UFG,* the balance of power between the galaxies will be destroyed. Worlds will be threatened by conquest or destruction, or subjected to brutal raids. We can't fail Maffei or our allies." She took a calming breath. "At least Tochar doesn't suspect a female agent is working against him. If he's on the alert for a spy, he shouldn't even glance in my direction. Correct?"

The android observed, recorded, and analyzed her words and mood. "He trusts you because you passed his truth serum test. He does not realize you are immune to it. All Elite Squad members have been rendered immune to it. The false identity and record you were given cannot be disproven. He believes you are a rough and tough loner who seeks wealth, adventure, and survival, and have committed many daring and illegal deeds to obtain them. Bree-Kayah Saar of Maffei is unknown to him, to those in Kalfa, and to all in Seri except their supreme ruler. That is why *Raz* Yakir and your Supreme Commander selected you for this mission. It is why Yakir gave you that special gift to use on them."

17

"This is the first time we have been loaned to a neighboring galaxy—a United Federation member—to carry out a mission, one which will also threaten our galaxy and planets if we fail."

Starla went over the gathered facts with Cypher. It was vital to their success and safety that only a few people knew of her assignment and location: Yakir, the Serian ruler; her superior in the Elite Squad; her family—the Saars—in Maffei; and her unique android. As far as everyone else was aware, Bree-Kayah Saar was on extended leave to rest following a series of difficult and exhausting missions.

"Do not forget: you infiltrated Tochar's band and earned their trust with skill and speed. If that is an inaccurate conclusion, Tochar would not allow you to go on raids on your ship and with only one teammate."

"But he doesn't permit me to use my ship to go after moonbeams, and secrets of those treks are withheld from me until the last *preon.* Isn't that suspicious, proof he doesn't fully believe me?"

"Tochar takes those actions because he is careful. The possibility of him learning the truth about you is minuscule. If he does, we have the means to dupe him and escape. I am your guardian. I monitor you at all times; you are safe from peril. Even if I were captured, he cannot extract information from me; my program is inaccessible to everyone except you."

"You've snatched me out of danger many times, Cypher, but no plan is totally foolproof and no person is totally unreachable by evil forces. If I'm exposed and his reaction time is swifter than ours, he could signal his attack stations to blast my shuttle or our ship into oblivion before I could reach it, cloak the *Liska,* vanish from their sensors, and flee."

"Do not fear, Bree-Kayah, I will not fail you or the Federation."

"I know, my friend. I'm fortunate to have you."

As she sipped a cool drink, Starla thought how lucky she was to have this particular android. It was the most advanced model available anywhere, one with a male appearance both in facial features and body build. His skin and visage revealed realistic human colorings, including his synthetic silver hair. The only giveaways he was non-human were his expressionless grey eyes and lack of sexual organs beneath his blue jumpsuit. His seventy-six *hapax* frame was strong and agile, made of an indestructible metal, thus far, until a moonbeam was discovered that could cut through known metals and materials. She did not want to imagine any *villite* slicing him apart to reach his chips and circuits, as that would initiate a self-destruct sequence and he would be lost to her. She did not want to think about an existence without him. She would do almost anything to protect him from harm, would kill to save him from evil, and Cypher was cognizant of that fact.

She was glad he had the capability to analyze any situation and to make decisions on his own when necessary. His flesh-colored face and silver-grey eyes revealed no presence of feelings, but he had been given an emotions chip to help him understand her and other humans. With it, he could be amusing and even vexing at times, as if he possessed a real personality. She loved, respected, and trusted him as if he were human. When others were present, she called him "Cypher-T" to alert the android to a caution/duplicity mode. As part of a test program, the technologically advanced unit had become her partner during her second mission for the undercover Elite Squad of the Maffei Galaxy. The pairing had worked so well that they had been left as a team. If he had been with her during her first assignment, she thought, perhaps Antarus would be alive and perhaps they would be lovers; and that auslander wouldn't have been so tempting, so unforgettable. *Don't think about him; he's gone forever.*

Starla looked at Cypher, sighed, and asked, "What if something goes wrong?"

"Relax, Bree-Kayah; you will succeed in your duty and mission. I will prevent failure and your destruction. It is unlike you to experience such doubts."

"I know, but this time it's different because so much is at risk, more than my life and the lives of those of my world. If only Tochar didn't have those incredible weapons on two ridges and atop his dwelling, Serian and Kalfan forces could attack and obliterate him. He is lucky his first crystal raid included them. Powered by such large white moonbeams, they can disable a fleet of starships, even with their deflective shields engaged. Those crystals don't require any maintenance or other driving force and will last for *yings.* They can fire in any direction by fast manual movement. He also has smaller laser guns on all four sides aimed landward to thwart any ground attack. When I witnessed their capabilities, I was astounded and frightened. Those structures are impregnable, Cypher, so there's no way we can reach and disable the *Destructoids.* Tochar doesn't allow anyone inside those sites except his Enforcer guards and his closest friends. The same is true for the smaller version atop his dwelling."

A weary Starla flopped down in a comfy seat and continued talking to the android. "I doubt I would be part of his band if his other backup team hadn't been terminated during that first raid and he needed to form a new one. Auken, Sach, and Moig were the only ones to escape that fierce battle, but—fortunately for Tochar and horrible for our side—the weapons and crystals were on Auken's ship."

"You have a powerful and secret weapon to aid you," Cypher reminded. "Yakir was intelligent to select you and to supply you with it."

"It feels strange when I become another woman in looks and voice, but it's also exciting."

"It is good shapeshifting does not cause pain."

"What's also good is that Yakir allowed me to have that Serian secret to use, as few know of its existence. Perhaps as Yana I can learn things Starla Vedris can't. We make a good team, Cypher; I'm glad you're with me. My world and family are so far away and no contact with them is possible. They must be worried about me, but they realize I had to come. I would be more afraid if I were here alone and doing all the work myself."

Cypher could not smile, but his emotions chip sent a good sensation through his circuits, one his unique program understood and appreciated. "Yes, Bree-Kayah Saar, we are a good team."

"I learned on the last crystal raid that no matter what precautions the Serians and Kalfans take, Tochar learns their plans. Our band's raids are connected in some crucial way with always having to use Auken's ship. Every time you cloak and follow us, nothing shows up on our sensors. We must look harder and closer, my friend, a clue is there somewhere."

"We will find it as you cozen them. Tochar is clever, but we are smarter."

Starla laughed and teased, "Is that conceit and boasting I hear?"

"I speak the truth as my program insists."

"Did I act wisely during that last raid with Moig? I was ordered to do whatever was necessary to obtain victory, but don't I have limits in some areas? What if that action returns to trouble me?"

Cypher scanned that incident file in his advanced system. "You did as you must, Bree-Kayah. Delete it from your memory cells."

"I lack an erase switch or command. He shouldn't have been aboard. I don't know who he was or why he was there. If you hadn't warned me and I hadn't dealt with him, Moig would have slain him, and Tochar would have kicked me out of his special unit."

"You must not do anything to expose your identity or endanger yourself; disobedience will provoke both." Cypher probed a matter he needed to understand. "Why did your vital signs register strange signals when you met and dealt with the intruder?"

Starla gazed at him. "What do you mean?"

"Your heart and pulse rates were fast and erratic. Body temperature fluctuated. Your chemical balance and brain wave pattern altered. Your muscles quivered. I have not picked up that mixture of signals before, and the sensors did not malfunction. Explain."

"I don't know what happened to me in that storage bay. He took me by surprise. We fought quite a battle. He underestimated me because I'm a woman and didn't fight his best. He was a magnificent specimen, Cypher, and he affected me in a strange manner. There was something about him that made me warm all over."

"It is physical attraction, the desire to mate."

Starla envisioned the handsome male with black hair and dark blue eyes and knew Cypher's conclusion was correct. She jested, "Don't be ridiculous. He was a stranger, a peril. I handled him in the only way open to me, with one of my little magic phials."

"I analyzed your reactions; my conclusions and program are accurate. You always speak the truth to me, Bree-Kayah; why is this time different?"

"Guilty of deceit, my friend, and I'm sorry. I just didn't want to confess my foolishness and don't want your deduction to be true. I admit he was handsome and virile and arousing, but..." *Stars afire. Just thinking and talking about him are stimulating. Careful, Bree.*

"Continue."

"I will never mate with an appealing stranger, and certainly not with a *villite.* Since he was hiding on that vessel, he must be a criminal on the run. Be sure to notify the Kalfans of his presence aboard so he can be taken prisoner by their *Sekis.* Under the circumstances, there was no way I could apprehend him, but he's captive aboard that transporter. He's gone, so I'm safe from temptation. Whatever it was that assailed me, let's drop the subject."

"Do you not want to understand or experience such emotions and pleasures? Are they not normal biological functions for your species?"

"Yes, but I haven't felt such emotions since that incident with Antarus before his death. Even then, my heart and will were barely involved since I was hurt and delirious," Starla answered, aware Cypher would grasp the reference to her first sexual experience, since he knew everything about her. She had no secrets from the trusted android; it was necessary for him to know how she would react under all circumstances. She also spent most of her time with him during missions, so many long and candid talks had taken place over the *yings.* "He made me uneasy, Cypher, and I don't like control and focus losses. I need only to think about Tochar and my mission. The sooner we finish it, the sooner we can go home. I miss my family and friends, and I hate this awful place and these horrible people. After I bathe and eat, we'll play a game of *resi* before I retire. You're in charge of the ship now. See you later."

Four days had passed when Starla was summoned to Tochar's dwelling. She entered his oblong work chamber in the elevated structure and approached him. She noticed someone was with him, his back to her. Black hair and his splendid physique told her it wasn't Moig, Auken, or Sach.

Tochar stood, smiled, and motioned her forward. "There is someone I want you to meet, Starla. Dagan Latu, this is Starla Vedris, one of my best pilots and raiders, and also a beautiful and fearless woman."

The male stood, then turned toward her. Starla's heart skipped several beats before pounding rapidly. She was relieved she did not gasp, flush, or pale as she faced the man Moig had ordered her to kill eleven *deegas* ago. She knew Cypher must be concerned over her erratic vital signs—reactions carried to him via her wrist device which always kept her in contact with him. Surely the android was deciding if her sudden distress indicated she was in danger and he should teleport her to safety, though she had not signaled him to do so.

Questions filled her mind in a rush: Who was he? How had he gotten there? Had she been exposed and walked into a trap? Was he one of Tochar's men, one she hadn't met until now? Had he been aboard the ship to test her loyalty and reflexes? No, she reasoned, or he would be dead if she had carried out Moig's order. Somehow the cunning stranger had escaped and would soon place her and her mission in jeopardy.

Well, Bree-Kayah Saar, how are you going to escape this threatening predicament?

24

Chapter Two

Starla was trained to think and react quickly to unexpected and hazardous circumstances. She warned herself not to panic and flee, as that would terminate her crucial mission and become her first failure during an assignment. She remained alert and prepared to signal Cypher to rescue her if the situation worsened. She tried to calm herself so the android would realize she had matters under control. Since the man had not spoken, Cypher had no clue as to why she was unsettled. No doubt the android was running his name through their computer bank at this moment, which would reveal Dagan's identity but not the reason behind her distress. The instant he spoke, however, Cypher would recognize his voice pattern and understand.

Even if he's told Tochar about the transporter incident, stay and bluff your way out. Starla moved forward and said, "It's a pleasure to meet any friend of Tochar's." She extended her hand and they clasped wrists in the usual manner of greeting. The stranger's grasp seemed too snug and lasted too long. She had seen surprise register in his blue eyes before one of amusement mingled with intrigue replaced it. She was relieved his back was to Tochar, so the leader missed Dagan's reaction. Her green gaze locked with his blue one for a few moments as if in challenge. She pulled her arm from his grip as it loosened, seemingly without his awareness or intent. His touch, face, and presence were disturbing, arousing, irritating.

As if he detected her reaction to him, he looked pleased and cocky. She shifted her gaze to Tochar and smiled. The leader grinned as if he assumed they had been evaluating each other and saw the sparks of physical attraction between them. She decided that was an advantage, as it would mask any departure from her normal behavior. *So what are you to him?*

The leader laughed and corrected, "Dagan is not a friend, but I am hoping he will become one and hire on to serve me as superbly as you do. I must tell you, Starla, his reputation spreads far, and is a colorful one. It will be good to have another brave and bold person working for me, if he accepts. According to his record, he will prove an excellent group member. I am sure you two will work remarkably and profitably together."

Good, he's a stranger. "I'll work with any man or woman you select. You are a generous and superior leader," she said in a smooth and professional tone, though she surmised the *fiendal* was using her to tempt Dagan Latu into becoming one of his hirelings.

Tochar chuckled. "I am the only potentate you have ever served." He glanced at Dagan. "Like you, Starla has been a loner, a success on her own. But I persuaded her to work for me and to enjoy the sanctuary and rewards I have to offer. I hope you will do the same."

"The offer you made sounds appealing," Dagan said, "especially the refuge and hefty payments, both of which I am in dire need of at present. As to Starla Vedris, she must be skilled in many ways to be thought and spoken of so highly by you. She is indeed beautiful, and a pleasure to meet. I'm certain I'll enjoy working with her at every available chance." He was fascinated by the desirable space pirate who appeared just as intrigued by and drawn to him, as he was to her.

"Starla is exquisite, but I must caution you, Dagan, to use care and respect. She is one of my best raiders, so I cannot allow anyone to provoke her into leaving me by offending her with an unwanted pursuit. Of course, she is free to select her companions and diversions."

"I catch your meaning, Tochar, and I'll honor it."

"Excellent, because you and Starla will make a fine pair for some of my most important treks. With you two as a unit and Auken, Sach, and Moig as another, I will have two superior teams to handle crucial raids. Sit and relax. Starla, would you care for a refreshment?"

She took the *seata* nearest Dagan's to prove to both men she was unafraid of the newcomer. *"Mumfresia* will be fine." She watched Tochar press a button on his control panel. The female slave appeared with haste, as if she feared a delay would anger her master and provoke punishment. Starla had seen bruises on Zarafa's yellow skin that implied abuse. She detested any male who used brutality on a helpless victim of any age or sex or race. Yet, she was not in a position to defend or rescue the alien slave. When she completed her mission, she would endeavor to do so.

"Mumfresia for Starla. Refills for me and Dagan."

She noticed the kindly behavior the cunning Tochar exhibited toward the slave to make a good impression on Dagan. She knew that the leader and this settlement had no automatic *servo* units to provide refreshments and meals by request using coded metallic cards and advanced technology, just as it lacked other facets to make work easier and life more enjoyable. Most of the living conditions and amenities were like those in her world more than two hundred *yings* ago. Neither Noy nor Tochara were places which attracted scientists and technicians to build, operate, and repair them. Yet, the primitive lifestyle suited the types of people who populated them. After the woman's departure, Starla asked Tochar, "Will we be going out again soon? I get itchy sitting around too long."

"You see, Dagan, Starla is as eager to get rich as you are, but for different reasons. Yes, my lovely creature, your next departure is in two *deegas.* It is another risky and profitable venture for you. Auken will give you the schedule; you will be using his ship this time."

That news told her their target was another cargo of moonbeams, but didn't reveal the crystals departure point: Seri or Kalfa. She would ponder the matter later. For now, she needed to stay alert for trouble from the handsome male nearby, who kept glancing at her and who probably was surprised to see her again. She could not guess so soon if he was going to expose her with the hope of gaining his new leader's gratitude and favor. Perhaps the appealing *villite* wanted her to sweat for a time out of revenge for defeating him, or perhaps he was repaying her for sparing his life. Or perhaps he assumed extorting her would be more profitable than revealing her defiance to Tochar, especially if she found a cunning way to excuse it. She also tried not to think about the audacious remarks she made to Dagan before she allegedly killed him, words he no doubt found amusing and enticing from his expressions.

As the slave returned and served them, Dagan pretended to listen to Starla and Tochar chat, but his mind kept drifting to the incident on the transporter and her provocative words. He couldn't surmise why she hadn't slain him, but he was grateful enough to conceal news of her defiance, no matter if revealing it would score him big points. She didn't seem worried, so her partner that *deega* must not have seen him, as she had covered his face with a sack. But if Moig recognized him, they were both in trouble for keeping secrets. Maybe he shouldn't take that risk; maybe he should expose her while he had time to joke it off. If he waited and Moig fingered him, Tochar would be suspicious of why he held silent and would send him on his way.

But, Dagan deduced, he might get Starla Vedris killed or punished for no reason, if Moig was ignorant. For certain, Tochar wasn't a man to dupe without an excellent motive, especially while sitting in his stronghold. He had noticed the discolored spots on the slave's face and arms and the terror in the poor creature's eyes. Any man who could do such despicable acts was an unpredictable and untrustworthy lowlife. If this job wasn't imperative, he would be gone on the next ship out. As to Starla, she was a mystery; he had never heard of her and her exploits. He wondered how and when and why she had linked up with Tochar and how she felt about the man. He needed to learn her secrets fast or she could be trouble for him if his guard rebelliously relaxed around her. It didn't sit well that he was so attracted to her, that he might jeopardize his wants and needs to save her life and skin.

Starla looked at three crystals lying on his desk. "Those are exquisite moonbeams, Tochar, but rather small. They would be breathtaking if they were gems and studded into a gold neck ring. Of course, they're too valuable and useful for mere adornment."

The leader fingered them almost erotically. "Dagan just sold them to me. He won them in a *resi* game from a cunning but stupid thief."

Dagan grinned. "If I had known those gems were so precious, I wouldn't have held on to them for so long. They're about the only thing I rescued after my little problem with those *Sekis.* Too bad my ship wouldn't fit in my pocket like they did. If I could get my hands on more of those, I'd be rich very soon with what you're willing to pay for them."

Tochar lifted one moonbeam, held it toward the light, and admired its color. These are the last ones you will be able to win in any game. No worker can sneak them out of the mines anymore because of security inspections. In addition, markets for them are rare and buyers are dangerous to seek."

"Ships transporting them make perfect targets," Dagan hinted, sorry he had been forced to sell them.

"Do not attempt to raid one unless you are ready to die or you know for certain it is safe to attack," Tochar warned. "The Serians and Kalfans are very protective of these beauties, very secretive about them. They tried to keep news of their discovery from general knowledge, but word always filters out about something so unique and potent. I crave every one in existence."

"What's so special about them? Why the secrecy surrounding them?" Dagan asked as he leaned forward to inspect the small crystals again.

"They have many uses. Research is being done to determine their full potential. But let us talk of other things to get better acquainted."

Starla deduced Tochar's reason for changing the subject: he didn't want Dagan—or anyone—to become fully aware of the moonbeams' enormous power and value. The two yellow ones could be ground into minute particles, then placed inside a tumor by surgery or injection to destroy it without damaging healthy cells or tissues and without side effects; yet, scientists did not know how the crystal differentiated between healthy and abnormal cells. The same was true for viral destruction when the moonbeams were ingested with liquid. It could repair broken bones in a few *horas* when inserted into their location. The blue crystal could be used on a scalpel to make thin incisions which instantly sealed vessels and capillaries to prevent bleeding. The cut would then heal within a *deega* after the operation and never became infected or left a scar. Other moonbeams, according to their sizes and colors, created powerful weapons and sources of heat and light that were long-lasting and safe. With such awesome capabilities, it was no wonder why the crystals were so valuable and craved, or a target for *villites* like Tochar. She wanted to know how Dagan had come across those three. She wondered if Tochar suspected the newcomer of being deceitful; if so, it was not revealed in the leader's expression or tone. If Dagan Latu *was* a liar or threat, that fact would be exposed as soon as Tochar used truth serum on him. She hoped that Dagan wasn't asked any questions about her while under that revealing drug's control.

Don't worry, Bree-Kayah, if Tochar puts you under again, with your immunity, you can lie your way out of trouble. As for you, Dagan Latu, if you're being deceitful, you're a dead man.

"How long have you been on Noy?" she asked him. She was amazed he or any man would enter Tochar's domain coated with red dust, his garment torn and rumpled, his hair uncombed, and his skin unwashed.

"Two *deegas.* I landed at another settlement, but decided I would like this one better. It isn't a secret that Tochar's is the best. I was hoping he would be willing to hire me until I earn enough for a new ship."

That information revealed to Starla he had left the transporter and headed there as soon as he awakened from the temporary cryogenic drug she had given him, a rare chemical from Yakir that had decreased his vital signs to the point Moig could not detect them. But how, she mused, had he gotten off the vessel, and what had become of it, and why land elsewhere if Tochara was his destination? "How did you cross the wasteland? From which direction? Did you have any trouble with the flesh-eating mutants who roam it?"

Dagan was stunned she would ask any questions about his travels. He glanced at his sorry appearance and answered, "I stole a landrover but, it malfunctioned before I reached Tochara, so I walked the rest of the way. I was lucky that one of Tochar's patrols sighted me and brought me to him. I didn't run into any mutants. I guess I was lucky I survived my little misadventure."

Starla was eager to return to the *Liska* and learn about Dagan Latu, as Cypher would have a report ready for her, but she must not appear nervous or in a rush to depart. "Yes, you were very lucky," she remarked. "I'm sure you're grateful to whatever force saved your life. What happened to your old ship?"

"Depletion of power forced me to abandon her, but I escaped a *Seki* before he could take me in to be sent to a penal colony. I caught a lift on a supply transporter to a Keezian colony. After I examined the place, I came here for rest, sanctuary, and work. What about—"

Auken, Sach, and Moig joined them and interrupted Dagan's query. As the three Icarians greeted their leader with respect and affection, Starla and Dagan sipped their drinks and listened.

The golden-haired Auken reported, "We'll get everything prepared tomorrow and leave the following *deega.* We should reach our target, grab its cargo, and return quickly. We'll take Starla with us."

She exchanged smiles with Auken.

Tochar introduced the newcomer to his men, "This is the infamous Dagan Latu, my friends: adventurer, *bijoni*, raider, and rogue. He barely escaped capture numerous times for some of his cunning and daring deeds. The *Sekis* would give a small fortune for his capture and destruction. If his reputation is accurate, he lives for pleasure, wealth, challenges, and excitement, as we do. Dagan will be going with you on the next trek. If he proves worthy, he will become a regular member of your special team."

Dagan clasped wrists with each of the men. He realized Tochar had checked his criminal record earlier when he was out of the chamber for a while, as this was his first time on Noy. "Where will we be heading?"

Tochar replied for his best friend, "Auken will tell you after you are under way. Why do you ask?"

Dagan chuckled. "Considering my recent brush with capture, I just want to make sure I'm not sticking my nose out too close to those Kalfans again. I kind of like it, so I don't want their *Sekis* to laser it off."

Tochar chuckled. "The danger and risks are small, and no space rangers will be in that sector. Starla, you work with Dagan and teach him how we operate. Make sure nothing happens to him during his first raid for me. I would like to keep him around for a long time."

Starla set aside her empty glass and nodded. "As you wish, Tochar."

Moig ventured with a grin, "Don't worry, Dagan, Vedris will watch out for you and get you back in one piece. She was with me on my last raid. She tricked a robot pilot into letting her come aboard his transporter and she disabled him as fast as a shooting star. Vedris isn't afraid of anybody or anything. She obeys orders and does her job well."

Dagan surmised from Moig's behavior that their secret was safe, and, oddly, it felt arousing to share it with the exquisite pirate. "I'll trust her to take excellent care of me and to be sure I don't make any mistakes."

"If there's nothing else to discuss, dismissed," Tochar said. "If you're in need of... diversion, Dagan, the Skull's Den is the best place to look. Radu, its owner, can find you a clean and quiet chamber to rent. If you need anything, ask Radu, and tell him you work for me. I will meet with all of you upon your successful return, except for you, Dagan. I want to see you here again tomorrow on the tenth *hora.*"

Dagan nodded, then spoke with Moig, Auken, and Sach for a few *preons.* Starla exited and was out of sight when he stepped from the *trans-to* with the other men. He wondered how she vanished so quickly.

Auken chuckled. "She returned to her ship, the *Liska.* She lives on it in orbit. She doesn't share a *sleeper* with any of the men here."

Dagan grinned, then laughed. "My interest in her is that obvious?"

Sach nodded. "She's beautiful but special," he told him. "Be careful with her. She's one of us, so we protect her from annoyances."

"What if I'm not an irritant to her?"

"That's for Starla to decide," Auken answered.

Dagan watched the men closely as he asked, "Any of you pursuing her? I don't want to intrude."

"We're just friends. Starla comes, goes, and does as she pleases. The inhabitants here know she works for Tochar, so they leave her alone. Only an outsider would dare to approach her in an offensive way."

"And then only one time." Moig chortled. "Vedris fights and shoots better than most men, so she can take care of herself. If not, that android of hers would lay a threat low."

Dagan was surprised by that news. "Android?"

"She has one she treats like a real person. Who knows? Maybe that's why she doesn't need a man. Maybe old Cypher takes care of her in all ways."

Sach scowled and cautioned, "Careful, Moig, you know that isn't true."

Dagan noticed how the shortest man defended Starla, and how the golden-haired Auken nodded agreement with Sach.

"I was only teasing. Everybody knows androids aren't equipped like that, only certain cyborgs."

"We don't have any cyborgs here," Auken said, "we don't allow them; they can't be trusted."

"Let's head for the drinker. I'm thirsty and I need a juicy female."

Sach concurred with Moig, "I'm ready for a few pleasures myself. I heard Radu hired two females with real special skills I'd like to try. Dagan?"

"What I need is a bath and clean garment."

Auken told the newcomer that Radu would take care of his needs, then reminded him not to forget his meeting with Tochar the following day.

"I'll be there," Dagan replied and wondered about the reason for it. . .

Starla rushed to the bridge of the *Liska* and took a seat next to Cypher. Her computer system had a memory bank and certain programs that no one could enter except the two of them and members of the Maffei Elite Squad; they didn't even show up on the screen unless a particular command was given. The advanced system—along with her security clearance level and her android's skills—had the capability and access codes for tapping in to numerous *UFG* and other sources without being traced back to her unit. She took a deep breath. "We came close to exposure, but he held silent about our first meeting for some reason. Who is Dagan Latu? I'm certain Tochar or his contacts have already checked his file. That *fiendal* seemed impressed by what he learned. That doesn't bode well for my impression of him and gives us an unneeded factor."

The intelligent android pressed a key to display the intruder's record and image onscreen. "Name: Dagan Latu. Age: Twenty-eight *yings.* Height: Seventy-five *hapaxs.* Weight: Two-twenty *pedis.* Hair: Black. Eyes: Blue. Scars: None. Origin: Gavas, Kalfa Galaxy. Mate status: None. Family status: All deceased. Current location: Unknown. Recently escaped from a Kalfan *Seki* after a fuel raid and his capture on Gavas."

The news he had no mate strangely pleased Starla, whose eyes were locked on the magnificent male's image as it was shown from all sides. *"Sekis* are well trained. Dagan must be cunning and skilled to perform such a feat. Few men have done so." She listened as Cypher spoke in the humanistic manner of his program, one which made him seem real to her.

"His criminal record is long, but the most serious parts consist of strong allegations and suspicions. No life-taking charges have been proven against him."

As she read the list and remarks, Starla realized why she had never heard of him in the past: he operated outside of her sectors. Language had not provided an enlightening clue, as all people had translator chips implanted in their ears at birth so that any tongue spoken was understandable. Too, an intergalactic form of visual language—*WEV*—was used in multiculture settings so that anyone could read names, signs, and messages. She was relieved *WEV* was used in Tochara where people from many planets and galaxies lived and worked, though she was skilled in the written and visual forms of several languages.

"If this record is only half accurate, Cypher, he's clever, careful, fearless, and intelligent; those traits are proven by his escape from one of the most sophisticated and highly trained law-enforcement units in Kalfa and in his ability to avoid detection and capture. It says he normally travels and works alone, but it's believed he occasionally hires on to bands of smugglers, raiders, adventurers, and *bijonis.* I can't see him as mercenary. His goals appear to be wealth, pleasure, excitement, challenges, and retaining freedom."

For a wild moment, she wondered what Dagan would say if she offered to pay him more than Tochar if he worked with her on her current assignment. She could provide more challenges and adventures than Tochar. As a man, he could get closer, faster, to the other band members and might gather facts she needed to complete her mission and fly home. Working together, perhaps they could find a way to disable the *fiendal's* defense system, which must take place simultaneously at the two sites; then, the Serians could attack. It was too risky for her and Cypher to make that attempt, as it would leave no one aboard her ship to rescue them if things went wrong. She was determined to win, but she was not foolish and reckless. *Villites* had crazy codes of honor and loyalty toward the men who hired them, she was aware, even for short spans of time and despite all perils involved. Perhaps a pardon would ensure Dagan's assistance, as a matter of such grave importance surely justified the rewarding of one.

The only way to determine his real character was to get close to him, but not as Starla, whom he surely would be watching after her defiance. Yet, a sensuous and seductive Yana might be able to entice facts from him if he was a boaster trying to impress her and lure her to a *sleeper* beneath him. If he lived past Tochar's truth serum test. That thought distressed her more than she cared to admit or consider.

"He's been a *bijoni* as Tochar said, a fighter for hire in matters which mean nothing to him except payment and stimulating risks. That strikes me as surprising and peculiar for the man he seems to be, self-contained and self-reliant. What is his loyalty record?"

"He has not betrayed any superior from his past; nor have they exposed him. Since leaving their hire, all are victims of annihilator units, captives on penal colonies, or are hiding in other galaxies. Use caution on him, Bree-Kayah. His physical effect on you can be perilous and distracting. I can detect every time your thoughts drift and you think about him; you did so before speaking again. Is that not accurate?"

"I should remove my wrist device when I'm with him so you can't read my mind and worry."

Cypher's silver visual sensors focused on the young woman whom he loved, if that was possible in his non-human state. At a height of seventy-six *hapaxs,* seven *hapaxs* taller than his companion, she had to look upward to meet his unreadable gaze. The expression in her eyes troubled him, as did the unknown factor who evoked it. "There is conflict within you concerning him. Do not forget who and what you are and why you are here. Do not forget he is an adversary, the same as Tochar and his space pirates."

"I know, my friend, and I'm grateful for your concern and affection; I'm glad your program allows you to experience such perceptions. I promise to be careful around Dagan, if he lives past tomorrow. Tochar will be giving him *Thorin* to test his credibility, and he might fail that examination. Wouldn't it be wonderful if I could infuse Tochar with a dose, question him, and finalize this mission? I doubt the *fiendal* has had access to *Rendelar* to make him immune; that chemical and process are guarded too well and only a skilled scientist like my mother can use them properly and safely. Besides, Tochar never allows anyone to get that close to him except Auken, Sach, Moig, and Palesa, who aren't threats to him. I wish his dwelling was penetrable by our probing devices so we could hear what is said at all times; he would have no secrets then to keep us here. Even with the needed coordinates recorded in our system, I can't transport into his chamber to search it, since we can't scan it for anyone's presence. I'm not worried about his session with Dagan tomorrow; I can elude any disclosure problems. But for some crazy reason I can't explain, I want him to survive it."

She changed the subject to her assignment. "We have one important advantage: from what I overheard between Auken and Sach, Tochar is storing moonbeams we've stolen so far. When he has an ample supply of the five types of crystals, he plans, to summon buyers from Ceyx and from his Thracian world. At least the crystals haven't fallen into enemy hands. If we can discover where they're hidden, perhaps we can destroy them before a deal takes place. If we can't recover them, that was *Raz* Yakir's order if the opportunity arose. To avoid suspicion, I haven't asked any questions about the moonbeams. If I can earn their complete trust, perhaps I will be told or shown where they are being kept."

"With the Latu complexity, it is good Tochar lacks the scientific ability and source to check for the detection of *Rendelar* in your body."

"If it were possible, he would know I overpower *Thorin* and can dupe him. But it would require one of the most intelligent and skilled scientists alive, secret formulas, and highly specialized equipment to do such an intricate test: things that *fiendal* doesn't have, thank the stars. It's also good that *Raz* Yakir wanted a female for this task. I believe, as he and my Elite Squad superior do, that a woman is less suspicious. This is a critical assignment, Cypher; we are lucky to be chosen for it. I hope we succeed soon. I miss my parents, my brother and sister, and their families. This is the longest time and distance I've been away from them."

Cypher placed his hand on her shoulder, knowing that action was used to supply encouragement and comfort. "It will be over soon. I will cloak the *Liska* and follow the *Adika* on its next trek. I will search for clues to solve this mystery. I will guard you from harm."

Starla smiled, reached for his hand, and clasped it between hers. "Thank you for being here with me. Now," she added as she released her grip and stood, "it's time for Yana to go to work for us. We are fortunate we have a treaty with Seri. Enemies took grim advantage of Yakir and almost convinced him to help destroy Maffei during the days of *Starlight And Splendor*. We made peace, and I have this useful gift from him."

Starla went to her quarters and stripped off her green jumpsuit. She opened the hidden compartment, retrieved a phial of unknown chemicals, and drank its contents. She stiffened as strange sensations assailed her body, flesh quivered and altered, colorings changed as the shapeshifting transformation took place. It was an uncomfortable and weird feeling, but not painful. *Raz* Yakir had given her an ample supply to use as needed, a secret and powerful discovery a Serian scientist had developed. While the chemicals completed their task, she selected her garment and accessories.

She entered the bathing unit and remained for a short time, then exited clean and refreshed. A familiar and yet totally different image greeted her gaze in the mirror as she completed her grooming and dressed. She placed a heady fragrance—Yana's scent—on her neck, wrists, and between her breasts, a bosom larger than her own. She strapped a *lazette* to her right thigh, a small weapon in a holder, to ward off trouble. The only time she was disarmed was when she entered Tochar's chamber and when she was aboard her ship. She made certain she had a second chemical—contained in what appeared to be a belt decoration—to return her normal image if needed before the transmutation's time span— twelve *horas*—elapsed.

After finishing her tasks, she joined Cypher at the transporter unit. "Is the women's private chamber at the Skull's Den unoccupied?" she asked the android.

"The coordinates are entered. Scanners register no presence there. It is safe to travel. Step onto the pad when you are ready to leave."

As Starla Vedris, she had gathered the coordinates earlier so she could beam in and out without being seen or followed. Since many ships came and went and orbited Noy, Yana's comings and goings could be explained without suspicion. To help protect her other identity, she had rented an abode from Radu where Yana supposedly lived, one which Cypher kept in order and stocked in case Yana had a visitor who needed to be duped. She had given Radu a false story as to why privacy about her whereabouts was needed. Since others often came to Tochara to conceal themselves for a while, her story and behavior were not suspicious. "How do I look?" she asked, turning for inspection.

"As Yana, you are perfect. The human saying is: you are a woman to evoke uncontrollable desire in most men and envy in other females."

Starla smiled and laughed. "Good, that's Yana's purpose. *Raz* Yakir certainly chose an alluring facade for me to assume. Bree-Kayah Saar cannot dress and behave as Yana does. I even sound different with the changes in my nose, mouth, and throat. No one can see through this

cunning disguise, not even Tochar with his wicked gaze."
She closed her eyes and repeated, "I'm Yana, I'm Yana, I
am Yana" to get herself into that identity's character. She
opened her eyes, took a deep breath, stepped onto the
sensor pad, and told Cypher she was ready to depart.
"Wish me luck."

The android did so before her presence shimmered
and vanished. He checked the scanners to make certain
she reached her destination without discovery. He
remained in the transporter room to be ready to retrieve
her in a hurry if necessary, monitoring her words via a
device in a neck ring of *plantinien* and fake jewels. He did
not like to depend on the wrist and neck devices to stay
in contact with and to monitor her, since they could be
removed or broken. Until this mission, a tiny unit had
been implanted under the skin of her right forearm, one
which had to be removed because of the shapeshifting
process. It was at times like this that his emotions chip
was a disadvantage, because it permitted him to
experience what must be worry.

In her Yana form, Starla left the women's chamber and
strolled into the large dome, the exterior of which, with
its strange shape and openings, resembled a skull. It was
occupied with people from many planets. It reverberated
with a variety of noises: voices, laughter, music, chair and
table movements, booted feet on the floor, and the clatter
of glasses and dishes. A variety of smells wafted in the air,
some pleasant and some foul. She walked to the long bar
and ordered a drink.

The owner smiled. "Haven't seen you for a while,
Yana. It's good to have you back; you give this place a
glow with your beauty."

"Your tongue is smooth; your words are pleasing to hear, Radu. I have been in my abode; I was in need of a few *deegas* rest and quiet."

As he drew her drink from one of the large kegs in a row on the wall, he said, "I was afraid you had started visiting another location."

Yana's gaze drifted over the rotund alien with gray hair and eyes, a Ceyxan of about sixty *yings.* His rippled forehead and the countless solid gray circles on his pale skin were traits of those of his race of a certain age. He was always genial to her and to most of his customers. One of a few men without a criminal past, she could not imagine why he would live in Tochara and serve evil. "There is no place here as nice and safe as yours, Radu. Others are rough and crowded for a woman. The Skull's Den is clean and secure and serves the best quality drinks and nourishments."

Radu returned the *plantinien* chip. "Those words and your adornment earned you a free drink."

"You are kind and generous, a good friend."

After the owner excused himself to serve others, Yana turned and glanced around the location that was separated into three areas. In one, games of various types were being played and enjoyed. In another, a few pairs danced, some of them doing little more than rubbing their bodies together in time to the music. Men outnumbered women; and most females were either visitors to Tochara, or were mates or lovers of *villites* who lived in the settlement. When Pleasure Givers were not sating men's desires upstairs, they served drinks for Radu. Most customers had to go to the bar for their needs, where two men assisted the owner. The third area was for drinkers and talkers, her location.

Yana recognized familiar faces, whether or not she knew their names and foul deeds. Many of them sold stolen goods to Tochar and paid him a yearly fee for the privilege of existing in this rugged haven. Others were buyers of those goods or had stopped by for rest and diversions. She didn't see any of the thirty Enforcers and assumed they were on guard at the defense sites and water sources or patrolling the settlement. Nor did she see Auken, Sach, or Moig and surmised they were secluded with Pleasure Givers on the next level. She had learned that a few of those desire-saters were males who dressed and looked like females, as some men preferred that type of erotic satisfaction.

Small chambers were located on the third level where patrons indulged in various drugs, alone or with a partner. Virtual reality devices were there in private cubicles; some, she had heard, offered sexual games which evoked incredible sensations when enhanced by drugs, but she had never been tempted to try them. She had a virtual reality unit on her ship for diversion and for practice sessions with assignments. It could be programed with any image and scene she desired and allowed her to either control the action or allowed the situation to travel where it willed.

Yana's roaming gaze paused and drifted over Dagan Latu who sat alone at a table with a drink before him and his gaze focused on her. She complimented herself for seizing his attention quickly—even though her Yana facade and manner were responsible—and before she got close enough for her special fragrance to ensnare him. One of the few unoccupied tables was beside his position, so she walked in that direction with a subtle sway to her hips.

Dagan observed the voluptuous creature with eyes as blue as a Kalfan sky in summer and features that were flawless in shape and size. Her hair was thick and long, with little curl, and as golden as the midnight sun that orbited his world. Her figure and movements were perfection. She was clad in a multicolored jumpsuit with flesh-revealing circles along the lengths of her arms and legs, and with matching cutouts at her abdomen and back. He noted a wide gold ring around her slender neck. It was her sole adornment, as no jewelry graced her ears, wrists, or fingers. A *lazette* was secured to one sleek thigh just above the knee, the fake jewels of its holder catching light and sparkling as she moved. There was a sultriness and allure about her that was arousing, especially since it had been a long time since he had enjoyed sex, a fact he had been reminded of during his two encounters with Starla. He had hoped Starla would appear, but it seemed unlikely now. Perhaps that denial was fortunate since he seemed to be susceptible to the enchanting brown-haired green-eyed pirate.

As the striking creature neared, Dagan smiled and stood to seat her, assuming from her thorough scan of his person that she was joining him. He was amused and bewildered when she broke their visual bond and claimed the next table, putting her back to him. Almost feeling foolish, he sat down. He realized she was from the Asisa Galaxy, as the faint blue tinge to her hair, skin, and sclera of her eyes were traits of that alien race. He couldn't help but wonder what she was doing in a rough and crude settlement like Tochara. He ruled out the position of a Pleasure Giver, as she would be occupied on the next level of the Skull's Den. He doubted she was anyone's steady companion, as no intelligent man would allow her to be there alone. A lack of a marriage band on her wrist told him she was mateless. She must be a regular, since Radu appeared well acquainted with her. She was not Tochar's lover; he had seen that redhead and knew she was *Binixe*, an hermaphroditic race from a planet in the Thracian Galaxy.

Dagan leaned back in his seat, sipped his drink, and tried to ignore her. He was about as successful as the other men present, who were almost drooling over the beauty. He decided that either she was off limits or had scorned them in the past because none approached her, which increased his curiosity. Her heady fragrance filled his nose, despite competition from the other smells in the area. It was as if she exuded a powerful pheromone which stimulated his sex glands and enticed him as potently as Starla Vedris did. He looked at her tresses flowing over the chair and halting near a slim waist. Vain and a teaser, he concluded. He wasn't in the mood for games, and conceit always cooled his physical interest in a female, no matter her beauty, or how badly he needed sexual release.

Yana sensed his potent gaze. She was not surprised he didn't approach her after a seeming rebuff on her part. She was glad he did not pour himself over her in an attempt to lure her into a casual sexual encounter. Yet, he must be fighting a battle to resist the Kalfan mating scent. Cypher had prepared the pheromone and mixed it with an exotic floral aroma, and she had applied it sparingly for this first encounter. Four men who were regular patrons asked her to dance or to join them; she told them she was waiting for a companion to arrive. After a stranger to Tochara proved difficult to discourage for a while, she turned and asked Dagan, "Would you mind, sitting with me while I have my drink so I can enjoy it without being bothered again?"

Dagan was taken off-guard by the request, spoken in a soft and polite tone. "I'm comfortable here, but you can join me if you wish. You'll be safe and untroubled at my table. Conversation is by your choice."

Yana took the seat across from him. "Thank you for the assistance. May I buy you a drink of gratitude?"

"If you're here when I finish this one. Name's Dagan Latu." He awaited her reaction with interest.

Remember only Starla met him. "I am Yana. Have you just arrived? I do not recall seeing you here."

Dagan lowered his glass, and his gaze met hers. Mysteries intrigued and challenged him, so he would play along with her ruse, because he was convinced she had intended to join him from the *preon* she had arrived. Perhaps she worked for Tochar, and he was being studied. "That means you must be a regular in here during stopovers or you live in Tochara." It was a statement on his part, not a question.

"Both. Is this a visit for you or a move here?"

"Both. I just hired on to work for Tochar."

Yana lifted her light-brown brows and widened her gaze to indicate surprise. "Every man in the settlement craves such an elite position, so you must possess many skills to catch Tochar's eye. He hires only the best."

He changed the subject. "I thought I caught your eye for a while there, but I guess I was mistaken."

That was not the response she expected, but her wits did not scatter for more than a few moments. She lowered long lashes and smiled before meeting his gaze again. "You did, but I don't approach strangers and do not accept their invitations to join them."

"Unless you require one's assistance or protection." He watched her eyes brighten and her lips give way to another radiant smile as she nodded.

"I don't like to cause noisy scenes, and Radu doesn't tolerate trouble. In a settlement where men outnumber women, it is difficult to be left alone when I only want to relax and have a drink."

"Even if females outnumbered males, you would have that problem. What do you do in Tochara?" he asked, wording his query with care.

47

"Very little. I'm only staying for a short time longer. There was a situation I had to escape and decided this was the last place anyone would search for me. I didn't realize Tochara was so... primitive. Fortunately, I know how to protect myself and to survive even under crude conditions." She laughed when he sent her a doubtful grin. "I meant, defend myself during perilous situations. Men like those five are nothing more than nuisances who need to be sent away quickly and quietly to avoid drawing unwanted attention and embarrassment to myself. Or to them, as some men do not take such predicaments well. As soon as matters are settled and it's safe, I'll return to where I came from."

Dagan leaned forward, propped his arms on the table, and ventured, "Which is the Asisa Galaxy."

She feigned a look of dismay to lure him into her spell. She reasoned that a man like him would be drawn to a woman in danger, snared by a challenging mystery, not to mention responsive to the sensuous image Yakir had given her, and weakened by a captivating fragrance. "You know me? Were you sent to locate and retrieve me? I rarely talk with anyone, and when I do, it's to the wrong man. You are cruel and deceitful. Your vile task will not be easy; I have sanctuary here."

Dagan grasped her hand and kept her from rising, noting how soft and warm her skin was. He was intrigued by her distress and hints, as he hadn't heard about a political upheaval in that location. No *bijonis* had been summoned, and its ruler had no daughters. That left him with the conclusion that the matter was a personal dilemma. "Don't panic, Yana; I'm not here because of you. I guessed from your colorings."

Her gaze searched his. "Is that the truth?"

He nodded and smiled. "You're still safe, so relax. Is it something you want to talk about with me? Can I help in some way? I'll guard your secret."

"Perhaps you would, but I'll keep it for now." As she finished her drink, she realized either he would be dead tomorrow or he would be one of her targets as Tochar's hireling. Both thoughts were unsettling. It was more strenuous than she had imagined to spend time with the appealing and disturbing man while on constant alert against slips. She had made initial contact and seized his interest; that was sufficient for now.

"Would you like another drink to calm you?"

"Thank you, but no. It's late and I need to leave."

"Will I see you again?"

"If you're alone next time, I'll join you and stay longer, or you can join me if I arrive first."

"Can I walk you to your dwelling?"

"Perhaps next time, after I know you better."

Dagan was unsure how to interpret her meaning. "If you need me for anything, *anything,* Yana, Radu knows where to find me."

She nodded acceptance of his offer, whatever it entailed. She stood and said, "Thank you for the rescue and I look forward to seeing you again."

"Any time, Yana." He saw her enter the women's private chamber. Radu arrived and blocked his view as he was deciding whether or not to follow her to see where she lived and check if she met with anyone. The Skull's Den owner interrupted his thoughts.

"Your abode is clean and ready to habitate," Radu said. "Drose will guide you there at your signal."

"Thank you. Tochar will be pleased by the good service I've received. I needed the bath, food, and fresh garment. Tell me, Radu, do you know who Yana is and why she is in Tochara?"

49

The stocky man knew her claims, but felt it was Yana's right and place to reveal those facts if she chose to do so. "My mouth does not travel across other's space. She visits here on occasion, but keeps to herself. You're a lucky man to have shared a drink with her; that's a rare event for Yana. I can tell you no more. Summon Drose when you're ready to leave."

Dagan realized the man knew more than he had revealed, but was glad Radu wasn't a loose talker. He watched for Yana to reappear, and finally decided she had left while his view was obstructed. A woman that beautiful and alluring couldn't be hard to locate if he decided to do so another time. Too restless for sleep, and the hour too early, he purchased another drink and settled back in his chair to observe some more. It remained to be seen if signing on with Tochar would be profitable, but it surely would be challenging, and he had no choice under the circumstances in any case.

Only an *hora* passed before Starla Vedris arrived, glanced around, and locked gazes with him. He lifted his hand and motioned for her to join him. From her expression and stroll to the bar, it appeared as if this wasn't his night to succeed with a woman. He realized he was wrong as he watched her purchase a drink, then walk toward him. His lagging energy was renewed and thoughts of Yana vanished just by looking at the beautiful and mysterious *spaceki*. His keen wits went on alert and he prepared to see what he could learn about the lovely space pirate and his other teammates.

Chapter Three

Dagan watched Starla approach in a green jumpsuit that matched her eyes. Long brown tresses tumbled over her shoulders. Her movements were fluid and graceful, confident. Her aura was feminine, despite the laser weapon strapped to her waist. She sat down and sipped her drink as they studied each other. "It's late. I had given up on seeing you tonight," he told her.

"We didn't have plans to meet."

"I know, but I was hoping you'd come."

She lowered her glass. "Why?"

"So you can tell me about Tochara and working for Tochar. I don't like walking into a new job blind."

"You'll learn what you need to know after your meeting with Tochar; that's when you'll be told if he accepts you or not and what's expected of you."

Dagan leaned forward and propped his arms on the table, catching a whiff of her fragrance, which was so different from Yana's heavier scent. "I was under the impression I was hired and you're my teacher."

"Not until he has a lengthy and private talk with you. He doesn't hire strangers or by reputation."

"Talk about what?" he asked, and took a long drink from his glass as he observed her observing him.

"That's between you and Tochar. I can't tell you or teach you anything until you're an insider, and he's certain you can be trusted."

Though the crowd had lessened at the Skull's Den, Dagan leaned closer and murmured in a low voice, "You know I can be trusted, since I didn't betray you. What's my continued silence worth?"

Starla walked her gaze over his grinning face with deliberate leisure. "Since I didn't take your life aboard that transporter, that should be ample payment."

"Weren't you just a little nervous and surprised when you saw me?"

"No more than you were when you saw me."

He locked gazes with her. "Aren't you afraid I'll change my mind and expose you?"

Starla leaned forward to bring their faces into close proximity. She whispered, "No, but do it and I'll kill you for certain next time because you wouldn't deserve this second chance. Moig is my witness I killed the intruder. He checked your vitals but never saw your face."

Dagan scrutinized her frosty gaze and heard her cold tone, but felt they were faked. She had been scared and tense during their earlier meeting, but she had concealed her feelings with skill and practice. Her full mouth was tempting and he wanted to taste it. He wanted to know everything about her, but not succumb to her many charms. "I believe you would attempt to kill me, so I'll try hard not to rub you wrong or be caught off guard again. Why exactly did you let me live?"

Starla's rebellious body and emotions responded to him and she ordered them to cease. "I don't want to have life-taking charges placed on my record. I don't kill unless my life is in jeopardy. I presumed you wouldn't be a future threat because you'd be long gone from this sector. I figured you must have been free-riding for a good reason. I was partly right."

"So, Moig didn't see me. We're both lucky."

"Yes," she admitted. "If you tell Tochar who you are, I doubt it will get me slain or exiled. I'm valuable to him. He'll consider it a weakness but not a fatal flaw. Don't forget, Tochar knows and trusts me."

"Will he, after learning you lied to him and Moig about my death? From my experiences, disobedience is more acceptable than deceit."

"I'll deal with that problem if it comes up. Besides you deceived him and would be exposed. Why did you hold silent about me, and why were you aboard?"

"I doubt Tochar would hire any man who was recently disabled by a woman, or by another man for that matter. That would tarnish my prowess, right? Surely you didn't expect me to admit you tricked me and stung my ego. Besides, I felt I owed you for sparing my life. If our positions had been reversed that *deega*, I would've taken your same course of action. Despite what we are, taking lives unnecessarily is dangerous and costly. What you did doesn't make me doubt your loyalty to Tochar, so why report it? Besides, Moig made that decision and gave my extermination order."

"Tochar agreed with it after our return and even rewarded me for killing you. Tell me, Dagan Latu: How did you get off that ship and get here?"

Why not earn her trust? "After I came to, hardly able to breathe thanks to you and that sack, I piloted the vessel close enough to use the escape pod, then sent it on its way out of this sector. Every pirate and rogue knows about Noy and Tochara. I came down in the wasteland, glimpsed the settlement, and walked toward it. Tochar's patrol found me and took me to him. I'm sure he's already checked me out thoroughly."

That's what you think, Dagan, but you're in for a shock tomorrow, especially if you're lying. "So, you were heading for Tochara all along?"

"It sounded like the best way to earn plenty in a short time and in a safe haven. I was going to take over that transporter, but you kinda intruded. Since we'll be working together, it will be nice to do it as friends. We already have a bond of protective secrecy."

"Let's keep it like that. Did you get a good price for those crystals?"

"I didn't know their value. Tochar does, so I assume they're targets during raids, despite his warning. I saw the way he looked at them and touched them, and he told me large ones supply the power for his defense system. What do you know about them?"

"If you join our team tomorrow, I'll tell you about the crystals and our raids."

As she took a swallow of the purple liquid, he asked, "Why do you keep saying *'if'*?" He watched her tongue collect a droplet from her upper lip and felt his loins quicken and flame at the enticing action.

"You're a clever man so you must realize Tochar wouldn't hire anyone on first sight. He'll want to question you further, in detail, in private."

That sounded like truth serum probing to him. "No problem; I'll tell him whatever he wants to know."

For certain and without control, my ignorant and sexy auslander. I wish you would stop looking at me like that. What is it about you that's so irresistible? His black hair seemingly begged her to hide her fingers in its depths. His full lips called to her to kiss them, as did his handsome face and throat. His dark-blue eyes were as potent and mesmerizing as a swirling vortex, drawing her ever toward it. But he was a criminal, one of her targets soon, so she must not lose herself in him.

"What's on your mind, Starla? You look puzzled." *Afraid I'll expose your deceit while drugged?*

"Somehow you don't strike me as a man who works for others. Why now? Why here?"

"I rarely do, but I have no choice if I want to buy a new ship. I heard Tochar pays well and he gives unreachable sanctuary to his men. Of course, if I could get my hands on a load of those crystals, I'd be rich."

"If you could find a buyer without being captured and terminated."

"They're that important?"

"You'll see if you're around the next time Tochar tests his weapons or gives a display of power and warning to would-be attackers. It's formidable; not even a fully armed fleet of starships can attack here. Those beams are so powerful they can penetrate force shields. They also have other abilities."

"So rich buyers are needed, and it's a risky venture to steal them. Why do you take such chances?"

"For payment and excitement, and I have nothing else to occupy me at this time. As you know, it requires a lot of money to keep a ship supplied and fueled, and there are only certain kinds of raids one can pull off alone. Tochara is the best place to rest and hide."

"Hide from what? From whom?"

"Anybody who's after me."

"Such as?"

"Lots of people, maybe some of the same ones who are seeking you." She was enflamed by his sexy grin and rich chuckle after her response. He certainly made it difficult to keep her mind where it should be!

"That's possible, since we're so much alike. Auken told me you have a ship and live on it, and Tochar said you're one of the best pilots he's seen."

"All true, and I'm not boasting."

"I believe you. How long have you been here?"

Starla shrugged. "Who keeps track of time without a reason?"

"How long do you plan to live and work here?"

"I'll stay until I'm bored or replaced, since I doubt I'll get a better offer anywhere else."

He noticed a tiny smile that time, but it didn't soften her steady gaze, so he decided it wasn't a natural one. "Where are you from?"

"All over, many places."

"I meant, what's your origin point?"

"I left it long ago and won't be returning."

Noting her sad expression, Dagan probed, "Any particular reason?"

"Several."

"Such as?"

"Nothing worth telling you. Besides, it's in the past, long gone."

Dagan realized he wasn't getting much information. She was as tight-lipped as a Kalfan leech, and was on tense alert. He wondered why he was making her so nervous, since she wasn't worried about him betraying her to Tochar. He finished his drink. "Any family?"

"No, all dead. What about you?"

"The same. My ship was my home and I miss her. She's probably been destroyed by now."

"Too bad. Our ships are like part of us. It's certainly impossible to come and go freely without one."

"Where and when did you learn to pilot a ship and a shuttle?"

"Long ago and by people special to me." *My father, sister, and my brother and his mate: all experts.*

While she seemed distracted, he probed, "How long have you been living and traveling alone?"

"Apparently not long enough, since I'm still doing it. What about you, Dagan?"

"Doesn't it get lonely and scary for a woman to exist in space by herself?"

"Is that how it affects you, why you're willing to become a lander for a while?"

Dagan realized she was amazingly quick and sly, an expert at this sort of get-nowhere conversation. He was more impressed and intrigued by the *preon.* "It happens on occasion to the best of us, doesn't it?"

"If you say so. But I'm not alone; I have an android for company and assistance."

"I know; Moig told me. But a robot isn't the same as a real person."

"Cypher is, and he's not a robot. He's the only companion I need, that I trust fully."

"You're a captivating and beautiful woman, Starla Vedris, but a wit-stealing mystery. Are you always this reserved and private with everyone?"

"I prefer it that way; work and diversion never mix well." *They definitely would not mingle safely and wisely with you, Dagan Latu.*

"Are you speaking from experience?"

"Let's say I'm convinced of that conclusion."

Dagan saw her green gaze widen and her enticing mouth part when he asked what must be a shocking query. "Are you interested in Tochar as a man?"

"Tochar has a longtime lover. Palesa. Beautiful and... feminine. I'm certain Palesa is very talented at servicing his needs." Cravings for both sexes would be his only reason for having a *Binixe* lover. At least his carnal preference had prevented any sexual overtures toward her. She had been ready to allege she was a lesbian if such an offensive predicament arose.

Dagan leaned closer to her from across the small table. His gaze meshed with hers. "You didn't reply to my query. Are you afraid to answer?"

Starla decided if she were compelled to get closer to Dagan for any reason, she mustn't allow him to think she was chasing after or was involved with their leader. "In the sense you mean, I'm not attracted to or bound to any

57

man, including Tochar, even if Palesa didn't exist. My sole interest here and in him is my work. Why would you ask such a personal question?"

"Are you annoyed you'll have to work with me?"

"Why should it bother me? One partner is as good as another, if he has the skills to be my equal and backup. If not, he doesn't work with me. So, why did you ask if I had any interest in Tochar or any man?"

"What if a teammate finds you lacking in some vital area? Can he refuse to work with you?"

"That hasn't happened so far. Now, reply to my previous query or our conversation is over."

Obviously she didn't fear his answer or she would stop pressing for it. Was she hoping he would admit to an interest in her? If so, he mused, why? "Just curious. I'd like to see your ship. Any chance for a visit?"

"You will, if you join our unit, because we use it sometimes. We were on the *Liksa* that *deega* we met. Tochar often pairs me with Moig."

"From your expression and tone, you would prefer Auken or Sach; right?"

"They have more skills, prowess and personality. Moig seems to enjoy harassing me under the guise of silly jokes. I find that annoying and insulting."

"I promise to make you an excellent partner when we travel as a team, very soon. How old are you?"

Stars afire, go trekking alone with you! "Twenty-two *yings,* why?" In her mother's time measurements, that was about two years older than Maffei's. She could not tell him she would be twenty-fourish on Earth.

"Just curious. I'm twenty-eight *yings.* Would you like another drink? Your glass is empty."

"No thanks." She needed to put distance between them after two lengthy and trying encounters in the same night. He was far too appealing to suit her, and she could not endure the stress any longer. It was a strain and risk to deal with him as two different people.

"Can I see you tomorrow to get better acquainted as a team?" Dagan asked. "We'll be leaving on our first raid in two *deegas* and I have much to learn. For safety and success, we must work as a single unit."

Those words and their meaning were familiar, but she cast them aside as coincidental. A bold idea entered her mind. "What if someone else joins you first?"

Dagan noted fast, but rapidly concealed, vexation with herself after that question slipped from her mouth. "Were you here earlier?"

She had not made a rash slip, but pretended she had. She reasoned, if he didn't want to risk offending Starla, suspecting her interest would keep him from making a premature move on Yana, as sexual overtures to Yana would force her into making a decision about how far she was willing to go for the success of her crucial mission. Too, Yana might not be able to extract clues if she didn't surrender to him. She also hoped that hearing she had sighted him with the sultry temptress would stress the point they were different women. A little encouragement might also pull him toward Starla in case he proved worthy of being trusted and asked to work with her on her assignment. Since he was a man who loved challenges, winning over a reluctant Starla should be enticing to him. If not, Yana would have to use him. "I'll see you around, Dagan Latu, if you stay past tomorrow," she said in parting.

Dagan grasped her hand, forcing her to stay seated. Realizing he had done the same thing with Yana gave him an eerie feeling. Her hands were a little larger than the golden-haired beauty's, but Starla's were cool and just as soft. Her green eyes glittered in warning, a contrast to Yana's alluring blue ones. Her complexion was darker, but flawless and supple. Her figure was as perfect as Yana's. Comparing the women was like trying to parallel night and day. Yana was desirable and provocative, but the space pirate had intoxicating spirit and vitality. Starla was strong; yet, feminine. Yana was the type of female perfect for enjoyable company and pleasure, but Starla Vedris was of value at any time and place. "You don't like being attracted to me, do you?"

She leaned so far forward that she knew he could smell the beverage on her breath and the fragrance she had applied after washing off Yana's scent. There was only a forearm's distance between their faces, and their challenging gazes were locked. "Let's get one thing straight: work is all we'll do together, and only if Tochar teams us up after your meeting with him. Keep your feelings and thoughts to yourself. Better still, find a woman who will be responsive to them."

Dagan did not release his grip when she tugged to get loose. He sensed her tension and saw the way her gaze engulfed him. Surely he wasn't mistaken about the desire glowing in her eyes. "If you're referring to Yana, she requested rescuing from nuisances."

"I'm sure she did, and you were eager to help her. Let's drop this topic because you two aren't of interest to me. You possess a disarming manner, Dagan, as you already know more about me than anyone here."

"As you see, Starla, I'm here and she's gone."

"I doubt that was your idea, so don't try to mislead or charm me. I've met men like you before, so don't think you can blast off with me."

"You're wrong, Starla, you've never met anyone like me, so don't be afraid to get to know me; I'll behave myself during that process." As if to prove his words, he released her hand and leaned back in his chair.

"If you give me trouble, Dagan, Tochar will have to choose between us. If you behave, we'll work together just fine. If not, I'm gone. Good night."

He warmed to her accidental clues. "Good night, Starla, and thanks again for saving my life."

"Just don't make me regret it," she quipped.

Starla passed Sach as she was departing for the landing grid. She halted to talk with him for a few *preons*. Afterward, while en route to her shuttle, she pondered her crazy feelings for Dagan Latu. Perhaps her strong attraction to him resulted from having his life in her hands and being able to save it, when she had been helpless to do the same for Antarus Hoy following the crash of their spacer three *yings* ago during an Elite Squad mission. Both injured and their supplies depleted and on the brink of death, she had surrendered to his need for her. Except for anguish over being unable to protect her and fearing she wouldn't survive, he had died a happy man, believing she loved him as much as he loved her. The mission had been a victory. She had been rescued, but she had lost her first teammate. She had been paired with Cypher, a successful arrangement which suited her just fine.

After Antarus's death, she had semi-enjoyed social evenings with other men, but none had affected her sexually as Dagan Latu did. What, she mused, was his special and potent appeal if not for her hand in his fate? Perhaps she had spared his life only to be forced to take it on a future *deega* if it came to a life-or-death battle for escape, or be forced to endure his loss to a annihilator unit or his exile to a penal colony after his capture, dependent upon which of his past charges were true and what he did while in Tochar's hire. She must not allow herself to become emotionally involved and ensnared by him. She must keep reminding herself he was a *villite*, a man out of her reach.

What if you can turn him from his nefarious ways? What if he can be persuaded to help you defeat Tochar? What if he can obtain a pardon for—Don't think such foolish things. Bree-Kayah, that's flying on a dangerous course for you and the entire UFG.

She reached her shuttle, prepared for lift-off, and went to her ship, her brain caught in a solar storm.

Sach joined Dagan. "You look better than you did earlier," he jested.

Dagan leaned back in his seat and smiled. "I feel better; trekking through that wasteland was rough. I'm lucky I didn't encounter any of those *Skalds;* from what I've been told, human flesh is a treat for them."

"Those mutants stay in the desert and don't trouble us, not since Tochar scared them from the fringes with a taste of his hot weapons. You'll be safe here, because nobody challenges him and those beamers."

"That's good news, since there are more than a few people who would like to get their greedy hands on me, and I'm grounded. I don't like feeling vulnerable. I'm eager to fill my pockets and get me a new ship; it feels strange not having a deck beneath my boots and warp drive at my fingertips. With what Tochar pays, that shouldn't take more than a *ying* or two, depending on what type I purchase next time. It will definitely have a cloaking device and lots of speed. That run-in at Gavas with a *Seki* is the closest I've come to getting caught, and it didn't flow over me well. That's the only time the old girl failed me and it wasn't her fault. I think I'm going to enjoy Tochara. It has plenty to offer; so does Tochar. I'd like to keep working for him and living in this haven even after I get a new ship, if that suits him. How long have you been with Tochar?"

"Tochar, Auken, and I have been a team since we were young. We've raided the Cosmos. Moig joined us about five *yings* ago, before we settled here." Sach tossed down his drink and purchased another one.

"What about Starla Vedris? She and I were just talking, but she isn't very communicative. Or maybe it's me she doesn't like," Dagan chuckled and downed the remainder of his drink.

Sach chuckled. He wasn't worried about chatting with Dagan, as the man would be silenced the following day if he didn't prove trustworthy. "She'll open up more after you get to know her. She was quiet and private when we met. She's been on her own for so long and staying just a few leaps ahead of capture that she's wary and used to keeping to herself. She's careful about who she gets close to and trusts. The good thing is that Tochar likes and wants you. He says you're perfect for our special unit."

"What is the 'special unit' and who's in it?"

Sach talked about his leader's Enforcers and how everyone who lived or traded in the colony paid Tochar for that privilege, for water, and for protection. "Only our team raids for him alone. There were four of us until you came along: me, Auken, Moig, and Starla. You'll learn more tomorrow and during our first raid."

Only four space pirates in the band... "Since there are so few of you going on raids, that speaks highly of the unit's skills. It's comforting to learn I'll be working with people who know how to take care of themselves and back up their teammates." Dagan watched Sach smile in pleasure. "I've never met a female pirate before Starla. I've seen women traveling and working with men, but never alone. What's her story?"

63

"She's grabbed your interest fast and hard, eh?"

Dagan grinned and nodded. "She's a beautiful, fascinating, and unique woman."

"You're right, Dagan, but don't treat her as an easy conquest. Starla Vedris flies by herself."

"Is there a reason why?"

"Auken thinks it's because she was either hurt by a man or lost one she loved. Probably doesn't want to get close to anybody she could lose again, and we do lead dangerous lives. Or could be she's just very selective. She doesn't talk much, if any, about her past."

Dagan noticed that Sach was becoming more and more relaxed and talkative, perhaps due to the many drinks he was consuming. He continued his questioning. "How long has she been here?"

"About three *malees.* She was trying to escape a Serian patrol after raiding an orbiting supply station for food, water, and fuel. They chased her across the entire sector, determined to capture her or blast her to pieces. We were on Auken's ship, returning from a raid, when they shot through the stargate, just missed hitting the *Adika,* and zoomed past us like speeding comets. You should have seen her evading their blasts; she's the best pilot I've ever encountered. We watched and listened to their exchanges. They ordered her to surrender, but she told them they had no authority across the boundary. They said she wasn't escaping them if they had to chase her across three galaxies. When she realized that patrol wasn't going to give up, she turned her ship and went straight at them, firing away. Blasted them into bits of debris. We contacted her and told her to head for Noy. It took a while to convince her she would be safe here, but she took a chance. Been with us ever-since."

"She actually destroyed a patrol ship and crew?"

"She had no choice if she wanted to survive, and the fools were in the Free-Zone. She probably confused them by turning and fighting. They didn't think a woman would respond that way. She was lucky to be on this side of the stargate when she destroyed them. That put them out of communication with their force, so life-taking charges didn't go on her record. All the Serians know is that one of their patrol ships vanished while in pursuit of a pirate. Starla's been real careful about working on the sly to keep her record short in case she's ever captured. She's tough, but she doesn't like to kill unless it can't be avoided."

"But she has an incriminating record?"

"Mostly of things like that Serian raid, enough to get her sent to a penal colony for life. She planned to leave us after she rested and resupplied, but Tochar convinced her staying would be safe and profitable."

"How long was she operating in Seri?" Dagan asked after Radu served them another drink.

"That was her third raid; she picked up weapons on one and a part for her cloaking device on the other. That's why she couldn't cloak and elude them. Since she's been here, Cypher repaired it."

"I'm curious. Where did she get the android?"

"It was being delivered to her father, a scientist on a skyball when the entire floating city was destroyed by a reactor malfunction. She was born and raised there, but she had gone with her brother to get the unit, the first time she had been off her world since birth. The android was ready for programing, so she ordered him to serve her. I don't know much about robots and computers and such, but that Cypher talks and acts so like a human sometimes that it's eerie. That's probably why Starla treats him as if he is alive. After that skyball exploded, she traveled with her brother for a couple of *yings.* He became a smuggler, but wasn't very successful. He taught her to fly, fight, and use weapons. After he and his men were killed by one of his buyers, she took off in his ship with Cypher as her crew."

"I haven't heard of her before; where was she operating before Seri?"

"Pyropea, Androas, Maffei, and other places. When it got hot for her in one sector, she left for another. She isn't rash, but she had no choice about that last raid; she needed supplies and fuel to vanish for a while. Tochar was impressed by her. He said we could use a pilot with a fast ship and somebody with courage, wits, and skills like hers. He offered her sanctuary and asked her to join us. She hasn't failed or disappointed him. The rest of us enjoy working with her; she's good, real good."

Dagan was learning a lot about Starla. He wanted to learn more, so he continued questioning Sach. "Was all of her family killed except her brother?"

Sach nodded. "She's lucky she was gone when its reactor went critical because there was no time for evacuation. The few ships that took flight were caught up in the blast; it must have been a huge explosion."

"That's a shame. Those incidents must have been tough for her, being a female and one so young."

Sach nodded again and downed his drink. "Starla's educated, intelligent, and well bred; her family was rich and powerful. I guess it's hard for a woman to lose everything and not change a lot."

"I understand how she feels. After those *Sekis* terminated my father and brother for alleged crimes, all I wanted to do was pay them back."

"It sounds like you've given them trouble for a long time. They don't take defeat and humiliation good, and you've given them plenty of both."

"That's part of the excitement and challenge: to bite and run, have them pursue, then elude them and leave them with singed pride. Do you think Starla's a permanent inhabitant here?"

"If she ever gets tired of being a pirate, she could have her looks changed and live elsewhere. I'm sure Tochara doesn't have much to offer a woman like her; that's why she lives on her ship. But after Tochar makes his improvements here, she might stay for good." Sach grinned and jested, "Unless you lure her away when you leave, if you do. You may want to stay after Tochara becomes a real city. All it needs is more time, wealth, and power, and some of those magic crystals. Best empty many glasses tonight and tomorrow, Dagan, because no drinking is allowed during raids."

"That's a wise precaution. Tell me, why does Moig call her Vedris?"

Sach laughed. "To keep him from thinking of her as a woman. Moig didn't stand a flick of a chance with her; he's finally accepted the fact he isn't her type."

"Am I?"

Sach chuckled as he toyed with his empty glass. "Don't know. As I said, she keeps to herself about men. About the only one here who could match her is Tochar, and he's involved with Palesa."

"He would be a tough competitor for her."

"You're lucky he doesn't desire Starla or she would belong to him. If all you need is a woman for your *sleeper* there are plenty of Pleasure Givers here."

"That isn't why Starla appeals to me." *Give it to him good, Dagan; nothing like supposedly sharing a secret to dupe a person into believing you like and trust him.* "To be truthful, Sach, I don't know why she gets to me and how she did it so fast. She has some kind of powerful magic and pull. I've never been tempted to go after a woman for serious reasons. Maybe that's a warning to avoid her before I'm snared in a crazy trap."

"Just take it slow and easy. Don't hurt her."

"I'll take that good advice. I guess I better turn in; it's late and I have to meet with Tochar in the morning. Been enjoyable talking with you."

"Same here, Dagan, and good luck."

"With my meeting or with Starla?"

"You'll need plenty of it to succeed with both."

After Sach stood and left, Dagan pondered the Icarian's parting words. He had a suspicion he was in for a life-depending challenge tomorrow.

It had been three *horas* since Starla took a seat in the Skull's Den to await news about Dagan. She didn't know if she wanted him to pass Tochar's *Thorin* test or not. If he failed, that meant he wasn't evil like the other *villites* or— even if he was proven to be just as wicked— wouldn't truly subject himself to the head *fiendal.* But failure meant his extermination. Yet, if he passed the truth and loyalty queries, he would become one of her targets to defeat and destroy. It would prove he was no different from them, prove her favorable impressions of him were wrong. By passing, he would be alive and in close proximity, until and if her mission succeeded. She felt trapped between two black holes in space, floating in peril, wondering if or when she would be sucked in and crushed by either one.

She knew from experience that the drug-induced interrogation and full recovery lasted for *horas:* thirty *preons* to be dazed completely, several *horas* of lengthy and detailed questions to learn his full history and motives, and one *hora* to return to complete awareness, plus travel time to and from the *fiendal's* abode.

According to that schedule he should have been finished five *horas* ago. Even if he had been taken on a tour of the defense sites and colony after he passed scrutiny, she reasoned, he should have appeared by now, if for nothing more than to have a drink and relax following his ordeal and perhaps to see if she and/or Yana awaited him. He wasn't with her Yana identity, but he could be celebrating on the second level with a Pleasure Giver. She attempted to quell the rash sparks of jealousy and anger that troubled her. It was a fact that most men believed they must have sex on a regular basis and, often, the face and name of the woman beneath them did not matter. Those carnal drives were strong in Tochara, where men lived and thrived on sating physical needs and thought only of the present.

She had played two games of *resi* with an off-duty Enforcer. She had eaten a rather tasty meal with the slowness of a *yema*'s pace to stall for time. She was on her second drink, the weakest type Radu stocked, as it seemed appropriate behavior for her Starla Vedris character to imbibe a little, and it gave her a plausible reason to remain in the place for a long period.

When she saw him enter the dome, her heart leapt with relief and happiness, uncontrollable reactions to learning he was alive. Of their own volition, her green gaze softened and almost misted; her heart beat faster; her lips parted. He was clad in a sleeveless top with a V neck in the front, the same shade as his blue eyes, a garment which displayed his muscled arms and shoulders and sun-darkened flesh. It fit him like a second skin, so his broad chest and flat abdomen were noticeable. His pants were snug, black like his boots and windblown hair, and hinted at sleek and strong legs beneath them. A weapon's belt was secured around his waist and hung low on the left side where a laser gun rested in a holster secured to his thigh. A sheathed knife was attached to the belt's right side. He was the epitome of a virile and handsome man, a pinnacle of strength and courage. He was a man to pursue...

As Dagan's roving gaze found her and he smiled, Starla returned the gesture without awareness, her wits scattering. Without taking his eyes from hers, she watched the Kalfan head toward her with an agile and confident stride. She stood entranced by his very presence, until Radu halted him for a brief word. As soon as their visual bond was severed and other thoughts invaded her mind, the strong and magical spell was broken and she became clearheaded. She scolded herself for being susceptible to Dagan's abundant charms. From now on, she reminded herself, he was one of her enemies; he must be viewed and treated as such, used in any way necessary to ensure the success of her mission. She took a swallow of her drink and did not look in his direction again.

Dagan sat down adjacent to her instead of across the small table. He was cognizant of her change in mood. There was no doubt in his mind that Starla had been excited and pleased to see him but had withdrawn into herself when Radu intruded on their spiritual connection. Now that he was acquainted with her history, that reaction was understandable. He thanked Radu for a drink the man delivered, compliments of Tochar, as was anything Dagan ordered tonight on either level of the Skull's Den. He ignored the beverage to ask, "How long have you been here?"

Starla was alert and calm; yet, strange sensations of sadness and weariness plagued her. "For a while."

"Were you worried about me?"

Starla leaned back and toward the right side of her chair to put more distance between them. "No, why would I be?" She watched him grin.

"Because you knew what I was facing. Too bad you couldn't warn me."

"Was one needed? Would it change anything?"

He chuckled. "If I wasn't who and what I claimed to be, I could have gotten out of Tochara before I was exposed and slain." That explained all her "ifs".

"There's no place you can hide from Tochar's reach and wrath. That's why no one betrays him."

"You didn't think I would pass scrutiny?"

She looked him straight in the eye. "No."

Dagan was pleased by her honesty and skepticism about his bad character, despite a criminal record and shady reputation. Yet, he sensed disappointment that her assessment of him had been proven wrong. "Why not? You passed interrogation when *Thorin* flowed in your veins. Afraid I would reveal my kill event?"

Unlike with you, his truth serum has no effect on me. "You struck me as being your own man, a loner, self-reliant, a leader, not a follower."

"Does taking orders from Tochar and being loyal to him me prevent me from having those traits?"

"Does it?"

"Not in your case, nor in mine. We're independent and self-reliant loners, but we bend and bond when we must. Under the circumstances, I have to work for him to get what I want and need." Dagan grinned to release their tensions and teased in a husky voice, "Unless you want to lure me away with a better offer."

Starla did not smile nor frown. "How would I accomplish that enormous feat?"

"You have the *Liska;* we can travel as partners, keep all we steal." *Access to your ship would give me a means of*

*escape if needed and would provide the opportunity for
private communication out of the Free-Zone. But that
would imperil you if I used them, used you for my needs,
which might become necessary if matters change.*

Starla wondered why Dagan was studying her so
strangely. "Why would I forfeit Tochar's generosity and
sanctuary to take risks with you? Besides, he would track
us and slay us for committing such treachery. As with me,
since you're alive, that means you told the truth about
being loyal to him, so you're only teasing me. It also
means you're part of our special unit."

Stars afire, woman, you're quick, captivating, clever!
To throw her off balance, he grinned. "Was I teasing?"
When Starla didn't smile or reply, he hinted, "No
congratulations? No welcome aboard? No glad you
survived? No thanks for not exposing me?"

Once more, Starla had the impression that Dagan
Latu was a cunning and complex male. If she didn't know
any better, she would think he had deluded Tochar. It
worried her that she could not depend upon her
normally keen instincts and gift for good judgment with
him. She took a swallow of her drink and eyed him over
the glass's rim before she lowered it and responded,
"Welcome to the special unit, Dagan. Since we're going to
be working together in dangerous situations, becoming
friends will be wise. I don't want an enemy or weakling
at my back."

"Being your enemy is the last thing I want, Starla,
and becoming friends will do for a start."

"What more do you want and expect from me?"

"Right to the point, a bold and direct woman."

"I'm pleased I have admirable qualities and traits."

"I made that discovery the first time we met; you're
an amazing woman. In case you're worried," he began in
a near whisper, though no one was nearby, "Tochar

didn't ask any questions about that incident, or about how I allegedly got to Noy, or about you. Except," he added and saw her tense, "he did ask if I knew you or anybody else before I came. It was easy to be honest because I didn't know you prior to my arrival."

She stared at him. Was it possible he was immune to *Thorin,* that he had tricked Tochar, that her initial appraisal of him was indeed accurate? And why tell her—one of Tochar's *Spacekis*—such a hazardous secret? "How can you know what he asked while you were under that drug?"

If you're wrong about her, Curran, you can be entrapping yourself. When she arrived here, she was truthful about her record and history and about giving fealty to Tochar or she would be dead now. Hopefully she's attracted enough to you to hold silent. "I had a recorder concealed in my boot and I listened to my session afterward." He witnessed an astonished look in Starla's green eyes, as well as something he decided was dismay, sadness. Why was she upset he had proven himself to be a criminal. . .

Chapter Four

The Kalfan's revelation took Starla by surprise and she responded before thinking, "That was taking a big risk, Dagan; Tochar isn't a fool, nor a man to deceive if you want to stay alive and work for him."

Her spontaneous reaction pleased him. It implied she cared about him and his survival. "If he was a dimwit, he wouldn't have control of this settlement and I wouldn't be interested in him. I had to be sure I didn't say anything disadvantageous or hazardous to me."

Starla regained her self-control. "Either you're daring and clever and fearless, or you're reckless and savor living on the edge." She saw him grin as if she had described him with accurate insight.

"I always try never to be reckless or impulsive." *But with you, woman, that's difficult. You're far too tempting and disarming. Maybe I should be worried that my interest in you equates with the one in Tochar, and that isn't smart. It can jeopardize the situation. Tochar has what Phaedrig wants, and I vowed to get it for him.*

Starla placed her glass on the table, unsettled by his intense mental study of her. "Do you use your little hidden unit very much? Is it on now?"

"Neither, and I destroyed that tape. Does he do more than one test?"

"Not to my knowledge. Afraid you'll change your mind, allow that independent streak to break through, and ruin future results?" She listened to his rich chuckles. She wished it wasn't such a fierce struggle to keep from staring at him and so strenuous a task to remain alert in his distracting presence.

"I just like to know what I'm up against. I don't like flying in a storm without sensors to guide me. I can use a friend while I'm grounded and a trusted co-pilot when we take flight, so I'm glad you aren't being defensive and distant anymore. I imagine you have your reasons for being that way, especially with strangers."

"I do. As a woman in my type of work, I have to be stronger, braver, smarter, and tougher than even the weakest of men to be accepted and respected. Or at least be a skilled pretender to dupe them into thinking I am. If I let down my guard, many try to take advantage of me or forget I have just as much prowess as they do and—in some cases— more."

He realized she wasn't bragging or exaggerating. Yet, he sensed her hard exterior was a protective shield for a unique and tender woman. Still, she was too enchanting and disarming to suit him. "I'm convinced you possess those traits; you took me down quick and easy. It was quite a shock and enlightenment. I remember every detail about our misadventure."

Starla didn't want to discuss their first meeting because of provocative things she had said to him, expecting never to confront him again and surely not as his teammate. "It's getting late, so I'll see you again at departure time."

"I hoped we could talk longer. You are supposed to edify me." He yearned to stretch out his fingers to fluff the tousled fringe of hair across her forehead. He wanted to touch and kiss her full lips and flawless skin, each exquisite feature on her face. He hungered to caress soft but firm flesh beneath a white jumpsuit which was a vivid contrast to dark-brown tresses that straight shoulders. Her green eyes enticed him to dive into their depths and search for the truth about her, to find and claim the real woman. Even the weapon she wore heightened his desire for the enigmatic and complex creature from a distant origin.

Starla knew it was futile to stop being attracted to him. "Don't you think you've seen and heard and done enough for one *deega?*" she asked in an attempt to control those intrusive emotions. "You were shown the defense sites and settlement, correct?"

"I got a tour. Those *Destructoids* are amazing. All it takes is removal of a cap to fire a formidable beam. I'm amazed such powers exist. Do you realize how mighty and invincible that makes Tochar and this colony?"

"That's why it's considered the safest haven for *villites* like us. Did they tell you the caps are the original encasements for those white crystals?" She waited for him to nod. "Whatever that rock is made of, it's the only thing that imprisons laser force. Crystals are round or oblong in their natural state. A ray can be created only after a white one is given a pointed end, and only a blue one can spall other moonbeams." She related medical facets of yellow crystals like he sold to Tochar. "Imagine how handy it would be to have that powder in your pocket during an accident. That blue one you had can be made into a scalpel with almost magical traits; it's the only color that can be cut by manmade instruments." After revealing its abilities, she said, "Nature is amazing; only one kind of crystal can give access to the powers and secrets of the others, and those capabilities depend upon their sizes and types."

"You know a lot about moonbeams. That *is* what they're called?"

"Yes, because their beams reminded discoverers of rays of moonlight, and their scientific name is long and hard to pronounce. You'll learn more during our raids; they're one of our targets. Despite their value and many uses, Tochar doesn't sell them or offer their magical powers here; to do so would cause a flood of buyers to come and that would attract too much attention. It would provoke others to steal them elsewhere and become competition. I learned all of this by keeping my eyes and ears open. It's good to gather any fact that might prove useful one *deega*. His most trusted men—his three closest friends—make tiny slips on occasion, especially during raids or post raid celebrations."

"Auken, Sach, and Moig?"

"That's correct, so never challenge them in any way or you're gone. Or slain."

"Thanks for the warning; I suspected as much. If what you say about crystals is accurate, if Tochar gets his hands on enough of them, he can rule the Universe, or enable his buyers to do so. One *ying* we could all be working for him or be under his subjection."

"If he has aspirations of conquest, I haven't heard them. His buyers will obtain the capability of preying on other worlds if he sells them the right type of crystals. I can't imagine him allowing anyone to gain such power; it could imperil him and his stronghold. As for me, I like the Universe as it is. Imagine how our existences will change if Tochar becomes a conqueror, or he enables others to destroy the current balance of power between the galaxies. We will have no say in our fates."

"Sounds scary and repulsive, almost a return to barbaric slavery."

"That's why the Serians and Kalfans tried so hard to protect that secret, but it slipped out, as most secrets do when profit is concerned. It hasn't been long since the crystals were discovered and mining began. But finding large specimens—especially the white hunks—is rare. Of course, without blue ones, the others are worthless. They make me think of colored ice."

"Why does either galaxy risk transporting them off their planets? That's reckless and tempting."

"Shipments of them are small, but research and testing must be done on secluded planetoids for safety and secrecy because their power is great and their potential not fully known. Tochar was fortunate that his first moonbeam raid resulted in acquiring those three awesome weapons."

"How did he accomplish that feat? Why weren't they guarded? How did he know about them?"

"The planetoid's force shield was disengaged during their transfer to a vessel for shipment to Ulux, Seri's head planet. Tochar's two units attacked them while they were vulnerable. His crafts were cloaked, so the androids and scientists didn't detect their presence until it was too late. Help was summoned, but the patrol's late arrival gave Tochar's band time to disable the androids and steal the cargo. One team and part of Auken's were trapped aboard the other vessel and wiped out during a battle and their craft destroyed, but the *Azoulay* cloaked and escaped with the *Destructoids;* that's what Tochar named his new weapons and it describes their power perfectly. Auken, Sach, and Moig were the only survivors. Tochar is rebuilding his special team; that's why he hired us. His Enforcers never go on raids; they remain here to protect him and Tochara."

"I'm surprised they told you such things when you joined up with them. Seems they would have kept quiet about such a disaster and the perilous risks you'd face; they didn't expose that information to me."

"When Sach is on Tochara, he likes to drink, drink heavily at times; that loosens his tongue to someone he trusts. Drinking is forbidden during treks. Sometimes all three get so accustomed to me being around that they forget I'm there and forget they aren't supposed to talk about such things in front of me, so they make slips. A dull-witted Sach once bragged about those being the only

Destructoids in existence because large white crystals are rare. Tochar never lets them leave his colony; that would make him vulnerable to attack. If he ever gets his hands on another one, he'll mount it on an attack ship; then no target will be unobtainable to him. I also keep my eyes and ears open without notice."

"I thought Auken's ship was named *Adika.*"

"It is, but they were using Tochar's that *deega;* it's faster, and has a better cloaking device and force shield. The *Azoulay* is useless until we steal a part needed for his energy system. It has only enough power left to stay in orbit and sustain life-support for a small crew. The parts he located are inaccessible and hazardous for a four-member team to go after. As we know from past experiences, power units or fuel can't be obtained without the proper papers and approval, and space stations are dangerous to raid."

"You're right, and I'm paying for that reality. Those moonbeams intrigue me, especially since I virtually gave away three out of ignorance. I'm curious. Why isn't their transportation guarded by huge forces?"

"How do you know they aren't?"

"Because four pirates couldn't attack a vessel or a planetoid and escape with any crystals if they were confronted by a large and well-armed force."

"You're very astute," Starla complimented. "The shipments are carried out in assumed secrecy, usually with only one or two androids aboard to prevent drawing attention to them or giving the impression of a vessel worthwhile to attack."

"Then how does Tochar know when and where to raid?" His questions flowed swiftly and fluently. "How do we get those android pilots to halt and lower their force shields? How does Tochar market something so secretive and dangerous?"

Starla noted how intelligent and educated he seemed, in particular for a space pirate, and how inquisitive. "Obviously he has contacts in Seri and Kalfa, important men in the know. You'll soon learn we have various ways of assaulting our targets. As to his buyers, I don't know anything about them, or if he's even sold any to date. I wouldn't advise asking questions about moonbeams or his sources; Tochar only shares that information with his three friends. Even I'm not told our destination and target until we reach them. I'm sure it will be the same with you."

"So, we're trusted, but we aren't. We're tested and accepted, but kept blinded. Interesting... I've never hired on with anybody who withheld information and didn't allow me to help plan our strategy. That makes me a little wary and edgy. How about you?" He saw Starla nod. "We can be of great help and protection to each other if we stick together."

Starla fused her gaze with his. "That's a tempting offer; just prove it's an honest one. Keep all I've told you to yourself, or we're both in deep trouble."

"I will, trust me."

"Give it time and patience. Good night, Dagan."

Starla looked at Cypher. "I wonder why Dagan disclosed such perilous things, if they're true. He doesn't seem the type to do anything without a good reason, one in his favor. If he thinks I'm so naive that allegedly sharing secrets will ensnare and bind me to him, he's wrong. I suspect he was trying to draw me toward him for a purpose I haven't grasped yet. Perhaps Tochar is suspicious of me and he's hired Dagan to get close enough to expose me. It's possible Dagan lost that struggle during the last raid by intention. On the other hand, Tochar knows I don't do life-taking. Although he believes I killed the crew chasing me when I was attempting to make my initial contact with him, and that ruse worked. What he doesn't know is those were advanced androids similar to you who only looked and sounded human. It's that traitor—or traitors—in Seri who have me concerned. *Raz* Yakir is supposed to be the only one who knows of my assignment and identity, but what if he let them slip to the wrong person, the one supplying Tochar with information about moonbeams and their shipments? Or maybe I said or did something to cause him to doubt me."

Cypher had not intruded on her rush of questions and remarks; he comprehended she was reasoning out matters to clarify them in her mind, and a means of letting him know her thoughts. "I require more data to classify Dagan Latu's character, motives, and goals. It is improbable Tochar doubts you; analysis of his voice patterns do not indicate suspicion in him or the others. It is illogical for *Raz* Yakir to expose you to anyone, even those close to him, because one is a traitor."

The android's words were reassuring. "If Dagan didn't know about the truth serum test, why did he take an undetectable recorder with him? And if he knew, why did he subject himself to uncontrollable scrutiny unless he was certain he would pass it?"

"He may have suspected *Thorin* would be--"

Before Cypher finished, Starla's gaze widened and she asked, "Do you suppose Dagan was sent here by an enemy of Tochar's to check his defenses and activities? To look for weaknesses? Perhaps to search for a way to disable his weapons so an attack can take place?"

"Tochar has many enemies and competitors. Those would be logical steps for a foe or rival to take if an attack or challenge is being planned. It is not known everywhere that Tochar has *Destructoids.*"

"You're right. That means Dagan could have been sent by a rival to study Tochar's strength and value. Do you think he's trying to lure me to his side?"

"He revealed suspicious things. Perhaps a strong attraction to you loosened his tongue and dazed his wits. If he is working for a rival, obtaining an ally or source of information will be of value to him."

Starla did not like the idea of being used by Dagan or anyone, but Cypher's second sentence did warm her from head to feet. "If he's an enemy or working for one, how can he dupe *Thorin?" Unless. . .*

"Many galaxies have secrets from others. He asked about future retesting; it can mean immunity is limited by time and induced by a temporary blocker. I do not know of such a chemical or treatment. That does not mean one does not exist elsewhere. He is of Kalfan origin, but his loyalties can be to another, for hire or another reason. He is a *villite* in his world and his record reveals he becomes a *bijoni* at times."

"Perhaps revenge for something Tochar did in the past is his motive."

"That is a possibility."

Starla realized an immunity to *Thorin* meant Dagan could have deceived Tochar and might not be as wicked as he alleged... But her speculations and Cypher's could be farfetched—and Dagan is, in reality, as bad as his record claims.

"Why did you reveal so much about moonbeams to him?" Cypher asked.

"So Dagan will grasp dangers involved in his new position and weigh the risks and his payments against Tochar's profits and safety. I'm hoping he'll decide they do not equate to suit him. If he leaves, it's one less *villite* to defeat." *And the removal of a disarming temptation.* "If he stays, it might cause dissension and disloyalty. Even a man like Dagan wouldn't want anybody to become so invincible he can never break free and any resemblance to life as he knows it will vanish."

Starla took a breath and a sip of soothing liquid. "He knows Tochar took advantage of his ignorance about moonbeams when the *fiendal* purchased them from him. No leader of honor would trick one of his men, and Tochar is hiring him. I doubt Dagan won the crystals in a *resi* game. Either he lucked up on a shipment and stole them, or one of Tochar's contacts is doubledealing. If he thinks I trust him—or irresistibly attracted to him—maybe he'll open up to me. If so, there might be a way to exploit it to aid our mission. I must confess, Cypher, no matter what Dagan Latu claims to be or how his record reads, my instincts tell me he can be trusted in a dark *hora. B*ut I promise I won't act on that impression until I am assured of its accuracy. If he is working for a rival or foe, maybe they will destroy each other and complete this mission for us."

"If that is a fact, be careful you do not get caught between adversaries in a violent takeover."

"I'll be careful. I have you to monitor and protect me. What did Dagan's voice pattern reveal to you?"

"An analysis is impossible without a base line of truth with which to compare his words and inflections for honesty and deception."

Starla pondered, "Is there any type of device I can press against him so you can obtain readings?"

"That is impossible. Without a foundation line for comparison, I can not differentiate between what is fact and what is prevarication."

"I'll have to go on my instincts and training."

"They have never failed you in the past."

83

"Hope and pray they don't desert me."

Dagan did a scan of his chamber for listening and observing mechanisms and found none. Afterward, he retrieved a cryptographic message awaiting him on the communications device concealed in his knife handle, the most advanced and smallest unit in existence. It told him that two perusals of his criminal record had been made, both from untraceable sources who had access codes to the same mass memory computer network into which he and his friend could tap. He was certain the first probe was Tochar's, but the second was a mystery. He deduced it was carried out by one of Tochar's cohorts from either Seri or Kalfa, contacts Starla had mentioned. The men must have supplied the data base password to the Icarian and may have double-checked Dagan Latu's identity and discovered he had a lengthy file, confirming his claims. He had expected to be examined thoroughly, but thanks to precautions, Tochar knew only what he wanted the man to learn.

Dagan pressed a button on the device to block detection of his out-going signal and transmitted a message to the man who had sent him there, though he had a personal reason for wanting to see Tochar slain. Before he could do so, he had to earn the trust of the leader and his band; that was how he could get close enough with a weapon to carry out that daring feat.

Dagan didn't need to ask for information about Tochar; he was well acquainted with the man's history and, thanks to a beautiful pirate, abreast of his present. He requested data on Starla Vedris and Yana of Asisa, as either or both could become impediments to him. With the aid of his secret contact and the man's access to the *I-GAF* computer network, he needed fingerprints to learn everything about them that use of their names—possibly fake ones--didn't provide. Of course, obtaining those prints could be difficult and entertaining, but he was looking forward to it. If his contact could not get answers using their purloined images via I-GAF files, he dared not circulate their faces and risk exposing either to peril. Until he received replies on the females, Dagan decided, he would study and deceive both women to determine which, if either, unknowingly or willingly could help him achieve his goal.

Eight *deegas* later as Dagan and Starla awaited the impending raid in the *Adika's* meeting compartment, Dagan glanced at their attire and down at their hands. "Why were we told to wear *I-GAF* uniforms and imprint these fake badges on the back of our hand? Though I admit, they look convincing. Even if false markings were put on Auken's ship, our target shouldn't halt or allow us to board her without the hailing frequency and watchword." *So where and how does he get them?*

From the corners of her eyes, Starla noticed how appealing Dagan Latu was in that deep-blue uniform which matched the color and potency of his gaze. The snug garment, all-powerful badge, and illustrious image of an Inter-Galactic Alliance Force officer suited him perfectly. She found herself aroused and wishing the implication was true. If so, he would be someone worthy of taking home to meet her family, someone within reach as a mate, someone she could team up with to defeat Tochar. He wasn't, so she cast those foolish fantasies aside and ventured an answer to his query, "Because Tochar knows them; he has ways of acquiring even the most secret and guarded information."

Dagan sensed her keen study, but he couldn't think about how tempting she looked or how he affected her. He had to quell his hunger for her and concentrate on his goal, so he continued, "How? From whom?"

Starla shrugged and clenched her fists. "I have no idea; they don't reveal such things to me."

"Why were we ordered to stay in here out of sight while we approach our target?"

"I suppose because there are things Tochar doesn't want us to see or hear. Perhaps he's afraid if we learn his secrets, we won't need him."

"That's logical and wise, but I don't like being kept in the shadows and maybe mistrusted when my life and payment are on the line. It makes me uneasy."

"Me, too. But if you want to stay in Tochar's hire, don't complain about or question his orders. You were given that advice, correct?"

He nodded. "How long does it take to be trusted and accepted fully?" He noted another shrug.

"I've been with them for over three *malees,* but I'm sitting here as ignorant as you, so wouldn't you agree I'm still being tested? For certain, if they promote a newcomer to the inner circle before me when I've earned that rank, I'm gone from Tochara." *That should convince you of my alleged identity and my motive for joining and staying in that* fiendal's *band.*

Before Dagan expressed an opinion, the door slid open. Auken instructed them to go to the transporter room. In the passageway, he asked, "You mean our target halted and will allow us to board her?"

The golden-haired man laughed and boasted, "Our disguises and ruse worked. Her engine is shut down and she's in a communications blackout as ordered. Let's hurry before somebody wonders why and sends a patrol to check out a problem. So far, nothing hazardous is registering on our sensors. No patrols are supposed to be in this sector for the next three *horas;* that's plenty of time to get what we came after and be gone. Starla, you and Sach will disable the androids while Dagan and I collect our prize and search the ship. We don't want another free-rider to intrude on this raid like that one did with you and Moig. We don't want any warnings sent or obstructions to arise."

Starla refused to let memories of that last raid cloud her mind. "Do you want us to delete their communication with us and record of our presence and put the vessel on automatic pilot as usual?"

"That won't be necessary; she'll be obliterated after our departure." Auken continued after he entered the transporter room. "Sach will handle that precaution; you assist him."

"Understood." She was shocked by his destructive intention. Yet, there was nothing she could do to save the vessel and the androids, unless she revealed herself and took the *villites* prisoner. She was a skilled, highly trained, multi-experienced fighter and authorized law enforcer. But to attempt to incapacitate four men with stun beams was too risky. Even if she succeeded, that would terminate her crucial mission. She knew Cypher was nearby in the cloaked *Liska,* protecting her and recording this incident as usual, but there was nothing he could do either or his presence would be exposed. The moment Auken divulged his plan, she slyly had pressed a button on her wrist device to signal Cypher to noninterference of the last statement.

Auken, Sach, Starla, and Dagan stepped onto the sensor pads so Moig could transfer them to the other ship, as he was to remain aboard to monitor their safety and operate the transportation unit.

It did not take long for Starla and Sach to disable the androids. Afterward, they headed to the engine room so the Icarian could set an explosive charge which would leave nothing behind except space debris. Then, the rugged man carried out an unexpected task.

Starla watched as he used a laser tool, powered by a white moonbeam, to open a recently installed and concealed flight recorder box. He poured Myozenic Acid inside to dissolve its contents and beacon. That action eliminated any clues about the incident and obliterated its tracking signal.

Sach contacted Auken by transmitter. "All tasks are done," he announced. "How long do you need before I switch on the timing device?"

"We're finished. Arm the charge and meet us in the transporter room. Let's get out of here."

Within five *preons,* the raid was completed and the group was sitting on the *Adika*'s bridge with Auken and Sach at the controls. They observed a distant explosion on the cloaked ship's viewing screen.

"That was too easy. No challenge at all."

"You're right, Auken, but I like easy and quick to protect my skin," Moig revealed. "That's a pretty view, bright colors and pieces flying in all directions, no evidence to point at us or Tochar. *Karlee* fire, those androids are stupid to be so smart; I love those glitches in their programs so we can bypass their orders."

Karlee was exactly where Starla wanted the evil *villites* to go one *deega,* as a hellish existence and punishment were what she felt they deserved. She made a mental note to report Tochar's knowledge of the investigative apparatus, a secret measure only certain people in Seri would be aware of, one that perhaps would provide the mistake needed to unmask its traitor. She would tell Cypher to add that discovery to their ever-growing file on this mission.

Dagan leaned back in his seat. "Auken's right; there were no challenges to stimulate the blood and test our skills. But I wouldn't mind keeping this uniform and marker; might come in handy for future use."

"You're planning on leaving us?" Auken asked.

"Not until I earn enough to buy a new ship. It will take a *ying* or two for what I want. Maybe I'll stay and hire on as a private raider. I like Tochar's generosity and sanctuary. He's smart, so he should be open to that suggestion. Having several teams working for him will bring in more profits. You think he will allow me to use the *Azoulay* if I can get her repaired?"

After checking his sensors and adjusting his course to head for a stargate into the Free-Zone, Auken asked, "How would you do that?"

"There's an old space station orbiting Gavas in the Kalfa system. I've made stops at Sion in the past. It's rarely used because others are newer, better equipped, and more advanced. The parts storage bay might have what Tochar needs to get her going again. Sion was well stocked the last time I was there, but it can be empty and abandoned by now. If not, only a skeleton crew will be manning it; they shouldn't give us any problem we can't overcome. If Tochar has trusted contacts in Kalfa, he can check out that possibility. If it's safe and the part he needs is there, we can get one for him. I'm sure I remember my way around that station, so we can be in and out in a hurry. We can use these disguises to obtain permission for docking."

Starla was dismayed by Dagan's suggestion, as it might endanger the lives of any humans assigned to Sion. If they were divided into teams, she could be given Moig as a partner and assigned raids that didn't include those for moonbeams, which would hinder her investigation and imperil her mission. If she and Moig used her ship while the others used the repaired *Azoulay,* which was superior to the *Adika,* that also would prevent Cypher's stealthy trackings. She mustn't allow that obstacle to thwart her.

"I'm pleased by your idea and offer of help, Dagan," Auken said, "but Tochar doesn't permit anybody to go anywhere in the *Azoulay* unless he's aboard. But he will be grateful to you for getting him that part."

Dagan grinned and shrugged as if in acceptance of the Icarian's words. He hoped Tochar would permit him to repair the ship and that the leader would be tempted to take a trek in it for diversion or testing, as that would get Tochar away from his formidable defenses and make him vulnerable to attack. "That's reason enough to do him a favor. That idea came to me after you mentioned the *Azoulay*'s troubles last night."

Starla was relieved to hear that news, as she feared Auken would ask how Dagan had learned about the *Azoulay's* problem and might wonder why she had mentioned that fact to the auslander. She suspected Dagan had made that statement to enlighten her. "If our job is completed," she said to Auken, "I'm going to change out of this uniform and scrub off this fake tattoo. It makes me nervous to be this close to them. I don't even want to imagine what an *I-GAF*er would do to us for impersonating one of their units. That ranks as one of the gravest offenses we can commit."

Auken increased their pace to starburst speed. "You're right, Starla, but who's going to find out with the evidence destroyed?"

Her gaze settled on Auken. "No secret or security is totally impregnable, my friend; somebody—somehow, someway—always finds a means to penetrate them. Our success on this trek proves that's a fact."

"Losing your courage, Vedris?"

She looked at the shorter man who was stroking his golden beard. "No, Moig, but it's good to be cautious, and healthy fear is wise. That's what keeps one from making fatal mistakes."

"She's right, Moig," Sach said, "so don't tease her or laugh. I would be nervous and worried too if I didn't know for certain our secret is safe. Starla doesn't have the same knowledge and advantage we do."

"It stokes her to be ignorant," Moig disclosed in vivid annoyance, "she told me so."

"Wouldn't being kept in the dark bother *you* when your life is at risk? If I were nothing more than a simple hireling, I wouldn't expect to be told things, but I'm a team-member for a long time. I just don't understand why I'm not fully trusted and enlightened."

"Don't worry, Starla; that won't be true for much longer. Moig, calm down and shut your flapper."

"Thanks, you're a good friend and teammate."

Sach smiled. "Thanks, so are you."

"I'm going to freshen up and change garments. I'll return soon. Anybody need anything?"

"You can relax and rest back there if you want. It's four *deegas* to the boundary and three to Tochara. Nothing much to do until we reach base."

"That's a good idea, Auken. Signal me if there's trouble." Starla left the bridge as they headed toward the boundary which separated the Free-Zone from Kalfa. The Zone had a small sun but only a few planets and planetoids orbited it every six *malees,* all close enough to the solar body to make their climates and landscapes extremely dry, but not uninhabitable. The Zone was surrounded by Kalfa, Seri, Thracia, and Ceyx; with stargates in each direction to provide fast and easy access from it to those galaxies, especially with certain planetary alignments and their various speeds: sublight, starlight, and starburst. Soon, she'd reach Noy.

After the journey ended and she was back aboard her ship, Cypher summoned Starla from her sleeping quarters to respond to an undetectable communication link with Thaine Sanger, Star Fleet Commander, head of Maffei's Elite Squad, son of her parents' best friends. He was still unattached, but like a brother to her.

"Lieutenant Bree-Kayah Saar responding, sir."

"Bree, I wanted to warn you somebody scanned Starla Vedris's record and requested data on Yana of Asisa. That cue I inserted in the program alerted me to the probes. The origin point was untraceable, so whoever did it has inside knowledge and sophisticated equipment. Do you have any speculations about the intruder's identity and motive?"

"I doubt it was Dagan Latu because he doesn't have access to communications. I'm sure he was searched by Tochar, so he couldn't have brought a device with him." She assumed he had gotten the recorder from one of the traders who was selling stolen goods in the colony. "The only explanation that comes to mind is that Tochar is doing a second scrutiny because he saw the two of us with Dagan. Perhaps that beast wants to make certain there are no connections between us."

"You've already used Yana to approach Latu?"

"I hoped she might learn things Starla can't, but I didn't extract anything useful during my attempt."

"Anything else to report?"

She told him about the recent raid and how it was accomplished using *I-GAF*er disguises and knowledge of

Seri's communications frequency and watchword. She told him about the concealed flight recorder's fate and about a possible raid on the Sion space station.

"I'll warn *Raz* Yakir to change his communications frequency and code word. I'll suggest he make a list of people who knew about the installation of that recorder and beacon, and to watch them carefully for clues of guilt. As to the Sion raid, I hope that succeeds; if Tochar gets his ship repaired, he might be tempted to take a voyage in her. If he does, we can lay a trap for him. You can't warn us about his trek if he takes you along, but Cypher can while he's cloaked and tracking you. If we get our hands on that *fiendal,* we can replace him with a lookalike cyborg and take control of Tochara's defense system and finalize this mission. I wish I could contact *Autorie* Zeev of Kalfa or the head of *I-GAF* to make certain a raid on Sion will work, but I can't risk them learning we have an agent inside Tochar's band because we don't know who or where the traitors are."

"I hadn't thought about entrapping Tochar away from Noy. I'll keep you informed on that angle. Who knows, maybe Dagan Latu will help us without knowing it? I agree with not telling the Kalfan ruler about my presence; we know Tochar has at least one contact there, somebody important and trusted." She revealed everything she had learned since their last talk, observations and facts that would be disclosed to Yakir. "The mission is progressing, but slowly."

"Don't get discouraged or take any risks," Thaine Sanger coaxed, "you're doing fine. At least we know more about Tochar and his settlement than we did before your arrival. You're getting closer to them and victory every *weg.* Be wary of Latu; he's cunning and dangerous, and obviously out to stick himself snugly to Tochar for profit and sanctuary."

93

"I'll be careful. If you learn anything else about him, send it to me. I don't want any unknown factors thwarting me. Now, tell me, how is my family?"

"Doing fine, just worried about you. I'll assure them you're safe and doing a superb job. I'm proud of you, Bree. If we weren't like siblings, I'd snag you."

She laughed with affection and respect. "Thank you. Anything important happening there?"

"Not at the present. But I don't want to imagine the troubles we'll face if Tochar continues to get his hands on moonbeams. As with every galaxy in existence, Maffei would be utterly helpless to repel his attacks and to protect itself. Yakir wishes he had never allowed those weapons to be invented and constructed, and he's distressed about them falling into enemy hands. He has no intention of ever using them against anyone; he just wanted to know the crystals full potential so he could guard against something like this happening."

"I like and respect *Raz* Yakir; he's a good man and superior ruler, despite how he unknowingly helped our enemies almost destroy us long ago. The Tri-Galaxy Alliance was fortunate when Seri and Kalfa decided to unite with Maffei, Androas, and Pyropea. It would be frightening to know those two galaxies possess such formidable crystals if we weren't allies. It must be a terrible burden for him and *Autorie* Zeev to be responsible for controlling such awesome power, to have the Microcosm's fate in their hands."

"There have been many times in the past when the fates of Maffei and the Tri-Galaxy rested in our fathers' hands, and in your mother's during that viral sabotage. I haven't forgotten the things your sister and her mate and Galen's mate did to save Maffei from our enemies' treacheries, and how our fathers saved your mother's home planet from destruction. Many of Star Fleet's best officers have come from your family and bloodline, including our past ruler. No *kadim* can ever be as wise and revered as your great-grandfather was. I hope Galen and I are as skilled and worthy of our ranks as our fathers were, as *you* are, Bree. We'd better sign off. The longer we stay in touch, the riskier it is for some unknown type of technology to detect our signal."

Thaine's reflections made Starla homesick for her family and friends, but sent a flood of pride in their accomplishments flowing through her. Her superior and her brother had been best friends since childhood and had carried out many crucial missions together. She had known Thaine and his family since her birth, twenty-six *yings* after her twin siblings—Galen and Amaya--were born to Supreme Commander Varian Saar of Maffei and scientist Jana Greyson Saar of Earth.

"Tell Father and Mother and the others I love them and miss them. I promise, Thaine, I'll do everything I can to defeat Tochar and to recover or destroy the moonbeams in his possession. Bree-Kayah out."

"Watch your back, Bree," the close friend in him advised. "I want to bring you home alive and safe and soon. Supreme Commander Sanger out."

As Starla deliberated their conversation and discussed matters with Cypher, another communication was received. It was from Tochar, an astonishing message to which she would react tomorrow.

Chapter Five

After finishing her talk with Tochar, Starla asked Cypher's input on the special and secret task Tochar wanted her to help the others carry out the next day. "Why would he signal me so late? If we're not going on another raid or leaving Noy, what can it be?"

"Insufficient data to theorize possibilities."

"I'll have to come up with a program to teach you to use gut instincts for making guesses," she teased. "Of course, intuition can be wrong, so perhaps it's best to base decisions on facts."

"It is rare for your perceptions to be wrong; in all instances when you made an error, it was not a serious or incorrectable one."

If Antarus had listened that deega, *he would be alive. At least our mission was achieved and he was awarded a posthumous commendation. If he had survived, would I have fallen in love with him and become his mate? I think not.* She took a deep breath and exhaled.

"Where do your thoughts and feelings travel, BreeKayah?"

"Into the past with Antarus where they do not belong. Thank you for your confidence in me and my abilities. I would be lost without you at my side."

"Even if I were not programed to serve and guard you, you have earned trust and loyalty."

"What a wonderful thing to say, Cypher. Now, back to our mystery: I think Tochar's plan has to do with buyers for the moonbeams we've stolen, at least for part of them. He doesn't want to involve his Enforcers and wants to keep them unaware of the crystals' power and value, so he needs his special team either to go with him or to carry out the sale and delivery. He wouldn't meet with them in Tochara and risk being seen by the wrong person. That indicates a probable rendezvous point in the desert. Do you have the device ready that *Raz* Yakir told you how to construct?"

"I completed it before I summoned you to speak with your superior." He lifted the tiny square and said, "I assembled it with the frequency *Raz* Yakir supplied. His theory of destablatory electromagnetic pulsations is rational, but there are no means by which to test the unit's prime function."

Starla was glad Cypher had many technological and scientific chips in his advanced system and had access to others in several computer networks' data bases. "If it works as Yakir's inventors say it will, all I have to do is get close enough to those moonbeam crates to attach it without getting caught. Do you believe the sound waves it emits can agitate the crystals' internal power source and cause them to shatter into particles too minute to be of use to Tochar? I don't understand the full concept, but it sounds as if it's some type of implosive sequence." Starla was glad Cypher always tried to explain things to her in a comprehensible way.

"*Raz* Yakir's report says it will do so."

"I thought moonbeams were infrangible."

"Nothing is indestructible. For each force in nature, there exists a counterforce if it can be found and mastered by thought and action." His control center told him to clarify his meaning in simple language. "Only a blue crystal can be cut by manmade instruments and only a blue crystal can penetrate the other crystals' surfaces. All crystals appear to have the same internal structure and power source, *heart,* as you humans would say. The color of its covering, its skin, alters, or decides capability. Their entire potentials, complexities, composition are still unknown."

"Perhaps the Serians and Kalfans have stumbled upon the Portal to Doom's *Deega* which can unleash the evil beyond it, because an intergalactic war with such awesome weapons will be catastrophic."

"If a doorway exists, we will close and seal it."

"How does one halt a solar storm after it begins and recall a laser's beam once it has been fired? It is the same with the crystals' power. It has been revealed and loosened upon a weaker mankind."

The android analyzed her words and grasped her meaning. "One who is intelligent, strong, brave, and agile can evade both forces. We will find a way to defeat your enemies and destroy their threat."

"If that device works, Cypher, why can't they create a larger unit with the same frequency band and aim it at those *Destructoids?* "

"Distance between the apparatus and its target will prevent success. *Raz* Yakir's communication stated it must be within a certain range to work."

"If I were allowed inside the defense sites, I could plant units there, but Tochar is too careful to imperil his treasures. As long as those weapons guard Tochara, an attack by our forces is impossible. Yet, the more raids we make, the more I help him to get stronger. Why can't the Serians and Kalfans halt shipment of those blasted crystals until Tochar is defeated, or at least increase their security and protection?"

"It is too late for research to be halted and it must be done in isolation. To use a show of force would draw attention to the transportation vessels and a valuable cargo; that would provoke bolder attacks by larger pirate bands. If raids are prevented, no clues are released and gathered; identities of the traitors cannot be discovered. Tochar would wait in safety on Noy until shipments were resumed. If Tochar is prevented access to all crystals, he could be tempted to attack to obtain them; there would be no defense against it."

Those were frustrating points Starla knew well, but reasoning aloud with an analytical Cypher often helped elicit new ideas which might prove helpful. "Your list of reasons is grim but accurate. It's a shame the Serians and Kalfans can't construct large devices and shatter the crystals in their possessions to prevent enemies from obtaining them, and seal the mines forever. That will prevent a threat from occurring again."

"Is it logical to destroy good to destroy bad? Recall what other crystals can do to help mankind."

"You're right; if mining continues, they can't control what types and sizes of moonbeams they locate. Still, the hazards of having such powers are enormous. Besides, if the mines are sealed, only Tochar will own *Destructoids,* Now, others must be built for a balance of power, if more large white crystals are found. Let's pray that little device works and slows Tochar's evil."

"I did as you ordered. I attached an adhesive circle for concealing it underneath a crate and disguised it as a metallic disk for your belt. It is ready for use."

"I'll take it tomorrow in case my speculation is accurate. This might be the only chance I have to get close to those crystals. Attach it to my belt while I'm sleeping, if I can sleep tonight."

"Take a *Calmer* if necessary; rest and renewed energy are needed."

"Don't follow us tomorrow, but keep us monitored and record the incident. We don't want to take more risks than necessary with our trick when you leave orbit to shadow me. I'm afraid somebody might discover we're using a hologram and fake signal and your absence would be revealed. If its auto-pilot or image maker malfunctioned, we would be exposed."

"I am programed to protect and assist you," Cypher reminded her. "I cannot accomplish that order from a great distance."

"I know. I'll be extra careful. Even if it seems I am in danger, do not interfere unless I signal you to help or rescue me. I don't want Tochar or the others to grasp the extent of your capabilities or constant observations. Victory is contingent upon duping them."

"Take no risks, Bree-Kayah; do not expose or endanger yourself."

"I promise, I won't attach or switch on the device unless it's safe. Don't worry, we may only be going on a weapons' or supply sale or buy."

"You cannot deceive me to prevent concern. Tochar handles such business in his abode."

Starla's eyes brightened. "What if he's going to meet with one of his contacts? If that's true, I can discover his identity and report it."

"Do not break contact to prevent concern."

"You've covered the warning angles, so relax and trust me. An Elite Squad member of Star Fleet will not jeopardize herself or her mission." She reminded, "Do not react in any way unless I signal you."

"What if you are unable to signal me?"

"Unless I'm dying or in chains, do not rescue me. Make sure they cannot handle the peril before revealing yourself to them. Even if the situation looks grim, wait until the last *preon* to take action. Understood?"

"Your meaning is explicit; I will obey."

"I'll sleep while you finish your task."

***

The next day, two landrovers with rear cargo holders headed to a secluded location beyond the busy colony.

Tochar, Auken, and Sach traveled in one; Moig, Dagan, and Starla rode in another to their left.

From her seat behind the two men, Starla made a quick and furtive study of Dagan Latu. He wore a thin and billowy white shirt with full long sleeves and corded ties below his throat. Earlier she had noticed those lacings had been left hanging free and loose, displaying a triangular expanse of hard chest covered with wispy dark hairs. His black pants were snug, their bottoms tucked inside matching boots. A weapons belt was secured around his waist and held a laser pistol and sheathed knife. His dark wind-tossed hair grazed broad shoulders, shorter from a recent cutting, very appealing. He had shaved recently, as well, and his strong jawline was smooth and free of stubble. Though he seemed to laze on the seat, she sensed he was ready to react in a flash if trouble threatened, and knew he possessed the skills and agility to do so. He was such a magnificent and virile male that his mere presence aroused her to forbidden desire. She was all too aware of the fact that if something went wrong later, this could be the last time she saw him, if they survived.

After they halted, a flurry of red dust created by their movements wafted past them or settled on their bodies and garments and on the transportation vehicles which lacked bubble covers. The arid canyon was hot and desolate, but the temperature cooled after sunset, which was imminent. The mostly flat terrain of semi-desert topography was altered in that area by clusters of burnt red rock formations and barren cliffs to their right and left; both revealed hollows in various sizes and shapes. Slashes of mountains were seen in the distance and the ridges on two sides of Tochara. In a few spots, gnarled scrubs and bunches of wiry grass grew low to the ground and close to odd configurations, as if cuddled against them for protection from these harsh conditions. The sky was a hazy red and no clouds were in view, indicating that no refreshing rain was forthcoming in the near future.

"Koteas and Terin are uneasy about this buy, so they will not land in their shuttle until the crates are in view and no one is near them except me," Tochar revealed to Auken and Sach. "Unload the rovers and move back to an acceptable distance," he instructed. "Stay alert, you two, but I do not anticipate any trouble or problems. I will not allow the crystals to be touched until I am paid and standing with you."

As she stepped from the vehicle, Starla overheard Tochar's words but pretended she was not listening as she glanced at the rugged setting with its forbidding aura and drab colors. She recognized the names of Koteas and Terin of Icaria—which also was the origin point for the *fiendal* and his three best friends, and the capital planet of the Thracian Empire. The leaders of Thracia had refused to join the United Federation of Galaxies; they claimed their solar system—beyond the Free-Zone— was too distant from the others for uniting with the *UFG* to be of benefit to their planets and people. She believed that was a devious excuse so the Thracians could continue doing as they pleased—continue their barbaric slavery practice and militaristic government—without interference and observation.

Auken passed along Tochar's orders, and the group obeyed them.

Although she acted calm, Starla's heart pounded fast and hard. Heightened tension plagued her as the moment for action arrived. While others were collecting more crates, Tochar was distracted. In a hasty and unseen motion, she removed the buttonlike disk from her belt and attached it beneath one of the moonbeam containers. That sly task was accomplished during her second delivery to a growing stack that included a large supply of a new pleasure-evoking drug from a past raid. She pressed the start button as she applied the device, but knew she had a safety interval of thirty *preons* to get out of danger's range. Thanks to the Icarians' demand for privacy, it was possible. By detonation time, since Tochar was in a rush to finish before dark, perhaps the *fiendals* would be standing near the crates when the crystals' internal pressure increased to a destructive level. The device's inaudible frequency transmission was undetectable except by a certain instrument, and no one here should have one. She prayed that Tochar's Serian spy had not learned of the device's existence and warned the pirate leader about it. She shoved that horrible thought from her mind. If she were injured or slain, she could be replaced, but she must not allow moonbeams to get into Thracian hands.

Starla grouped with the others beside the empty landrovers, aware precious *preons* were clicking off on an imaginary timer inside her head.

"That's all of them," Sach said. "Where do you want us to stand guard?"

Tochar glanced at the hovering shuttle before he pointed to a cluster of contoured rocks with odd-looking apertures in their red surfaces. "Move over there and stay alert. Weapons at the ready. I will join you after I make my deal. They will land as soon as I am alone with the crates."

The five obeyed their leader's words as the last rays of sunshine vanished, allowing sufficient light for visibility for another *hora.*

With the others, Starla watched the shuttle touch down, blowing about sand as it did so. Two men exited and approached Tochar, who was spanking debris from his garments. As with the *fiendal* and his friends, the other two Icarians had various shades of golden hair and black eyes, genetic traits of their race. As the three *villites* talked, she observed with fingers grazing the butt of her laser weapon. She wished she could draw it and put an end to the crimes in progress, but chances of defeating seven armed enemies were slim to none. She knew Cypher was positioned in the *Liska* to witness and record this secret meeting as evidence and for clues. She was glad no one nearby was speaking, as that might intrude on her android's ability to pick up the *nefariants* conversation via her wrist communicator. After it was recorded, other sounds were deleted, and those three voices were amplified, she and Cypher and their superiors could listen to the incriminating talk.

Starla's intense concentration intrigued Dagan, just as he was intrigued by the woman herself. She was not clad in her usual jumpsuit. She wore a bronze top that covered her torso from armpit to waist and bared her shoulders front and back. The band was fitted to her figure, so no straps were necessary to hold the garment in place. Her hips were covered by a matching short skirt with many pointed ends at the hem; underneath it was a pair of flesh-colored leggings covering long and sleek limbs. The top and skirt were decorated with dull *plantinien* disks at their borders. Her feet were encased in knee-high bronze boots. Her slim waist was encircled with a wide and studded belt with weapons attached. He assumed she had secured her brown hair into a long, thick plait which dangled down her spine to prevent strands from blowing into her eyes and for keeping her cool in the arid location.

Dagan's body heat was rising, but not because of the weather; it was Starla's effect on him. Her skin looked soft and he saw nothing to mar its smooth surface, not even the dirty red smudges where she had wiped away grime and salt-tinged perspiration. She was the most beautiful, desirable, and fascinating female he had met in all of his travels. He enjoyed her company, even when she was being aloof or wary or falsely spurning him. She had a smile, voice, and manner that summoned enormous cravings within him, emotions and sensations that were unfamiliar and close to alarming. She would be a prize for any man who was lucky enough to win her heart and loyalty, but that couldn't be him, wouldn't be him... It was as if she didn't know he was alive and standing beside her, so focused were her attention and green eyes on the meeting beyond their hearing range. But there was something unusual, contradictory, about the beauty that he couldn't put his finger on...

"I'm thirsty and my throat is dry," Starla remarked, praying her voice didn't expose her anxiety, results of Dagan's keen examination and the impending blast. Did the Kalfan not realize that his gaze was so potent that she sensed it? She was concerned because his interest seemed to be more than a casual or merely sexual one. Perhaps he wasn't duped by her Starla identity. She forced her thoughts back to her bodily discomfort. "I wish we had brought along something to drink."

"I didn't think about it," Auken admitted.

"Neither did I, so you aren't to blame."

"This business won't take much longer. It's getting dark. You'll be soothing that dry mouth soon."

"At least a breeze is stirring now and cooling me off, but it's kicking up more dust. I feel as if I'm covered in it. A bath will be wonderful," she said as she received two vibration signals from Cypher on her wrist unit. *One* meant danger at a distance and *two* meant peril was close by. It told her that his sensors had detected something unusual. She heightened her alert and glanced around as she tried to discover the hazard. It sounded like movements and whispers were coming from inside the cavities in the rocks.

Dagan also heard the eerie noise, become vigilant, and caught a glimpse of something in the shadowy recess before it vanished into the darkness. He warned the others they weren't alone, be it man or beast.

The five backed away from formations and eyed them as they drew their weapons to prepare for trouble and self-defense. Suddenly, numerous unkempt men in filthy, ragged garments leapt from the closest orifices as they sent forth strange clickings with their tongues. The horrible looking creatures brandished clubs and spears in hands covered with new and old sores. Mutants also poured into the large clearing from hollows on the other side of the canyon and from others on the space pirates' side, continuously flowing from the dark holes like the yellowy fluid oozing from their pustules.

"Skalds!" Auken's black gaze widened.

"Tochar! Take cover! We're under attack!" Starla shouted to dupe the leader with feigned affection and loyalty as she took refuge with her companions between the landrovers, and signaled Cypher not to panic.

The team ducked and dodged the rocks that were thrown at them as they fired at the mutants running toward their leader. Koteas and Terin, cut off from their shuttle, raced toward the armed pirates with Tochar. The Skalds darted with such speed and nimbleness that even skilled shooters like Auken, Sach, and Moig had trouble hitting their targets; but Starla and Dagan struck down attackers with each blast.

Laser fire buzzed in all directions, but the freaks kept coming, almost tripping over bodies of their fallen pack. Their wild eyes and scabby faces exposed fierce determination to capture and devour them. Their arms and tattered clothing were beyond dirty. Their feet were bare, but the sand had cooled, allowing comfort to their strides. Beneath layers of slime and grime, it was impossible to tell their skins were pale, as were their ghostly eyes. Nocturnal beings who could not take the blazing sun, they had waited and watched their chosen quarry until the safety of dusk appeared.

"They've never come this close before or tried to attack our fringes or patrols," Auken exclaimed. "They usually prey on less guarded colonies."

"This will be the last time they attack us!" Tochar used a communicator to order *Destructoid* beams from his mountaintop defense sites to slay and repel the flesh-eating *Skalds*, and for Enforcers to come rescue them. When he saw howling savages going after the crates of crystals and drugs, his black gaze narrowed in fury. "Aim near the crates!" he shouted to the men controlling the *Destructoids*. "They're trying to steal my delivery! Stop them! Kill them all!"

Bursts from the *Destructoids* chewed into the dirt near the stack of containers as the team fired in rapid succession at feral brutes closing in on their location. Then a loud explosion occurred that terrified the *Skalds*, killing those in the blast's vicinity and causing others to flee for the rocks. The air was filled with minute debris from shattered crystals and scattered drugs, small pieces of the containers, and red sand.

Tochar gaped at the costly destruction and cursed his losses. "We will be lucky if we can find even a few of those crystals. Probably all of them are buried in the sand or concealed in crevices, and those drugs are history. As soon as it is light tomorrow, I want a large, well-armed unit out here to search for those crystals; nothing can destroy them, so they still exist."

A suspenseful silence surrounded the group for a few *preons* after the rumble landed and Tochar spoke. With targets gone, the *Destructoids* had ceased firing. Except for sounds of their mingled breathing and gusts of wind, nothing could be heard. Everyone glanced about, but no live enemies were in view.

"Let's take the rovers and get out of here," Auken suggested. "It's almost dark and they might return. We're too outnumbered."

"The Enforcers will be here soon. Nypeer should have them gathered and en route by now."

"Nypeer better hurry, Tochar, because they're coming again!" Sach shouted.

As *Skalds* crept from the orifices, showing caution and wariness this time, an enraged Tochar ordered more blasts from the *Destructoids* and demanded the rescuers get there fast.

Starla looked at Tochar. "Do you want me to see if I can reach Cypher-T, get him to lock in on my signal, and give us added firepower?" she asked. Before the leader could respond, a sharp pain stabbed her head and her senses gave way to blackness.

Dagan grabbed her body as it slumped forward. "They hit her with a rock," he told the others as he examined the injury.

Between blasts at attackers, Auken asked Dagan about her condition.

The worried Kalfan replied, "Out cold and has a head cut, but breathing. We'd better get her back to the colony fast in case she has a concussion."

"We will after my unit arrives and finishes off these ugly creatures," Tochar said. "I see dust rising, so my Enforcers will be here soon."

"Not soon enough if they don't hurry!" Moig yelled. "Those beasts are almost on top of us! *Karlee,* we can't kill them fast enough!"

Dagan positioned himself between Starla and the new threat. "Those carnivorous brutes won't get their hands on you, if I have to die preventing it." He twisted and turned as he shot countless targets. When his energy pack was drained, he grabbed another from his belt and shoved it into place. Two *Skalds* almost reached them, but the quick and accurate Dagan terminated those perils. He was amazed that the mutants lived and preyed so near the settlement without being seen—or smelled, as their bodies and breaths reeked of the damp muskiness of underground, foul stench of unwashed bodies, and of rotten meat and unbrushed teeth. Before the next rush at him, he glanced at her, stroked her cheek, inhaled her fragrance to clear his nostrils of the creatures' offensive odors, and whispered, "Hang in there, Starla. I promise I'll get you out of here."

Destructoids fired away at the attackers, as did the Enforcers, who arrived before a cloud of red dust and using weapons more powerful than those of their entrapped friends. The sounds of laser beams, shouts, yelps of pain, and shattered rock filled the air. Wind, laser impacts, and rapid movements stirred up more dust. Light was vanishing fast, but the Enforcers were wearing night vision gear.

Within *preons,* all mutants were dead, had lethal wounds, or were hiding in their apertures.

Koteas and Terin were eager to leave the dangerous setting, and did so after the shuttle was checked to make certain no *Skalds* were lurking there. The craft lifted off to return to its ship and to head for their planet to await news from Tochar that more crystals and drugs were available.

While the Enforcers stood guard, Tochar and his team climbed into rovers. Dagan lifted Starla in his arms and carried her to a vehicle, placing her in his lap for the swift and bumpy ride. Darkness engulfed the canyon as they drove toward the settlement in the next one.

Starla was awakened by the jostlings. While her wits were still dazed, she sighed dreamily and nestled closer to Dagan, whose smell was familiar to her. She liked being held in his strong and possessive embrace. She just wished those intrusive noises, bounces, and ache in her head would go away.

"Starla, are you all right? How does your head feel? You took quite a hard hit on it back there."

Starla realized she was not dreaming or fantasizing. She opened her eyes and stared into Dagan Latu's blue gaze, one filled with concern and desire. She was sitting in his lap, in the landrover. Except for the vehicle's lights, it was dark, night. They were traveling, safe, alive, with Moig. She lifted her hand to check the sore area on the back left side of her head.

Dagan captured her hand and said, "Don't touch it. We'll let a doctor look it over when we reach Tochara. That mutant's rock struck you hard."

Moig glanced over. "Glad you're alive, Vedris. You had us worried. Those *Skalds* about did us all in."

"What happened?" Starla gathered her wits to ask, "Is everyone safe?"

Dagan related the events that took place after she was rendered unconscious. "Tochar's planning to have those rock formations shattered by *Destructoids* to prevent mutants from having places to live and hide so close to his settlement. It will be done late tomorrow after the area is searched for crystals, though he doubts any can be found. After a blast like that one, they're probably lost in the sand and rocks."

Starla could imagine how angry Tochar was about their loss. If the device worked as Yakir said, there wouldn't be any crystals to recover, and no evidence of the unit to find. "I guess that means we'll be going after more to replace them. At least no one was hurt during the blast and attack."

"Except you." Dagan smiled at her.

Starla was aroused by his touch and gaze. She felt safe in his embrace, but that was a perilous place to be. Since there were only two seats in the front of the vehicle, she did not make a futile attempt to leave his lap and arms. Getting into the backseat while moving was impossible and ridiculous. "I'll be fine by tomorrow. Thanks for taking care of me."

Dagan winked. "Despite the grim circumstances, it was an enjoyable task."

The group reached the settlement and halted at the Enforcers' command station. Tochar approached Starla to check on her condition and to suggest she visit the only doctor in the colony, one with a lost license.

"Thanks, but Cypher has a medical program and my ship has a sick bay with equipment so he can check me out and take care of this minor injury. All I want are a bath, clean clothes, a cool drink, and rest. That was quite an intimidating adventure. We expect to confront dangers and risks during raids, but not in or near our base. We weren't prepared to battle that much trouble. I'm glad everyone is safe and unharmed."

"That hazard will be destroyed tomorrow, so you must not worry about being safe in Tochara."

She smiled at the leader. "We are all grateful to you for taking good care of everyone. What happened to cause that explosion?" She saw him frown.

"I do not know." Tochar clenched his teeth. "Nypeer vows it was not from *Destructoid* fire."

"Perhaps since it's powered by a crystal, its blasts so close to the others destabilized them. Too, sitting in the hot sun so close together might have created some type of chain reaction. My father was a scientist," Starla alleged, "but I don't know much about those kinds of things or those moonbeams."

"Whatever it was, Starla, they are gone now and my sale is lost."

"Only until we can replace them for you."

"I was smart to hire you, Starla Vedris. If you need anything tonight or your android cannot handle that injury, contact me."

"I will, and thank you. Can one of the men take me to my shuttle?"

"Dagan, will you see that Starla gets to the landing grid safely?" Tochar requested.

"It will be an honor and a pleasure. I'll see you tomorrow, Tochar."

The leader grinned at Dagan as if to say, *you owe me for this favor.*

Starla and Dagan left in a rover and traveled toward the landing grid, both holding silent for a time and cognizant of their close proximity.

Starla evaluated their surroundings to keep her mind off being alone with Dagan. They passed single and multi-unit dwellings and a variety of businesses, none over two levels. Several nightspots sent forth loud music and most were crowded with customers, obvious from views through large clear *transascreens.* Small groups of people gathered here and there. She overheard them chatting or discussing sales or relating news of recent raids as the rover moved along slowly to avoid hitting walkers. Old-style signs, some painted and some illuminated, revealed what one could buy or the service one could obtain inside those places. The only ground transportation available was rental landrovers, offered by a man that paid Tochar for that privilege. The streets and walks were made of a hard white material, and were spray-washed frequently to get rid of the red dust accumulation.

Dagan sneaked a glance at her. "You're mighty quiet, Starla. Are you sure you're all right?"

"I'm fine, thanks. Were you told that if caught stealing here," she began to end the strained silence, "means one's choice of exile into the desert or the loss of a hand? No fights—either with fists or weapons—are allowed, and the penalty is the same. If men disagree to such a strong point, they must leave the colony to settle the matter. The punishment for murder is execution. Cheating another in a deal results in the loss of the defrauder's possessions and subsequent exile. Littering is against Tochar's orders, so the settlement is clean and rather neat except for the outer fringes where the less fortunate live and hardly anyone visits. No one lands on or visits Tochara without our leader's and his Enforcers' permission. It seems as if Tochar has created a safe place for him and his inhabitants to live and for guests to visit, a rough sort of civilization. I was told it isn't the same in the other settlements on Noy where it's every male or female for themselves, so crimes are rampant and conditions are crude in those places."

When Starla paused, Dagan asked, "That's what you were thinking about so hard and long?"

She laughed, but didn't look at him. "That, and how lucky we are to be stranded in Tochara instead of one of the other settlements on a near primitive planet. Unless you've seen them in the past, you have no idea how horrible they are. That's what the others told me."

"Even this colony doesn't seem like the place for a woman like you."

"What is a 'woman like' me?" she asked, warmed by his implication and husky tone of voice.

"You're civilized, educated, intelligent, well mannered, and gentle-spirited, though you try to hide that last trait."

Starla noted how mellow and tender his voice had become, and the sound of it sent tingles over her body. "Where does a woman like me belong?"

"Not in this rough setting or this type of work, and not with these kinds of people."

"That isn't my choice; this is where I have to be." *For now.*

"You can change your appearance and identity and start a new life."

"Until forged ident papers are exposed."

"The Microcosm is big, Starla; there's someplace you can be safe, someplace where you can live the kind of life you deserve."

"Are you trying to get me to quit and leave so you can take my place in Tochar's band?" she jested. "Do you dislike having a female teamer?"

"Not for those reasons. I'd like to see you live longer and happier."

"Who says my life will be short and sad?"

"What else can it be in this line of work?"

"Is that how you see yourself, Dagan, dying young and unhappy?"

He chuckled as he halted the vehicle. "Yes. Unless I change my ways, or I make another mistake. We can only elude capture and escape death so many times."

Starla stepped out and thanked him for his help and escort, dropping the confusing subject. Dagan halted her departure with a question.

"If you're feeling all right after Cypher checks you over, why don't you meet me at the Skull's Den for food and drinks?"

"Thanks, Dagan, but not tonight. I'm tired and tense. That was the closest I've ever come to getting killed." She saw him grimace as if that thought troubled him, but perhaps he was only trying to beguile her.

"What about tomorrow night?" There were things he needed to learn from and about her.

"Maybe. If so, I'll see you there about dusk."

"I'll be waiting, so please join me. Get inside and close the door before I leave."

"Worried about my safety?" she teased.

"Tochar will punish me if I allow anything to harm you, and you are supposed to be my teacher."

"From what I've seen, Dagan Latu, there is nothing I can tell or show you that you don't already know or do expertly. Good night." She sealed the shuttle door for takeoff. She wanted to get to the *Liska* and Cypher fast because there were important things to do.

Chapter Six

"I'm glad you stayed calm when I was hurt or they would have wondered how you knew to come and rescue me," Starla told Cypher.

"The sensors in your wrist monitor indicated your injury was minor. Your vital signs remained normal. You ordered me not to expose our contact unless you signaled for help or your life was in imminent danger. I locked on to your coordinates to transport you if the *Skalds* reached your location or your condition changed. I moved into position to provide assistance if the threat increased. I must examine your injury."

"After we finish checking things here; my head's sore but there's no headache or dizziness or blurred vision. That vibrator signal is an excellent idea, Cypher; it's worked for us many times. If Tochar suspects sabotage, he shouldn't look in my direction after my offer of help during the attack and he knows I was never alone with the crates while traveling with Moig and Dagan. Besides, he should doubt I—or any of the others—would risk death or injury to betray him in his stronghold and with his armed men nearby. Let's listen to his talk with Koteas and Terin. Is it ready?"

"Yes." He pressed a key to start the recording.

Starla listened and frowned. "Nothing of help there, no clues about his raids or contacts, but it gives us evidence against him and we learned who two of his potential buyers are."

As Cypher reached his hand forward to switch off the button, she stayed it and said, "Wait, I want to hear what happened after I was knocked out." She listened to combined sounds of men's voices, mutants' yells, and laser discharges, "It was a fierce battle, wasn't it?"

"I detected many *Skalds* on my sensors, but rescue was near and the Kalfan was guarding you, so I did not make my presence known. I would have done so the *preon* your life was in peril."

"You acted wisely, Cypher. Your analysis program is excellent. I'm glad you're able to make those kinds of imperative decisions."

"Your speculations concerning the explosion were clever. The Kalfan affected you strangely again while you were in physical contact with him after the attack and during your ride to the shuttle."

"That doesn't surprise me since I was practically held captive by his body. He's a unique and complex male. I'm certain there is far more to Dagan Latu than we see on his surface. He may be a *nefariant,* but he has good traits. I wonder if he can be turned around."

"That is possible, but improbable. From my many observations, few men like him change."

Starla was warmed by the things Dagan had said to and about her when he didn't know she would discover them and wasn't trying to charm her for a selfish reason. He had seemed surprised by her garments and appearance. She had purchased the outfit in Tochara from a trader. Though it was sexy and feminine, it looked appropriate for that setting and her alleged identity. Perhaps it had sent the point home to him that she was a woman. Yet, his remarks in the rover still befuddled her. If he found her desirable, why would he attempt to persuade her to leave Noy? Unless it was with him or because he feared for her safety. *Don't be ridiculous, Bree, he isn't the mating kind. He's a carefree loner and a villite to be defeated.*

"Let's go to sickbay so you can examine my injury. I have a hard head," Starla said and laughed, "but I don't want any problems with it."

"Your immunity levels are in the upper range, but we do not want to risk an infection. We are far from base, and unknown germs or viruses could exist in this sector and in such primitive conditions."

Cypher cleaned, sterilized, and sealed the wound with a *latron* beam. A communication signaled from the Serian ruler. "Bree-Kayah Saar here, sir."

"I wanted to make certain you are safe and well and the mission is progressing. Are the dangers too great for you to continue working there?"

"I'm fine, sir. I appreciate your solicitude and your faith in me." She told him about the destruction of a few of the crystals using the device design he had provided. The elderly leader was happy and relieved by that news. "Do not tell anyone—even your advisors and closest friends—about Koteas and Terin and our first triumph. We don't know who the traitor is and he could reveal it to our enemy. Only Dagan and I were present besides those *villites*, so Tochar would realize one of us betrayed him. I'm sure you don't want to believe it's someone close to you, but only a man in the know can tell Tochar the secrets he learns and uses: for example, that flight recording device, and the watchword to convince those androids to let us board the vessel on the last raid. With the evidence destroyed, Tochar assumes it's a mystery to the I-GAF as to how we accomplished our feat and who's responsible for the theft."

"Your conclusion is logical and must be accurate, though it pains my old heart to experience doubts. Iverk is investigating for leaks. He has found none, perhaps because I do not share my knowledge with him."

Starla recognized the name of the Serian *Ysolte*, head of Seri's galactic defense and third in line for rulership.

"I'm sorry you must keep secrets from Iverk, but he mustn't learn of my existence and mission. He can make a slip or ask the wrong person a revealing question. If that happens and I'm exposed, I'm dead and the mission is destroyed."

"Do not worry, Bree-Kayah," *Raz* Yakir assured. "I keep my lips sealed to protect you and your mission. Supreme Commander Sanger keeps me informed of your reports to him. It is safer for you and our critical task because his conversations appear to be about Federation business or friendly chats. I contacted you this time because I needed to hear your voice to make certain you are safe and all is well."

"It is, sir, and I'm grateful for your concern. I think I know where Tochar is hiding the moonbeams we steal. The cave I suspect he's using is well-guarded and inaccessible. The cavern is located in the same ridge as his dwelling, but not within close proximity to it. So far, we've only seen Tochar, Auken, and Sach enter it following moonbeam raids. If I'm given an opportunity, I'll destroy the remaining crystals. Cypher will have another device ready by tomorrow for me to use if an occasion arises. There is no way I can recover them and return them to you and *Autorie* Zeev."

"The crucial point is to prevent Tochar and other criminals from having them."

"Is there any progress on matching or bettering his firepower?"

"To date, we have not located any white crystals large enough for constructing more weapons like the ones he stole from us."

"They have terrifying capabilities, sir. There's no way I can get near them to plant destructive devices; they're guarded and off-limits."

119

"Do not take dangerous risks, Bree-Kayah; I want you to remain alive."

"Cypher and I are being careful, sir."

"Have you experienced any problems with the shapeshifting?"

"None, sir; I've used it several times with success and secrecy. I still have an ample supply of the chemical needed for the alteration process."

"Be sure to keep one phial for an emergency, in the event Starla Vedris must vanish to escape danger."

"I carry that one with me at all times; and Cypher monitors me every *preon* in case I need assistance or a swift rescue."

"I am glad he is there with you and his intelligence is so advanced."

"So am I, sir."

"I will terminate our transmission now. Farewell and survive, Bree-Kayah Saar of Maffei. I will reward you greatly whether you succeed or not."

"That isn't necessary, sir; my reward is in defeating Tochar and saving the Federation from his threat. Bree-Kayah signing off."

"*Raz* Yakir signing off."

Starla looked at Cypher. "I think I'll get cleaned up and see if I can gather any clues from Dagan."

"You told him you would not return tonight."

Starla grinned. "I'm not; Yana is."

"What clues do you seek to extract from him?"

"I want to know what kind of man he really is."

"How will you discern that fact?"

"By seeing how he reacts to Yana when Starla's back is turned."

Cypher analyzed and grasped that response. "What if your plan fails?"

"How can it fail?"

"If he surrenders to Yana's magic, that action will harm you."

"How so, my friend?"

"It will injure your emotions and perhaps become distracting. You do not want him to unite bodies with Yana, but you tempt him to do so. That is contradictory and hazardous."

"I know, but it's the only way to study him because I can't do such things as Starla. If Starla ensnares him, he won't divulge anything to her. As Yana, many secrets escape on a *sleeper;* or so I'm told. Please don't worry," she assured her trusted android. "I haven't made that decision yet. I won't make it lightly or impulsively or unless it seems imperative to my mission."

"Take care with the mating scent application. Do not use so much that he cannot control his physical responses and actions."

"I'll use it sparingly. I don't want to bring out the carnal beast in him. I only want to enchant him for a while, dull his wits, loosen his tongue."

Yana looked up at light coming through the apertures of the skull-like facade of her destination. She had transported to the rental abode where Yana allegedly lived, and left from there. Music and other sounds of merriment came from speakers in the "skull's ears" to entice regular and new customers inside. She walked between "teeth" columns to enter, and took a deep breath to prepare herself to share time with Dagan if he was present. Even with his back to her, she recognized his black hair and magnificent physique. She strolled to his table. "May I join you?"

Dagan knew that sultry voice and smell. He turned, smiled, and stood to assist her with a chair next to him. "It's nice to see you, Yana."

"It's nice to see you, Dagan. I was hoping you would be here. I stay mostly to myself, but I need diversion at times. I hope you don't mind my intrusion, but I feel safe when I'm with you." She watched his blue eyes sparkle and a sexy grin curl the corners of his full mouth. His teeth were white and straight. His clothes were clean and neat, brown pants and a tan shirt in a material that stretched taut over his muscled torso. He hadn't shaved, so dark stubble was visible on his angular jawline, making him appear rakish.

Dagan was aware of her keen study. "That's a stimulating and pleasing compliment, Yana. Why don't I get you a drink? What would you like?"

"Radu knows my favorite drink if it's available. Thank you." She watched the captivating Kalfan almost swagger to the bar and lean against it in a nonchalant posture. He possessed such a commanding aura that no one else in the place could match him in looks or manner, in her opinion.

While Radu fetched a glass and filled it with *Clearian* wine, Dagan's gaze roved Yana's lovely profile and long sunny gold mane, almost the same shade—minus the faint blue tinge--as his hair without his Dagan Latu disguise. Even the aquamarine tone of her bodysuit beneath a multihued flowing garment in a diaphanous material, a garment as ethereal as the stunning creature herself, matched the real color of his eyes—a fusion of pale blue and pale green--before they were chemically dyed for this crucial mission. Yana, he concluded, was created and adorned by some mischievous force to be an intoxicating temptation to men. Her appeal to him was purely physical, though she was a likable female. She was so different from Starla Vedris, a greater and many-faceted temptation. He didn't normally take up time with women during an assignment and he moved around too frequently and rapidly to be ensnared by romance and never by love, not since a terrible tragedy *yings* ago played havoc with his emotions and life.

Yet, his gut instinct—which rarely failed him—warned him not to trust her. It told him she wanted something from him, something he needed to discern, and fast. He suspected she was either a spy for Tochar or was a cunning scout for one of the man's many enemies, or a rival who wanted to take control of this settlement and the *fiendal's* possessions. If the latter was true, she or her employer could be the person who ran that second check on his Dagan Latu record—an unquestionable one—to see if he was for real or was approachable as an ally against Tochar.

Perhaps the Asisan ruler had sent her to check out Tochar's weapons and moonbeams, but Yana had been unable to get close to Tochar since the man had a satisfying lover. Perhaps—though he could not imagine how—she had failed to entice Auken or Sach into her clutches to extract needed information, so she was focused on beguiling him. There was an almost irresistible allure about the beauty, but no matter how tantalizing or talented she was, Yana would never extricate his secret identity and goal or sway him from it. With his special immunities, neither could Tochar nor anybody else, even with the aid of torture or their ineffective truth serums.

Yana took the glass he handed to her, smiled, and thanked him. "What was the commotion about earlier this evening outside the settlement? I saw and heard those mountaintop weapons firing into the desert. Did Tochara come under attack?"

"It was just a test of the defense system. Perhaps Tochar should have announced it so people wouldn't worry. I'll point out his oversight to him."

"I'm glad that's all it was. It frightened me. To be honest, I'll be happy when I leave this place. It's much too primitive and rough for me."

"When will you be leaving?"

"In another *malee* or two, or as soon as I receive a certain message. Do you have to leave often for work and remain gone for long periods?"

Dagan was amused and intrigued. "I never know my schedule until the last minute. Why?"

She sent him a radiant smile and laughed in a sultry tone. "I won't have a trusted escort and bodyguard while you're gone."

Dagan's keen intuition and training told him that wasn't her purpose for signaling him out to receive her attentions. He would not underestimate Yana's cunning and talents, as he had with Starla on that transporter. As she chatted for a few *preons* with Radu, his mind scoffed that he didn't think any of the other I-GAF secret agents would believe her. Officers like him were selected, tested, trained, and skilled at investigating and solving tough and perilous interplanetary and intergalactic crimes An *I-GAF*er was hard, if not impossible, to dupe or defeat. They had never failed to succeed in their assignments, and he would not fail in this mission to destroy Tochar and those dangerous crystals. He must destroy the *fiendal* responsible for his own personal torment *yings* ago. His target was a man he hated and wanted dead, but after his victory was ensured.

Whatever it required Tochar's reign of terror must be terminated before it reached a critical level. As an *I-GAF* covert agent, he had the power and authority to do anything necessary to achieve his goal. He reported only to his superior, commander of an awesome force that was almost a law unto itself. His work and methods could not be questioned and reprimanded by anyone else. Only his superior and the other special agents knew who and what he was. For some cases, his birth face was surgically or chemically altered. Though he used a different disguise for every mission, between assignments he worked and lived as Dagan Latu to keep that role well-established and credible.

Dagan briefly recalled how that *I-GAF* uniform had felt familiar. He had experienced anger at dishonoring it during the commission of a crime. But Tochar lacked the secret of how to create and conceal an *I-GAF*er hand badge. The symbol was tattooed into the flesh on the back of the right hand with an invisible dye. It was made evident as needed by smearing a particular chemical over it and was re-concealed with a different one. Those chemicals and dye were unreproducible formulas; for that reason, a pretender was easy to unmask.

As he watched Yana work her charms on Radu, Dagan decided he might have to take daring steps to beguile her into dropping needed clues. Yet, something intangible about her was making his job difficult and uncomfortable, as it was an unfamiliar struggle to keep his arousal in check. The alien beauty was having a potent effect on him. He could not surmise why his body was battling with his mind. Perhaps Asisan women had a magical pull about which he hadn't heard. Perhaps one could exude an irresistible pheromone to enslave her victim. For certain, the next time he lay on a *sleeper* with a female, he wanted it to be Starla, even if she was one of Tochar's hirelings and his targets.

Dagan spoke with Radu before the man departed. His gaze met hers as he asked, "Who are you, Yana? What or whom are you hiding from?"

Yana went on alert. "I can't divulge that data."

"So, you only trust me to a certain degree?"

"I'm sorry, but privacy is a must until a particular matter is resolved."

"You won't leave Noy before saying good-bye?"

"I promise, unless you're away when I must depart. When do you take another journey? And how long will you be gone?" she asked to see if Tochar had confided anything of interest to his new hireling.

"I don't know. I'm awaiting Tochar's orders."

"Impatiently? You appear to love traveling."

He lowered his glass and locked their gazes. "What gives you that impression?"

"You always seem a little... restless."

He grinned as she lowered her gaze. "Not when I'm in such entertaining and ravishing company."

She traced her forefinger around the glass's rim as she fused her gaze to his. "That was a quick and smooth response. Do you enchant all of the women you meet so easily and swiftly?"

"Does that mean our attraction is mutual?"

She halted her movement to prevent tipping over the glass when her hand trembled. "Yes, but I think, where relationships are concerned, I move more slowly and carefully than you do."

Dagan chuckled and sipped his drink. "Impulsive and reckless I'm not, Yana."

"Neither am I, Dagan. Now, why don't you tell me about yourself and your work."

He downed the last swallow of his drink. "It's getting late and I've had a long and busy *deega.* We can get better acquainted next time. What if I escort you to your dwelling to ensure your safety?"

Is that all you have in mind? "That will be kind."

They left the Skull's Den in silence as she led the way to Yana's abode.

"It's located there," she said, pointing to a small domeshaped pod. At the entrance, she slid a metallic card into a slot and the door swished open. She turned and asked, "Would you like to visit for a while?" She half expected and needed him to refuse, but he did not.

"For a few *preons*; it's late, and we're both tired. But I wouldn't mind seeing your surroundings and having a last drink with you."

"There isn't much to see," Yana remarked as they entered the rental unit. "It's plain and serviceable and clean. Radu owns it." As she poured two glasses of *Clearian* wine, she told him, "I was fortunate to arrive when I did because the person who habitated it before me had to leave that *deega.*"

"That was a stroke of good luck," he said, taking the drink from her, their fingers touching for a moment.

Yana watched him stroll around as if looking for things that would give him clues about her. She sat down, wondering what would happen next. She saw him glance over a waist-high partition into the sleeping and dressing area, then into another where the cooking and eating area was located. He didn't have to ask where the one door went: into the bathing chamber.

Dagan sat beside her on a small but cozy *seata* and sipped his drink. She was right, there wasn't much to see or anything to provide clues about her. That told him she was clever and cautious about her privacy; perhaps she stayed ready to flee at *a preon's* notice.

"You don't like to talk about yourself, do you?"

Dagan shrugged and grinned. "There isn't much to tell. And you're just as tight-lipped as I am."

"I promise I will tell you everything about me later. In any case, since we'll know each other for such a short time, do facts about me really matter?"

"I'll decide as we go along." He nodded toward an odd-looking figurine. "That's an interesting piece of sculpture. Is it yours?" he asked.

"No, it's part of the decor."

"May I see it?"

"Of course." She fetched the item.

With her back to him, he switched their glasses, having been careful to keep his liquid even with hers. Dagan examined the object and said, "Looks like an artist's strange interpretation of a Thracian *kilitar*." He handed it to her as if asking for her opinion. As she made her decision, he pretended to absently toy with a paper casing on the lower part of the glass for capturing moisture and preventing a slippery surface.

"It does slightly resemble that six-legged beast." Immediately after Dagan downed the remainder of his drink, she asked him if he wanted another one.

"No thanks. I'll be leaving now, but I'll see you again soon." He stood and stretched as if weary, then furtively stuffed the glass's wrap into his pocket, the one with Yana's fingerprints on it, retrievable with a special process he knew. Added to the voice print he had made that evening on his recorder, Yana's identity wouldn't remain a mystery much longer.

She was half relieved and half disappointed that he was departing without attempting to seduce Yana, her. She craved to feel his arms about her, to taste his lips, to join her body with his. She walked him to the door, but he turned before he pressed the open button.

Dagan gazed into her rich blue eyes and scanned her faint blue skin and blond hair with the same blue tinge.

"You're a beautiful and desirable woman, Yana; I hope we'll see a lot of each other before you're gone."

"That will please me," she responded, though not totally true, not as Yana.

Without releasing her captive gaze, Dagan cupped her face between his hands, lowered his head, and sealed their lips. He couldn't help but close his eyes and pretend she was Starla, which proved to be a mistake. As his body flamed with fiery cravings and she yielded her mouth to his, he told himself if he didn't leave soon, his control would vanish.

Yana's wits danced and her body quivered. The kiss was everything she had imagined and more: tender, delicious, arousing. His manly scent pervaded her senses. His hands were strong, yet gentle, as was he. But the kiss was too short to suit her.

Dagan leaned back and smiled. "Good night, Yana. I'll see you soon."

She trailed her fingers up his jawline. "Good night, Dagan. I enjoyed our brief evening together."

"Perhaps it will last longer next time."

Yana watched him disappear into the shadows, then closed the door and leaned against it as she tried to quell her tremblings of excitement. So, he didn't leap into a *sleeper* with a woman just because she was "beautiful and desirable"; that was excellent, and it prevented her from making that serious choice tonight in a weakened state. She called to mind the romance, sex, and love teachings from her mother, sister Amaya, and her brother's mate Renah. Each had experienced powerful and forbidden emotions and actions. Was she destined to follow in their footsteps? Was Dagan Latu as irresistible as Varian Saar, Jason Carlisle, Galen Saar? Each family member was from a different planet, galaxy, than their mates. Just as she and Dagan were... Each couple had met under dangerous and adventurous conditions, just as she and Dagan had done... As Jason of Earth loved to say, "Hold your horses, Bree."

She communicated with Cypher; her android had overheard everything via her monitor, "I'll wait for a while to make sure he doesn't return and wonder where I am or how I departed if he's lurking outside."

"It is unnecessary. I took a body reading and am following it. He is returning to his chamber."

"Then I'm ready for transport."

Starla entered the Skull's Den shortly after dusk the following day, purchased a drink, and took a seat near the dome's outer shell. It was a slow night for business on the first level and in that area, so it was quieter than usual. Even the music from the adjoining section wasn't loud, nor the voices and laughter of the few patrons there. She wondered how long Starla and/or Yana could hold Dagan Latu's attention if one or both of them failed to share a *sleeper* with him. Should she, *could* she, in either form, surrender to temptation? Did her sense of duty and the importance of her mission justify using her body to obtain victory? She was so lost in thought that she didn't notice Dagan's arrival until his commanding presence filled her line of vision as he joined her.

"Looks as if you were mentally trekking far away," he murmured as he leaned back in his chair and gazed at her. A strange warmth flowed over him every time he was near her, one that worried and pleased him.

Starla yanked herself back to reality. "A hazard of our fate-altered lives, wouldn't you agree?"

"I suppose so," he replied, then sipped his drink. He wished he could convince her to leave Tochar and Noy, remove herself as one of his targets. As soon as Tochar was defeated and slain, she would have no leader and this settlement would be destroyed to scatter and weaken the remaining *villites* who used it. Afterward, she would be thrust into space on her own again or be caught up in the whirling vortex which would swallow and crush the wicked elements in Tochara.

In his opinion, Starla couldn't be held totally to blame for her illegal actions. She had gotten entrapped in this dangerous existence while in a vulnerable state, pulled in by her brother. He hoped Tochar's influence wasn't too strong and she would escape it; if not, there would be no way he could ignore her position in *the fiendal's* band and her participation in its crimes, even though the ravishing pirate enflamed his passions and touched his emotions. Her effect on him evoked a battle of personal feelings vying against professional ones.

"Is your real name Starla Vedris?"

Following his long and intense and arousing study of her, she had not expected that odd question. She stared at him for a moment. "Why, does it really matter? One name is as good as another in our work."

He propped his elbows on the table. "I like you, Starla, so I want to get to know you better."

"That takes time, Dagan, time we might not have in our risky lives."

"Since our fates are uncertain, my lovely space pirate, we should enjoy every *preon* we have."

Was that a sexual overture? "If those diversions don't shorten or worsen our existences. I think it is unwise to live only for the *deega,* as so many do here. Indulgence can be self-destructive."

Dagan locked his cobalt gaze to her green one. "What kind of future do you want? Any desire for a normal one with a mate and offspring?"

A romantic overture? Her heart raced at his odd queries and his desire-igniting expression. She fought to keep the trembling of strong emotion from her voice. "Is that what you want? Do you ask because I'm a woman and you assume that's what all females crave?"

Dagan felt himself heating up beneath her sultry gaze. The fates have mercy, he wanted her badly, and was sure she felt the same. "Why do you always reply to certain queries with a question so you can avoid sharing something personal about yourself?"

Starla laughed to release tension. "You answered your own question. Rule One: protect thyself."

"I sense you're a private person and probably have reason to be, but is it just me or everyone you want to keep at a defensive distance?"

"Would you think me vain if I said no man on Noy has interested me in that way since my arrival? Unless I'm wrong about your meaning."

"Your conclusion is accurate." Before he could halt himself, he challenged, "Does 'no man' include me?"

Starla's shiny gaze roamed his face. She found his expression unreadable except for glimmers of fiery desire which matched the flames searing her. "I haven't decided what I think or feel about you. I try not to make hasty judgments; that can be rash and hazardous."

"Thanks for being honest; and it isn't vain to be discriminating. I hope I didn't sound brazen."

Starla thought it was best to change the subject. "I want to thank you again for being willing to sacrifice your life to save me from those carnivorous brutes."

"I'm sure you would do the same thing for one of your teammates." *But how do you know what I said when you were out cold?* Dagan withdrew his knife and extended it toward Starla. "You should get one of these. It comes in handy if you run out of power packs. It's good for close range fighting and for throwing a long distance. Has lots of other uses in a bind." He watched her take the knife and examine it, supplying him with her fingerprints. Added to the voice pattern he was recording, soon he would know everything about Starla Vedris or whoever she was, as she would be registered in the *I-GAF* data base, as were all *UFG* citizens.

"If you don't know how to use one, I'll be glad to teach you," he offered.

Starla returned the weapon and noted how he handled it: his fingers didn't touch any area hers had done so... "Thanks, but I do know how. You might want to change to a curved hilt for a better grip."

Her practical idea impressed him. "Has Auken told you we're leaving tomorrow to head for the Sion space station to get that part for Tochar's ship?"

"No, I haven't seen or heard from him. I take it Tochar has checked and knows the part is available and the station is approachable. He amazes me with the number of contacts he has in other places. It seems as if there is little he can't learn, so they must hold high and trusted positions." She laughed. "If I had his sources, I wouldn't need to work for him or anyone."

"We take lots of risks and steal valuable cargoes for such small cuts of the profits. Not that he doesn't pay well, better than most leaders, but he sells those hauls for huge amounts. Our services should be worth more, don't you agree?"

"Too bad it's dangerous to leave his employ or we could venture out on our own. He has long arms and a good memory, so any departure has to be agreeable to him. Can you repair his ship after we get that part he needs?" she asked.

"Yes, I checked it over this morning; nothing to it. Being on my own for so long, I have to know a ship from top to bottom. I can't exactly call for help if something malfunctions, and I don't want to drift alone in space until death claims me. You're lucky you have an android for company and assistance."

"I'm fortunate to have Cypher for many reasons." After she enumerated a few, she asked, "Did Auken say whether or not I'll be going along on the raid?"

"The entire unit is going. Why?"

"Since we're leaving tomorrow and I haven't been told, I wondered. I don't like disclusions."

"He's probably been busy getting the *Adika* ready to depart."

"I hope that's the only reason."

Dagan didn't tell her he had hinted to Auken that only three or four of them were needed to carry out the raid, one which would be allowed to succeed with the hope of enticing Tochar off his stronghold. Though there shouldn't be any risks involved, unless something unforeseen came up, he wanted her kept away from as many dangers and punishable crimes as possible. But Auken was loyal and ignored his words.

"Would you care for a fresh drink?"

"No thanks. Since we're leaving tomorrow, I won't even finish this one, and I need to get back to my ship to rest and prepare. Good night, Dagan."

"Good night; I'll see you at sun-high at the landing grid." He watched her rise and exit, her departure evoking an odd feeling of loneliness. *Stop letting her get to you so fast and easy; she's a* villite, *Curran, despite good traits. Don't forget, she's in the forbidden zone. And get moving before Yana appears. You don't want to deal with her tonight, not even for sexual release.*

Starla took a seat on the bridge of her ship with Cypher. "I'm relieved Auken sent a message about the band leaving tomorrow. I can't allow them to shut me out now that they have Dagan. If necessary, I'll find a way to disable one of the men to prevent it from happening. Don't follow us this time and do something small to make your presence in orbit known while I'm gone, maybe purchase supplies to restock the *servo* and have them delivered by shuttle. Since we aren't going after moonbeams, there won't be any clues dropped for you to collect, so let's not risk using the hologram and beacon. I'm convinced that Tochar has made certain the needed part is there and it's safe to raid that space station, so I'm certain I won't be taking any risks going without you in the shadows."

"Your reasoning is logical," Cypher affirmed. "I will obey. Keep alert for entanglements."

"I will, so don't worry. And report our imminent trek to my superior."

From the bridge of the *Adika,* Starla watched the docking procedure after they were given permission to stop at Sion. She noted that Auken had the correct hailing frequency and password and wished she knew how Tochar had obtained them. She glanced at Dagan and the others, who were clad as *I-GAF* officers, just as she was. She surmised she and Dagan had been allowed to remain on the bridge because the secret moonbeam codes weren't being used today. She hoped the raid went smoothly and that no humans were inside, as Tochar was told.

"Connection complete and ready to enter the station," Moig announced.

Auken thanked Moig and told him to remain ready for a swift take-off if needed. "The rest of you come with me. You know what we're after and where those parts are stored. Let's move fast and get going."

Inside the entry corridor, Starla watched Auken and Sach head in one direction while she and Dagan walked in the other to collect certain items. The tubular hallway was long and dim, with only one series of well-spaced lights illuminated. Their booted steps echoed against the metallic flooring. Their fingers grazed the butts of their laser weapons, ready to thwart any unknown threats. The android in the control room wouldn't trouble them, as it was duped.

"The fuel rods we want are down the next corridor and on the left," Dagan informed Starla. "Stay alert in case Tochar's information isn't accurate."

Starla acknowledged his words and kept glancing over her shoulder for any sign of trouble. She followed him into the storage bay and helped him load the rods onto a carrier. She saw him gather other items Tochar wanted for future use or sales.

They returned to the ship and unloaded their haul, then headed down another corridor for a second and last pickup in a bay on the far side.

Shortly after leaving the second storage area, Starla tensed as she overheard a shocking message from Moig to Auken via their transmitters. She and Dagan paused and exchanged looks of surprise and displeasure.

"We've got a problem, Auken. I have a *Spacer* on the sensors. It just decloaked. The pilot is communicating with a man inside the station somewhere; they're *I-GAFers.* Sounds like he was dropped off by another craft and this one's picking him up. He's already gotten permission to dock from that android controller and he's coming in. We have five *preons* or less to disengage our connection and get cloaked."

"Starla, Dagan, did you hear that message?"

"We heard, Auken," Starla responded, "and we're heading back in a hurry. It'll take a while; we're almost on the other side of the ring."

"Leave everything and move fast, but we won't leave without you two."

After the communication ended, Starla murmured, "Do you think they'll hang around very long with an *I-GAFer* aboard and another one coming? If we don't rush, we'll be stuck here and in big trouble. These uniforms and fake badges won't fool those clever agents."

"Don't worry, we'll bluff our way out if the one here sees us. Just don't act suspicious."

"I won't have to: I'm a woman. There are no female *I-GAFers.*"

"Yes, there are, a few, so behave like you're one. All we need is enough time to disarm them if they approach and challenge us. If Auken deserts us, we'll just have to steal their *Spacer* and escape."

Starla pressed her fingertips to his lips and whispered, "Somebody's coming."

"Get down!" Dagan shouted, and pushed her to the floor. Almost in the same sweeping motion, he drew his laser gun and fired at the agent who rounded the corner at the end of the corridor. He had to stun the man before he was seen, recognized, and perhaps exposed.

Starla grabbed her gun and fired in the opposite direction after the second agent came into view, his own weapon drawn. The man got off one blast, which zinged against the metal carrier near Dagan after she had kicked it between him and the shot's angle. Dagan whirled to check out the peril, saw the downed agent, and looked at her oddly. "He's only stunned," Starla announced. "I'm not killing an *IGAF*er. If you do, you're a fool, Dagan. Tochar doesn't pay me or scare me enough to murder one of them. Or anybody."

"I only stunned mine; I don't kill unless necessary." He called Auken and said, "The agents are down, so relax and wait for us. We're bringing our haul; no need to abandon it now."

After the loading and disengaging procedures were carried out, the *Adika* took flight and cloaked. Auken and Sach were at the controls, and the other three were sitting nearby trying to calm themselves.

Moig, his thick brow sweaty and his face flushed, complained, "I thought there wasn't going to be any threats in this sector. That was too close."

"Tochar was told there wouldn't be any Kalfan *Sekis,*" Auken said, "but he can't control or learn the actions of the *I-GAFers.* Did you kill them?"

There was no hesitation in Dagan's response, "No, we stunned them, because they didn't get a chance to see our faces. One docked at the portal nearest us and the other was going to meet him; we were caught between them. Saw no need for murder charges."

Auken shrugged and related, "Wouldn't matter if they had seen you."

"Yes, it would, my friend. As for me, I don't want them eager for my blood," Starla refuted.

"Look at the rearview screen and you'll stop worrying," Auken told her.

Starla's gaze widened as the orbiting space station exploded and sent debris flying. She reflexively blinked at the bright light and gasped in astonishment. "Why did you do that, Auken? They didn't see us. There will be *karlee* to pay for this reckless deed."

"When that *Spacer* appeared, we lost time to get to the internal recording system to wipe out the record of our transmission, and our faces and voices. We had no choice. We can't leave evidence behind."

Starla watched the debris slow and begin to float in endless space. Two Inter-Galactic Alliance Force officers had been murdered to conceal their identities and operation methods. At least, she thought sadly, the men had been unconscious and hadn't suffered.

"I know you don't like life-taking, Starla, but it couldn't be helped. They shouldn't have been there, and I wish they hadn't been."

Starla realized it was foolish to argue with the *villite*. She must not let him think she lacked the courage to do whatever was needed to protect the unit and their leader or she could be ousted.

"Do you understand?" Auken asked.

"As you said, we had no choice. At least we got what we came after." Starla realized something Auken didn't notice: if a detonation wasn't planned, why had explosives been planted before the officer came...

Dagan observed with keen senses and surmised how upset she was, which pleased him. He was furious with Auken and Sach, and tempted to slay them on the spot. He couldn't; too much was at stake. Later, he would take revenge for the two fellow officers, though they were not close friends of his. If Auken had revealed his lethal intention earlier, he would have captured the band and returned to rescue the two agents. He would have turned the prisoners over to them, then headed for Tochara to delude their leader. Or he could have pretended they were all slain, altered his guise, and headed for Noy to become the first member of Tochar's new unit. No matter, it was too late to save their lives. Obviously his superior hadn't warned them to stay clear of Sion or hadn't known they were in the area.

Auken called over his shoulder to Dagan. "What about you? Any problem with that course of action?"

"Things happen; they can't be avoided."

Starla slyly noted how Dagan's fingers gripped his kneecaps, his jawline clenched, and his gaze narrowed and chilled as he replied to Auken's query. She guessed the gesture was an indication of Dagan's anger about the two deaths, which relieved her following his disturbing remarks. *Maybe you are different from them. Maybe you can be turned around after all.*

Dagan looked at Starla. "Thanks for saving my butt. That was quick thinking. I owe you for my life."

"You're valuable to Tochar and our unit. I'm glad I could help. Consider it payback for saving mine."

"What about being valuable to you?"

"Friends are important to me, too."

"I think Dagan wants to be a real close friend, Vedris," Moig teased.

"Don't start; I'm tired and tense for games."

"Speaking of games, how about we play *resi* to help us relax?" Dagan suggested.

"Sounds good to me. I'll get the chips," Starla said to silence Moig. She wasn't looking forward to the lengthy trip back to base: seven *deegas* to the Kalfa/Free-Zone stargate, then four to Noy in their current alignments. She didn't like the tight confinement with the men... and especially with the enticing Dagan.

After they landed at Tochara, for the first time, Starla was asked to help transport the load to a cave their leader used for storage, one guarded by Tochar's Enforcers. Yet, she and Dagan were allowed only to place the crates in the entry cavern, and the many recesses beyond it weren't visible for inspection. As she worked, she pressed a button on her wrist device so Cypher could lock in on and record the coordinates for future use, as she was positive this was where the crystals were being kept.

When the task was finished, Dagan asked Starla to join him later for the evening meal and drinks. First, he needed to report the two agents' deaths and see what Phaedrig had discovered about Starla and Yana from their fingerprints and voice patterns. He was eager for those facts, but dreaded what he might learn.

Starla politely declined. "Thanks, but I want to rest. I'll see you tomorrow around dusk at the Skull's Den. I just need to be alone for a while."

"After being caged with four men for *deegas* and what we went through at that station, I understand. See you tomorrow, I hope."

Starla nodded and left in her shuttle to make a report to Supreme Commander Thaine Sanger about the fatal incident at Sion. She knew that Cypher would be concerned when he heard the bad news, but there wouldn't have been anything he could have done to save those men. By the time Auken exposed his action, it had been too late even for *her* to save them. She yearned to know how that episode was sitting with Dagan, but doubted he would reveal anything to Starla. Yet, perhaps Yana could extract facts and feelings from him about the incident and Tochar, especially if she used an alluring splash of her irresistible fragrance...

Chapter Seven

Yana took a deep breath and pressed a button near the door to Dagan's chamber, after making certain no one was close to witness her bold visit. He was renting one of four dwellings in a tubular-shaped pod of a heat-resistant material. Its entrance was on the back, facing the ridge, and the passageway was deserted at present. Yana's abode wasn't far away, so she had transported there and slipped to this location without being seen. When Dagan did not respond to her signal within a short span, she assumed he wasn't there and started to leave. As she turned, wondering where he was and if she should seek him out, the door swished open.

"Yana, what are you doing here?"

"I haven't seen you for *wegs.* Have you been gone or evading me?"

"We returned from a long trek this evening."

"You must be tired. I'll let you rest. Please excuse my intrusion. I wanted to see you. I've missed you."

What are you up to, woman? You didn't come here dressed like that just to talk. His gaze noticed the visually impenetrable but thin and silky garment in a multi-colored pattern. Thick, shiny tresses flowed around her shoulders and framed her beautiful face like liquid sun. Blue smeared on her lids intensified the hue of her eyes and its faint tinge to her flesh and hair. Her lips were full and pink, and parted slightly. He must detain her to see why she had come. He had made certain his secrets were concealed before he answered the summons. "Would you like to come inside for a while?"

"If you're alone and it won't intrude on your relaxation schedule."

Dagan grasped her hand and led her into the multi-purpose room. "Have a seat. Would you like something to drink? I have *Clearian* wine."

Yana saw him smile, but the action did not reach his remarkable eyes. Was it her imagination or was he displeased to see Yana in his quarters? "That will be nice." She sat down on the only *seata* in the small and sparsely furnished dwelling, which was sectioned off by waist-high partitions, much like her rental pod. She watched him fetch a bottle from a cooling unit, and two glasses. She put her daring wile into motion as she pretended to toy with her neck ring.

As he poured two glasses of purple liquid, Dagan asked, "What have you been doing lately?"

"The usual, nothing, very little."

"Life on Tochara is boring for you?"

She laughed and nodded as he put away the bottle. "There aren't many quality diversions here."

"Not the kind you're accustomed to?"

"Thank you," she said as she accepted the proffered glass. "True, but I can manage for a while longer."

"How long?" he asked, and sipped his drink.

"I don't know; things that affect me and departure are happening very slowly."

A talented beguiler. Why were your fingerprints surgically or chemically eradicated and why is there no record of you or your voice pattern? It's strange that both you and Starla have no fingerprints on your lovely hands, but at least there's a file on her, and thankfully it's a nonpriority one. The whorls, arches, and loops on his finger pads had been obliterated to protect his many identities. That was often the case with *villites. Perhaps Starla's were removed to conceal past crimes which are more hazardous than I realize, but I hope not.* "You still don't want to discuss your problems with me?"

"I hope that situation will change soon."

"So do I; mysteries can be as frustrating as they are intriguing." He chuckled and grinned to disarm her. Yet, a strange feeling assailed him. His body was becoming hot and eager for mating, and his mind told him she was within reach and enticing him. *Control yourself, Curran, and see what you can learn.*

Yana saw his cheeks flush, his eyes brighten, and his respiration alter. He was trying to appear calm, but she sensed his apprehension. She watched him lick his lips, shift his position, and twist the glass in his grasp. She knew her ploy was working on him. "Did you have a successful trek? Was it dangerous?"

Right to the point? Although his race had lost the ability to exude at will an ancient mating pheromone and his nostrils didn't detect any odor other than her heady fragrance, it was as if her skin had been bathed in that titillating chemical. It was if the air and his lungs were filled with it, as if that stimulus was gushing through his pulsing body. His erotic need was making it difficult to concentrate on his goal of unmasking her and her ruse. He was troubled by his inability to ignore those irresistible sensations. He wanted to remove her temptation, but couldn't allow himself to be thwarted and overpowered by carnal urgings. He summoned his wits to answer, "Both."

"I'm happy you survived whatever perils you confronted. What do you do when you're away from the settlement, if that isn't a secret?"

"Maybe I can tell you about it some *deega.*"

"I doubt we will see each other after I depart."

Dagan watched her tease soft fingertips over his arm as he battled her potent allure. Every *hapax* of him craved to undress and seduce her. He scolded himself for not casting aside such an absurd weakness. "That means

144

you won't be returning to Tochara after matters are settled?" he asked, trying not to stumble over his words as his wits were clouding steadily.

"This will be my one and only visit." She put aside her glass. Should she leave, remove temptation?

"Do you have a lover or mate waiting for you somewhere in Asisa?"

Yana placed a hand on his taut thigh and pretended to absently stroke it. "No. Do *you* have someone special in your life?" He was trying hard to resist her. Why?

"Not yet, but perhaps I will in the distant future." *If Starla doesn't get killed, exterminated, or incarcerated on a penal colony. That's it, Curran, think about Starla so you can disregard Yana's eerie magic.*

Yana fastened her gaze to his muscled thigh as she drew finger circles on it. "Do you ever get lonely or dissatisfied with your existence?"

Dagan set his glass on a side table. "Do you?"

Yana lifted her hand and moved aside a strayed lock of black hair from his cheek, brushing a finger against his flesh as she did so. "Yes, but you're making my time here pass swifter and easier."

You're one talented temptress, Yana, but two can play at your little game. Let's see how far you're willing to take it to charm me over to your side. He grasped her hand and stroked her thumb with his. "But not enough to entice you to stay longer than planned?"

"This isn't the kind of life I want for myself. What about you?"

Dagan noticed that her chest seemed to rise and fall at a swifter pace and her breathing pattern altered. Her cheeks flushed and she began to fidget on the seat, seemingly unaware of responding to his trick. Taut points stood out on her breasts, the thin material unable to restrain them. Her fingers tightened around his hand.

Her gaze filled with readable desire and glued to his captivating one. So, he mused, she was susceptible to him; it wasn't just an act. "Presently, I'm right where I want and need to be."

Enchanted by the virile and handsome Kalfan, she couldn't help but ask, "What do you want and need most at this *preon?*"

He realized he was snared by his own verbal trap. "I'm not sure," he murmured.

Yana noted his husky tone and the hunger gnawing in his eyes, the same ravenous one which chewed at her wits and will. She—Bree-Kayah Saar, Star Fleet officer, Elite Squad member, agent on a crucial mission—wanted this perilous and forbidden prize with every fiber of her being. The words leapt from her lips, "You want and need me, isn't that true?"

"Is this what you want?" *Say no and leave fast!*

She slipped one leg over his hips and sat across his lap. Their privates touched through the materials of their garments, hot, eager, moist. Her hands cupped his strong jawline and she fused her gaze to his. "Yes," she murmured before she meshed her mouth with his, knowing the scent on her face would fill his nostrils and remove any lingering self-control.

Dagan's senses whirled as if he were caught in a spinning vortex. His arms banded her waist and pressed her against him. He spread kisses over her face and the soft column of her throat. As she rubbed herself against his throbbing groin, he lost the battle to resist. His hands grasped the hem of her flowing garment, lifted it over her head, and cast it to the floor. His deft fingers quivered as they released the lacy band around her full breasts before he nestled his face between them. His mouth wandered over each luscious mound and his lips teased at both pinnacles in turn as his hands caressed her sleek

146

back. He had no choice except to possess her or surely he would zone out forever.

Dagan created blissful sensations within Yana and exhilarated her with his actions. Her fingers roamed his broad shoulders; they played in his dark mane; they drew his head closer to her taut peaks, encouraging him to ravish them. She moaned and writhed across his lap, aware of the hardness straining against his jumpsuit and pulsing against her private domain. She had planned to ensnare him and loosen his lips with Yana's surrender; but now, only thoughts of seizing great pleasure for herself filled her mind.

They stood in unison and together they peeled off her panties, then his boots, jumpsuit, and briefs in a feverish rush. They kissed and caressed, naked and enflamed. Soon, they sidled as if one entity to his *sleeper* and fell upon it with Dagan atop her, rubbing their ignited bodies together to heighten their flames.

He fondled and kissed her in an almost mindless frenzy. Results, she knew, of the potent pheromone and her brazen enticements. He was her sex captive.

Enthralled and tantalized, Dagan could not stop himself from entering her. He sank deep into the core of her until his hardness was surrounded by her delicate folds and soft triangle of bluish-blond hair. He explored that exciting terrain as his hips undulated with haste and greed. Though skilled at giving sensual delights, he could not help but seek his own satisfaction, dazed beyond thinking about sating hers first.

It was unnecessary for Dagan to guide Yana to her pinnacle because she was so stimulated that her body responded to his of its own volition. Her eager and supple limbs imprisoned him. Sweet ecstasy coiled steadily within her pleading loins and prepared itself to unwind when she could endure the glorious torment no longer. She matched each perfect thrust he sent into her receptive body and coaxed him with murmurings and movements to continue his pace.

She had just enough presence of mind to realize this experience was nothing like the one she had shared with Antarus *yings* ago. While weakened in body and wits and believed death was imminent, she had allowed Antarus to take her so he could die happy. His kisses and caresses had not evoked the potent effect Dagan's did. She had not craved or responded to Antarus in a wild and eager way, nor to any other male. She was glad she didn't have to worry about pregnancy, as Maffeian females were given a chemical upon reaching puberty to halt the release of ovums; that measure required the infusion of another chemical after bonding to a lifelong mate to restore reproductive ability or at a selected period when she was ready for children. That action wasn't taken to promote or condone promiscuity, but to prevent unwanted pregnancies either from carelessness or a tragic criminal attack. Due to innoculations at age five, STDs no longer existed in their world.

Both reached the brink of release. They labored as one until they were rewarded with rapturous climaxes. Yana gasped and arched her back as she clung to him. Dagan rode her with wild fervor until gratification was complete, his enormous craving slaked. For a few *preons,* their mouths and flesh remained united as their senses and bodies returned to normal.

Fulfilled, Dagan was astonished and dismayed by his crazed behavior. This wasn't the woman he wanted lying beneath him, not the woman he wanted to share such moments and feelings. He dreaded to imagine the damage this carnal episode could do to his budding relationship with Starla Vedris, if she discovered it. Yet, how could he conceal it from her and others, if Yana started to cling to him in a possessive and intimate manner? On the other hand, how could he learn Yana's secrets if he sent the Asisan on her way? He berated himself for falling into such a perilous and costly trap. If he didn't know better, he would believe his immunities to all known drugs and tricks had failed him. Whatever Yana's allure was, it was potent, and he cautioned himself to be on alert against it in the future.

"You are quiet and distant, Dagan," Yana observed. "Is something wrong? Did I fail to please you? Do you think badly of me for succumbing to your charms?" *Did I use too much of the pheromone?*

The *I-GAF* officer realized he had no choice now except to take advantage of the unwanted predicament. "I'm just relaxed. You were more than satisfying, Yana, and my opinion of you hasn't changed."

She noted that he didn't relate what that "opinion" was, and sensed he was being careful with his words, perhaps deceitful. "I'm glad, because I want to remain close to you while I'm here, if that's agreeable. But we must be careful about being seen together too often or appearing to be too close."

"Why is that?" he asked, then wished he had agreed immediately.

"If other men learn we've shared a *sleeper,* they may become sexually overt. Some might become jealous and angry that you succeeded with me where they failed; that can cause nasty situations."

"I concur with your logic and precautions. In public, we'll act like friends. As to sharing moments like this one, we should wait a while before doing so again. I don't think it's a good idea for either of us to be seen coming and going from private dwellings."

Yana pressed a kiss to his bare shoulder. "Thank you for being understanding. A woman cannot be too careful in a place like Tochara where most men seek only the pleasures of the present. Now, tell me: How long do you plan to remain in the colony and work for Tochar? Where will you go and what will you do after you leave them?"

Hadn't they, he mused, covered those areas? Maybe she was making small talk to get past an unsettling moment. Yet, he believed she had enjoyed their sexual encounter, perhaps too much and unexpectedly to suit her. "I'll stay until I get bored and restless," he responded, "or earn enough to replace the ship I lost, whichever comes first, I suppose."

"What if living and working here remains exciting and rewarding, even after you buy your own ship?"

"Tochara will have to improve greatly to keep me here longer than necessary to accomplish my goals."

She continued her probe. "What if Tochar doesn't want you to leave his employ, ever?"

"That isn't his decision."

"What if he makes it his decision? I've never heard of any man leaving his force, alive. Won't he fear you revealing secrets you learn about him? And won't he attempt to prevent you from becoming stiff competition by using his secrets for your own gains?"

"You believe he's dangerous and unpredictable?" Dagan asked.

"I overhear alarming things on occasion. I don't want you to get hurt."

"I doubt Tochar will live here permanently unless he can make it a nicer settlement. Rich and powerful men prefer better living conditions."

"If he resettled elsewhere, would you go with him?"

"I don't like to deal in unknowns, so I can't say."

"Perhaps if you decide to leave Noy at the same time I do, you can deliver me to my destination. Traveling together would be fun."

"Perhaps, when the time comes for you to leave, if I'm available."

"I hope you're gone by then."

"Why?"

"Because Tochar is gathering many enemies from both sides of the law. I don't want you caught up in a fierce rivalry or attack."

Who was she thinking of? "Do you have a particular force, enemy, or rival in mind?"

"A man like him must be craved by the authorities and enemies. Other men like him must envy his position and possessions."

"That's logical and probably true, but it's unlikely anybody will challenge him."

"Why? Because of those weapons he has to guard himself and Tochara?"

"What do you know about his *Destructoids?* "

"I've been here long enough to witness their power several times. It's frightening to realize what he can do with them if he used them elsewhere, such as in my world. Doesn't it worry you to be connected to such a wicked man, a destroyer, an enslaver?"

"Only if Tochar is that kind of person; he hasn't shown me that side."

"Won't it be too late to escape him after he does expose his evil nature? Would you help him conquer and ravage other worlds?"

"Why would I? Do you think I match your dark opinion of him?"

"No, that's why I hate to see you get so entangled with him. Be careful and wary, Dagan."

"Are you afraid he'll attack your planet?"

Yana rolled to her back, fluffed her long golden hair, and adjusted her neck ring. "Yes, because we have many things greedy men crave. Despite our strength, we cannot defend ourselves against his assault."

Dagan rolled to his side, propped on his elbow, and gazed down at her as he questioned, "Did the Asisan leader send you here to spy on him?"

She stared at him. "Of course not; I swear it."

"Did one of those shadowy rivals or a fierce enemy send you here for study?"

"No, I swear that, too. You must believe me; I came for other reasons."

"Reasons you'll confide in me one *deega?*"

"Yes, when the time is right."

She sounded honest, which surprised him and increased his intrigue. Was it possible she had told him the truth about everything except her name? Was she only hiding out on Noy for personal reasons? Was she truly drawn to him as a man and had no ulterior stimulus for yielding to him? Could she be falling in love with him? If those speculations were accurate, his association with her could both evoke problems with Starla and endanger Yana's life if he was exposed. If she was what she claimed to be, he didn't want to mislead her about his feelings. As he gazed into her limpid eyes and ravishing face, a searing heat and inexplicable urge to possess her overwhelmed him again. Before he was cognizant of what he was doing, he leaned forward and sealed their mouths. Soon, he was a sexual slave of her sweet lips, roving hands, and ardent surrender. Yet, with his eyes closed, it was an exquisite pirate whom his mind saw and touched and possessed.

Yana knew he had not seen her press the added disk on her neck ring to release more of the ancient pheromone. Though Kalfans and other races had lost the ability to produce and release it, he had not acquired an immunity to the chemical stimulus which Cypher had

152

duplicated for her. She had used the trick again to end their conversation, and she needed to have him once more, as she had no idea when they could unite their bodies again. Within moments, she also was lost in the wonder and flames of raging passion with the only man who had stolen her heart and will.

Twice in a short span, Dagan had behaved like a rutting and thoughtless animal for the first time in his life. Yet, he realized—from the flush on Yana's face and chest, her actions, and her gaze—she had received enormous pleasure and gratification. He was certain an unknown force had dazed and provoked him to fulfill this raw and unbridled passion, though he could not surmise what it was. Perhaps Asisan women emitted a mating scent when aroused which affected males in such a manner. His body had been snared, but his heart and mind had not wanted either encounter. With Starla, it was different; he desired her with total clarity and yearned to make love to her. Perhaps he had ruined any chance of that happening.

Relaxed in an afterglow of the exquisite experience, Yana cuddled in his embrace and drifted off to sleep.

When Dagan noticed her peaceful slumber, he didn't awaken her, as it was too late for her to return safely to her abode. And, at this *hora,* their presence outside if he escorted her there would be noticed by those still up and around. It would be easier for her to slip out tomorrow morning. He closed his eyes and soon was asleep, exhausted from his confusing exertions.

Aboard the *Liksa,* Cypher was worried and helpless. He knew the shapeshifting chemical's time span was twelve *horas,* and she was asleep. The problem was, with her wearing Yana's one-way neck ring unit instead of Starla's two-way wrist device, he could not send her a vibrating signal or contact her. If Bree-Kayah failed to awaken and escape before transmutation occurred, she would be exposed to Dagan, as her emergency phial could not be used for continuation of her current state. He was concerned by the fact she had been emotionally involved in her ruse, revealed by the physiological readings in his monitoring system. It was his duty to enlighten her to the hazards and distractions of such behavior and emotions after her return to the ship.

The android watched the timer until only forty-five *preons* remained to be spent, and Bree-Kayah was still asleep. He analyzed the dilemma, but could not deduce a way in which to warn her to come to her senses. It was illogical for him to transport into Latu's quarters and expose himself to the *villite* when his intelligent partner might find a way to protect their mission even if she were unmasked to him. He concluded he should not lock on to her coordinates and teleport her out prematurely, as that action would evoke Dagan's suspicions. Though she was not thinking clearly or acting wisely, he reasoned he must have faith in her and her abilities.

Still, the *preons* continued to vanish from the timer, one by one and the couple slept on...

Chapter Eight

Dagan's eyes opened shortly after sunup. He turned his head to find Yana still slumbering nearby, her breathing slow and even. His gaze roamed her serene face and naked body, and he was pleased his did not go crazy with another surge of mating lust. To ensure that wouldn't happen this morning, he slipped from the *sleeper* to shower and dress. He had to get out of there before she could enspell him again.

Yana pretended to be asleep when Dagan arose, though it was a struggle to keep her expression calm and breathing controlled. She had seen—via slits in her eyelids—light outside the overhead *transascreen* and almost panicked. Lying on her side and facing him, her panic had lessened when she saw bluish-blond hair spread on the pillow instead of brown tresses. As she pondered an escape plan, he had risen and entered the privacy chamber. She glanced at the timepiece on a far wall and her gaze widened in renewed alarm; Yana had less than thirty *preons* to get out of there, hopefully without being seen by others or being delayed by Dagan. She heard water running and knew he was using the old-fashioned bathing method in this primitive place that lacked automatic cleansing cubicles.

"I'm awake, Cypher," she whispered. "Lock on to my coordinates and await my signal to transport me." She yanked on her garments and entered a message for Dagan in the communication system nearby. She pressed a signal button on the neck-ring to catch his attention. "Get me out of here fast, Cypher."

As soon as she reached her ship, Starla assured him she would never lower her guard that far again. "It was stupid and reckless. I don't know what Dagan would have done if I had changed before his eyes. I'm sure he would have been furious with me for tricking him. I can't imagine what I would have told him to protect myself and our mission. You heard the answers he gave to me after we... had sex. I haven't decided if he is trustworthy or not, or worthy of saving. I do have another plan in mind for this evening. I'll relate it to you and tell me what you think about it."

After she finished, Cypher said, "It is dangerous from two angles, but both are clever ideas. If you are cautious and no hazards are present, you can succeed. Your second idea contains the same level of risk."

"But I will go as Starla this time."

"No matter which identity you use, you are too susceptible to him."

"Dagan caught me off-guard; I didn't expect him to be so irresistible. I didn't realize my attraction to him was so potent. Even though I probably used too much of the pheromone on him to fault him with his behavior, my conduct was foolish, and forbidden under these grim circumstances. I'm only human, Cypher, I lost self-control for a time. I've never faced this kind of situation and challenge before. I'm aware I didn't handle them right. Now that I know how strongly the mating scent affects him and how strongly he disarms me, I'll be on alert to thwart our weaknesses."

"It is not your behavior that was imprudent and prohibited. It is your carnal emotions which war against your intelligence. Your heart and body are in intense conflict with your head. As was Dagan's. He had no immunity to the pheromone, or experience with it. He had no choice except to seduce and surrender."

"You're right, Cypher. I'll have to find a way to halt my struggle, and to prevent his. I was wrong to make him helpless to resist Yana. Even as he made love to Yana, I sensed a conflict within him. When he climaxed, I thought I heard him murmur Starla's name."

"I have been studying human emotions and sexual drives. Do you love and desire this Kalfan?"

"Pralu, my friend, but the truth is... yes, yes, yes. Is there a drug or treatment you can perform to make me immune to him and these feelings?"

"I cannot help you resolve this serious problem. It will be propitious if he does not love you. Reciprocation can be detrimental to you and to our mission."

"If he says he loves me, I will not believe him."

"It can be true, or he can be convincing."

"Pray that neither of those traps appear."

"I do not possess a religious program."

"Then I'll pray hard enough for both of us." *Kahala, save me, if that perilous snare approaches me. Don't forget, Bree, Dagan Latu is an enemy. Isn't he?*

"I'm going to refresh myself and prepare for my tasks later. Take care of your part while I'm gone. And, Cypher, thanks for everything. I love you."

The android watched her leave through grey orbs. Was it possible to understand and empathize with her as if on a human level? What program could he access to learn the truth? To grasp how best to serve and save Bree-Kayah Saar? The upgrades given to him by *Raz Yakir* were... were what? He felt—felt?—strange and confused at times. How was it possible, when Bree said "I love you," to grasp her true meaning? A best and most trusted friend above all others in the Universe.

***

Dagan's tension diminished when he found Yana gone after he left the privacy chamber: showered, shaved, and dressed to depart in an alleged hurry. He heard the message unit beeping and checked it. Again, relief filled him after learning she thought it was best they avoid each other for a few *deegas*. He needed time and privacy to decide how to discourage her interest in him. He didn't want Yana to fall in love with him, if that was the case. It was possible she had selected him as a protector and companion if matters failed to be resolved in her world and she could never return there. Even if she was stranded on Noy, she couldn't dock at his bay and latch on to him for security. Yet, after his mission was over and if she was still present and in trouble, he decided he would get Phaedrig to settle her elsewhere. Maybe he did owe Yana something for last night—if she hadn't tricked him-—but assistance into another life was as far as he could go to repay her.

Dagan discarded those worries for now, as he was to report to Tochar's ship this morning to begin the repairs on it. He still had not decided if he was going to tamper with other parts, because Tochar had said he would not make an ensuing test run which might place him in harm's way before his vessel was armed with an invincible weapon. Since someone else might be assigned to test the *Azoulay* before Tochar was tempted to go trekking, problems would be suspicious. He must bide his time while making observations and getting closer to the band to cull clues. He couldn't make a move against Tochar or his men until he unmasked the Kalfan traitor who was feeding the *fiendal* secret information and helping him obtain moonbeams from their mines on the planet Orr. Or act against the *villites* until he weakened or destroyed the colony's defense system. But, he vowed, somehow and some way, he would achieve those goals; and he would slay Tochar and his friends for their personal offenses *yings* ago.

Don't get in my way, Starla, or you'll have to go down with them. I hope you'll leave this place before the end arrives, which it will. If I was convinced you would take my side and help me, I would confide in you. After we get to know each other better, I can make that decision. For certain, I cannot trust Yana.

At dusk, Staria stepped onto a sensor pad and looked at Cypher who was standing at the transporter's control panel and watching her. She took a deep breath and gave her plan one last mental going-over. What she had in mind was risky; she could lose her life and destroy her mission if she failed. "If I don't survive, my friend, cloak and leave for home immediately. Report my fate and our findings and suspicions to Supreme Commander Sanger, and hand over our evidence to him. Only to him, Cypher. There's a message for my parents, my brother, and my sister in the computer; make certain it reaches them if I never return. If I'm captured and we lose contact, cloak and wait three *deegas* for my escape. I'll shapeshift to Yana and hide in her abode, so monitor it for my arrival and rescue."

"What if you cannot escape in three *deegas?*"

"If I haven't freed myself by then, either I'll be dead or flight will be impossible. If that occurs, obey my first order to cloak and leave. Be safe and survive."

"I am programmed to protect and assist you; I cannot desert you."

"The mission must take precedence over my life and safety if anything goes wrong this evening. We do not have all of the answers to this mystery, but we have things which will be helpful to the agent who takes my place. You are responsible for getting those facts and speculations to Thaine. Do this for me."

Strange, but he understood. "I will obey. Use caution, Bree-Kayah, and return unharmed."

"I'll do my best, Cypher. Always remember our friendship and my love for you. I could not have done all I have in the past without you."

"I will not delete my memory chip of you."

"Let's do it. Ready to go."

Starla watched his image and the location vanish and the cavern appear before her line of vision. She drew her weapon and placed her finger near the button to signal Cypher for rescue if necessary since speaking could be perilous if anyone was nearby. Her gaze scanned the dim recess and she listened for any hint of a threat, but saw and heard nothing to alarm her. She inched her way to the rock corridor, flattened herself against the hard surface, and peered around its edge into the next hollow section. Again, she heard and saw nothing to indicate danger or anyone's presence.

Using caution, she made her way to the targets, recognizing them from their containers during raids. She saw crates of weapons, the parts they had stolen from the space station, holders with drugs, and other pirated items. Since Tochar had tried to sell crystals to the Thracians, she assumed he would make another attempt soon and she could not allow the moonbeams to fall into enemy or rival hands. She knew Enforcers were standing guard outside the cave's mouth and could enter for a check at any time, so she must hurry with her daring task. If anyone did arrive, she must slay him to avoid exposure and to achieve her goal.

The Elite Squad officer put away her weapon and withdrew three devices Cypher had constructed, two extra ones to make certain the job was accomplished. She placed the tiny units underneath the crystals containers and pressed the initiation buttons to begin their sequences. In one *hora,* if the devices did not malfunction, a massive explosion would occur and everything in the cave would be gone. The only thing left to do was get out of there fast and set up her alibi, with Dagan or some other person.

As she headed to the coordinates for her beaming point, she heard voices and froze. She prayed it wasn't Dagan and they wouldn't stay long in case she had to take drastic measures for escape. She concealed herself, listened, and waited, aware the timers were running and she was trapped within the detonation range. She mustn't signal Cypher to lock on to new coordinates unless she was certain she could not make it back to the original ones, as the light and sound of the transporter would expose someone's presence and treachery. She wanted the explosion to be a mystery, not compel Tochar to look for an enemy or to go on alert.

Starla caught the voices of two of Tochar's Enforcers. She tensed as they paused to chat and joke not far from her hidden location. She willed them to hush and leave, but they didn't get her mental message. She waited in mounting anxiety as her heart pounded and her body trembled.

At last, the men strolled outside to enter a guard shelter. In a rush, she returned to her spot and signaled Cypher to extract her. The moment she was aboard her ship, she yelled, "I have to hurry. See you later or in the morning." She ran down the corridor to a shuttle and piloted it to the landing grid. Fortunately, Auken was leaving the *trans-to* to Tochar's dwelling. She hailed him and received a ride into the settlement, making him a superb witness to her whereabouts if one was needed.

"Would you like a drink and play *resi?*"

161

"Thanks, Starla, but I have other plans with a friend. Another time?"

"Of course, my friend. I'm sure I can find somebody to lose to me tonight."

Auken laughed at her jest and humorous tone. "I'm sure you can."

They entered the Skull's Den together and parted for Auken to go to the second level where the Pleasure Givers plied their trade.

Starla glanced around the interior and saw Dagan motioning to her. Without halting to purchase a drink at the bar, she walked straight toward him.

"I was afraid you'd forgotten we agreed to meet tonight." He prayed Yana had not told her…

"I think I only said *perhaps* we would."

"Back on alert against me, are you?"

"If so, I didn't realize I was. Are you going to buy me a drink or do you want me to get it myself?"

"What about if I serve you one at my place?"

Starla's gaze met his. "Go to your place?"

"We can talk there in private; it's getting busy and noisy. I give you my word of honor to behave."

"Behave like what?" she teased.

Dagan warmed to the sparkle in her green eyes and the sexy curve to her mouth as she smiled again. "You're in a good mood tonight."

"I didn't realize I was always in a bad one."

"No, but you seem more relaxed and happier. I hope it's because of the company you're in."

"You did save my life on that space station."

"And you saved mine twice," Dagan reminded.

"That means you owe me one."

"I hope we're never put in the position of you having to collect it."

"I'd rather collect it than suffer the consequences," Starla quipped.

"Well, do we stay or go?" he inquired, wanting to leave in case Yana appeared on the scene. He could only hope the Asisan did not attempt to visit him.

"We can go if we take food with us; I'm hungry."

He chuckled as his happy mood increased. "I'll order something from Radu. Any suggestions?"

She licked her lips and said, "Surprise me."

"I hope your likes and dislikes match mine if I'm making the choices."

"You are, so we'll soon find out, won't we?"

"That we will. I've taken one swallow from my drink if you'd like to finish it while I get our meals."

"Thanks," she said. Starla lifted the glass and took a sip, passing her tongue over her mouth afterward. "So, you like *paonee* with *arple*. Nice flavor."

"I asked Radu not to make it too strong; I like to keep a clear head."

"So do I. It's a shame we sometimes allow certain things to dull our wits, isn't it?"

"I suppose it's according to what or whom dulls them." Before Dagan reached the bar, he halted to speak with Sach as the Icarian headed for the second level.

As the men talked, an explosion was heard over the music and voices, then a continuous rumbling noise. The dome shook. Tables and chairs rattled, and some overturned. Glasses and bottles tinkled; several fell over and broke. Clients from the second and third levels rushed down the steps. Light fixtures swayed, and a painting on one wall crashed to the floor.

"What was that?" Dagan exclaimed as he glanced around the room as Radu delievered their meals.

"We're under attack! Let's see what's happening."

Starla joined Dagan and Sach. "What's wrong?"

"We don't know," Sach muttered, his eyes wide in alarm, "but we're going to find out."

"I'm coming with you two," Starla said.

Dagan told Radu, "Hold those meals for me!"

They hurried outside and sighted a huge dust cloud near Tochar's dwelling, which appeared unharmed. Rocks still tumbled down the ridges. They looked skyward for signs of enemy vessels and laser fire, but none were present. Other people crowded around and asked questions, some pointing to the fiery-colored dust drifting upward.

"That's where the storage cave is located. Let's see what happened."

Starla and Dagan climbed into the landrover with Sach and rode toward the scene. Within a *preon* Auken came behind them, still adjusting his garment and fingercombing his tousled hair. Enforcers, those on and off duty, gathered at the site, their black uniforms a stark contrast against the reds of the landscape. Tochar was there, his expression filled with fury.

"What's the trouble?" Sach asked him.

"There was an explosion in the storage cavern; the entrance is sealed off by a cave-in. Without tunneling equipment and expert technicians, we will never be able to clear that rubble or recover what is inside."

"What caused the blast?" Auken asked.

"I do not know. Perhaps some of those starbursts or crystals were volatile. A check was made of the area not long before this happened, and nothing unusual was detected. No one was inside or had been inside lately except for the two guards."

"So you're ruling out sabotage?" Sach queried.

"I do not see how an enemy could have done this, but I want the area and settlement inspected for any

164

suspicious signs. I also want those guards questioned under *Thorin* to make certain they are loyal to me."

"We'll handle that matter for you tonight."

Tochar nodded agreement to Auken's words.

"Is there anything you need us to do?" Starla offered, feigning a tone of concern.

Tochar shook his head. "Nothing I can think of. Where were all of you? Did you see or hear anything strange before the explosion?"

"Me, Sach, Dagan, and Starla were at the Skull's Den," Auken replied. "I don't know about Moig. We heard the noise and felt the vibrations and came as fast as we could. Anybody have any speculations?"

With cunning, Starla suggested, "Do you think some type of detonation device could have been concealed in one of the crates we brought here? Perhaps one with a delayed timer which was set to explode if not switched off by a certain *hora* or *deega?*"

"It is possible a device was hidden in one of those shipments. If so, it was done cleverly, as all crates are checked before storage. But that is a good idea, Starla, one we will watch more carefully in the future."

"There's another plausible angle, Tochar," she continued. "What if the crystals require special handling or storage measures to prevent destabilization when kept close together for a long period and out of their rock casings? What if they overload with some type of energy force that must be restrained in a particular manner? Perhaps your contact can investigate that angle, since we know so little about them. If they're dangerous when mishandled, they can explode on the ship before we reach base. Especially if secret devices are being planted in the cargoes."

"I have not been alerted to any new security measures, but it is a possibility I need to study," Tochar stated. "But from here on, all crates will be examined before loading them on the ship, and all crystals will be stored in separate containers, with space between them and preferably in their rock casings. Each cargo must be stored in different locations to prevent such a massive loss again. If another incident occurs, we will know which item and person caused the trouble."

"It will be wise to get a list of the ships in orbit and names of visitors in the settlement," Dagan said, "then we can make sure they're all trustworthy. Is there more than one entrance to the cave?" he asked.

"No, and without the right coordinates, it would be dangerous for anyone to transport into a cavern. He could materialize inside solid rock."

"Somebody might have thought that was a risk worth taking or might have found a way to get the coordinates. The items stored there were of enormous value. On the other hand, perhaps one of the weapons or other containers had a beacon implanted for obtaining the right coordinates."

"That is excellent reasoning, Dagan. Auken, get that list of ships and names for me. But there is no way we can look for trickery this time."

"Which caves will we use in the future?"

"Not those with water, Sach; their resources are too precious to imperil."

"Using more than one will spread the Enforcer guards thin."

"That cannot be avoided, Sach; safety measures must be taken."

"Don't store those crates in your dwelling."

"Perhaps that is what an unknown enemy or rival hoped I would do and I would be destroyed. I will not take any risks in the future."

"It could have been only an accident."

"That is possible, Auken, but I want to make certain it was, and it does not happen again."

"What about the *Destructoids?* " Auken hinted. "Do you think they're unstable or will become unstable? If so, we'll be defenseless."

"So far, nothing suspicious has occurred. Examine them tonight."

"They're kept covered with their rock casings. Maybe that controls their energy force. If transporting crystals out of their casings is dangerous, they should be ensheathed when we steal them. Perhaps it has to do with a certain time span of safety."

"I will check into that matter immediately. Starla, Dagan, you two can leave; there is nothing more to be done here. Auken, Sach, you two handle those other matters for me. Tell Nypeer to put the Enforcers on full alert and watch everybody's comings and goings for a while. Find Moig and see why he did not join us; his absence is strange."

"I saw him enter the Skull's Den earlier and go to the second level," Dagan said.

Auken frowned. "He must be engrossed in a virtual-reality game with a drug inducer; he's becoming addicted to them. If he's in one of those cubicles and dazed, he doesn't know what's going on."

"Make certain that is where he is."

"I will, Tochar," Auken replied.

Dagan and Starla returned to the Skull's Den to purchase meals before entering Dagan's chamber. They sat down at his table to eat and drink.

To lessen any uneasiness, he remarked, "That was some unexpected excitement, wasn't it?"

Starla finished chewing before she said, "Yes, and Tochar is lucky he didn't have those crystals stored in his abode or he would be dead."

"If the moonbeams are responsible for that blast." Dagan could not divulge that he had not heard of such a possibility. If the Serians knew that secret, they had not shared it with his people. Yet, if Nature was giving them a helping hand, he did not object and was grateful. The first moment of privacy he obtained, he would inform Phaedrig of the strange incident. With the thefts destroyed, that left only the *Destructoids* to handle. He hoped those weapons would self-terminate and make Tochar and Tochara vulnerable.

Starla was thinking along similar lines, yet, she could not imagine how she could destroy those weapons. If she did find a way, she could finalize her mission soon and be gone. No, there still remained the mystery of who was supplying Tochar with secrets. "I wonder if Tochar knew or suspected the crystals were dangerous," Starla mused. "If so, he didn't tell us and he put our lives at great risk."

Dagan shook his head. "He might endanger us, but I doubt he would imperil his friends. I think those two explosive episodes have him confused and worried. I'm sure he assumed he had lucked out on a valuable, powerful, safe product."

"I wonder if his contacts know the truth, but took a chance they could make a large profit before the crystals' flaws were discovered," Starla said.

As Dagan poured them more *Clearian* wine, he reasoned, "If that were true, they wouldn't have let him get his hands on such powerful weapons, then provoke him to revenge. That would be stupid."

They ate for a short span before Dagan looked up at Starla and suggested, "Maybe you should think about leaving the settlement. If those weapons malfunction, Tochara will be vulnerable to attack. Anybody here when that happens will be slain or captured."

"What about you?" she asked in dread. "Are you thinking of leaving soon?"

"I can't; I have to stay until I earn what I came after. You have a ship, so you can depart at any time, work or resettle somewhere safer."

Finished with her meal, Starla stood to discard the container. "Is there a safe place for people like us?"

Dagan rose and tossed away his container as he answered, "You can change your identity and begin a new life, a legal one, a safe one."

"So can you," Starla retorted with a smile as she took a seat in the adjoining area. "For now, this seems to be the best place to stay."

Dagan sat down and eyed her. "I don't want you to get hurt, Starla."

"That's nice of you to say."

"It has nothing to do with being nice or with you saving my life."

"What does it have to do with?"

"You, as a person, a woman, a friend, a..."

"A *what*, Dagan?" She locked her gaze to his.

"Somebody I want to get to know better."

"How so if I take your suggestion and leave?"

He stroked her cheek under the guise of pushing aside a stray lock. "I'd rather see you live and be happy than to see you..."

"Why do you keep stopping? Than to, what?"

"Than to have a chance to get closer to you."

"How close do you want to get?"

He grasped her hand and held it, noticing its sudden chill. "I want to make love to you; I have since the first *deega* we met."

Starla stared at him, surprised, and yet not, by his words. She no longer needed him as an alibi, so she could escape suspicion. But she needed—wanted—him in

169

another way. How else could she discover what kind of man he truly was unless she stayed with him tonight? "What if it doesn't work between us?"

"How and why would that happen?"

"I don't know. It's hard to think of a good reason with you looking at me like that."

"Like what?" Dagan murmured in a husky tone.

"Like you want to kiss me, devour me."

"I do," he murmured, then slowly leaned toward her. When she did not retreat, he sealed his mouth to hers. He pulled her into his embrace and savored the taste and feel of her.

Starla looped her arms around his neck and guided her fingers into his dark mane, drawing his head closer. She loved his soft, tender kisses. She was both weakened and enflamed as his mouth roved her face and neck. She felt his embrace tighten and his kisses become urgent and deeper after his lips returned to hers. His strong and gentle hands stroked her arms and back, making her aware of every part of her yearning body. When his hand roamed over her shoulder to her breast and cupped it, heat and tingles raced over her flesh. Her mammillas grew taut. The essence of her being called out for appeasement.

Dagan halted his actions, stood, and extended his hand, his message clear and enticing. He hoped she would respond because he craved her beyond belief. "You need not fear me, Starla; I will do everything within my power never to hurt you in any way."

Starla gazed at his hand, then looked into his beckoning blue eyes. "Your skills and experience in this area far outweigh mine, so you might be disappointed you initiated this encounter." As he shook his head, she placed her hand in his and was helped to her feet, her knees shaky and weak. She let him guide her to his *sleeper*, where he halted to kiss her.

As he had dreamed of doing many times, he peeled off her garments. To lessen the tension he sensed within her and read within her green eyes, he kept his gaze fastened to hers as she lay down and he removed his boots and jumpsuit. As fast as possible, he joined her, pulled her into his embrace, and kissed her again.

"Relax, Starla; I do want to devour you, but it will be a painless deed."

The warmth of his breath and huskiness of his voice in her ear caused her to quiver. Somehow she knew his promise of ecstasy would come true.

They surrendered to their soaring passions. They yielded to the glorious torment of wanting each other so deeply and strongly they would risk entanglements with their missions. Fervent needs consumed them as they kissed countless times and fondled scorching bodies. They savored the wonder and rapture of a compelling episode. It seemed right, natural, for them to bond in this physical and emotional manner. Embers of desire were fueled to ignite into a roaring blaze which neither could nor wanted to douse or control.

Starla felt the sleek strands of his black hair as she twirled them around her fingers. She eyed his perfect features, and her fingers and lips trekked them with ardor. She relished his kisses and caresses, which were slow, seductive, and dazing. There was not a spot on her that did not burn or quiver with longing and pleasure. Nestled in his strong embrace, his fingers wandered over her from head to knee—admiring, teasing, enflaming. Her head lolled on the pillow as his deft lips fastened to one breast and tantalized its peak to taut eagerness as his hand kneaded the other mound to anticipation of that same action. She wanted this man with all of her heart

171

and soul. She responded to the signal from his nudging hand to part her thighs so it could drift up and down those sensitive lengths before one tenderly approached her woman's domain. She sighed in bliss as the peak hardened under his masterful touch. There was a quickening in her stomach and a sweet tension building in her ingress. His preparatory finger slipped within her, delving, thrusting, moistening her, assailing her passage. She moaned and thrashed and drew every drop of splendor from that new experience and eagerly awaited many more.

Dagan brushed his fingers over her rib cage and traveled the curves and planes of her pliant body. She caressed his shoulders, arms, and back with light but highly arousing gestures. He ached to bury himself inside her, but he did not want to rush this cherished event. First, he wanted to titillate her to great heights. His fingers dove into the shiny, thick waves of her brown hair. Her lips brushed kisses over his neck, throat, and face while he did the same to hers. He loved feeling her naked flesh next to his. Once more his mouth captured her breast and claimed its summit. He kissed, teethed, and brought it to full attention.

Starla savored the magic of his deft tongue and talented hands. A blast of searing heat stormed her body, one so demanding and swift that it astonished her. She felt the tautness and erotic heat of his protruding desire against her hip. "Take me, Dagan."

He moved atop her, the force of his weight controlled. She wrapped her arms around his back and pressed her fingers near his spine to entice him to unite their bodies and relieve their longings. His mouth melded with hers as their lips tantalized and their tongues teased. He slid the tip of his erection into her, paused a moment to draw a deep and needed breath for renewed restraint, then thrust past her delicate folds until his arousal was concealed by her soft and damp haven. He was stimulated by the way she captured him between her legs with overlapped ankles.

Starla felt no shame or modesty with the man she loved. Yes, she admitted, *loved.* A flood of suspenseful rapture washed over her, one so powerful that she could deny him nothing he wanted from her. The proof of his matching hunger feasted on and within her. She trailed her fingers over the rippling muscles of his back where no scars marred his flesh. He entered and departed her open body, making many journeys to and from it as their mutual passions soared. It was as if primal urgings trapped within them surfaced and demanded a swift mating. She matched his pace and pattern, clinging to him, refusing to allow him to withdraw for any distance or any length of time.

Dagan's ravenous appetite heightened. When he felt her stiffen and heard her gasp for air, he knew she was in the thralls of sweet release. He hastened and strengthened his thrusts to give her supreme pleasure. As she writhed and moaned, he knew he had succeeded, and joy suffused him. He was so enraptured by her and their ecstatic bonding that nothing and no one could have seized his attention at that moment.

A spinning vortex of exquisite splendor carried them away as they climaxed within minutes of each other, their releases overlapping, then subsiding as one. Their greedy mouths and questing hands continued to send delightful and receptive messages; signals of satisfaction and serenity. They remained cuddled and quiet for a time.

Dagan propped on his side, leaned forward and kissed the tip of her nose. "I was right."

Starla eyed his confident expression. "You were right about what?"

"Us being a perfect match."

"In what area?"

Dagan trailed his fingertips over her collarbone and grinned. "In every area. Don't you agree?"

Starla captured his hand to halt its distracting motion. "I think it's too soon to make a judgment. We don't know each other that well."

"If your instincts and impressions are as good as mine, I'm right." He pulled their clasped hands to his lips and kissed hers.

His mood and motive confused her. "Have you ever been wrong?"

He chuckled. "Not many times, and they weren't important." *All except one, yings ago, and I'll correct that error very soon...*

"What if this—I'm—one of your mistakes?"

"Is it? Are you?"

"I don't know, yet. We're almost strangers."

"Then why is it that I feel as if we've known each other for a long time?"

"We have been working together and closely for quite a while."

Dagan noted she contradicted an earlier statement, that they were "almost strangers." They had known each other for over seven *wegs*. "Working together doesn't explain our quick and easy rapport."

"We haven't been friends for very long."

"There was a spark between us the first time we met, Starla. Accept it and admit it."

"I don't deny I find you attractive, but..."

"But, what? You have my full attention."

"I never expected this to happen between us. In fact, I never expected to see you again after our initial encounter on that vessel."

"Fate brought us together for a purpose."

"What kind of purpose?"

"That's something we'll have to wait to learn."

"Perhaps you're reading too much into what just happened between us."

"Perhaps you're not reading enough into it."

"You're confusing me and making me nervous."

"Because you don't want to get this close? You're the most fascinating, beautiful, and enchanting woman I've met. I don't want you to slip through my fingers." *Or get hurt by your connection to Tochar.*

Starla was bewildered and alarmed. This was not how he had behaved with Yana, even while dazed by the pheromone! Was he being honest or was he trying to beguile her for some reason? Either way, she could not fall under his spell and become disarmed. "Don't expect me to become your lover, Dagan; I'm not ready for that kind of commitment."

He challenged, "Maybe your head isn't, but your heart and body are. Just as mine are."

As he leaned forward to kiss her, Starla placed her hand on his chest to stay him. "Please, don't do this. I can't begin a relationship with you."

"You already have, so why run scared now?"

"You don't understand."

"Then, explain what you mean so I can."

"This is... too sudden. Too... unexpected. Too... frightening," she stammered her excuses.

"I promise not to hurt you, so trust me."

"I can't, not this soon. Give me time, Dagan, or it's over now. This is all so new to me."

175

He studied her near-panicked expression. "I won't pressure you, but I will continue to pursue you."

"To what end?" The question leapt from her mouth before she could stop it or reword it.

"To become my mate one *deega.*" He hadn't meant to go that far, though the words were true; yet, he didn't retreat from his statement.

Starla's gaze widened. "You can't be serious?"

Maybe that was the only reason she would leave Tochar and the colony, so he continued. "Why not? We can't live this kind of life until death."

She studied his expression. "You would alter your existence and character to have me?"

"When the time is right, yes." *If I can extricate you from the charges against you, and if you don't make them worse, and if I can get you away before the end comes.* He needed to get a better grasp of her true character, so he challenged, "Would you do the same for me?"

With their gazes locked and in his embrace, Starla deliberated how she should respond, as an answer in either direction seemed hazardous.

Chapter Nine

Starla formed a reply slowly. "When and if the time is right," *but I doubt it ever will be with us on opposite sides of the law,* "and if we truly are compatible, perhaps a future together is possible after we retire from our current lifestyle. As for me, it still remains to be proven that we are a good match for a serious relationship. Many changes will be required, and I can't imagine a man like you settling down and beginning a family, if you can even locate a safe place to do so and find another means of support."

Dagan was cognizant she responded with caution. "That's sufficient encouragement; a slow and easy course makes sense to me. After you get to know me better, you'll probably be surprised by what you learn. I have many unseen facets, Starla, just as you do."

I hope so, my love. I truly hope so. "We'll see."

"That we will, my irresistible teammate."

Dagan kissed and caressed her, and soon they were making passionate and glorious love again.

In the golden aftermath of their union, they cuddled for a while in silence, sated and content. Yet, each was troubled by what loomed before them: their missions and what victory could cost them.

When Starla left his arms, he tried to coax her not to go. "Stay tonight," he implored.

As she pulled on her garments, she glanced at him and said, "That wouldn't be wise; someone might see me departing in the morning."

He grinned. "Want to keep our relationship a secret from everybody?"

"Until it is a relationship, I do. Good night, Dagan. See you tomorrow; Tochar has a task for us to do."

"I'll escort you to the landing grid."

"That isn't necessary; it isn't that late; and I'm well armed. Almost everyone here knows I work for Tochar, so no one will dare attack me. If anyone tries, I can protect myself."

"I remember your superior skills from when you battled me, but I will slay anyone who harms you."

"Thanks, Dagan, but revenge can be a dangerous and self-destructive task."

Not if one is careful, and justice is a must for peace of mind. I'll have it after Tochar is destroyed, just as I'll find a way to have you. "Good night, Starla. Be careful."

She allowed her gaze to roam his handsome face and virile unclothed body. Every facet of him was enormously appealing; and she was susceptible to him in all ways. *Get moving, Bree, before you weaken and succumb again!* "I will. See you tomorrow."

The next morning, Starla sent *Raz* Yakir a message via Thaine Sanger to warn the Serlan ruler to be on alert for an incoming communication from Tochar to his spy on the capital planet of Ulux or crystal mining planet of Kian. Yet, she suspected his signal could not be detected or traced, just as hers couldn't. She wished the *fiendal* did not possess that technology and instrument so the traitor could be unmasked. She reported to her superior and friend in Maffei that all moonbeams stolen so far had been destroyed by the secret devices. She told him to expect imminent raids for more, though she had not been informed as to dates and sites for them.

After that task was finished, Starla looked at Cypher and said, "All we can do now is wait and watch for clues. If only we can discover the leaks in Seri and Kalfa, destroy the weapons protecting Tochara, and prevent more crystal raids, we can complete our mission here and go home. I need to get away from these terrible people and this awful place. I want to see my family." *I need to talk with Mother; she will know what I should do about Dagan. When she and Father met, they were antagonists from different worlds, and their relationship appeared doomed. Now, no two can be more in love or happier. Despite their past dissimilarities and problems, they are matched perfectly and everything was resolved between them.* That also was true for her brother, Galen, and his mate, Renah; and for her sister, Amaya, and her mate, Jason of Earth. All three couples had overcome seemingly impossible and tormenting obstacles and had been bonded for *yings. If only it can be that way for me and Dagan.* She reminded herself, her love was a criminal, a willing hireling of Tochar; and his future seemed grim. None of her family had been evil, except for one, and she was pardoned.

The android analyzed from her expression she was thinking and reasoning on a dilemma and allowed her time to do so. When she looked at him, he said, "You want to escape Dagan Latu because you fear him."

"Not him, Cypher, but his powerful effect on me. My uncontrollable feelings for him grow stronger and run deeper every *deega.* It's an inexplicable bond between us, as if we're matched in a strange and potent way. It's more than a physical attraction, at least for me, and he appears to be telling the truth about his feelings. Yet, I can't say for certain if he is falling in love with me or he's only beguiling me for an unknown or selfish reason. Either angle can create trouble and torment for me."

Starla lazed back in her chair and frowned. "He makes it difficult for me to concentrate on my duty and to remember he's one of our targets. I love him and I want him, Cypher, but I know that's wrong for me and perilous for my mission. Soon, I may be forced to betray him. If that happens, he'll hate me and curse the *deega* we met. You can't imagine how tempted I am to warn him to flee while there's time for escape or to attempt to convince him to side with us, but he could expose me to Tochar. I'm certain he holds no kind feelings for that *fiendal,* but men like him have a strange code of honor to the leaders who hire them. Dagan's record says his father and brother were slain by *Sekis* after a suspicious incident of treachery, and that's when he turned wicked. I wonder if he can be turned again. Even so, there are many charges and allegations against him; and I'm not certain I can get him a pardon for helping us."

"If you request a pardon and it is denied, then he escapes or you allow him to flee punishment for his crimes, you will come under suspicion. An investigation will ensue. You must not dishonor yourself, your rank, and your family; or breach their faith in you."

"I know; as hard as it will be, I will do my duty. But it torments me to think of him being terminated forever or being confined for life on a barbaric penal colony. I know there is much good in Dagan Latu if he is given the chance to show it."

"You cannot alter his fate, Bree-Kayah; he chose his evil way of life. If there are grim consequences from his choice, he must suffer them."

"My head tells me you are right, but my heart rebels against bitter reality. If only I can persuade him or trick him into leaving Tochar's hire and settlement, my dilemma will resolve itself. There isn't enough time left for him to earn enough to purchase a new ship to return to work for himself. If he can steal one from somewhere, he can leave."

"It is a remote possibility for Tochar to permit him to quit and depart. There is a chance Latu will ask you to leave with him. If he loves you and you refused to go, he will not depart and will remain in Tochar's hire."

"I had not reasoned it out that way. He said I was running scared. He's accurate; he just doesn't know the correct reason for my contradictory behavior. I should not have become physically involved with him as Starla or as Yana. Being so close to him confuses my emotions and dulls my instincts. I must find the strength and wits to resist him, without arousing suspicions in him for my sudden rejection."

"When the time comes for you to make a decision about his fate, you will make the right one."

Starla looked at the intelligent android, her eyes misty, her soul in anguish. "Will I, Cypher? Can I trust my head to overrule my heart when the moment of truth arrives?"

"You are Bree-Kayah Saar, daughter of legends, sister of legends; you will do your duty."

"Promise you'll make certain I do what is right."

"I will prevent an error in judgment."

"Thank you, Cypher." She took a deep breath and wiped the moisture from her eyes. "I'm going to eat and freshen up before it's time to leave to do that futile task for Tochar. You're in control of the ship."

Starla left the bridge to order a meal from the automated *servo* that had been restocked recently by a traveling supply vessel. She dreaded what she must do to Dagan later, but she had no choice.

As he dressed, Dagan pondered the report from his superior early this morning. The two *I-GAF* officers who had been slain on the Sion space station had been there without Phaedrig's knowledge, en route from a secret assignment, so a warning to stay clear had not been issued to them. As the Kalfan combed his black hair, he mused upon a mystery: Sach had told him Starla had destroyed a Serian patrol ship and its crew three *malees* ago before joining Tochar. Yet, there was no record of that incident in *I-GAF* files. He could not surmise why the Serians had not reported an intergalactic episode, but was glad a serious charge wasn't registered against her. If murder was committed during the commission of a crime, Starla Vedris was doomed, if he exposed her. Dagan knew it was his duty as an *I-GAF* officer to do so. Yet, he realized what that exposure would cost Starla and himself: her death. With every fiber of his being, he believed she loved him and was a good person, and would change her existence if given the chance. If only, he brooded, he could keep her out of trouble and danger from now until he completed his assignment, one progressing too slowly to suit him. True, the stolen crystals had been destroyed, but not because of him. He was no closer to solving the mystery of the traitor or to defeating Tochar than when he arrived. The longer he took to finalize this crucial case, the deeper Starla was drawn into it, and the farther she was pushed from his reach. He had to do something and fast to get the situation resolved. But what, he did not know.

Starla, Dagan, Auken, Sach, Moig, and members of the Enforcers searched the area around the demolished cave for clues to the cause of the explosion and for any signs of enemy involvement. None were found, much to their leader's annoyance, as that would explain the mystery. Even so, Tochar ordered his men to remain on full alert and to take extra precautions when storing future stolen goods.

After they were dismissed and left the others, Dagan asked Starla to join him for the evening meal at the Skull's Den. He was surprised and disappointed when she refused his invitation, and was dismayed by her chilly aura. "What's wrong?" he asked as they reached her shuttle.

"I need time to think about what you said to me and what happened between us. I'm not sure I want the same things you do. If we go into this with different expectations and feelings, it will cause problems."

Dagan became wary. "What kind of problems?"

"Resentment, spitefulness, a lack of concentration and loyalty during raids. That will be dangerous for us and the others. Dissension will irritate Tochar, possibly to the point of getting rid of us."

"I'm confused, Starla; I thought you wanted me as much as I want you. I thought our desires and goals matched perfectly."

"I don't understand or know you, Dagan. One *preon,* you seem like one person and the next, you're totally different. I've never met a man like you, enigmatic and captivating. You make me... think and behave in foreign ways, and that alarms me. I want to give you and any future relationship deep and careful study."

"How can you get to know me if you refuse to spend time with me? Besides, we can't avoid each other, since we have to work together."

"I meant, see each other like we did last night. I'm not ready to get that close. And, I get the impression you aren't ready for love and romance, either. I suppose what I'm trying to say is... I'm not into casual sex."

"That isn't what I want from you. Do you think I'm unworthy of your attention and affections?"

"That isn't what I meant to imply. If I did, I'm sorry. Look at how and where we live, Dagan. We can't change or move, at least not anytime soon. To initiate a serious affair at this time will evoke complexities."

"Do I understand correctly: you aren't jettisoning your feelings for me, only docking them for a while?"

"I suppose you can put it that way."

Maybe, he reasoned, she had a good point. He was in a precarious position and shouldn't drag her into it and endanger her life. He eyed her sad expression and perceived her mixed emotions, things he suspected she did not realize she was revealing. Something inspired intense conflict within her, but he could not deduce the cause. "Take the time you need, Starla; I'll be patient. I'm not going anywhere. Just let me know when you change your mind." After she nodded, he smiled and left her standing there, aware her gaze was fastened to his back as he walked away, her pain palpable in the air...

Starla was relieved when Cypher told her Dagan had not tried to visit Yana's abode that night or the following one. She remained on her ship so she would not be tempted to surrender to her lover, but she had been prepared to shapeshift and transport to Yana's dwelling if a signal came Dagan or another approached it. She had decided that she also must rebuff him in that form, as Yana could not extract any secrets from him, and to unite Yana's body with his was just as precarious to her.

On the following morning, Starla was ordered to attend a meeting at Tochar's. She found the *fiendal* and Moig awaiting her upon her arrival.

"There is a task I want you and Moig to do. You will leave in your ship after our talk. Serian patrols have stored a large supply of confiscated drugs on Zumali.

Two androids are guarding them. I want you to help Moig get them to replace those I lost during that curious incident with the *Skalds.* Moig has the details. There should not be any problem stealing them."

"You want us to go alone?" Starla asked.

"Yes, the rest of my team is doing another task for me. You should return within two *deegas* of each other. Is your ship supplied and ready for a flight?"

"It was serviced by a supply vessel while I was gone on our last trek; my android handled it for me." Starla knew she could not refuse Tochar's order, and thought it unwise to ask probing and suspicious questions. She would delve for clues with Moig during their journey. She was vexed about the unit being divided and sent on separate raids. She assumed the other men had gone after more crystals, but she concealed her annoyance. If she didn't learn anything useful from Moig, she would be forced to seek information later from Dagan, and there was only one way to accomplish that feat... "We can be ready to depart within the *hora.*"

Tochar smiled. "You always please me, Starla."

She faked a bright smile of gratitude. "Thank you, sir. Moig, are you coming with me now or do you want me to return for you later?"

"I'm ready to go," the bearded man replied.

"Have a safe and successful journey."

"We will," Moig boasted with a grin.

Seven *deegas* later, Starla and Moig transported to a clearing on the snowy surface of Zumali, a small planet on the edge of the Seri Galaxy, far from its solar body. She pointed to the square complex a lengthy distance away, nestled against a white-covered ridge. Gusts of cold wind yanked at their synthetic fur garments, but protective helmets with visors shielded their faces from the weather and exposure of their identity. Cypher reported that no lifeforms registered amidst the rocks and hills nearby, so they headed toward their target, trudging slowly and gingerly in ankle-deep snow.

Before they reached the structure and used their faked papers and uniforms to obtain entrance from the android guards, Cypher contacted Starla. "A Serian patrol is approaching; arrival in five *preons.* Abort raid and return to the ship. There is insufficient time to carry out your task and the risks are increasing with haste. Three officers are transporting to the surface; ten *leongs* from the complex entrance. Departure is crucial."

Starla saw three Serians materialize, spot them, and shout a warning to surrender or be attacked. She could not slay them or allow herself to be taken captive and be exposed to Tochar's spy. "Take cover behind that large rock, Moig, fast!" she ordered.

She did the same, then told Cypher, "Lock on to our coordinates and bring us aboard. The *preon* we're safe, cloak, raise defense shield, and go to starlight speed." The android could handle only one task at a time: the cloaker and shield must be lowered to retrieve them, making her ship vulnerable to destruction during that period. Even with Cypher's intelligence and abilities, the series of actions had to be scheduled just right to prevent perils and would take a few moments to set into motion. She knew if an attack came while the ship's defenses were lowered and she was in transport, her life-force would be lost forever.

Laser weapons were fired at their location, striking and spalling rock and tossing about snow and ice. Moig was hit in the arm by a stun-beam as he tried to return their blasts before Starla could halt him. The patrol carried oblong defense shields, so the Icarian's fire was deflected as he was knocked unconscious.

The setting vanished as the *Liska's* transporter beam rescued them just as the protective rock was destroyed. The moment she materialized on the sensor pad on her ship, Starla glanced to her right and saw Moig's frame. "Get us out of here quick, Cypher! Evade them as necessary, but do not fire upon them."

Cypher reported to her as he worked, "Shield up. Cloaker engaged. Patrol firing a broad sweep of beams at our last visible location. Going to starburst speed in one *preon.*" A minute later, he said, "Clear of danger. Course laid in for stargate to Noy. Patrol heading in opposite direction."

"Excellent, Cypher. Moig was stunned, so I'll remain with him until he arouses. You know what to do, and thanks for saving my life again."

"What happened?" Moig asked an *hora* later.

"A cloaked Serian ship appeared as if by magic. Their sensors must have detected us. They were told no authorization had been given for a landing. We barely escaped before they shattered the rock we were hiding behind. Cypher grabbed us off the surface, got my ship cloaked and left fast. We're on the way to base."

"Tochar will be angry we failed him."

"Somebody gave him bad information. It almost got us killed or captured. He wouldn't expect us to make a second attempt with a patrol lurking nearby. Besides, you had the code. You were wounded, out cold."

"Not our fault, but he'll be riled. He needs those drugs for his buyers. The meeting is already scheduled. He promised them drugs and crystals."

Starla realized the still woozy Moig was making slips. "He can't blame us; we did our part. I'll play the record of our attack so he can grasp our peril. We had no choice except to abort the raid. Cypher picked up their communications. They know two people were involved and one was injured, but they couldn't see our faces through our visors. How's the head, Moig? You struck it hard after you were stunned."

"It hurts like *karlee*."

"I'll give you something for the pain and to prevent infection. As soon as Cypher can leave the bridge, he'll seal the cut with a *latron* beam. He has a medical program and he's repaired me many times."

"Thanks, Vedris, for saving my life."

"That's what partners do for each other."

Starla prepared the injector with a clear liquid and infused it in Moig's arm. She chatted with him while the potent chemical took effect. As soon as the Icarian was dazed by the *Thorin*, she said, "Moig, you will answer my questions with total honesty. Do you understand?"

Controlled by truth serum, he replied, "Yes."

Starla knew her action was daring and dangerous, but she needed information and this might be the last time she could extract it. She had the attack record in her possession to play for Tochar, and another clever ruse to keep Moig disabled... "Where did Auken's team go? What was his target?"

"Moonbeams in Kalfa."

"Are they for Koteas and Terin?"

"Yes."

"When is the meeting with them scheduled?"

"Four *deegas* after our return to Tochara."

"Is it set to take place near the settlement?"

"Yes."

"Do you know Tochar's contact in Seri?"

"No."

"How does Auken know when it's safe to approach a ship carrying moonbeams? Is there a special reason why we use his ship for those raids?"

"Yes. A device on the transport vessel sends Auken a signal. He has a unit to pick up that signal."

"Is that why no one is allowed on the bridge when approaching a target except you, Auken, and Sach?"

"Yes."

"Does Tochar trust Starla Vedris?"

"Yes."

"Does Tochar trust Dagan Latu?"

"Yes."

"Do you know who is Tochar's Kalfa contact?"

"Yes."

Anticipation flooded her. "What is his name?"

"Syrkin."

Starla gaped at the drugged man. "The officer in charge of crystal mining and shipments?"

"Yes."

"Why does Syrkin help Tochar steal moonbeams?"

"After Tochar is rich and powerful, Syrkin will join him as a partner and will rule Kalfa."

"Does Tochar have contacts or partners in other places besides Kalfa and Seri?"

"Yes, in Maffei."

Astonished and dismayed, she asked, "Who?"

"I do not know."

Starla did not have the time to ponder who from her world could be a traitor or why. She would leave that investigation up to Thaine. "Is there any way to disarm or destroy Tochar's defense weapons?"

"No."

"Do you know that for certain or is that what you were told?"

"What I was told, what Tochar was told."

"Why did Tochar divide the team and send us on separate raids?"

"He needed drugs and crystals fast, soon. The *Adika* and *Liksa* were needed to carry out two raids."

"Why did Tochar send you with Starla instead of one of the others?"

"Vedris and Latu are attracted to each other and might be distracted by their feelings during a trek."

"Is he angry they like each other?"

"No, he does not care, if it does not distract them from work."

Starla thought hard to make certain there were no other questions she wanted to ask before she placed him in a chemical coma, one from which he could not arouse until given the antidote; that would not be until after her mission was completed. She knew the doctor on Noy could not detect Moig's true condition or treat it. With Moig out of the way, she reasoned, Tochar could not divide the band again and exclude her from crystal raids. She had not dared use this tactic sooner because there had been no previous occurrence to explain a coma until this incident provided one.

After Cypher joined her, Starla told him everything Moig had said. "Bandage his head but do not seal the wound," she instructed the android. "I want Tochar and the settlement doctor to see it. They should assume he has a severe concussion and possible brain damage. Connect a feeding tube and vital-signs monitors. One *villite* down and many to go."

"This was a clever move, Bree-Kayah. On the next crystal raid, I will scan for the signal he mentioned and record its frequency."

She smiled. "At long last, my friend, we're making valuable progress. I must report these findings and what

I've done to Supreme Commander Sanger. Thaine can have either a Serian or *I-GAF* unit cloaked and standing by to capture Koteas and Terin after they obtain those moonbeams and leave Noy. I dare not risk exploding another load, if Tochar allows anybody to get near them again. Thaine or Yakir will have to either let Syrkin continue his ruse for a while or find a way to remove him without anybody learning how Syrkin's treachery was uncovered. We can't risk the wrong person discovering an agent has infiltrated Tochar's band. At least that nefarious *fiendal* doesn't suspect me. What I can't understand is why Tochar has a contact in Maffei, since we don't have a crystal mine."

"Perhaps the Maffeian supplies him with other data and needs."

"He'll be hard to unmask since his motive isn't obvious. I'm glad Tochar didn't send me with the others; we accomplished far more on our trek."

"It is good to see you smile."

"I feel wonderful, Cypher, but I have another hard task ahead. I might have to dupe Dagan again to see if he learned anything during their trek, and you know there's only one way I can ensnare him. First, I might let Yana give it a try; if she fails, it will be up to Starla."

As they approached the harsh planet of Noy, Starla contacted Tochar with her bad news.

"I have been informed of the trouble at Zumali," he responded. "I will have the doctor awaiting your shuttle. We will talk after your arrival."

After landing, Tochar and the doctor came aboard her craft. "I'm sorry, sir, but we were trapped and attacked," Starla explained. "Cypher and I have done all we can for him." She handed Tochar a disk and said, "This

191

is a recording of the communications between the Serian patrol and the complex, and the patrol and their base. You will hear how and why we failed you."

"A patrol was not supposed to be in that sector, so I do not blame you and Moig for what happened. When I was warned of its presence, it was too late to alert you in your communications void. I am glad you were not slain or captured. You did well, Starla, as always."

"Thank you." She turned to the doctor who was examining Moig to ask about his condition, but was told to wait outside. Though the doctor spoke to Tochar in whispers, Starla knew Cypher was picking up their words as the communications switch had been left on in preparation for such an incident. She walked a short distance away so the two men would talk freely, and was stunned when they joined her shortly and reported that Moig had "died from his injury."

"But I got him here fast and kept him nourished. I do not know what more I could have done."

"It is sad to lose a longtime friend," Tochar said, "but life makes such demands of us." He motioned for two Enforcers to come forward, then told them to collect Moig's body for burial. "I know you did all you could to keep him alive, but he is gone now," he said to Starla. "When the others return, I will contact you for a meeting. Rest, Starla, this trek was hard on you."

"I'm sorry things went wrong." She faked grief and an apology. "I'll be on my ship if you need me."

Starla returned to the *Liska.* She hurried to the bridge to join Cypher. "What happened to Moig? His death isn't natural. His injury and condition weren't terminal. What could have happened?"

The android replayed the shocking scene.

The doctor's words came first. "His condition is serious, Tochar. I'm not qualified to treat it. I lack the proper medical facility and means to do anything for him. I do not think he can recover or even live very long, at least not here. Perhaps you can send him to Icaria for treatment. Perhaps they can help him."

"I cannot risk anyone there extracting my secrets," Tochar's words were firm, "and Moig knows most of them. Too, he is delving too deeply into drugs. He is beyond our help and should not be forced to live in this state, so do as I ordered."

"Give him a lethal injection?"

"I have no choice. Put him out of his misery. I cannot allow him to become a threat to me. After it is done, forget it happened. Do you understand me?"

"I understand; I won't tell anyone."

"So," Starla murmured, "they killed Moig to silence him. So much for friendship and loyalty."

"He was a *villite*, Bree-Kayah. If Tochar had sent him to Icaria and he was diagnosed correctly and was given the antidote, the truth would have imperiled you. His death serves us well, just as his data will serve us well. You are not responsible for his fate."

Two days later, Starla was summoned to Tochar's elevated dwelling. Dagan, Auken, and Sach had returned and were present. Dagan passed his gaze over her as if making certain she was unharmed, but it was Auken who spoke first.

"Tochar told us about the trouble on your raid, Starla. We're all glad you're alive and uninjured."

"Thank you, Auken; it was scary there for a while. I'm sorry about Moig's loss; I know he was a close friend to you three for *yings.*"

"Tochar said you did all you could to save him."

"Obviously it wasn't enough, Auken, or he wouldn't be dead."

"Don't blame yourself; it was that patrol's fault."

"Thank you, Sach, but we were on my ship, so I feel responsible. I didn't know how to help him. Cypher did all his medical program allowed, but he lacks the in-depth knowledge required for that injury." She needed to change the subject. "Was your raid successful? Did you encounter any trouble?"

Auken grinned. "In and out like a comet."

"Let's get our business handled," Tochar said, "then all of you can seek rest and diversions, both of which are needed and well deserved. My buyers arrive in two *deegas* for the crystals. In three *deegas,* you will leave again and bring me another supply of drugs for them. This time, there will not be a patrol in that sector."

"We're going back to Zumali?" Starla inquired.

"I have been assured it will be safe this time. They will not expect you to strike at the same place and so soon; they will be guarding other sites."

"Who will go with me this time?" she asked.

"The entire unit will make the trek together."

She nodded understanding and agreement.

"Meet for departure at the landing grid on the morning of the third *deega* from this one. Until then, do as you please."

"Don't you need us to guard you for the buyer meeting?" Dagan asked.

"No, I am taking a large and well-armed unit of Enforcers with me. Unless you have other questions, you may leave and enjoy yourselves. Dagan, stay behind for a while; I have more to talk about with you."

Starla left with the others and walked to her shuttle. She was glad she had warned Thaine to prepare a surprise attack on the Thracians who were coming for the crystals, since she would not have an opportunity to destroy them, and doing so again would be reckless. When she returned to her ship, she would send Thaine an update to confirm that delivery schedule and would report Moig's death, as she had waited for this meeting to take place before contacting her superior. She hoped no Serians would be near Zumali during the next drug raid, as she wanted to avoid a lethal battle. She would warn *Raz* Yakir via Thaine, as it would be dangerous for the ruler to give his forces a command to stay clear of the planet since that information could enter the wrong ears. She would ask both men not to act upon that news and risk exposing her to the Serian traitor, and she was certain they would concur with her precaution. So far, Yakir had kept his word about protecting her identity and mission; because she was still alive and free.

She decided against waiting for Dagan to finish his talk with Tochar. She would return to her ship, make her report to Thaine, and change into Yana before seeing him tonight.

Dagan rounded the corner of the structure to head for his chamber and sighted the sultry creature leaning against the wall near his door. She looked up and smiled, then straightened her posture and fingered her long golden hair. *Blast it all, you're the last person I want to encounter tonight. I need to file a report with Phaedrig and try to reach Starla.* "Yana, what are you doing here?" Annoyance dripped from his words.

"I saw Auken and Sach in the Skull's Den, so I knew you had returned. When you didn't appear or answer my signal, I waited for you. It's been a long time since we saw each other. Can we visit tonight?"

"Come inside; we need to talk." Dagan slid the metallic card into a slot and the door swished open. He stepped aside for Yana to enter first, her scent teasing into his nostrils as she did so. He felt his body warm, and he was annoyed by her effect on him. *Keep your distance from her!* He walked to the eating area and fetched himself a cool drink which he downed with haste. He offered her no refreshment. He looked at the sensual woman who took a seat and gazed at him.

"You're angry with me for coming here, aren't you?" she asked.

"Not exactly," he replied, staying where he was, a partition between them. "I don't want to hurt you or mislead you, Yana, but nothing can happen between us again. From here on, let's keep our distance."

Yana widened her fake blue gaze. "Why? What have I done to be rejected like this? We're a good match. I thought you were as attracted to me as I am to you. We enjoyed each other. Am I being too forward and easy? Did I displease you on the *sleeper?*"

"I'm involved with another woman, so I can't see you again."

"Surely a virile male like you can have more than one relationship." She watched him shake his head.

"This one is serious and important to me."

"If you love and want another woman, why did you have sex with me? You cannot tell me you did not find pleasure and satisfaction with me."

As she stood to approach him, he ordered in a stern tone, "Stay where you are."

Yana halted and stared at him. "What's wrong with you? I am not an enemy; why are you afraid of me?"

"I don't know how you did it, and maybe it was unintentional, but you ensnared me in some unknown trap. That's the only way to explain what happened with you. Perhaps Asisan females possess some biological magic. It won't happen again. If you're in trouble or danger, I'll try to help you; but that's as far as our relationship can go."

"You think I tricked you into surrendering?"

"I didn't want you that night and I don't want you tonight, but there's something you emit that makes you irresistible at close proximity."

"There is a special chemistry between us, Dagan, so why fight it? You affect me in the same way; that is why I came to you both times."

He chilled his tone. "Leave, Yana, and don't return again. I love and desire another woman. I won't allow you to destroy my chances with her."

Yana was astonished and aroused by his words and expression. It would be wrong to use the pheromone on him again, and she was glad she had sprayed it on so lightly he could battle it. "You sound determined. True love is rare and valuable, so I will not intrude on your life again. I'm sorry you don't trust me. I will not bother you in the future unless I am in dire need of your help. Good-bye, Dagan."

"Good-bye, Yana, and I'm sorry if your feelings are injured by me."

"I am a survivor, Dagan, so do not worry."

He watched Yana leave and hoped she wouldn't cause him trouble with Starla. It seemed she had given up too easily to be trusted. If a problem arose, he told himself, he would handle it. Right now, he had work to do. He checked the security of his chamber, filed his report, and awaited a reply as he thought about Starla and how close she had come to death. Even so, the incident had not frightened or convinced her to terminate her work. How, he worried, could he protect her when they were separated, if that happened again? How could he coax her away from Noy and Tochar?

Dagan was astonished by Phaedrig's response: an *I-GAF* unit was already standing by to prevent Koteas and Terin from returning to Icaria with the crystals they had stolen recently. Phaedrig did not know where the information had come from; it had been entered into their private network from an untraceable source, one using the proper code and password. In case the data was true, Phaedrig had sent a cloaked ship and special team to handle the matter in guarded secrecy.

Dagan could not imagine who had gotten the facts in time to put his superior's plan into motion, when he and the others had been told only less than an *hora* ago. Was it possible there was an agent working in Icaria, he mused, or could Tochar's lover be a traitor to him? Who else could know the *fiendal's* plans so far in advance except someone close to Tochar or to his buyers? At least he wouldn't have to worry about the crystals being used by Thracians, but a further mystery had arisen. If another agent was working on this same mission, who was he? Who had hired him and what was his location and why the secrecy from *I-GAF?* He needed to be on alert for clues to the answers to those questions.

Dagan showered and changed, then headed for the Skull's Den to ask Auken or Sach how he could contact Starla on her ship. He hoped Yana had not returned as he didn't want to confront her again. He was relieved when he sighted Starla sitting alone at a side table.

Dagan joined her and smiled. "I was coming to search for you, woman. I've been zoned out since I heard about your close brush with peril. Are you sure you're all right?"

"I'm fine; I can take care of myself." Starla sipped her drink and avoided fusing their gazes.

"Still chilly from your Zumali visit? I hoped you had changed your mind and softened toward me."

Her gaze met his as she challenged, "Do you really need two women at one time to sate you?"

He tensed. "What do you mean?"

"I came to see you earlier, but you were busy."

Dagan's heart lurched in panic and dread. "You have it wrong, Starla; please, let me explain."

"Then explain, if you can. I will not share you. Even forbidden love cannot survive betrayal."

Chapter Ten

Dagan glanced around the rustic room which was becoming crowded and noisy. "Not here. In private, at my place or on your ship," he whispered.

"Cypher is on my ship. I know he's an android, but he's like a real person to me, like a brother; so I don't want to go there to talk."

"Will you come to my chamber?"

"What if she returns?" Starla asked to impress upon him they were different entities, even though it was unlikely he would suspect shapeshifting.

"I can promise you she won't, if she leaves me alone as I ordered her to do. I didn't invite Yana there and didn't want to see her; I swear."

Starla pretended to study him for a moment. She needed to learn if he had discovered any clues during his last raid which he might share with her, by accident or volition. She also wanted to draw him closer to her in case his help and protection were needed soon, if he truly loved her and would provide them. "Let's go. I'll hear you out this one time."

They left the Skull's Den and walked the short distance to Dagan's chamber.

Dagan took a position facing her. He rested his right arm along the back of the *seata,* his fingers touching her shoulder. He gazed into her green eyes. "Yana was waiting for me when I returned. I asked her to come inside so I could settle the matter with her. Despite, what I am, Starla, I'm not a cruel person. I didn't want to hurt her and didn't mean to mislead her. I told her I'm involved with another woman and made it clear nothing can happen between us. I suppose she's never been rebuffed before. She looked confused and surprised by my rejection, and maybe her feelings were injured. I told her I love and desire only you, and I wouldn't allow her to cause trouble between us by making it appear as if I am betraying you in secret." Dagan noticed Starla's controlled expression and reaction. When she didn't respond to his last sentence, he continued with his explanation.

"I don't know who she is or why she's here. There seems to be a serious problem where she habitates. I get the impression something important must take place before she can return home. She puts on a good facade of being brave. I think she's afraid and lonely, and that's why she turned to me. I offered to help her if she got into trouble, but that's all. She said she believed me and wouldn't approach me again unless she was threatened. I hope she told the truth. If not, please don't misread any contact between us. In fact, if you see us together, join me and prove to her I'm off-limits, prove to yourself I'm not chasing her." Dagan thought it best not to reveal their sexual encounter and his suspicions about how and why it happened. "I love you, Starla Vedris, and I want you, only you, and forever. I hope you either feel the same way, or will some *deega*."

Starla took a deep breath and kept her gaze locked to his blue one. She knew an intimate relationship with him was hazardous, but it seemed necessary. Yet, she felt guilty about deceiving him and worse about using him. She couldn't imagine her torment if she had to betray and arrest him.

"Do you believe me?" Dagan asked, his chest tight with dread and his emotions in a freefall.

"Yes, I do." She saw him exhale in relief, then smile. "I don't understand this rapid and potent attraction between us, but—I admit--it exists. Let's move slowly and carefully and see where it takes us."

Dagan clasped her hand in his. "It will guide us to our future if we don't resist its power and magic."

"Our future?" We have none as long as your trajectory is bad. Recalibrate it, my love. Decontaminate yourself, Dagan, so I can have you, if it's not already too late for you to escape your nefarious past.

Her silence and intense study worried him, as did the chilled flesh on her hand. "Yield to me, Starla; bond to me as you have to no other man. Let me love you, protect you, cherish you above all females who have lived or will live. I will do everything in my power to defend you and to keep you at my side forever, this I swear with all my heart and soul."

As she gazed into his blue eyes and listened to his words, she was convinced he was being serious and honest. Yet, obstacles between them were enormous, seemingly insurmountable. *Why did cruel fate send you here to create havoc with my emotions and mission? Why did I fall in love with a forbidden rogue?* She felt the vibration in her wrist unit as Cypher signaled a warning she was losing control of herself and the situation, a fact the android had deduced from monitoring her physiological reactions. Starla pressed a tiny button to let Cypher know she had gotten his message, the response masked by her rise from the *seata.*

Dagan grasped her arm, "Don't leave."

"I was heading there," she replied, nodding toward his *sleeper.*

Dagan stood and embraced her. "I feared I had panicked you with my confession and the revelation of my great need for you."

Starla rested her head against his chest and wrapped her arms around his waist. "The only thing I fear at this *preon* is that this mysterious bond between us won't be strong or tight enough to hold us together for the rest of our lives. I don't want to lose you, Dagan, but I'm afraid something or someone will tear us apart; that would evoke terrible anguish."

He hugged her and kissed the top of her head. "We won't allow that to happen, my love."

"There are forces in the Cosmos stronger than we are, so that choice might not be ours to make."

Dagan lifted her chin and fused their gazes. "If necessary, my ravishing moonbeam, I will battle both *Kahala* and *Karlee* to have you."

"Moonbeam," her mind echoed, the endearment her father used for her golden-haired mother and the crux of her mission: a word with such disparate meanings: love and unity, death and separation. "Whatever happens beyond this night, Dagan, know I love and desire only you."

"I have no doubt you are the perfect woman for me, my destined mate, my partner in all things," Dagan murmured. *I must find a way to keep you, but also do my duty. How, I don't know at this time.*

Dagan's mouth slanted across Starla's in a tender kiss to which she responded with eagerness. Many others followed, the pressure of his lips varying from gentle and soft to firm and demanding. His deft hands roamed her back and his mouth soon journeyed down her neck and over her ears, driving her wild with feverish cravings.

Starla yearned to feel her bare skin making contact with his. She wriggled her fingers between them and removed her top, then his, with Dagan helping her peel off their garments. Her senses were alive, responsive, enchanted. She pressed her hips to his, bringing their fiery loins into snug and tantalizing proximity.

His body begged for appeasement. He trembled from need and in a battle for self-control. Her mouth seemed to ravish his with undeniable urgency. His tension increased and he wondered if he could explode just from touching her and being touched by her. No female had aroused him to such great heights of hunger, to such near mindless abandonment of will and wits. His knees felt weak and shaky, so he lifted her and carried her to his *sleeper* where they reclined.

His hands fondled and kneaded her breasts, their buds growing hard beneath his fingers. His mouth joined them to labor lovingly on their points, to circle their mounds, and to delve into the valley between them. Soon, one hand drifted down her rib cage, making a slow and sensuous trek over each bone. His palm flattened over her stomach and moved from hipbone to hipbone as he relished the smooth and warm surface, each trip carrying it lower and lower.

Starla quivered in anticipation. She squirmed in delight as his fingers explored the pulsing nub and silky folds surrounding it. She trailed her fingertips over his broad back and shoulders, stroking the soft covering over his hard frame. She wanted him to continue this thrilling sport, but her body begged to have him within her. "Take me, Dagan," she panted. "Make me yours forever; I can wait no longer to bond with you."

His mouth trekked back to hers and melded their lips as he moved atop her. He entered her feminine domain and reveled in the welcome he received. He began to thrust and withdraw as he kissed and caressed her. His desires heightened, his pleasures intensified. When passion threatened to overwhelm him, he paused and took several deep breaths, retreating until only the tip of his organ was poised at her rosy portal. But Starla's hands and mouth protested the delay. Her hips and legs urged him to resume his previous actions. "Easy, my love,

I want you so fiercely I can barely stay within you without losing all control."

Starla murmured in his ear, "There's no need for control or hesitation, my beloved."

Heat and suspense rose in her loins. Sparks of ecstasy licked her body and dazed her mind. Tiny jolts built into powerful ones that staggered her senses and swept her away to a glorious climax. She gave herself totally to him and the blissful experience.

For a weird minute, Dagan speculated that her responses were oddly and strongly similar to Yana's. Though the sultry Asisan was pleasurable and beautiful in a physical sense, Starla had so much more to offer him. Again, he briefly worried about his love and desire for the space pirate conflicting with his duty. Even so, his wits scattered and his heart pounded as she once more confessed her feelings for him.

"I love you, Dagan Latu. I've never wanted a man as I desire you. This might be the craziest thing I've ever done, but I can't help myself."

He echoed her fiery sentiments. "I love and desire you, Starla Vedris, more than you know or can imagine." He buried his face in her brown hair and thrust into her until every drop of love's nectar was spent. *This may be the most reality-impaired thing I've done, but I can't help myself, either. Whatever your magic is, my radiant and potent moonbeam, I'm enchanted by it and you.*

Almost breathless from their exertions but sated to a supreme level, they cuddled in each other's arms, sharing and savoring their closeness and serenity.

"You're mine, Starla, tonight and forever."

"If it's possible one *deega*, I do want a future with you," she said with certainty.

"As soon as I earn enough to buy another ship, we're gone from this perilous place and existence." *What if*, he

worried, *she offers you her ship? Clear your head, Curran!*
He tried to prevent that predicament by saying, "Call it
ego or male pride, but I have to get on my feet again using
my own skills. Right now, I have little to offer you except
me, but we can't live on love, as delicious as it is. When
I'm back in full control of my life, I'll have the means to
support and protect you."

Starla was relieved he gave her an excuse not to
suggest they depart on her ship, as she had not
considered that reaction when her last words escaped
her lips. *Uncloud your mind, Bree, and get back to work;
that's why you're here tonight.* "I understand and agree
with your reasoning and motives. We also have to be
cautious, Dagan. We can't flaunt our relationship or it
might worry Tochar. He could think it might be
distracting for us or may fear we'll pair up and leave
him." She faked soft laughter and a jest, "He needs us, so
we don't want him to be tempted to harm one of us to
keep the other here. Seriously, those recent incidents
might have his thinking reality impaired. If he has an
enemy or rival working against him, the man is clever
and leaves no clues. I'm afraid that if anything else
happens, suspicion could fall upon either of us as the
newest members of his unit. In view of those two
explosions and my thwarted raid on Zumali, Tochar
might use that truth serum on us again. If he does, there
is no guessing what we will say if our feelings and
thoughts have changed since joining up with him and
after meeting each other. Too bad there's no way around
such a powerful and precarious probing." Starla knew
she was immune to *Thorin,* but she could not reveal
anything to Dagan that might be extracted by the *fiendal,*
which was why she had changed her mind about
mentioning a suspicion about Moig's death.

Dagan was thinking much the same; he must not tell Starla anything that Tochar could learn from her during another drug questioning. "Tochar knows I'm working for him only for a limited time, so my eventual departure won't be news to him if he tests us again, and I'm always loyal to whoever hires me."

"Tochar is my first leader, but I would never betray him after I've given him my word of honor to be loyal," Starla fabricated, "and I try to do everything he expects of me. It wasn't my fault that drug raid failed and Moig died from his injury, so I hope he doesn't blame me or think less of my skills."

Dagan caressed her still-flushed cheek. "There's no way he or the others can blame you. I'm happy you escaped alive and unharmed."

"I'm glad you weren't harmed. It's risky to send small teams on raids. I hope he doesn't divide us again. Where did your team go? What did you do? Tochar wouldn't give me any details. I was worried about you facing perils with only two men as back-up."

"I didn't know why you and Moig weren't along until we were heading back after our raid. Then I couldn't get here fast enough to check on you. I suppose Auken didn't reveal that news so I wouldn't be distracted. They kept me in the transporter room during our approach. I don't know why Auken doesn't want me to witness the initial contact with our targets. We made a raid on Orr. We pretended we were there for a secret pick-up of crystals. We had convincing papers, codes, watchword, identification, and uniforms which duped the guards. It was quick and simple, and the crystals were handed to us without trouble. That's terrible security for something so valuable."

"You're right, Dagan. We've never raided at a mine before; that boldness surprises me. I wonder how and where Tochar gets his information."

"It has to come from somebody in an elite and trusted position."

"I'd rather be a pirate than a traitor; a betrayer's fate is worse than death if or when he's exposed."

Dagan concurred. "Is there any way I can persuade you to go some place safe until I can join you later? With all these strange incidents occurring, I don't like you taking so many risks."

She trailed her fingers over his collarbone. "How can we get to know each other and test our feelings if we're separated? It would be a long and lonely time before you can join me. Besides, you need somebody you can trust completely to guard your back, especially if matters worsen. It's naive to believe the Serians and Kalfans and *I-GAF* will continue to allow us to raid them without taking action against us, despite our defense system here."

She played with dark curls on his chest. "In fact, I'm amazed that at least one if not all of those forces hasn't laid traps for us. Our goals and tactics must be clear to them. If they have set snares, Tochar is kept informed about how to elude them; that's probably what Auken checks on when we're exiled from the bridge, some unknown measure he doesn't want us to discover."

When Dagan failed to respond to her evocative statements, she said, "There's another angle to consider: Tochar may not allow me to leave or he could send a team of his men after me if I did. With his elite sources, I'm certain he could locate me wherever I went. Until he has the invincible power he wants and I'm no threat to him, he might refuse to release me, refuse to release both of us."

Dagan was impressed by her wits. "You're right. Be careful you don't do anything to get into trouble with Tochar or to make your record worse. When we leave, we don't want anybody in hot pursuit."

"The same applies to you. So far, our records aren't that bad, so let's keep it that way. No life-taking charges against us, agreed? As long as we don't do anything to get us terminated if we're captured, there's always a chance for escape or rescue and being reunited."

"That will be our safeguard for survival. You're a smart and intuitive woman, my love."

Starla's yearning for him was enflamed by his endearment. "You're an intelligent and clever man, so perhaps we are a good match as you claimed."

He smiled and murmured, "Trust me, my ravishing delight, we are."

As he kissed and caressed Starla, he planned, *Before our next trek and after I see if Tochar will use Thorin to interrogate you again, I'll set up a meeting place in case we get separated.* Since she had a ship and possessed great prowess, there was a strong possibility she could escape during a crisis or attack, especially if he decided to warn her about one in advance, and if that daring assault came from *I-GAF* teammates. What concerned him was an unexpected intrusion by the mysterious person also working on this mission, one whose name and goal were still unknown to Phaedrig. At least only his superior and other Inter-Galactic Alliance Force members had access to the *I-GAF* computer files which contained their personnel and assignments records, so his identity and mission were safe. Their headquarters—computer/data center, strategy chambers, medical labs, between missions quarters, armory, recreation and training facilities, and ship storage—were located underground on a barren-appearing planetoid in Kalfa. It was protected by an impenetrable force shield, and only *I-GAF* members knew the entry code. Even if a foe learned the password, no one could get beyond the main portal without the proper retinal and digital scans. If only he had a *Spacer* at his disposal, he could stay prepared to thwart trouble. His was in a storage bay at headquarters until he completed this mission and retrieved it—a swift and sleek craft with advanced cloaking ability to conceal his comings and goings, and a weapons system that could defeat any force except Tochar's.

He wondered if Starla would find Curran Thaiter as appealing as she found Dagan Latu, as their looks and characters were so different. He wondered if he was deluding himself about her feelings for him and about sharing a future with her. There were barriers between them to crush and hurdles to vault. After this mission was over, a difficult talk with her loomed before him. He was certain she would be angry and hurt and would feel betrayed and used. Somehow, he must find a way to convince her he had no choice except to do his duty: to destroy Tochar and his threat to the United Federation of Galaxies, and to seek personal revenge against the *fiendal* for a lethal crime against his loved ones. Yet, the joy of having justice within his impending reach was overshadowed by the grim possibility of his victory costing him the woman he loved.

He didn't know how he was going to accomplish the gigantic task, but he was determined to find a way to save Starla from a black fate so she could share a golden one with him. He loved her. He wanted her. He needed her. With *Kahala*'s help, he would have her at his side forever. *I can't lose you, Starla, but neither can I fail my duty and the UFG. I hope and pray it never comes to a choice between you and them because there's far more at stake than our lives, happiness, and our love.*

Dreamily her fingers grazed through the ebony waves on his head, deserting that location only to roam a supple terrain of bronze lean and hard flesh. She adored the smooth and strong body touching hers. Yet, she was painfully aware this could be the last time she enjoyed such a union if anything went wrong during her mission or if it terminated soon. She didn't know how she could exist without him and didn't want to envision that horrible event, not tonight.

Dagan trailed his lips and hands over her face and throat, returning time and time again to ravish her tasty mouth. He had never taken such a perilous risk during a mission but he could not help himself. His kisses became deep, greedy, as were hers. She had become a vital part of him, one he could not excise from his life without slaying his soul. His left hand cupped a breast before sliding past a hip to grasp her buttocks to lock her groin against his. He savored how her sleek legs imprisoned him and the ardent way she surrendered to him. Love her? Yes, with all his being.

Starla writhed in exquisite delight, as if it had been *wegs* or *malees* since they had last united their bodies. Such a great hunger attacked her again. She knew his restraint was stretched tightly, precariously. She soared with pleasure at his great need of her. She meshed her mouth to his as the sensations mounting within her waxed achingly sweet and potent. Her hands pulled him closer, and Dagan's mouth fastened to hers as their passions burned higher and hotter until they were engulfed in rapturous flames. He felt her tense, arch her back, and cling to him as she moaned a glorious victory. Without delay, he rushed to join her, to conquer the same pinnacle of magic. When the last spasms ceased, he rolled to his back and carried her with him, cradling her in his strong and possessive arms.

Spent and sated, neither spoke nor moved.

Finally, Starla lifted her head and looked at him. Her heart warmed at his glowing smile and tranquil gaze. "I have to leave; it's late."

"Will I see you tomorrow?"

"Yes, same time, same place." She smiled.

As did Curran Thaiter before he kissed her.

Two days later while en route from the landing grid to the settlement, Starla saw Tochar and a group of well-armed Enforcers leave his dwelling to rendezvous with Koteas and Terin near shattered rock formations where the last thwarted encounter had been held. Since she could not destroy the new supply of crystals, she prayed the *I-GAF* team was standing by to defeat the Thracians and to send the crystals hurling into the vast Cosmos where they would float forever among space debris. She was certain that the *I-GAF* commander must wonder who had gathered that data and how it had been entered into his communication system, one which *Raz* Yakir was privy to with its files and secret code. The leader had performed the task through an untraceable method. By now, the commander must have initiated an investigation into the mystery and possibly changed the password. Even so, she reasoned, a man of that elite rank would be compelled to check out the anonymous lead in case it was authentic. Soon, Duald Phaedrig would be convinced, and one more victory would be obtained for her side. Perhaps at this very moment, a cloaked *I-GAF* ship and team were witnessing the exchange of crystals for payment.

Once Syrkin and the Kalfan mine were eliminated from Tochar's reach, Starla deduced, the *fiendal* would be constrained to lean toward his Serian nexus. When that happened, perhaps a slip would be made by the conspirator. If that source could be eradicated, that left only the indomitable weapons here to be obliterated. Without his *Destructoids* and contacts, Tochar would be vulnerable to a full-scale assault.

Starla wanted her work on Tochara to be finalized soon, but cautioned herself against reckless action and rash mistakes. She was getting too close to victory to risk a setback or defeat. She was aware success limited her time with Dagan, perhaps limited his existence in the Universe. She didn't want to think about that grave cost and shoved it from her mind.

She headed for Dagan's chamber to spend a few *horas* with him before their scheduled departure for Zumali in the morning. Her lengthy union with him last night had been as wonderful as the two couplings the night before. She didn't know how it was possible, but each new fusion of their bodies was more exciting than the last. They had shared new and bold experiences only *horas* ago, seeking and exploring various carnal delights. It was as if she had become insatiable, though every climax was rapturous and satisfying. The way he touched her, kissed her, looked at her drove her wild with desire. There were so many ways to make love and she wanted to enjoy every one of them with him.

Cypher had cautioned her not to trust Dagan completely, as a proud man who felt betrayed and used would not protect her or take her side during a crisis. She did not know how her lover would react if she were exposed and imperiled, but she hoped he would stand by her, would believe she loved him. Even so, she took Cypher's words to heart and kept Dagan ignorant of the truth about her identity, rank, and mission.

At the landing grid, Tochar told Starla to remove her wrist device and leave it in her shuttle since she was traveling with Auken on the *Adika* and it would not be needed for communication with her android.

Starla concealed her sudden tension. She smiled and shrugged. "I wear it all the time, so I never think to remove it. If it concerns you, I'll leave it behind. Do you want to examine it for a problem?" she asked as she held the wrist monitor/communicator out to him, knowing it would not function without contact with her right forefinger and certain signals.

"That is unnecessary. I just want to prevent any frequency it might emit from being detected by the wrong person and endangering my team."

"Is that what you think happened on Zumali? You think that Serian patrol intercepted a communication between me and Cypher? It shouldn't have."

"It is not worth taking a risk. Correct?"

"Of course, you're right, and I'll comply since it isn't needed this time." Starla entered her shuttle and placed the device in her pilot's seat. She whispered to Cypher, "Don't worry, I'll be fine. Don't follow us; Tochar is in an odd mood and might check on you." Even without a response, she knew the android heard her and would obey. Starla closed the shuttle door and joined the others to leave in another craft for Auken's ship in stationary orbit over the settlement. After boarding the vessel and as she was settling in to her assigned quarters for the trek, she relaxed by envisioning the lovemaking with Dagan last night. She tried not to fret about Tochar's motive for his odd request and told herself it was nothing more than a precaution following several strange incidents. She hoped the *fiendal* was not suspicious of her or testing her. No matter, she would be on constant alert against a slip. She would be on her own this time without

Cypher's guard, but she had Dagan as a back-up if needed.

A *weg* later and beyond the Free-Zone on the snowy surface of Zumali, Auken told the android guards at the complex that they had been sent to transfer the drugs stored there to another location because a second raid would be attempted within a few *deegas.* Using official-looking papers and uniforms and issuing the proper code words, they were given access to the structure and its valuable contents. The minute they were inside, the androids were disabled and their memory chips were dissolved by a highly corrosive acid. The video/audio monitoring system was destroyed to prevent their exposure as the perpetrators.

Auken, Starla, and Dagan gathered the drugs for conveyance to the *Adika* while Sach stayed aboard to watch the sensors for danger and to be prepared to transport them to safety if trouble arrived.

During their task, Starla and Dagan were given their first moments of privacy since leaving Noy. "Why was Tochar so interested in your wrist device?"

Starla noticed his anxious expression. "I don't know, but it was strange and scary. Maybe he's only looking for someone or something to blame for those weird incidents. We'll discuss it later. We don't want Auken to catch us whispering and think we're sharing secrets or conspiring."

"Be careful, and I'll watch your back. I won't let them fault you or harm you for what's happened."

She sent him a smile of gratitude and love.

After the drugs were transferred to the ship, Auken took a final precaution: he placed explosive *sunbursts*— those stolen by Starla and Moig when she met Dagan—

215

around the complex and set their timers to destroy it, to make certain all evidence or clues were eliminated.

"Let's go!" he shouted to Dagan and Starla. "We want to be far away when this place blows."

As they were leaving, Dagan snagged his shirt on a sharp object and cut his arm. He wrapped his fingers around the area to halt the bleeding.

"Wait," Starla told Auken. "Let me sear this jagged spot to obliterate Dagan's blood or his presence could be exposed if it's found and tested."

"No need. The blast will take care of it."

"Are you sure?" she asked Auken, but it was Dagan who responded to her panic.

"He's right, Starla. Hurry before we get trapped and killed here."

Later in the *Adika*'s medical bay, after sterilizing the location, Starla used a *latron* beam to seal her lover's wound: techniques she had learned from her scientist mother and sister.

"Where did you learn to do that?"

"When one is a loner and on the run, one must know such tricks for survival. Cypher taught me. I learned by watching him repair me a few times following accidents. I also remember my father... doing a repair procedure before his death," she was compelled to lie after Auken entered the bay during Dagan's query. "I hope I did it correctly. The bleeding has stopped and the skin color is good. Does it hurt?"

Dagan flexed his fingers. "Not at all. Thanks. They taught you well. She's an excellent asset to our team, isn't she, Auken?"

"That she is; both of you are. Tochar is pleased with your work and skills. He's hoping you two will remain with us for a long time."

Dagan grinned. "Considering the amount I need to purchase a ship, I certainly will be. You aren't tired of us and our adventures, are you, Starla?"

"This team consists of the best and only friends I have," she alleged. "Where else would I go and earn such large payments and have a safe haven? Besides, after Tochar is rich and powerful, he'll make the settlement a nicer place to live; or he'll relocate us to a wonderful stronghold. Either way, I'm with him for as long as he wants me and I please him."

"That's good news," Auken said. "He'll be happy to hear it. Why don't we go test our wits and skills with a few hands of *resi?* "

"That sounds fun to me," Starla responded.

"Me, too," Dagan added, intrigued and concerned by the easy way Starla had deluded Auken, which he was certain she had done.

After they reach Noy and the others departed from the landing grid, Starla suggested Dagan freshen up while she did the same. "I'll return for you in two *horas.* Then I'll treat you to a meal and a tour aboard my ship." That plan would give Cypher a chance to observe the man who had stolen her heart. First, she needed to make a report to Thaine and to check with Cypher about any incidents while she was gone.

"Tochar contacted me twice during your absence," the android related. "One *deega* after your departure, he said a *mechano* vessel was in orbit and wanted to know

217

if we required any repairs. I responded in the negative. Three *deegas* later, he said a *servo* vessel was in orbit and asked if we required any supplies or service. I responded in the negative. He has not communicated with me since that *deega*."

"Surely he knows we were serviced recently. Do you think he was checking to see if you followed me or had anything to do with the attack on Koteas and Terin? It did take place, didn't it?"

"The Thracian vessel and all aboard were eliminated on schedule. A communication came from *Raz* Yakir to confirm that action was taken. The destruction was done in a manner to appear an internal problem and accident; no warning to be picked up by other sources was issued."

"They believed our information and observed the Icarians's guilt or they wouldn't have taken lethal and covert action."

"That is a logical assumption. The *I-GAF* network code was changed, but *Raz* Yakir is privy to the new one if it is needed."

"Let's hope it isn't necessary as that will narrow down the possibilities of who's inserting our clues. I'm sure the *I-GAF* commander will investigate everyone with access to the code and computer network, but if Phaedrig sends an agent here to investigate, *Raz* Yakir will warn us."

"That would be a logical conclusion and course of action," Cypher concurred.

"It's a good thing you stayed behind with the ship or we would be exposed by now. Maybe Tochar is only checking out any possibility of an enemy or agent working against him. It would be sensible to start with any newcomers, especially one with a private vessel. Anything else happen?"

"I constructed a one-way communication device in case Tochar refuses to permit you to wear your wrist monitor again. I will attach it to whatever garment you select to wear; its size and shape will delude them."

"You're so intelligent and foresighted, my friend. Now, I must get ready for our guest. I want you to remain with us until we retire for the night to my quarters; that way, you can observe Dagan and tell me what you think about him later." Starla filled her trusted android in on what happened during the trek, then said, "Inform our superior of our current status and my safe return from Zumali while I freshen up."

Starla headed for her quarters in a mixture of excitement and suspense. Soon, Dagan would view how she lived and they would share a sublime night on her *sleeper.* Yet, worries about Tochar's actions troubled her. Positive she was in for another encounter with his truth serum, she wasn't concerned about passing his test, but she dreaded Dagan's submission to it. Tonight, she cunningly must prepare him for facing that hazard or he could endanger both of them.

Chapter Eleven

Dagan was impressed by Starla's spaceship which was a larger and more advanced vessel than he had expected. The four-*ying*-old model was sleek and swift. Its color was an almost perfect match to the gray-blue space encasing it, far above the reddish atmosphere of the planet. He learned many surprising facets of the *Liska:* its potent power source, superior force shield, and phenomenal weapons capability. It contained the best quality sensors, communications, and instruments; a superb bridge with two pilot seats; a well-fitted medical room; a shuttle bay with a small landing craft, and two emergency escape pods. He noted the top-notch decontamination unit and a transporter room.

He was shown an eating location with automated *servo* and disposal equipment, one sufficiently-sized guest suite, and her femininely decorated quarters with a grooming chamber. Near her *sleeper* he noticed a control/communications panel and, on the adjacent wall, he saw a viewing monitor and audio system for amusement. There was a short *seata* with a square table beside it. A small *servo* unit was located in a wall nearby for quick access to refreshments. He saw a collection of miniature animals and image disks of an older man, a lovely woman, and younger male on a wall shelf; he decided to study them closer another time since her family was deceased and speaking about them could cause her pain. Yet from a glance, she favored her mother. Variegated tints of ivory, blue, and green were the colors of her quarters, which gave them a light and relaxing aura. He noted a panel above her *sleeper* which covered a *transascreen* for exterior viewing.

All doors and controls were voice activated by either her command or by Cypher's rather than by floor-pressure panels; no doubt, he assumed, because Moig had journeyed on her ship on occasion and she wanted to ensure her privacy. The environmental system was automatically controlled; lights came on and went off when someone entered or left a room or area, unless their sensors were overridden by voice command, such as for sleeping.

Dagan smiled. "I'm almost speechless, Starla; this ship is a beauty. I can see why you prefer to habitate here instead of in the settlement."

From his reactions, he appeared to believe her ruse. The spacecraft—styled in the manner, marked appropriately, and registered to the obliterated skycity where she allegedly had been born and reared—was decorated to convince anyone who came aboard of her false identity and origin, down to faked family image disks. Everything inside and outside the *Liska* had been skillfully "aged" to four *yings,* the purported date of her survival and the loss of her world. "I feel safer and more comfortable in my own surroundings," Starla admitted, then switched to another subject. "Do you have any questions for Cypher-T? I asked him to accompany us in case you did, since he knows more about the ship and its functions than I do. I learn more every *weg,* but I would be lost without his help and lonely without his companionship. As many times as he's either rescued me or warned me of danger, I would probably be a captive by now if not for his assistance and protection. He can do just about everything, even any maintenance required on himself."

Starla observed Dagan as he walked down the passageway with her android and probed the unit for information about their weapons, force shield, power source, and speed capability. She was amused when he asked Cypher about himself, and Cypher—intentionally, she surmised—related his abilities in scientific and technological terms to prevent clarity. She assumed Dagan didn't ask Cypher to explain in words he could understand because her lover didn't wish to appear as if he lacked intelligence and comprehension.

They reached the eating area and made selections from a row of metallic cards which were inserted into an order slot, marked with words or symbols in *WEV* the universal language for communication. There were four recessed spaces, of which three, contained units with smoky doors: the first for dispensing liquids, a second for serving hot foods, and a third for serving cold ones. The last was for disposing of containers which were cleaned and returned to stock for future use. Leftovers and wrappings were disintegrated by an internal device, commands given by a memory chip.

As they ate, Dagan was cognizant of the android's continued presence, as Starla had not dismissed him. Cypher's expressionless silver eyes seemed to remain focused on him as the android stood at attention near the door. Cypher was male in appearance—even his silver hair, body covering, limbs, and features looked real. Dagan had an eerie sensation that the advanced unit was analyzing him as if he were a complex problem to be solved. He also had the weird idea that the android didn't like having him aboard and with Starla, as if the sophisticated automaton actually possessed feelings and they were in conflict with his logical, nonemotional programming. He observed the almost human rapport between his lover and her longtime companion, one who clearly was protective of her. At times, he found himself forgetting the android wasn't alive, so Dagan fully understood why Starla thought of Cypher as a living being. Foolish as it seemed, he was almost jealous of their tight bond and cohabitation arrangement.

Between bites, Dagan said, "I'm surprised Tochar doesn't let us use your ship or his during raids since both are superior to Auken's."

"Even with the *Azoulay* repaired, thanks to you, Tochar wouldn't risk its loss during an attack; and mine is too small to carry a crew of five—four now that Moig is gone—and any large amount of stolen cargo."

Dagan finished chewing before he said, "I suppose you're right. I must say, this food is delicious, better than the colony's fare."

Starla smiled and thanked him after lowering her liquid container. "You're lucky my supplies were restocked recently. A traveling vessel arrived during our last raid and Cypher handled the task for me."

Dagan glanced at the android before he told her, "You're fortunate you have him to take care of the *Liska* while you're gone. No matter how good an automatic pilot system is, they can malfunction and cost you your ship." Before taking another bite, he asked Starla, "Do you think we'll be going on another raid soon?"

"Tochar doesn't inform me in advance."

"Why is that?"

"I suppose he has to wait until his contacts supply him with needed data on our targets. He's a clever and cautious leader."

"Do you think he trusts us?"

Starla swallowed as she eyed him. "I don't see why not; we've given him no reason to doubt us."

"Do *you* trust *him?*" He watched her think, take a cleansing breath, then shrug.

"He hasn't given me a reason to doubt or defy him, or done anything to provoke me to leave his hire. Working for him and living here have many advantages

I'm certain I couldn't find elsewhere. As for Auken and Sach, they're excellent teammates. I didn't care for Moig, but that was personal."

"You think and feel much like I do; that's good."

"Yes, it is."

They finished eating in silence, each pleased with their necessary performances. Yet, both experienced qualms of guilt over their deceptions. They disposed of their containers and she wiped off the bar.

"Cypher-T, control the bridge. If you need me, we'll be in my quarters. That's all for tonight."

"Affirmative." Cypher left the room.

Dagan pulled Starla into his arms. "Alone at last," he murmured. "It's been *wegs* since I last held you and kissed you; I've missed those pleasures."

"So have I." As he nuzzled her neck and she laughed at the ticklish sensations, she murmured, "Let's retire to my quarters and get comfortable."

"Sounds perfect to me," he responded in a husky tone. He was ready and willing to forget everything and everyone except her for the next few *horas.*

Inside the private haven and as they undressed, Dagan motioned to her wrist device. "Do you need that here? Is he listening to us?" He hadn't thought about the device until Tochar expressed interest, but recalled she hadn't taken it off during their previous encounters.

Starla laughed as she removed the unit and put it aside. "I see you're also forgetting he isn't real."

"Isn't he?" Dagan quipped. "I was beginning to think he wasn't going to give us any privacy. He doesn't have a jealousy chip, does he?"

"Not to my knowledge, but I'm not that educated on androids. He is loyal and he takes excellent care of me; that's how he was programmed."

"Just so he isn't too possessive and doesn't consider me a threat to you. I would hate to battle with him to win you; he's bigger and stronger, and no doubt knows every trick and skill in existence. From the way you fought with me the first time we met, he's taught you most of them."

"I bested you because you didn't take me seriously as an opponent."

"Maybe and maybe not, but I won't underestimate you again, woman."

"And I won't misjudge you. Soon, I want you to tell me everything there is to know about you."

"Craving all of my secrets?"

"Yes."

Dagan looked at her and jested, "You sure they won't change your nice opinion of me?"

"How can they? You did say we're perfectly matched, alike."

Dagan's gaze roamed her unclothed body. "Not alike in all ways, thank goodness. I was referring to our good sides and traits."

Starla leaned against him, the unobstructed contact stirring. "Have you ever done anything that was bad, really horrible?"

Dagan lifted a strand of lustrous brown hair and toyed with it. "In whose opinion? Mine or that of the authorities, or my targets?"

"I'm only interested in yours, for now."

He shrugged and said, "I don't think so."

"Good, because I haven't, either."

Dagan recalled her destruction of the Serian patrol ship and crew before she hired on with Tochar. He was tempted to question her about it, but decided this wasn't the right time. Though the incident wasn't listed against her in the *I-GAF* files, he—an *I-GAF* officer—knew about it and it troubled him, as did her apparent lie moments ago. He reasoned she didn't know he had been enlightened and had deceived him to protect her image. If she could lie at this point and look so innocent, she could have duped him in other areas. No, he had to be understanding and lenient, considering her past tragic history and her love for him.

Dagan backed her to the *sleeper* with a sexy grin on his face. "Now, it's time for my dessert: you, woman."

"That's why I didn't serve you one in the eating room," she jested, her forefinger touching his lips.

"Then, I suppose I'll have to taste you *hapax* by *hapax* until I find the best treat to sate my empty spot. Get ready, my love, this greedy space pirate is about to go araiding for real treasures."

"I stay ready for you, shameless and bold."

Dagan pulled her against him and sealed their mouths with a tender and leisurely kiss. It melded into one that became swift, passionate, and ardent as his hands roamed her bare flesh. He savored her response. She was so disarming and enchanting as she swayed against him that his intense yearnings increased. For a time, duty didn't exist; nothing beyond his rampant desire for this woman. The eternal flame of love had been ignited in his heart and it would burn forever. He felt her tremble with a mutual longing and he knew this bond between them was meant to be.

Starla clasped his handsome face between her hands and almost ravished his lips. He was tantalizing and tempting her beyond reason and reality. Her arms looped his neck and she pressed closer to him. She rubbed her body against his to titillate and pleasure him. She leaned her head back when he trekked down her throat and trailed kisses over her pulse point, then willingly lay on the *sleeper*.

Dagan's mouth traveled her body with skill and persistence. He kissed the straining points on her breasts and stroked them with his cheek. He heard her moan with delight. His hand took a sensuous path down her body to the fuzzy triangle between her thighs. His palm flattened over her mons and absorbed its heat before drifting up and down the soft surface from her groin to her knees. He ached for her. His lips covered the same terrain his hands had just traveled...

She abandoned herself to his rapturous and daring conquest. Her nails gently raked at his shoulders. Then, she buried her fingers in his hair, relishing the way the strands wound around them in a possessive embrace. Her core tensed as her need for release mounted. She opened herself to his actions. She encouraged him to do as he pleased with her, because anything he did to her was gratifying. As his fingers and tongue trekked her essence, she experienced exquisite thrills. She wanted to relax, but she couldn't; his actions wouldn't allow it. Her stomach muscles tightened. She could not help but fall over the precipice she had climbed, the one he had pushed her toward with expertise and generosity.

She urged him up beside her. Her hands roved his hard chest, flat belly, and lower abdomen. Her fingers played in dark hair around his manhood. She captured the rigid erection and stimulated him with hands and lips until he groaned and wriggled in pleasure.

Dagan knew that only total fulfillment could be sweeter than this splendid prelude. He reached for her arms and lifted her, his arousal penetrating her fully as he seated her upon it. In a near dazed state, he watched her rock back and forth, every fiber of his being alive and pleading for more. He didn't want to stop but knew he must or she would get left behind. "I can't hold out much longer, my love," he admitted in a ragged tone.

"Neither can I," she revealed in a husky tone, "so come with me. Now, Dagan, now."

He rolled them to her back. Their gazes fused. Their passions soared and hearts pounded. Their mouths meshed and they kissed with urgency. They climaxed in unison this time, their loins throbbing and contracting as they found their gratification.

As they rested and their bodies cooled, they lay nestled together, her fingers stroking his damp chest, and his drifting up and down her back.

"You have a magic and allure I can't resist, Starla. I've never been tempted to settle down until I met you. I wish this had happened at a different time and place in our lives because we're stuck for a while longer. We have to remain loyal to Tochar for many reasons."

"I understand. One *deega* it will change for us, so we must be patient, and careful. Now tell me, my lover, how did you get into this kind of existence?"

Dagan wasn't in the mood to lie to her tonight, not after what they had just shared. "I promise to tell you all about me another time. It's late, so I should return to the settlement. We have that early meeting with Tochar in the morning; we need to be fresh and alert."

"You're right. It slipped my mind; you're much too distracting and enticing, Latu," she teased as she sat up and gazed down at him.

"You're the one who's disarming. You capture and enspell me as easily as you take a breath."

"I am under the impression you did the chasing and ensnaring. You were the predator and I, the prey."

"Once we met on that transporter and tangled, I doubt either of us stood a chance of escaping the other's interest. I couldn't stop thinking about you."

"It must have been fate, Dagan, so why fight it?"

"My thoughts and feelings exactly. Let's get dressed and moving. The beast awaits us in the morning."

"Yes, sir," she said, and gave him a mock salute. "Your shuttle will be ready and waiting in fifteen *preons,* so you best get off this *sleeper* before I'm tempted to change my mind and hold you prisoner."

The *Spaceki* team—Starla, Dagan, Auken, and Sach—met with Tochar the following morning. As they sat before him, his piercing black eyes passed over each one in turn, then he stared downward. The four sensed a problem and exchanged curious glances.

Starla masked her anxiety, but she knew without a doubt that trouble was brewing. She hoped and prayed she wasn't about to be unmasked, and slain.

"I have bad news and it troubles me deeply."

Auken asked, "What is it, my friend?"

Tochar looked at his lead man and close friend. "Koteas and Terin are dead; their vessel was destroyed, one *deega* after your departure."

All four team members stared at their leader as if in disbelief. Then, they glanced at each other again.

"What happened? Were they attacked?"

"I do not know, Sach, but the matter is suspicious, highly suspicious. Their vessel was still registering on our sensors when it exploded."

"Did our sensors pick up a ship or laser blast?"

"No, Auken; that is the mystery. One *preon* it was there; then a fiery detonation; then it was gone, leaving only debris to drift forever." Tochar slapped his hands together, causing all except Dagan to jump in surprise. "Blam, and no more Koteas, Terin, or moonbeams."

"If sensors didn't detect another ship or weapons fire, it must have been an accident," Sach surmised.

"That is possible, but coming atop the other strange events, I am unconvinced. Any speculations?" Auken shook his head and so did Sach. "What about you two," Tochar asked Starla and Dagan, "Any theories?"

Starla knew from Yakir's report to Cypher during her absence that the smaller *I-GAF* ship had been obscured from Noy's sensors by the larger Thracian vessel when it briefly decloaked to fire a destructive beam. "Perhaps the crystals are unstable under certain conditions. Or perhaps your buyers mishandled them in a hazardous manner. The cave and desert are hot and dry locations which may have affected them. We haven't experienced trouble transporting them where humidity and temperature are controlled. What if your buyers stored theirs in a compartment without environmental control or their system malfunctioned? In light of three losses, it must have something to do with conditions or how the crystals are handled. Have you questioned your contact? If there's something we don't know and we're doing wrong, that jeopardizes us during raids, and you and the settlement after delivery."

"These incidents will make future buyers nervous," Dagan added. "Whatever the trouble is, it needs to be discovered and resolved. Our lives and profits are in jeopardy. Sounds like something destabilizes them."

"My contact vows there is no known problem with destabilizing; nor do they require special handling."

"If that's true or accurate, Tochar, what causes the strange explosions? Do you trust this contact?"

"That is what I am determined to learn, Starla. I hope none of you take offense or become provoked to leave me, but I must check my security. To do so, everyone around me—my special unit, my Enforcers, and even my Palesa—must be questioned with truth serum. Does anyone object?"

Starla, Dagan, Auken, and Sach shook their heads simultaneously. Tochar nodded. "Excellent, because this precaution is necessary for everyone who will continue to work for me. We will begin the tests immediately. Starla, will you go first?"

"That's fine with me, Tochar."

"Dagan, you'll go next; then, Sach and Auken. It requires thirty *preons* to go under and thirty for questioning. Recovery can be done in an antechamber to save time. After I complete your tests, Auken and Sach can assist me with those for the Enforcers. Any tests not completed before your departure in two *deegas* will be carried out by me and Palesa during your absence. The rest of you can await your turns in the recreation chamber so Starla and I can get started and get this annoying but necessary matter behind us. Your cooperation and understanding are appreciated."

Starla exchanged smiles with the team members before they left the room. She followed Tochar to a smaller one which had an oblong padded table, cabinets on one wall, a counter with recording equipment and a tray with an *Airosyringe,* and a tall sitting stool. After the door closed behind them, the man told her to take her place on the table. She obeyed his order and calmed her tension as much as possible.

"I am sorry this must be done again, Starla."

As Tochar placed the *Airosyringe* against her right arm and pressed the button to infuse her with *Thorin,* she said, "I understand. If you were not a smart and cautious man, I would not be working for you."

"I am grateful for your trust in me. Put your arms at your sides. As you recall, these straps are to prevent you from falling off the table while you are drugged. Relax, and I shall return soon."

231

She nodded as he secured bands across her chest, hips, and ankles. She watched him exit, then closed her eyes. The drug required twenty *preons* to take affect on anyone not immune via the *Rendelar* chemical and process, as were her world's leaders and all members of the Elite Squad. That chemical and procedure belonged to Maffei and were inventions of her father's deceased half-brother, made in his laboratory on the planetoid of Darkar. Her mother had once owned the powerful and impregnable complex where unreproducible chemicals and formulas were created, but Jana Greyson Triloni Saar had turned it over to the Maffeian government after her marriage to Varian Saar.

Starla was certain Tochar would give a fortune to own or to be able to raid Trilabs—which also produced other drugs and weapons—but no one could penetrate Darkar's advanced defense system. Unless, Tochar got his hands on a portable laser cannon powered by a large white moonbeam which could pierce its force shield and blast through the complex's doors. She could not allow that, as Trilabs was vital to her world's survival and too dangerous in a *villite's* control.

She had witnessed many interrogations of suspects under *Thorin's* influence, so she knew how to act and speak to dupe him, as she had done once before. She was not worried about revealing any secrets, but she did not like feeling vulnerable and helpless in this imprisoned state. She also fretted over what Dagan might expose to the *fiendal*.

She heard the door swish open and knew Tochar had returned. She was prepared to deceive him, thanks in part to a harmless tablet she had secreted in her belt for this anticipated occasion and had slipped into her mouth without notice while following Tochar to this location. The tiny tablet created a flush on her cheeks and a glazed look in her green eyes. She commanded her body to go limp and her breathing to slow. She saw Tochar when he opened her lids to check her eyes, then allowed them to close again. She heard him approach the counter to turn on the recorder and return to take a seat on the stool beside her.

"What is your name?"

"Starla Vedris," she said in a slow and soft tone.

"Who is your leader? Where does he habitate?"

"Tochar Glaic. He lives in Tochara on the planet Noy in the Free-Zone."

"Are you loyal to him?"

"Yes." She was glad he hadn't told her to open her eyes and look at him, as concentration on her responses was easier with them closed.

"Do you know anything about the recent explosions and mysterious events, those so-called accidents which have plagued Tochar?"

Starla related what she was supposed to know. When he asked who and what she held responsible, she repeated the speculations she had fabricated earlier.

"Do you know if any enemies or rivals are working against Tochar?"

"No."

"Have you ever disobeyed Tochar's orders or been lax during raids?"

"No."

"What do you know about moonbeams?"

She related facts she had overheard by accident or been told by him and his friends. "I fear them because they could be unstable and dangerous; their power is enormous and destructive. I would not approach or handle them if I were not ordered to do so."

"Do you know the identities of Tochar's contacts in Seri and Kalfa and Maffei?"

"No."

"Do you know Dagan Latu?"

"Yes."

"Can Dagan be trusted?"

"I believe so."

"Do you love Dagan?"

Starla decided she should respond honestly in order to fool Tochar completely. "Yes, I think so."

"Why hide your feelings and affair? Explain."

"Such new and powerful feelings alarm me. I have never loved a man. These emotions are strange and confusing, and we have not known each other very long. I lost everyone I loved in the past and I fear that can happen again if I put myself in a vulnerable position. It is hard to explain how I feel."

"Does Dagan love you?"

"He told me he does."

"Do you believe him?"

"I do not know."

"Will you become his mate and leave Tochar?"

"One *deega* in the future if we remain alive and uncaptured and if he is the man he appears to be. I would like to bond with him to have a real life."

"If you decide to bond with him, when do you plan to leave Tochara?"

"After Dagan purchases another ship."

"Why not use your ship to depart?"

"Dagan is proud. He lost everything before he came to Noy. He thinks he must raise himself again before he's worthy to claim me." She heard Tochar chuckle at what he must consider silly romantic notions.

"Do you intend to work against Tochar as a rival after your departure?"

"No; we will settle where it is safe and begin a new life. We may work for hire for Tochar."

"Have you shared a *sleeper* with Dagan?"

Starla didn't want to reveal such a private matter but it was possible Tochar had discovered or suspected the truth, and would learn it when he asked Dagan that same nosy query. "Yes."

"Why hide your relationship from Tochar?"

"I do not want Tochar to worry about my loyalty or distraction during raids. I want to be sure a relationship is solid before it becomes known. It will be humiliating if Dagan parts with me. Other men could think me an easy conquest and approach me for sex."

"Will you remain loyal to Tochar even if Dagan turns against him?"

"Yes; Tochar is my leader; he protects and supports me. If Dagan turned against him, Dagan would not be a good and honest man. I could not mate with one who is untrustworthy and wicked."

"Was Moig's death an accident?"

She was glad he left his prior topic. "Yes and no."

"Explain."

"We were fired upon by a Serian patrol; he fell and struck his head. We were attacked, but he was not slain by laser fire. I rescued him and tended him, but I lacked the knowledge to treat his injury. He died."

"Do you know of any man or woman whom Tochar cannot trust?"

"No."

"If you learn Tochar's secrets, will you steal or reveal them?"

"No, I gave him my word of honor, and it is wrong to betray a leader. He does not confide his secrets to me, only to his friends and perhaps his lover."

"Why is that?"

"Perhaps I have not earned his total trust."

"Do you deserve Tochar's complete trust?"

"Yes."

"What are your feelings for Tochar?"

"I admire and respect him; he is a superior and intelligent leader."

"Do you have any sexual feelings for Tochar?"

That query made her nervous. "He is handsome and virile, but my heart belongs to Dagan." She heard Tochar murmur his approval to her response. She waited while the *fiendal* apparently scanned his mind for any remaining questions and was relieved when he seemed to find none. She heard him rise, turn off the recorder, and leave the room. She wanted to take a few deep cleansing breaths, but was uncertain about the security in the chamber. She remained still.

It wasn't long before Dagan entered with Tochar, unfastened her straps, and carried her to a guest chamber. As her lover placed her on a *sleeper,* she was glad Tochar was with him so Dagan couldn't ask her any questions while she was allegedly under the influence of a truth serum. The men departed, and she turned to her side to relax until the drug supposedly wore off.

Starla fretted over Dagan's answers to some of the questions Tochar asked her. She prayed he wouldn't expose anything detrimental to him or anything that might make her appear to have lied, which would be suspicious to Tochar. She cautioned herself to remain ready to signal Cypher for a rescue if necessary.

Chapter Twelve

Dagan lay on a *sleeper* in another chamber after his session with Tochar. He was amused and annoyed by the man's probings into his private life. He had admitted to a love and desire for Starla, but he didn't believe he had won her totally as of this time. He admitted to plans to make her his legal mate in the far future, but wanted time to have more adventures and to earn his own way before he settled down. What vexed him was Tochar's queries about Yana; they had been seen together and the perverted Icarian wanted to know if he had shared sex with the Asisan beauty. Needing to dupe Tochar and to prevent suspicions, he had felt compelled to confess he had done so on one occasion but would not do so again because he didn't want to risk losing Starla.

Tochar had asked the expected questions, probably the same ones used on Starla. Dagan hoped she had satisfied the leader's curiosity and assuaged any doubts without revealing any harmful information. He would learn soon enough by Tochar's reactions in the next two *deegas*. If Starla made slips during her interrogation, he could not extricate her when surrounded by Tochar's men. That feeling of helplessness when his love might be imperiled angered him. He cautioned himself to stay alert and try to come up with an escape plan if one was needed, though escape from Noy was unlikely without a ship at his disposal. Should he, Dagan wondered, trust Starla with the truth about himself and his mission in case her ship was required for either or both of them to flee? Would she feel betrayed, accuse him of using her as a cover to obtain information? He could not decide how she would react, so he told himself he should be patient and watchful a while longer.

237

At least Tochar couldn't extract any secrets from him, not with the immunity supplied to him and all *I-GAF* members from Trilabs in Maffei, the strongest member of the United Federation of Galaxies. He didn't understand exactly how *Rendelar* worked, but it did, and *Thorin* had no effect on him. If only that were true for his cherished Starla, he wouldn't have to worry about her safety and survival.

Dagan wasn't surprised Tochar was skeptical of recent incidents. Though he could not venture a guess as to how an enemy or agent had reached and destroyed them, he didn't believe those crystals had exploded on their own. Nor did Phaedrig, but his superior could not ask Syrkin about the possibility of that occurrence since Syrkin was being investigated for alleged complicity with Tochar and to do so would reveal an agent was present on Noy and working against Tochar. If Syrkin was guilty of treachery, he would be arrested and terminated as soon as he made a slip. Somehow Dagan wasn't shocked by Syrkin's probable conspiracy; he had lost trust, admiration, and respect for the man when Syrkin was his *Seki* superior. He realized that a longtime connection between the two men would explain several frustrating episodes when Tochar eluded capture and revenge by Curran Thaiter. It was advantageous to him that Syrkin believed Thaiter was dead and that Syrkin had no idea he was Dagan Latu or an *I-GAF* agent.

If Syrkin was taken down, Tochar would lose the traitor's assistance. That meant the Icarian would be forced to focus raids on Serian crystals, which should make it easier to discover the second conspirator. With his sources cut off, Tochar could not become more powerful than he was. That still left the *Destructoids* to battle, and no weapon existed that could do so, not until and unless more large white crystals were found. At least by being there, maybe he could prevent Tochar from mounting one on a spacecraft and attacking elsewhere with it. As long as the *fiendal* was compelled to protect his settlement and life with the three weapons in his possession, Dagan reasoned, Tochar wouldn't attempt that daring feat.

He had hoped to work his way closer to Tochar, but the man was leery since those strange incidents. He knew from Phaedrig that Koteas and Terin had been exposed by an unknown person, and the Thracians's destruction was carried out by an *I-GAF* team in an undetectable manner. He was getting nowhere on his mission, but somebody was having splendid success.

Who and where was this sly person? How had he gathered his data about Syrkin and the Thracians? How had he inserted it into a computer network to which only certain people in power knew the entry code? If the secret agent— or whatever he was—destroyed the crystals, how had he done so when Kalfan scientists claimed it was impossible? Yet, if moonbeams weren't indestructible, neither was Tochar's defense system. Who possessed such a powerful secret, and why not share it or even sell it to his people and the Serians? If *Raz* Yakir had been approached with that crucial news or a sale offer, Yakir should have told Phaedrig and *Autorie* Zeev. The honorable and sage Serian ruler knew an *I-GAF* agent had been assigned to the imperative mission, so surely Yakir would help defeat a mutual threat. If moonbeams weren't indestructible, and that seemed a proven fact, why didn't the unknown factor blast Tochar's *Destructoids* into oblivion and render him helpless? It was frustrating to be faced by such an enigma, to be uncertain as to whether he had an ally in the shadows or another deadly problem to handle...

When his recovery time elapsed, Dagan rose from the surface of the *sleeper* and went to locate Starla to see what she thought about her *Thorin* session. He was told she had left Tochar's dwelling after she aroused and had returned to the *Liska*. Dagan went to his dwelling to await her arrival, hoping and assuming she would visit him soon.

Starla's hands clasped Dagan's head and she whispered in his ear, "Is your abode private? Totally private?"

He fused their gazes. "Yes, I check it every *deega*. I'm familiar with all types of spying devices. Are you worried about something? Are you afraid you revealed secrets during your drugged meeting with Tochar?"

Following her reply, Dagan gaped at her. "You did what? Tell me that again, woman."

"The same thing you did during your first *Thorin* session. Since my wrist unit makes Tochar nervous, I didn't wear it. I wore a device that Cypher constructed for me in the shape of a disk on my belt. It transmitted my session to him and he recorded it."

After Starla walked to the *seata* and sat down, Dagan joined her. "So?" he hinted. "What did he ask and how did you respond?"

"Why don't I play the scssion for you?" she asked, having edited the tape to exclude anything she didn't want him to learn, such as the query about rejecting Dagan if he betrayed Tochar and her vow of loyalty.

He saw her take a thin instrument from a pouch suspended from her belt. "You brought it with you?" After she nodded, he scolded, "Do you realize how dangerous it is to get caught with that disk?"

"I'm not foolish or reckless, my beloved. Cypher rigged the release switch to initiate a self-destruct sequence if not opened correctly."

"That was very clever of him, but what if Tochar had asked you about such a measure while you were ensnared by truth serum?"

"If he had, I wouldn't be here at this *preon.*"

Dagan frowned. "What about your promise not to endanger yourself?"

"Wouldn't it be far more perilous to not know I revealed a secret or I expressed a feeling Tochar didn't like or trust? It was a necessary precaution."

"I can't refute your point, but be careful if you take such a chance again." As Dagan listened to the tape, her answers about him pleased him, but Tochar asking those questions evoked annoyance. "He seems greatly interested in our personal relationship." He saw her nod agreement as he listened to the remainder of her encounter. With the drugging hazard removed, it was time to pull Starla closer and away from the *fiendal.* "It's good he didn't ask if you trust him fully, because I don't think you do. Neither do I. This is the first time I've distrusted a leader, and that doesn't trek well with me, especially when you're also involved with him."

His words delighted her and evoked her to reveal, "What relieved me was when he interrupted my reply about Moig's death and leapt to his next query: if I knew of any man he couldn't trust. I would have told him what I suspect about Moig's death and other things."

"Do you mean there is a mystery about it?"

"I think he killed Moig because there was no way to treat him on Noy, and Tochar couldn't allow Moig to be taken to a place where Moig might expose his secrets." Starla revealed he had a private conversation with the doctor, and later they told her Moig had died during the examination. "The timing was suspicious to me, and I saw an *Airosyringe* mark on Moig's arm when he was carried past me by Enforcers."

"Why didn't you tell me this sooner? This darkens Tochar's image and tells me he's more untrustworthy and dangerous than I imagined."

"I kept quiet because it was a horrible suspicion I didn't want to believe. The infusion could have been medicine, but I doubt it. I feared you'd reveal it during a *Thorin* test, and be endangered. After those incidents, I was positive we were in for a second one."

"What I thought you were going to tell me was that Tochar suspected Moig of being behind his troubles, so he had Moig disposed of in a clever way. Are you sure it was a Serian patrol that attacked you and Moig?"

"Yes, because Tochar needs drugs. If he wanted to get rid of Moig or me for any reason, he would have used another way and time. If somebody is creating problems for Tochar, I doubt it's one of his best friends. If I were Tochar, the one I would watch is Palesa; she's Thracian like Koteas and Terin, though their planets have long been restrained adversaries. Palesa is in the best position to learn Tochar's secrets, and she has access to a means of sending messages from Noy."

Dagan mused if Palesa could be the unknown factor in the enigma. Yet, it seemed unlikely since Palesa was in a position to kill Tochar and claim his possessions. "Thank the stars he didn't ask if there was any woman he shouldn't trust or you might have mentioned your doubts of Palesa and vexed him." *He certainly asked me about possible enemies from both sexes.*

"I wouldn't have mentioned her because Palesa is neither male nor female to me. I refer to Palesa as a 'her' and 'she' because she plays a female's role in public. But she's *Binixe,* from a race of hermaphrodites."

"I know; I've met several in the past. I recognized the marks on her neck when her hair moved aside. Tochar's choice of that type of lover explains why he hasn't pursued a beautiful female like you."

"He wouldn't stand a *flick* with me. Seriously, we must stay alert and watch each other's back, earn as much profit as possible until we can leave. Departure too soon will be suspicious and unacceptable. We must not forget he has powerful contacts in other galaxies he can use against us. No doubt he would alert the Serian, Kalfan, and *I-GAF* patrols to our locations. Or he'd send Enforcers after us. If I left, you could be endangered, now that he knows about our relationship. If we both left, he would consider us treacherous and threatening. We don't want to end up like Moig or others who've crossed ways with him. The safest and wisest thing for us to do is to appear loyal to him, to fake respect, and to have patience. At least Auken and Sach like us."

Dagan was thrilled to have Starla opening up to him, proving her trust in him and love for him. But a few of her revelations alarmed him. He realized that if Tochar had asked her some of the same questions the *fiendal* had asked him, Starla would've exposed the perilous thoughts and feelings she just related to him. It worried Dagan that he might be the cause of Starla changing her mind and emotions about Tochar, as they could get her slain. "You're right, my love; we have to concentrate on survival during raids and while we're living here. But in the event Tochar turns against either or both of us, do everything you can to escape Noy. I promise I'll find a way to escape and join you, so don't worry about me. Believe me, Starla, I'm an expert in that area, so don't endanger yourself trying to rescue or warn me. Cloak and fly to Karteal and wait for me there." He gave her coordinates for the location he had in mind as an emergency rendezvous point.

As soon as she had recorded them in her wrist device, Starla asked, "What if you don't come within an acceptable time frame?"

"Whatever happens, love, don't ever return to Noy for any reason. If I haven't joined you within two *malees,* begin a new and safe life without me. But," he added, pressing his fingers to her lips to silence her protest, "in case I'm delayed, leave a message about where you're heading beneath the rock shaped like a *winger;* you'll find it without any trouble."

Starla grimaced. "I don't want to talk or think about such a disturbing occurrence. Did you record your session with Tochar? Can you play it for me?"

"I did, but I've already destroyed the tape," he was compelled to lie, the taste of the deception sour in his mouth. "I didn't say anything harmful to us because he didn't ask any questions that required such responses. In fact, he asked me the almost identical things he asked you. It's a good thing the words *loyalty* and *trust* have different meanings in my mind. He used *loyalty* or I would have been in deep trouble with him. Or if we had had this talk before I was put under. We don't want to give him any reason to use that serum on us again, not with the way we feel and think. Agreed?"

"Absolutely, or we'll become space debris." As she nestled against his chest and he stroked her hair, Starla wondered if Tochar had asked him any questions about Yana and, if so, what his replies had been. It was time for Yana to make an appearance to Radu and others, which she would do tomorrow. For tonight, all she wanted was to make love to Dagan. She lifted her head and gazed at him. "I love you and want you."

Dagan leaned forward and fastened his mouth to hers. Between kisses, he said, "I love you and want you, Starla, so much it almost scares me." He swept aside her bangs and kissed her forehead. "I'm convinced we were destined to meet and bond."

"I hope so, Dagan," she said, clinging to him.

"I know so." *But I'm unconvinced fickled fate will be kind to us. Destiny be damned if I lose you.* He carried her to his *sleeper* where he made tender love to her.

The following afternoon in her Yana life-form, Starla visited with Radu at the Skull's Den. During their talk, she hinted she might be taking a short trip with a "new and close friend," but she would return soon. She hoped the excuse would conceal her impending absence with the other space pirates, a trek which would take longer than the recent ones.

Between sips, the sexy blond with shiny blue eyes murmured, "Sometimes it's difficult to keep to myself for long periods, but I don't want to evoke trouble with any of those in the settlement by showing myself too frequently. I shouldn't be here much longer than another *malee* or two, so I'll continue to be patient and reclusive. At least I'm learning a great deal from the computer programs that keep me company."

"I think you are wise for such a beautiful woman; men often do crazy things when they are tempted by one such as you, Yana. I shall miss you after your departure, but Tochara isn't the right place for you."

"I know, Radu, and I appreciate all you've done for me while I've been entrapped here."

"It is easy to be kind to a gentle creature."

"Thank you, my friend."

They chatted another few minutes before she returned to Yana's dwelling and transported to her ship from that location.

Starla and Dagan ate at the Skull's Den before they retired to his chamber to make passionate love before the next day's departure. They lay on his *sleeper,* kissing and caressing. They savored close contact, and dreaded the imminent *wegs-long* denial looming ahead.

Starla's arms encircled the virile Kalfan's waist, her palms flattened against his broad and sleek back. Her fingers slid into the fullness of his ebony hair; she liked the way the thick mane buried and tickled them. She was hot and tingly from head to feet. She relished his cool and supple bare skin next to hers.

Dagan's right hand traversed her torso and caused her to quiver. He ached to bury himself inside her, but he did not want to rush this event as it would be their last one for a long time. His mouth wandered down the enticing column of her throat at a *yema*'s crawl, brushed over her collarbone, and climbed a beckoning mound. He thrilled to giving her such exquisite delight.

When he trailed fingers over her rib cage, across her abdomen, and toward the beckoning place between her thighs, she tingled in suspenseful anticipation. She was willing and eager to give her all to him. She parted her thighs to allow him the space and freedom to do as he pleased, as it greatly pleased her.

His kisses were deep and hungry as he enflamed her body with his skilled fingers. He savored how she murmured and wiggled and stroked his back. His tongue played with hers and he nibbled at her lips.

Fervent and scorching needs consumed Starla and Dagan. They kissed and caressed each other as they yielded to the radiant torment of wanting each other so intensely they would risk their lives and careers to steal such overpowering moments together. Desires had smoldered since their last fervid union; now, they were encouraged, stoked, and enticed to ignite into a roaring wildfire which neither could nor wanted to douse.

Starla felt the sleek strands of his ebony hair as she twirled them around her fingers and inhaled his masculine scent. She looked into his blue gaze, then admired his perfect features. She relished his kisses and caresses which were deliberate, seductive, and dazing. Her arms looped his neck and drew his mouth closer and tighter to hers. There was not a spot on her that did not burn or quiver with longing and elation. She was nestled in his strong embrace as her fingers wandered over him for as far as she could reach. She cherished this man with all of her heart and soul, and surrendered fully to his tender conquest. There was a quickening in her abdomen and a sweet tension in her loins as he explored her feminine core. She sighed, craved, and tasted every morsel of splendor from that experience.

Starla's lips brushed kisses over his neck, ears, and face. Her wits were devoured by love and desire for him, a yearning to pleasure him. She grasped his straining erection and massaged it, causing him to groan and writhe in enjoyment as she titillated his body and tried to daze his senses, as he had done with her.

Dagan's achings were intense; he was feverish to cool his scorching eagerness within her. But first, he wanted to stimulate her to rapture again.

Starla savored the magic of his tongue and hands. A blast of searing heat stormed her, one so potent and demanding and swift that it astonished her coming so close to her previous release. "Take me, my love."

Dagan moved atop her. His mouth melded with hers as he slid the tip of his probe past her seductive portal, then paused a moment to draw a needed breath for renewed restraint. When he obtained it, he thrust further until he was fully encased within her.

Starla's legs encircled his muscled thighs and locked him in that location. They undulated as one. He entered and half withdrew many times with her coaxing him onward to greater swiftness, depth, and strength.

Starla felt no shame or restraint. A flood of bliss washed over her, one so powerful that she could deny him nothing he wanted from her. She matched his pace and pattern, clinging to him, almost plundering his mouth, refusing to let him withdraw completely or for any span of time.

Dagan's ravenous appetite for her increased. He kissed her slow and gentle; sometimes fast, ardent, and firm. His passions soared and the sensations were magnificent as he delved into her receptive body. He labored with love and tenderness until he knew she was ready to seek the next level of satisfaction. He was glad he knew how to enflame and how to sate her. He wanted every encounter to be as special and satisfying for her as it was for him. He wanted to share such unions many times in the future, and he wanted her at his side forever. Somehow he must accomplish that personal goal. He realized when she was on the brink of release as she writhed beneath him, her kisses deepened, and her breathing quickened. He flew with speed and purpose to carry her over the last boundary into a splendid sector she hadn't visited before.

Starla clung to him and collected many sensations which flooded her quivering body. She had believed the experience would be enjoyable, but it was *magnificent.* Unless her wits and instincts had been destroyed, it was obvious she had won the man of her heart. She belonged to Dagan Latu in every way except one: legal bonding, a marital state which might never occur. But she would love and desire this galactic-hopping rogue until her soul lived among the stars in *Kahala.*

Dagan moaned and tensed as his climactic moment arrived. A landslide of pleasure carried him away as he found intoxicating release. He cherished every thrust and spasm to the fullest, and the woman who provided them. His mouth and hands continued to send sweet and receptive messages; they were ones of intermingled elation and serenity. His heart brimmed with love and jubilation. His mind preened with pride. His spirit soared with victory. Starla was his of her own free will, until his mission was finalized. But she would remain his forever if he could find a way to extricate her from her past mistakes. "I love you, Starla Vedris. I've never known such pleasure and peace of mind."

She saw his engulfing gaze and was convinced he spoke the truth, evoking mixed emotions. Her fingers traced his sensual lips as she said, "I love you, too, Dagan; I always will, no matter our fates."

Many *deegas* passed before Starla and Dagan found themselves waiting in the *Adika's* teleportation room to carry out their next moonbeam raid.

She glanced at the authentic-looking *Seki* emblem on the dark-green Space Ranger jumpsuit. "I presume these uniforms and insignia mean we're attacking somewhere in Kalfa. We—" Starla halted and shrieked, *"Pralu.* Dagan, we're under attack! That was a photon blast! Let's get to the bridge and save ourselves." She raced out the door with him behind her and yelling for her to wait for him and to be careful.

After they joined the Icarians, they found a panicked Sach piloting the ship while an injured Auken handled the weapon's controls with one hand.

While trying to evade enemy fire and escape a larger and slower vessel, the less than superb pilot shouted, "It's a trap! We veered off when she lacked the proper signal, but she came after us and fired on us!"

That told Starla and Dagan they had decloaked to send some type of signal to their target, and hadn't received the desired response.

A worried Auken glanced up. "Glad you came. I haven't had time to summon you since things went wrong. Starla, take over as pilot and get us out of here. At least get an obstacle between us and them. Our force shield and cloaking device aren't functioning."

As she took the captain's seat from Sach, Starla sent a furtive signal to Cypher in the concealed *Liska* which indicated he was not to interfere in the grim situation unless she requested help or a rescue. Her darting gaze rapidly scanned the ship's instruments and monitors as her keen mind plotted an escape course and assessed the extent of their current peril. She was relieved to have such superior skills and training from her sister, brother, father, and Star Fleet of Maffei.

With the skilled female at the helm and putting distance between the *Adika* and the transporter, Auken continued. "Dagan, see what you can do about the problems with my force shield and cloaker. Sach will help you repair them while I operate the weapons. We have speed and agility and an expert pilot on our side while you're getting the ship back to normal."

"I'm heading for that astroid belt twenty *preons* away," Starla revealed. "It's dangerous to challenge one, but it might be our only chance for escape and survival with our deflectors down. Since you're hurt and your reactions might be delayed or restricted, Dagan should be in charge of our defense until we're out of their range. With luck, they won't follow us into that hurtling maze. Sach can be checking out our problems while we head for our destination; then Dagan can join him after we reach it." After Auken nodded agreement, Starla advised, "Dagan, fire only if absolutely necessary. With our shield and cloaker malfunctioning, any drain on our power source can overload it and shut down our engine or life-support unit. Besides, if we strike them with a blast, that will only provoke them into pursuing us at all costs, especially if those are *Sekis* or *I-GAF*ers."

"She's right," Auken concurred. "Defend but don't attack." He looked at his second best friend and said, "Get started on those repairs, Sach; Dagan will join you soon. I'll watch the monitors for them."

No one spoke again in an attempt to prevent distracting Starla from her evasive course of action as she closed the distance to her target. With Dagan and Auken's helpful warnings, she dodged all incoming blasts with maneuvers that elated her teammates and astonished her pursuers.

Dagan was glad his lover's defense suggestion sounded logical so he wouldn't have to fire on the other ship. He was relieved that even though their survivals were in jeopardy, she had tried to avoid having life-taking charges added to their records as they had agreed. That told him she loved him and wanted a future with him. If it came down to a fierce battle, could he, Dagan mused, *should* he destroy the other ship and crew to save their lives and to protect his crucial mission? He hoped he didn't have to confront that awesome dilemma, nor endure her capture. He realized there was another possible peril: he recognized the location as being near the planet of Orr in his world's galaxy; if *Sekis* or *I-GAF* agents weren't in current pursuit, those forces could be soon if their persistent opponents summoned help while the *Adika* was vulnerable and their retreat was hindered. He dared not look at or speak to his cherished love, as he could cause either or both of them to lose focus on their critical tasks. His hands itched to take charge of the controls, but he couldn't do a better job than she was doing, though it would keep him from feeling so helpless.

Starla's anxiety and suspense mounted by the *preon* as she struggled to concentrate on getting them to safety. She must avoid exposure of herself and her mission, and certainly prevent the deaths of whoever was assailing them. The traveling expanse of scattered space debris and irregular-shaped bodies which ranged from a few to several hundred *migs* in diameter loomed ahead of them. She was afraid the next photon blast would disable the ship before they could reach cover. If that happened, Dagan would be captured and... *Stay alert, Bree! You have to get yourself and your beloved out of this perilous trap!*

Chapter Thirteen

The *Adika* reached the asteroid field before the other vessel could overtake it. "If Cypher-T were here, he could get us through this belt without a problem and he could handle our repairs with haste and skill. But I'm glad he isn't here and won't be entering this perilous region because it could interfere with his circuits and damage him. I'm relieved he's at Noy and I hope he's replacing the water in my ship's system in case we need the *Liska* for our next raid." She knew the intelligent android would grasp her clues and not follow the *Adika;* she was certain he would understand she wanted him to return to the Free-Zone.

Starla guided the ship into the belt, then positioned it behind and kept pace with an asymmetrical body for a while. She observed the other objects moving around them, eluding them as necessary. Within *preons,* it was obvious the Kalfans didn't enter the hazardous location, at least not at the same penetration point. She glanced at the golden-haired male whose black gaze was locked on the forward screen and said, "Auken, it should be safe for Dagan to initiate our repairs. You and I can monitor the sensors."

Auken agreed, and Dagan left the bridge for the engineering section.

"How's your hand? Do you need to go bind it for comfort?" Auken shook his head, and she asked, "What happened back there?"

"I was taking my seat after I... stood to scan the transporter when she fired on us. The unexpected jolt knocked me down and I twisted my wrist. That's why Sach took over as pilot until you arrived."

"Why did they attack? Were you given the wrong code word or signal?"

"They fired the *preon* we decloaked to check her out. I wasn't given a chance to communicate with them, and they didn't issue a warning."

Starla knew he didn't have to stand to look out the viewer screen, so Auken had needed to be near the *transascreen*— perhaps with the strange black box still laying nearby—to check for that signal Moig had mentioned to her before she placed him in an ill-fated coma. With luck, Starla hoped, Cypher had picked up the frequency when he recorded the incident for evidence. Since the raid had been foiled, she wondered if that meant Syrkin had exposed himself, been removed, and hadn't been able to alert Tochar or Auken to trouble before his downfall. "Did you say anything to them after they fired on us?" she asked. "Do you know who's aboard that ship?"

"I used the watchword we were given. It must have been changed because it didn't halt their attack, and they never identified themselves."

"That's strange," she murmured, keeping an eye on a big asteroid as she began to weave her way through the in-motion maze.

"More than strange if you ask me. Don't worry; Tochar will find out what happened and make certain it doesn't occur again."

"If we get out of this trap alive," she muttered with a frown as she evaded collision with another large asteroid. She guessed their pursuers were *Sekis* and doubted Space Rangers would give up the chase this soon. She tried to surmise their opponent's strategy so she could outwit it. She didn't want Dagan captured along with Auken and Sach as that wouldn't give her the time or opportunity to explain the truth to him as she

254

struggled to convince those officers of her identity and mission. Until she proved herself, she would be locked away like one of the *villites* on this craft.

The passage of time seemed contradictory: snailish, yet swift. Starla perceived the heightening of Auken's tension and suspected he was afraid, a condition which the alien must find vexing. She also was apprehensive, but neither summoned aid from their busy teammates and waited in silence as they watched for hazards.

Dagan communicated with Auken to relate he was checking on several solenoids, triaxial connectors, transducers, multiplexer interface adapter, and two inverters. He had replaced a couple of damaged parts, bypassed a module he didn't have a replacement for, and repaired another component. "I'm re-engaging the deflector shield now, but she has a weak spot in section three, so keep that side away from the enemy if they return. Most of the sensors and scanners are back to normal. The indicators seem to be functioning correctly, but I can't be certain without the right kind of flow meter; there's one on Tochar's ship I can use after we return to base. I'll replace these substitutes I've rigged and the other damaged parts from those we got from Sion if Tochar hasn't sold them during our absence. Sach has sealed those two small ruptures, and pressure in all compartments has stabilized. We're still working on the cloaker; the interface coupling is fused solid; I'm trying to reroute it around that segment."

"You're doing your best, Dagan," Starla urged, "but we need it functioning fast so they can't detect our exit point and intercept us when we come out of this belt. We can't stay in here much longer. The field is getting very tight and crowded and navigation is becoming difficult. At least with the force shield up, we can bounce the

255

smallest ones off our hull if necessary, but the large bodies are increasing in number and in velocity."

Dagan wished he could say something comforting and intimate to her, but that was unwise. He responded on the internal com-system, "If this idea works, I'll have it repaired in about ten to twenty *preons.* Don't worry, Starla, you can do it, you're one of the best pilots I've seen. I'll hurry."

"Why don't we halt and wait here for him to finish? Conserve our power," Sach asked Auken. "If those Kalfans are trying to get ahead of us and lay another trap, we don't want to zoom right into their snare."

"We can't," Starla replied. "Natural drift will crash us into a big asteroid, or pull us into that radiation belt to our right and knock out instrumentation. We have to keep going slowly and dodging these obstacles. If it gets worse, I'll have to turn around and keep pace with the original entry point. But we shouldn't exit without that cloaker. If there are *Sekis or parsec jumpers* aboard that vessel, by now, they could have an entire unit laying in wait for us along both perimeters. I can't get an accurate reading for other lifeforms with so much interference from this field of debris."

More time passed, and Starla noticed that Auken was showing signs of extreme tension. She knew why: she had been compelled to retreat along their previous course to escape the increase of asteroids; and he feared the Kalfans knew that action would be mandatory and would be waiting ahead to seize them.

"What's that?" she dared to ask, motioning to the apparatus near him.

"Something personal of mine," Auken replied, and put it away.

So, she mused, still not trusted completely…

Dagan and Sach arrived on the bridge, and the ebony haired male said, "Engage her and see if she responds. We've done all we can. If she fails, we'll have to make a run for it."

"Hope for the best, my friends," Starla said as she pressed the button. She smiled and whooped with joy. "She seems to work. Let's get out of here and put some distance between us and this quadrant."

"My suggestion exactly before that device realizes Sach and I tricked her and she gets angry and quits on us for spite," Dagan jested with a broad grin to help calm everyone's tension. "With that said, I'll hush so I won't distract our superior pilot."

As soon as the ship cleared the asteroid field, Starla cloaked them and went to starlight speed. As she performed those tasks, Auken, Sach, and Dagan scanned their monitors and sensors for the presence of other ships, but found none. Even so, each of them knew that another cloaked vessel could be lurking nearby; for that reason, she kept the *Adika* obscured until they were far away from their thwarted raid.

"Those were excellent maneuvers, Starla. We're lucky to have you," Auken complimented her.

"Thank you, my friend. I'm going to decloak soon so I won't put stress on Dagan's repairs in case the device is needed later."

"Sounds like a smart precaution to me," the band leader replied, and the others concurred.

Dagan looked at his weary lover and offered, "Why don't I take over for a while, Starla? You must be tense and sore from all the strain and pressure back there. I'm sure you can use a break."

"That will be appreciated, Dagan." She sent him a glowing smile and mouthed she loved him as they exchanged places. She knew he couldn't respond in like kind because he was facing the others, but he did give her arm a gentle squeeze as he assisted her to her feet. Once more they had survived near-death, Starla mused, but more perils loomed before them, and the possibility of eternal and agonizing separation.

Three days later, Starla and Sach were summoned from their quarters and told a medical wares ship was within their reach for a raid.

"If we take her cargo to Tochar," Auken reasoned, "this trek won't be a waste of time and supplies."

And it will help appease that fiendal's fury. Starla's mind reasoned.

"Medical products and drugs sell for high prices in secluded ports," Auken continued. "She should be a simple challenge with little risk."

"What if she's a trap?" Sach wondered aloud. "Been put between us and the boundary to tempt us to take her to avoid going back empty-handed?"

"What do you think, Starla?"

"Sach could be right; it would be a cunning tactic." She pretended to concur, in case the medical goods were in desperate need somewhere.

"What do you think, Dagan?"

"I say we slip into our *Seki* uniforms and lay claim to her haul," the Kalfan agent answered; he would explain his clever reason to Starla later.

Auken grinned. "Dagan's right; we take her load."

After everyone was deceptively attired as Space Rangers, the raid was carried out without a problem, and a semi-valuable cargo was taken aboard the *Adika*.

***

When the group reached Noy, it was late at night, so they did not meet with their leader or unload their cargo. Instead, Sach, Dagan, and Starla took a shuttle to the landing grid while Auken remained aboard his "injured" ship to sleep there. A fatigued Sach bid the couple farewell and headed for a nightspot to enjoy several drinks before retiring to his abode.

Starla decided, much as she loved and craved Dagan, she needed to concentrate on her mission and duty tonight, not on him. "I don't think you should come to my ship and I shouldn't go to your chamber tonight," she said, then searched her mind for a plausible excuse. "I'm certain Tochar is furious about our failure and will be looking for somebody to blame for our trouble. We not only didn't get those crystals he wanted, but we almost fell into a lethal trap. I suspect his Kalfan contact failed him. Since we were assaulted, he might have been exposed and captured. If that's the reason, Tochar will be reality-impaired and furious. It could look suspicious for two of his newest team members to be so close so fast, despite our admissions during *Thorin* tests. I know we haven't been alone for *wegs*, Dagan, but we don't want to take any risks of displeasing him. I doubt that medical haul will assuage him when it's moonbeams he wants. We should let him settle down tomorrow, then get together the following *deega*. Do you concur?"

Dagan, who needed to send and receive a report from Phaedrig, was compelled to deny his throbbing loins and respond, "I think that's wise. For all we know, he can be watching us this very moment and wondering if we're plotting against him. We should hug and kiss and go our separate ways tonight."

Starla decided to ask him tomorrow why he agreed with, actually coaxed Auken, to raid that medical ship, as she did not want to get into that offensive matter at this late *hora.* She smiled, shared an embrace and kiss with him, whispered she loved him, and headed for her shuttle. She heard Dagan leave in a landrover which had been left there by someone.

After reaching her ship, Starla found Cypher ready to pass along a message from Supreme Commander Thaine Sanger. She listened with relief and interest as the android told her that Syrkin had exposed himself while attaching a signaling device to a crystal shipment and had been arrested. "That explains why the evil traitor couldn't give the cue to Auken," Starla reasoned. "He was placing his world and many others in terrible jeopardy for selfish reasons. I wouldn't have been surprised if Tochar had destroyed him after Syrkin was no longer useful to him. Tochar wouldn't allow an equal to work with him later; those are the kinds of men who eventually become rivals and threats and assassinators. It will be marvelous if we can create a breach between Tochar and his Serian contact, make them believe they can't trust each other. But that's impossible without knowing the man's identity. I don't know how we can obtain it, not yet anyway. Somehow, I must get closer to Tochar, Sach, and Auken; then, perhaps one of them will let that crucial name slip."

"Do not increase your mission velocity, Bree. Haste or impatience evokes dangerous mistakes. We are making progress. Our accomplishments are many and important. I understand your desires to defeat Tochar and to return home as quickly as possible, but do not rush your task and imperil it. The feat you performed in the asteroid belt will elicit praise and admiration in the *villites.* It is possible that episode will achieve a bonding goal and the rewards which accompany one." Cypher explained how he analyzed she was in no danger from the Kalfans when he saw their vessel depart in the opposite direction to continue to their destination. "I assessed the damage to the *Adika* and concluded it was not beyond the capabilities of Dagan Latu and Sach to repair or bypass them. Our instruments detected the signal Auken sent to the other vessel, the one Moig revealed to us. I recorded the frequency and incident as evidence. Following my return to Noy, I had our water system flushed and refilled; it has been decontaminated and sterilized for your consumption."

"Have you filed a report to Thaine?"

"Negative. In the event he made a verbal response, I did not think it was intelligent for him to learn I left you behind in possible peril. The disk is ready for you to complete the data; I will send it to our superior."

"You're the best teammate I could have, Cypher. I'll add my news in *a preon.* Anything else happen during our separation?"

"On the preceding *deega,* I used a holographic image of Yana to dupe Radu and others with him into believing Yana was in the settlement while Starla was absent. All illusions were carried out at a distance to which the aliens could not approach her image and discover my tricks."

"You're so clever, my friend," Starla complimented the android. "No one should suspect Yana and Starla are the same person. We need to keep her around until we're certain we won't have a special use for her." She took a deep breath. "I'll finish that report so you can send it to Thaine. By the time I finish my cleansing and having a refreshment, if he intends to respond, he can do so before I take to my *sleeper.* I'm exhausted."

***

On the planet's surface, Dagan awaited a reply from Dauld Phaedrig concerning the communication he had sent out earlier. He sipped a drink and lazed on the *seata* while he let his troubled mind drift to Starla. He wished he was with the intoxicating *spaceki* tonight, but realized he must put duty and this pivotal assignment above his personal desires for one *deega.* He had to discover what was going on; if mission matters were heating up and perils were increasing, Starla could be in danger and time with her could be shortening faster than he knew. He could not surmise why Phaedrig had allowed shots to be fired on them with him aboard, and he was angry and alarmed because Starla could have been injured or killed, or captured.

When the encrypted message came through from his superior in a code only *I-GAF* members knew, the skilled agent learned about Syrkin's fate. It was clear to him that the unknown factor's lead had been accurate again; yet, Phaedrig still had no idea who or where that source was. In regard to why an attack had occurred against the *Adika* with him aboard, the answer was that the *Seki* superior from the capital planet in Kalfa had put several of his Space Rangers aboard after Syrkin's exposure and arrest.

Phaedrig's symbols deciphered to explain how he couldn't order the *Sekis* to cancel counterstrike plans because doing so would reveal there was an *I-GAF* agent in Tochar's band. Their orders were to "disable and capture but not kill, so the *spacekis* can be interrogated before punishment": if an assault was hazardous, the Rangers were to break off their pursuit and safeguard the crystals to their destination. "No more clues received from anonymous informant. No further data located on Starla Verdris, Yana, or Palesa."

Dagan wished he could recall his rash comments about Starla's piloting skills and prowess; that she would make a good agent; that she didn't believe in life-taking and resisted doing excess damage; that from how he saw it, she was into something over her head and didn't know how to get out; that he was certain Tocher wouldn't let her go alive; and how she had endured a hard life and made mistakes.

Phaedrig had cautioned if he was "getting too involved with one of your targets, Curran, don't forget she's a wanted *villite,* one of Tochar's band."

Dagan sent a short reply that he wished wasn't true, if it was. "I haven't forgotten and I won't."

The following morning, Auken took Starla to a site where they were to place the cargo they had collected earlier from his ship. They had been assigned to unload and store their haul while Dagan and Sach worked on Auken's craft using parts stolen during the raid on the Sion space station. While aboard the *Adika,* the band leader related to Starla and Dagan he had told Tochar how they had saved the team and his ship during the ill-fated trek. Auken had grinned and hinted they shouldn't be surprised if Tochar rewarded them for their courage and prowess. Starla and Dagan hadn't been given an opportunity to speak privately, but each was cognizant they had plans to meet that night in his abode.

At the cavern entrance, too narrow for a landrover to drive through, Auken stood beside two vehicles and recorded the items and drugs before Starla carried them into a storage cave. The natural corridor used to reach the correct chamber was long and twisted. It was illuminated by hanging lanterns, a light source which was predated long before her parents' births, but a necessary one in this primitive location. It prevented her from taking a wrong passageway along the winding course, since there were many paths and recesses in the dark red grotto's interior.

Starla wondered why Tochar had not commanded some of his Enforcers to assist them in order to lessen their time and labor. These weren't the type of products the leader needed to keep a secret; and the site—one of several—was always under guard. Perhaps, she mused, there were items amassed in other cavities that the *fiendal* didn't want his hirelings to see. While alone, she whispered for Cypher to take a coordinate reading so she could return later to investigate that idea.

As she approached the cavern's opening to get another load, Starla heard Tochar's voice and halted before rounding the last bend. She hoped to learn something vital. She signaled Cypher to go on alert and to record the conversation. She kept out of sight and eavesdropped as the *villite* leader told someone— perhaps Auken, but she didn't think so from his tone— about Syrkin's loss in Kalfa. When Tochar spoke about the thwarted moonbeam raid and boasted of how his special team had eluded Kalfan Rangers, she knew his companion was not the other Icarian. She heard her leader brag about his loyal *spaceki* team which cunningly had substituted a raid for medical supplies so they wouldn't return to him empty-handed.

"Our accomplice on Ulux contacted me to relate the ill-timed news Serian mines and shipments have been put under heavy guard by *Raz* Yakir's order, so no crystal raids are possible any time soon. Unless, my thrall on Kian finds a way around that precaution. In the event that does not occur, my friend, I am considering a plan to mount the smallest *Destructoid* from atop my dwelling to my ship so my team can strike at will. That will leave me

264

with my two largest ones for protection. If Dagan Latu—
one of my recent hirelings and best men—cannot do that
kind of work, I will get my special team to abduct a
scientist from Seri who can."

Starla was horrified by that news and prayed her
beloved would not be an accessory to such evil. She
wished she knew who was with Tochar, but she dared
not peek around the rocky corner and risk being seen.
The other person hadn't spoken, but no one interrupted
Tochar and the *fiendal* was still speaking.

"I cannot wait any longer for a big white crystal to
be found and another *Destructoid* to be built so I can
recover my losses," Tochar continued. "If we are going to
get control of Trilabs and make use of its products, we
must have one of those weapons to penetrate Darkar's
force shield and complex structures. With Trilabs and the
moonbeams in our possession, we will have great wealth
and power, more than we can imagine or ever use. These
are serious and pressing matters, my friend, but we will
discuss them later. Go and look over the items stored
inside to see if there is anything you want or need. I will
join you soon in the lighted chamber. Starla Vedris is
inside and will guide you around. Do not allow certain
lust for her to show, my friend, she must not be offended;
she is my best pilot and an elite member of my special
team."

Before the man responded or reacted to Tochar, she
hurried down the winding passageway. She did not want
to be caught near the entrance and be suspected of
spying. As she made preparations, she whispered them
to the ever-vigilant android aboard her orbiting ship,
then awaited a new adversary's arrival and exposure.

"Starla Vedris, Tochar sent me to-—"

As she turned from her faked task, her startled gaze
widened as much as the Maffeian's did as his shock sliced

265

off the remainder of his sentence. Starla felt as if the blood drained from her face, her entire body, as she confronted Acharius, son of *Avatar* Faeroe, son of the planetary leader of Caguas in her Galaxy, a man near her age who knew and desired her.

"What in *Gehenna* are you doing here?"

Starla mutely cursed the traitor before her who was jeopardizing her mission, who surreptitiously had aligned himself with the forces of evil and darkness. As he gaped at her in shock, it gave her time to think rapidly about what to do. She wondered if she should slay him and try to bluff it out with Tochar; or let the *nefariant* live, escape fast, and admit defeat. In order to safeguard her mission, could she, Starla mused, kill the son of a Maffeian *Avatar*, a man whose father was a respected leader and a close friend of her parents? If she didn't eliminate him, sparing Acharius's life could cost innumerable ones on the planets in the United Federation of Galaxies, and her own after he exposed her to Tochar, which he surely would do.

"Great *Gehenna*, you're on a secret assignment! Aren't you?" Reality returned to her opponent and the grim truth settled in on him. He didn't give her time to answer before he shouted into the rocky corridor behind him, "Tochar, come quick! We have a spy!"

Starla leapt aside as Acharius drew his laser weapon and fired at her, the beam zinging off the wall behind her and scattering debris. Cypher sent a vibratory warning signal via her wrist device that more danger was approaching. She heard Tochar and Auken racing toward, them and yelling questions.

As Acharius steadied his weapon to fire again, Starla knew decision time had expired...

266

Chapter Fourteen

Due to past mysterious incidents, team members had been told to wear their weapons at all times. That was advantageous for Starla, unfortunate for her crazed assailant. She was given no choice except to draw her weapon and fire in self-defense, as Acharius never entreated or demanded her surrender. She lacked time to reason with him, to try to persuade him not to unmask her. It was clear to her that the reality-impaired man was trying to eliminate the only witness who could bind him to Tochar. Her dexterous fingers worked the weapon's settings in resolved haste, and she fired a lethal and accurate beam into his evil heart which sent his jolted body tumbling backward to the ground. She signaled Cypher to delay any attempt to transport her out of jeopardy, as she hoped she could salvage the situation with the threat of exposure removed.

Tochar and Auken reached the astonishing scene. Auken went down on one knee to check the man for signs of life and found none. He looked at Tochar and shook his head, then eyed Starla in confusion.

Tochar stared at her and demanded, "Why did you kill my friend Acharius?"

Starla lowered the laser weapon to her side instead of holstering it, and left a finger on the trigger. She remained where she was, keeping a safe distance between them and feigning an expression of dismay. "Before I came here, I robbed him during a stop at Caguas in Maffei. He recognized me and attacked like he was zoned out. Look at the wall behind me; he fired at me twice, and his weapon wasn't set on *Stun*. The damage and sound of his blasts revealed his intent to kill me. I was only trying to defend myself. I must have pressed the wrong button when I panicked and drew my weapon. Things happened fast. I hope he wasn't a close friend. If so, I'm sorry about his loss." She noticed how cold and piercing Tochar's gaze and tone were when he replied to her desperate fabrications.

"I think there is a good reason why Acharius tried to kill you, Starla, and it has nothing to do with a simple theft. Acharius would find that coincidence amusing, even sexually arousing. You are too highly skilled and in control of your prowess to slay anyone by error or to panic in any situation. If he was a threat, you would have stunned him and allowed me to handle the matter. I heard what he shouted, so I think you silenced him for a good reason. Tell me who you work for, my spy?"

Starla feigned dismay. "I can't believe you would call me a liar and threaten me. Haven't I proven my fealty to you countless times and in countless ways? Perhaps he mistook me for someone else. I gave him no reason to react as he did. When I'm on a raid, I'm on full alert; my guard was lowered during this accident since I felt safe in here. Have you forgotten the troubles we've had, those so-called 'mysterious' incidents? The way he suddenly appeared and attacked me, he could have been an enemy, a saboteur. Your suspicions trouble and hurt me deeply. I can tell you want to punish me or perhaps terminate me without just cause, based on the rantings of a reality-impaired man who tried to kill me. I have done nothing to deserve such wicked treatment, and I will not endure it. I shall leave your settlement and hire this very *deega*. I will be a great loss, my previous leader, for no one has been a better or truer raider for you than I have, including your friends. I shall return to work for myself, since you think I can't be trusted." *Let's see if you apologize and beg me to stay...*

"What if she's telling the truth?" Auken reasoned. "She's never given me a reason to mistrust her. She's been an excellent teammate. She saved my life."

"We both heard what Acharius shouted about having a spy in here. That is something I have suspected for many *wegs* since those incidents."

"How can it be Starla? She couldn't have done those attacks. Maybe Acharius did zone out for a *preon*."

Tochar kept a dark and chilly gaze on her. "Perhaps you are right, Auken, but I am skeptical. She will have to find a way to convince me I should take her word over that of Acharius. I shall have a long and serious talk with Starla in private. Take her to my—"

Starla glared at him. "If you distrust me, you are unworthy of my fealty. I will not let you torture me for a false and absurd reason." She darted into the nearest corridor, ignored shouts for her to halt, and vanished into engulfing darkness. She knew she didn't have much time before Tochar summoned Enforcers and they used lanterns to search for her. She didn't dare to imagine what the vicious *fiendal* would do to her if she was caught. Not even Dagan with all his elite prowess or claims of love could save her from such an enormous and powerful force. *Dagan, my love, be safe and...*

Stop it, Bree, and focus on saving your skin! He's lost to you. She prayed no *Skalds* were lurking nearby, since the cannibalistic mutants were compelled to avoid the sun and favored caves. Her hands found the wall and guided her deeper into the location until she felt it was safe to stop. "Cypher, lock on to my coordinates and get me out of here. Be ready to cloak the ship as soon as I'm aboard, then change her location fast."

Starla paced the bridge of her cloaked spacecraft, still shaky from a close call with death and the gloomy destruction of her mission. Before she contacted her superior with the bad news, she had to settle down and clear her wits. "I don't understand how a man with his bloodline and status could have turned out so wicked. Many times he tried to be my companion for private evenings. Many times we've been at the same special functions, even sat together at a few of them. I know his parents. He knows mine. Our parents are friends. I'm certain Acharius would have pursued me as a legal mate if I had allowed or coaxed him to do so, but he did not appeal to me in that way."

She halted aimless movements and asked Cypher, "How could he attempt to slay me like that when he has vowed love for me? My rejection of him was never done in a cold or cruel manner, and he seemed to understand and accept the fact my feelings did not match his."

"My data on human behavior and emotions—in particular, those of *villites*—suggests he panicked and reacted from fear, shame, a survival instinct. I deduce his love was not pure, strong, self-sacrificing."

Starla did not want to discuss that emotion. "Your logic is accurate, as always. I have misused and betrayed the man I love. I fear for Dagan's safety and survival in light of our intimate relationship, of which Tochar is aware. Dagan may be imperiled by my actions. If Tochar uses *Thorin* on him, at least the *fiendal* will learn he has no idea about me having another identity or committing treachery. I dare not warn my beloved on the *Adika,* as there is no way he can escape. Contacting him will make him appear to be my accomplice in whatever Tochar suspects me of doing. I will find a way to check on him tomorrow after things settled down on the surface. If his life is in jeopardy, Cypher, we must find a way to rescue him."

She sighed. "When Tochar challenged me after I eliminated Acharius, it was reckless for me to stay and attempt to convince him of a false story. As long as he enters my image and voice into the network files, only data about Starla Vedris will be accessed and he'll remain ignorant of who I truly am. With that override command Thaine inserted in all databases, information about Bree-Kayah Saar will be prevented from being retrieved. I'm vulnerable to exposure only if he shows or sends my image to someone who knows me. I can't return to the surface as Starla, but I don't want Tochar getting too nervous and taking precautions which can hinder the work of the next agent they send to defeat him. With luck, I have convinced Tochar of my fealty, which may prevent him from running another check. Auken believed me, so maybe he can convince Tochar I escaped out of anger and a fear of being unable to prove my innocence. I never foresaw Acharius's intrusion." In frustration, she slapped her thigh with her palm. "Blast him, Cypher! He's ruined everything we've worked for; we're useless now."

"Have you forgotten about your transmutation identity?" the android asked. "There are things Yana can do and facts she can gather. We can follow the pirates, observe their raids, and record them for evidence."

Starla grasped his metallic hand covered in realistic synthetic flesh. "You're right, Cypher. Our goal is too important for us to give up without first trying other tactics. We must not fail ourselves, our ranks, and our superior." She didn't reiterate she hated to leave Dagan, whose life might be imperiled and who might vanish forever if he left Tochar's hire to avoid being slain by the *fiendal*, but she suspected the android guessed her additional motive. "I have an ample supply of phials from

Yakir, so I can return to the surface as Yana and spy on them. Tochar should assume Starla is eaten, lost or gone. The colony is crowded and busy. Yana is known there, so no one should pay attention to her."

She smiled at the silent Cypher and said, "Thanks, my friend, for clearing my head and giving me comfort. After I refresh myself, I will contact Thaine."

In her quarters, Starla wondered again if there was a chance she could persuade Dagan Latu to join her side and cause. She pondered if she could trust him if he agreed, and what to do if he attempted to capture her. If she confessed to being both Starla and Yana, would bruised pride and ego cause him to feel as if she had made a fool of him and provoke him to react badly? Did Dagan possess that unpredictable and perilous code of honor and loyalty toward an employer like most of his kind did? By returning to him, even as Yana, she could obtain information about Tochar's actions. In her heart, she knew he was trustworthy, but she would confide in him only if she was given proof she was right.

On the planet's surface, Dagan entered Tochar's dwelling and asked why he had been summoned—almost by force—from his work on Auken's ship. "Sach acted strange when he brought me here. Is there a problem?" He took the *seata* Tochar gestured to and observed the man's odd behavior. He hoped he had not fallen under suspicion for any reason. That dilemma seemed scant, yet, his gut instinct and keen perceptions warned him a solar storm was brewing. He feigned a look of curiosity and calm, but was on alert.

"My response is yes, if—as I do—you consider the treachery of Starla Vedris a problem."

Dagan was taken by surprise and did not conceal his reaction. He stared at Tochar and realized he was serious. His love was being called... His heart pounded and his insides twisted in dread. "What are you talking about? There must be a grave misunderstanding. Starla is as loyal to you as the rest of us are."

"I hope that is only a figure of speech, Dagan, since she has revealed herself to be my enemy."

"Your... enemy? How can that be? What happened to evoke such an astonishing accusation?"

Tochar related the incident that took place in the cave two *horas* ago. "Despite an intensified quest for her which is still in progress, Starla has eluded my men and vanished. Perhaps mutants found her."

Dagan was stunned and alarmed by all Tochar told him of Acharius's accusation of Starla and the shocking incidents that had ensued. Tochar revealed how Auken had argued briefly in her favor, until she "proved to us she is guilty by fleeing."

"Are you positive she's done something wrong? If so, what treacheries did she commit?"

"She looked and behaved culpable before she fled my investigation. She is a spy for somebody."

"What if she told you the truth like Auken said? If she believed you doubted her and intended to harm her, maybe she was scared and panicked. She's a female, a very young one at that, and alone. I can't imagine her being daring or foolish enough to spy on you. She never acted as if she was observing us or stealing information. And there's no way she could carry out those attacks. It sounds incredible she fooled all of us and for so long."

"She did, Dagan, I am certain of it."

The Kalfan knew an unknown factor was working against Tochar, but his beloved Starla? "How? Why? For whom? What could she have learned and how could she pass on your secrets to anybody? This doesn't click."

"I will know after she is captured. If she's still alive or captured alive. You know Starla's skills. Do you think she could make such a blatant mistake as to slay a man by error or in panic? Neither do I," Tochar replied for him. "I know you two became close, so it is time for you to choose between us. Do you know who she is working for or where she will seek a hiding place, on Noy or on another planet?"

"This is a mystery and shock to me, Tochar. I have no idea about her guilt or her whereabouts. She never gave me any reason to doubt or suspect her of being anything other than the woman I… believed her to be." Dagan made an intentional pause to imply the words he omitted: loved and trusted, feelings known to the *fiendal*. He was cognizant a denial of them would cast doubts on him. "My mind's in a daze. It's incredible," he murmured again. He wondered who and what Starla was: an agent for an alien galactic force who feared the man's increasing power? A hireling for a rival who wanted to seize the man's possessions, or one for a disloyal partner? Or an innocent ensnared by Tochar's suspicions. How could she have duped a lover and a skilled *I-GAFer* with such ease, if guilty? If not, why had she fled and to what location? Had Tochar harmed her and this was only a cunning ruse to cover his dark deed? If so, Dagan vowed he would punish the *fiendal*. As if he had been analyzing her and the matter, he said, "If what you say is right, we all misjudged her and she's one of the cleverest people alive."

"I never doubted her courage, daring, or prowess; that is why she was working for me. No one has ever deceived me as she has, so her punishment must be severe as an example to others who might be tempted to do the same. I have ordered my contacts to watch for her in Kalfa and Seri in case she reached her ship, fled, and goes to either galaxy. I have given orders to kill her on sight before she meets with her accomplice. If she is found here, she will be thrown to *Skalds.* My Enforcers are guarding my defense sites, storage caves, and dwelling in the event she tries to destroy any of them. I am certain she is responsible for those mysterious incidents, but I do not know yet how she accomplished it. My men are searching the colony and surrounding area; all chambers in the cave have been examined. Her image has been placed on papers and hung in numerous locations. Anyone caught hiding or helping her will share her fate. I know you have strong feelings for her, but I cannot permit her to endanger us by divulging the secrets she gathered while working for me."

"Those measures sound harsh and hasty, Tochar, and I can't help but hope she isn't guilty. But if she is a betrayer to us, you have no choice but to--"

"Trust me, Dagan, she is a traitor. Are you going to look for her?"

Dagan forced a frown and shook his head. "I'm sure your men will find her if she's in Tochara or on Noy. I'm still in shock; I need a few strong drinks at the Skull's Den while I let this grim reality settle in. If you or your contacts elsewhere get your hands on her, I think she should be questioned before she's terminated. In your position, I'd want to know who hired her and why, and I'd make certain she isn't replaced." *Convince him to keep her alive, Curran, until you or other agents can rescue or arrest her.* "I'll be more than happy to question her. Within five *preons,* I'll have answers for you. For me, too. If she duped and used me and made a fool of me, she'll regret that error. Blast it all! I should have known better than to mix work and pleasure. This is the first time I've been blinded, and it won't happen again."

Tochar mused on Dagan's suggestion. "Perhaps you are right about interrogating her before her death; I will consider it. I hope you will understand why I must speak with you using *Thorin.* You and Starla were very close, so I have to make certain you are still loyal."

Dagan eyed him for *a preon* as if vexed, which would be a normal reaction. "I'm being honest with you; but if that's how it has to be in this difficult situation, let's get it over with so I can visit the drinker."

Dagan was not surprised by the questions he was asked. The Kalfan used his immunity to truth serum and his cunning to convince Tochar of allegedly conflicting emotions. He said he didn't want to believe the many accusations were true, though they must be because Tochar wouldn't be so positive if he didn't have proof on which to base them. He related anger at Starla for using him as a cover for her selfish desires, for enticing him to fall in love with her if she detested men like him and wanted to destroy him along with Tochar. He pretended to be humiliated and furious for not seeing through her ruse; if she loved him and wanted to protect him, she would have confided in him, warned him of peril if she was exposed. He spoke about how she knew he would be incriminated by her actions and perhaps slain but she hadn't cared. He said he might harm her if saw her again, though he didn't lean toward harming anyone, to which his Dagan Latu reputation attested. He said he shouldn't have weakened toward a female; he should have held to his opinion that women were for pleasure. The next time he was in need of sex, he would use Yana or one of the Pleasure Givers at the Skull's Den, but he wouldn't become emotionally involved with another woman and would try to forget the deceitful creature whose treachery was gnawing at him and evoking an unfamiliar hunger for cruel revenge.

When Tochar asked if he knew anything about her plans against him or who she really was, he responded, "No." And when the leader asked him to speculate on those two areas, Dagan said, "Nothing comes to mind. This seems inconceivable. It's baffling."

Tochar asked him if he had any questions, and he answered, "I want to know who Starla is and who she works for. I want to know why she betrayed Tochar and how she passed multiple *Thorin* tests if she was lying." To which he heard Tochar mutter, "So do I."

Dagan continued as if talking to his lost lover, "Why did you betray me, Starla? How could you make love to me, then endanger me like this? Do you really love me? Am I expendable to you? Why did you do this?"

Dagan was relieved when Tochar halted his lists of queries before he asked again, "Do you believe she is guilty of Tochar's accusations?"

"I'm not sure. I'm too confused to think straight. I guess she wouldn't have run if she didn't have things to hide. If she's innocent, why didn't she stay and ask me to help her prove herself to Tochar?"

"If Tochar cannot give you proof, what then?"

"I must accept his word, agree to his precaution. Dagan Latu is loyal to the man who hires him."

"Do you love and desire Starla above all else?"

"There are limits to what a man does for a woman, unless he is a weakling or a fool. He must not dishonor himself or break his word or crawl on his knees to please her or to win her or even to protect her."

After Tochar halted the draining session, Dagan recovered on the table before heading for the Skull's Den to appease his woes with strong drink.

Aboard the *Liska,* Starla contacted Thaine with the grim news about her exposure and how it had occurred. She related how she would remain on the case as Yana and revealed facts about Acharius's treachery and death. She observed Thaine's shock as he listened to the recording of the conversation outside the cave between the two men and the events inside involving her. It was obvious how concerned Thaine was about a Maffeian being an accomplice to Tochar's evil, and the discovery that the *fiendal* had his wicked eye on Trilabs.

"At least we now know his Serian contact habitates on the capital planet of Ulux, and that traitor has a helper on the mining planet of Kian; perhaps those will be useful clues to *Raz* Yakir. You must warn him to put his scientists under guard to prevent their abductions." She then voiced an important question to Thaine: "Why did Yakir add new security to the mines and shipments without telling me?"

"I was to relate that news when we communicated after your return from Kalfa. *Raz* Yakir made that decision after Syrkin's evil was laid bare. He reasoned, with both sources cut off, Tochar might become desperate and make mistakes or try to mount a weapon on his ship, which he has plans to do according to what you overheard. Yakir reasoned that during a transfer process, the weapon is vulnerable to destruction."

Starla's voice was firm with conviction. "Not with me exiled from his band and settlement; there's no way that Yana can get near any of those weapons." *But perhaps there is someone who can...* "Keep the news about Acharius's death and treason a secret for now. I don't want Tochar to realize it's been reported and suspect I did it. Also tell *Raz* Yakir to use a plausible explanation for placing guards on his scientists; advise him to trust no one with the truth, as his traitor can be a disloyal friend or someone high in his government. It will be useful to me and our cause if Tochar remains confused about who and what I am and whether or not I'm innocent of his suspicions about me."

"Two of Tochar's cohorts are dead, Bree, so you've done an excellent job. You've destroyed all crystals from previous raids. Be proud of your accomplishments, even if they are your last ones there. We need to unmask and terminate accomplice number three in Seri, and Tochar will be without a means to get his hands on more crystals while we seek his defeat."

"But Tochar still has three invincible weapons, Thaine. I don't know how to get to them and eliminate them, but I'll try; then you can attack. And check out Dagan Latu for me again; see if there is anything in his record to indicate he can be coaxed to join our side. If I can achieve that goal, it will give us someone on the inside, someone who can get to at least one of those weapons during its mounting on Tochar's ship. Then, maybe he and I—with Cypher's help in teleportation—can find a way to eradicate the other two."

"Don't take any unnecessary risks, Bree, or trust Latu without proof he can be turned."

"I'll work in Yana's form as long as possible and keep you informed of my progress and discoveries."

"I'll report these developments and your new strategy to *Raz* Yakir as soon as possible. Now that Tochar is wary, be more alert than ever, Bree."

"I will, Thaine. Please tell my family I love them and miss them."

***

That night in his abode on Noy, Dagan pondered the mystery surrounding Starla. If she wasn't who and what she claimed to be, how could he discover the truth? He recalled her mock salute on her ship during his visit, remembered she had no fingerprints to expose her. He reflected on her astute mind and countless skills. If she was an agent or enemy hireling, how had she duped him so easily? Or had he been too blinded by love for her to notice the clues she dropped or the slips she made, if there were any? Why, if she loved him as she vowed, hadn't she confided in him? If she was innocent and merely had panicked, or if Tochar had harmed her as the *fiendal* had done to his family *yings* ago, Dagan swore he would slay Tochar with his bare hands. One of the reasons he had become an *I-GAF* agent was to find a way to get to Tochar, but their paths had not converged until this mission. Yet, if Tochar had killed her, why was the *fiendal* furious, unsettled and eager to find her? He worried about Starla's survival, but he couldn't desert his mission to go search for her. Although tempted, he lacked the means to do so. He just wished he knew if she were alive and safe.

If only there was a way she could contact him to explain her actions and to appease his fears. Suddenly he realized there was: she had a ship with an android who could transport her into and out of his chamber. *If* she had the coordinates. Coming to him in that manner wouldn't be any more hazardous than the predicament their relationship had placed him in. Maybe her love was false and his usefulness was past. But he didn't want to think along that tormenting line.

He had contacted his superior earlier and told Phaedrig the incredible news. He had asked Phaedrig to investigate the matter, to find her if possible, and to hold her for his interrogation. Yet, when a response had come only *preons* ago, it had revealed that only her Starla Vedris record was retrieved when all data bases were accessed. That seemed impossible unless she had told him and Tochar the truth... He was relieved that Phaedrig had put his men on alert to watch for her and her ship, especially at Karteal, but he couldn't relax until the enigma was solved.

His identity and assignment were safe, so he would be sent on further raids where he might gather evidence to defeat the *nefariant.* He would concentrate on that, as there was nothing he could do about Starla until she reappeared. He hoped she wasn't on Noy and within Tochar's reach. If so, there was no way he or her side could rescue her, not with him being outnumbered by *villites.* Not with those *Destructoids* preventing an attack by her friends or his. Was she lost to him? Dead?

The next morning, Starla teleported to Yana's dwelling and gave the place a more lived-in appearance in case she had visitors while using that identity on a frequent basis. Afterward, Yana strolled in the busiest area of the settlement and went to the Skull's Den to observe the continued search for Starla Vedris. She saw the old-time "wanted posters" and heard Radu and others talking about the threats against anyone who befriended her. She chatted with the alien from Mu so she would be familiar with the alleged facts about Starla's treachery and escape. She hoped Dagan would arrive soon so she could witness how he was reacting to the shocking news. She wanted to see if Dagan would turn to Yana or another woman to ease his anguish and to pretend to others he wasn't hurting deeply from her betrayal.

When she was left alone with Radu for a short time, Yana asked in a whisper, "How is Dagan taking such a terrible situation?"

The speckle-faced alien with rippled forehead was aware of the Asisan beauty's interest in Dagan and also knew Dagan had seemed to stop seeing Yana after he became close with Starla. "He was in here last night, drinking heavily and brooding. He sat alone in a corner for *horas*. I think he is as confused by the incredible event as others are. I have known Starla for *malees* and believed her to be trustworthy. Tochar has not revealed the charges against her, but they must be serious for him to order her death."

She noted a gleam of concern in his gray eyes, one seemingly mixed with disbelief and affection, and his reaction touched her heart. "I wonder why Tochar does not want her captured and questioned. Papers hanging around the colony say she can be slain on sight."

"If I were Starla, I would prefer death to capture and torture. It is said that Tochar is strict and harsh where enemies are concerned." He leaned closer across the bar and warned, "Never provoke him to anger."

Yana nodded. "I have seen Starla, but we have not spoken. From seeing her at a distance, I cannot imagine what horrid deeds she committed to enrage her leader. It is said she is one of Tochar's special team members, one of his elite *spacekis*. Do you think Dagan will imperil himself to help her if she's captured?"

Radu shook his head, the multiple folds on his face jiggling. "Dagan Latu is not a fool. To an adventurer and rogue like him, survival and honor come first."

Yana daintily took a sip of her drink. "I wonder if he would resent my approaching him to offer comfort and friendship. Perhaps he will trust no female after being shamed and hurt, perhaps imperiled."

Radu grinned. "A ravishing and interesting woman is just what he needs to help him forget Starla."

Yana smiled as if that opinion pleased her and to imply she still found the Kalfan desirable. "Thank you, Radu; you give good advice. I am fortunate to know you." *Fortunate to have a source of information like you and a safe place to conduct observations.*

"How much longer will you be here?"

"Perhaps a *malee;* I doubt more than two. Matters are resolving themselves at home, so I hope to return there soon. But I shall miss you after my departure, and I will not leave without saying farewell."

Radu smiled before he left her to greet and serve several men who entered.

In her Yana guise, Starla felt safe and confident against discovery; and Cypher was on standby to rescue her at the first sign of peril. Yet, tension and remorse nibbled at her nerves as she planned her next move, the difficult task of confronting her lost lover without letting her true emotions show.

Dagan opened the door to his chamber, stared at the Asisan beauty standing there, and asked, "What are you doing here, Yana?"

"I want to be sure you aren't suffering badly."

He noticed the look of empathy in her crystal-blue eyes and heard it in her voice, but he wasn't in the mood to talk with her or to accept such seemingly authentic kindness. For a moment he had hoped it was Starla in his chamber, but knew it was too dangerous for her to visit him. "Suffering over what?" he asked, irritable from lack of sleep and worry, and unaccustomed libation of too much strong drink last night.

Yana studied his annoyed reaction at seeing her. She had refused to use the pheromone to weaken him. "The betrayal and loss of Starla Vedris."

Dagan grabbed her arm and yanked her inside. "What do you know about Starla and me?"

She ignored his firm grip on her arm, one with pale-blue skin in this form. She softened her startled blue gaze and in a gentle tone--a voice so different from Starla's— replied, "It isn't a secret, Dagan. Everyone has been warned not to give her help or to conceal her. Anyone caught doing so will be terminated, thrown to the *Skalds* for food. Talk spread fast about her alleged perfidy and disappearance. I was visiting with Radu and heard plenty from him and others in the Skull's Den. I'm sorry she hurt you."

Dagan caught her use of the word "alleged" and wondered why she had used it. "I'm not in torment, Yana; I've survived worse incidents. It isn't fatal to lose one's relationship partner. I'll find another when I'm ready for diversion or sexual gratification."

"You don't have to pretend or lie to me, Dagan; you love her; you told me so."

Dagan narrowed his false blue gaze and asked in a gruff tone, "Did someone send you here to examine me or to give me comfort?"

"I came because I am concerned. This incident is strange, and many are whispering about it. Those who know her are... mystified and dismayed by what sounds like... an incomprehensible occurrence. Our paths have not crossed, but her reputation and my sightings of her do not match what this situation implies."

He was intrigued by her pauses and word choices, and amazed by her revelations. "That's dangerous talk, Yana, if it's reported to Tochar."

284

"Yes, but I thought you should know how others feel. I do not believe you are the kind of man who will imperil me for telling you. What will you do if she comes to you for help?"

Dagan backed Yana against the wall and pinned her voluptuous body there. "I don't want to discuss Starla Vedris with you or anyone; not ever, understand? She is beautiful and satisfying, but she duped us. She isn't for real, and I detest pretenders and despise being used. If we meet again, she'll be sorry she pulled me into her little scheme. If she expected to turn Tochar and others against me and get me killed, she failed, because he trusts me completely, and is right to do so. I don't want to hear anything else about your suspicions or those of anyone else or I'll be forced to report them to Tochar." *Tell the fiendal that, if he's the one who sent you!*

"I'm sorry if I anger or offend you, Dagan; that is not my intention. I can help you forget her, if you'll allow me to do so. I swear to you I am a loyal friend."

He released her and stepped backward. "Thanks for the generous and kind offer, Yana, but I'm not in the mood for this kind of talk right now. Please leave before I say or do something I'll regret."

"May I return in a few *deegas* to visit with you? As friends, if that's all you want. You helped me in a time of trouble, so I would like to help you."

Dagan reasoned he might need Yana as a cover against being implicated as Starla's accomplice or as a source of information, so he replied, "You can come see me again, but give me a few *deegas* alone."

She sent him a glowing smile and nodded. At least he hadn't turned to the alluring creature yet, and he did give her the impression he was hurting inside. Twinges of guilt chewed at her and desire blazed within her as she returned to Yana's dwelling.

***

Later, Dagan was warned by a message from Phaedrig that somebody in Seri and in Maffei had retrieved data from Dagan Latu's file by accessing the official network using an untraceable frequency and the correct password again, which meant the encroachers were in positions of power. His superior had been alerted by the cue Phaedrig had inserted to call his attention to any time an undercover *I-GAF* agent was checked out, but the procedures were carried out and terminated too fast for him to reach a terminal to determine their origins. Phaedrig was concerned about the intruders' motives and Dagan's safety. He asked Dagan if he should be extracted via a fake trading vessel or if he wanted to stay and bluff it out; the resolute agent said he would complete his assignment.

Dagan wondered if one check was done by Tochar's accomplice in Seri and the second by another contact in Maffei. Tochar had asked during his *Thorin* test if he knew Acharius Faeroe of Caguas, so Dagan had asked Phaedrig to run a surreptitious probe on the Maffeian. It was possible that Acharius and/or Tochar had an additional conspirator in that same galaxy. Since he had been subjected to truth serum again, he was surprised they would remain suspicious of him, though he'd had an intimate and close connection to Starla. Perhaps they were making certain he was loyal before drawing him deeper into their band.

Perhaps Starla was an agent of some type or the hireling of a rival. He was aware her ship had cloaking ability but she couldn't linger for very long without supplies and surely wouldn't be so reckless as to make an appearance to get them. But if she had lingered, he mused, would she come to him? If so, what would her story be? If she had deluded Tochar several times, she was immune to *Thorin*... Then his speculations took a wild turn: What if the same was true of Yana? What if Starla and Yana were confederates? That would explain why Yana had backed away from him without causing trouble and why Yana seemingly had defended Starla to him... Or perhaps the two women were working for the same person without each other's awareness. That would be a cunning and unsuspected ruse: two females assigned to defeat Tochar.

"Who, where, and what are you, Starla?" he murmured. "And you, Yana, there's no info available on you. Perhaps I should draw you closer, my seductive Asisan, and see what I can extract from you."

Cypher summoned Starla to her ship that night to communicate with *Raz* Yakir, galactic ruler of Seri, the man who had initiated this mission, one of two men who had selected her for this critical and perilous task, the man who had gifted her with the transmutation ability and chemical.

Starla listened to his astonishing words. "What do you mean, there's another agent working on this assignment, one from *I-GAF?* Why wasn't I informed about such an important fact? Who is he?"

"I do not know who the *I-GAF* agent is," *Raz* Yakir's voice wavered not at all in indecision, "their identities and mission records are inaccessible to me, to everyone except members of that force. I do not know if it is a male or a female. I do not know if the agent has been in Tochar's band for a long time, or if one arrived after you did and joined it, or if one has yet to infiltrate it. I was away resting when Supreme Commander Sanger tried to contact me, and he could not reach me until I returned late this *deega*. When Thaine related what had occurred there, I knew I should reveal this fact to you. There is no reason for you to further endanger yourself, Bree-Kayah; return home and allow the *I-GAF* agent to handle the mission from henceforth."

"I don't want to quit and leave, sir," Starla said in an emotion-choked voice, "this mission is too crucial to both of our worlds. I can still observe and gather facts in my Yana disguise."

"Only if your life and safety are not imperiled. You have done a superior job for us and I do not want to see you harmed. I have great respect and affection for you and I trust you without question or hesitation."

"Thank you, sir, but why didn't you tell me about the other agent?"

"I had selected you and planned your mission before the ruler of Kalfa asked for an *I-GAF* agent to be assigned to defeating Tochar and recovering the stolen crystals and weapons. I know the *I-GAF* is in charge of solving intergalactic crimes and pursuing intergalactic *villites,* but I wanted someone working solely for me on this vital matter. It is obvious there is a traitor high in my rulership and I—with the help of my agent—must be the one to expose and punish him. I also believe there is a better chance of success if separate agents are on the job, and without each other's knowledge so they cannot influence each other's findings or jeopardize each other's role. I want a resolution to this problem because of the value, power, and danger of moonbeams in the wrong hands and to prevent a flood of them across the nearest galaxies."

Yakir took a deep breath before he continued. "I believe a second agent—mine—can gather clues their agent misses or ignores. After I was informed of the other agent's assignment, mine was already on the case. I feared if I extracted you when you were already in place and the *I-GAF* agent was either exposed or killed, all progress would be lost; and that despicable *fiendal* would be on alert to an investigation and anticipate the agent's replacement and make it impossible. I chose you because I think a woman might make discoveries a man cannot, and a gentle female will attract less suspicion. My pride is involved, Bree-Kayah. I feel a loss of control in my own responsibilities if I allow an *I-GAF* agent to be in total charge when it is my world and rulership being attacked and weakened. My pride urges me to be the one to solve the crimes committed against Seri because the *villites* dared to steal from us and because one of my subjects has betrayed me and my people. I ask your forgiveness for withholding this secret from you."

"I understand your motives, and I agree with them. Does Thaine know of this other agent's existence?"

"He was informed at the same time I was, but I requested he keep that news to himself and he obeyed. When we spoke earlier, I told him I would reveal the secret to you. I considered asking Dauld Phaedrig to let his agent contact Yana and allow you two to work together. That way he will know I have one there and will learn about our shapeshifting secret. Since we do not know the identities of all traitors but we do know they are men in elite positions, I feared what might happen to you if the wrong person intercepted my message to him and learned of Yana's existence and location. Commander Phaedrig will be annoyed with me for taking the action I have and for failing to inform him about it, but, after all, I am the ruler of Seri and it is my right, my duty. There is the possibility that Commander Phaedrig will want you off the mission and away from Noy; he can order his agent to expose Yana to force you to leave and let *I-GAF* handle the case. What action do you think I should take, Bree-Kayah?"

"In my opinion, sir, we should keep Phaedrig in the dark for the time being, and I shall continue to work here as Yana. Perhaps I can uncover his agent's identity and decide if it will be productive for us to work as a team. I will keep you and Thaine informed."

"That is acceptable to me, Bree-Kayah. Be careful, and withdraw any time you feel your Yana identity has been imperiled. I have great admiration and esteem for your parents; even this monumental mission's success is not worth the cost of your life."

"I will be careful, sir, and thank you for confiding in me and for your kind words about me and my parents. Both spoke highly of you when I was approached about taking this assignment. Bree-Kayah Saar out."

Starla and Cypher discussed the ruler's revelations and her plans for the next *deega* before she returned to Yana's dwelling. She got little sleep as she speculated on the *I-GAF* agent's identity. She hoped and prayed it was Dagan Latu and that was how he had passed his *Thorin* tests, but that could be wishful thinking.

Tomorrow she would test her wild theory, after she inspected the cave where she had slain Acharius and escaped Tochar's revenge. Surely by now, it had been searched and eliminated and deserted.

Chapter Fifteen

Cypher transported Starla to Yana's dwelling after a rapid examination of the cave where she found nothing unusual among the stolen items stored there. After shapeshifting into Yana, she prepared herself for a momentous visit with Dagan Latu. She attired herself in a multicolored garment that ended just above her knees and bared her shoulders and arms. The bottom had a slight flare below her hips and a fitted waist. A stretchy band above her breasts and thin straps held the top in place. Her feet were clad in sandals with ties which overlapped several times before they were secured above her calves. The cosmetics she selected enhanced the shade of Yana's eyes and the pale-blue tint to Yana's flesh. Thick and wavy golden hair with a faint blue tinge flowed midway down her back. She used a fragrant scent but avoided using the pheromone, as there was no intent to dupe or entice Dagan on this occasion. She fastened the neck ring at the base of her throat, one of its "gems" a miniaturized transmitter to keep her in touch with the android in case of an emergency.

Starla gazed at her Asisan image and took a deep breath. She closed her eyes for a moment to pray her perceptions about Dagan were right, as that would put her lover within her reach, then contacted her android. "I'm ready, Cypher, and leaving for his chamber. Stay alert but do not interfere unless I signal you by saying, 'This is futile and I want to leave,' then beam me out without delay." She knew her longtime companion heard her order but could not respond since the neck unit was a one-way device. She checked the *lazette* strapped to her right thigh beneath the garment to make certain it was set on *Stun;* not *terminate,* as she doubted she could slay the man she loved for any reason. If he failed to prove he was an *I-GAF* agent, she would not expose her true identity or Starla form, so eliminating him as a threat would be unnecessary.

Dagan stared at the lovely Yana in shock. "Why did you return this soon? I thought we agreed you would not come again for a few *deegas*."

"I had to see you, Dagan. It is important. May I come inside for a few *preons?*"

"Why?" He was cognizant—and suspicious—of the absence of her previous magical and irresistible allure, an unnatural weakness which still vexed him. Until he knew the truth about his lost love, he couldn't initiate even a casual affair with Yana to assure Tochar of his fealty. He hoped one wouldn't become necessary, and dreaded making that repulsive decision. He had never misused a female before during a mission, yet, he was certain Yana was somehow connected to this situation, and a great deal was at stake: the safety of the United Federation of Galaxies.

She stressed, "I must speak with you in private. It is important, very important."

Dagan caught the urgency to her words, so he stepped back and allowed her to enter his chamber. He followed her to where she halted near the room's waist-high partition that separated the sitting and eating areas. He saw her lean against it, as if requiring the divider's support. "Well?"

"Does Starla know the truth about you?"

Dagan was baffled by the unexpected query, and realized his reaction was evident. "I didn't tell her about us, but somebody may have. Why is that important?"

Yana moistened her lips. "I didn't mean the truth about us; she knew that fact."

Dagan's dark-blue gaze widened in surprise, then narrowed. "You told her about our one encounter?" Was that why Starla didn't trust him and confide in him, or return to make certain Tochar hadn't slain him, because she doubted his love and commitment to her?

"No, she told me after it happened."

His alert heightened, as did his intrigue. "But you said you two aren't acquainted."

"I thought it best not to reveal we are, given the danger of that fact, especially now. I don't want to induce Tochar to investigate and shadow me."

Dagan needed a reply fast. "Why is that, Yana? Do you have something hazardous to conceal?"

"I have my reasons which I will explain later."

"Have you seen or spoken to her since this trouble began? Do you know if she's alive and safe?"

"She disappeared from everybody's sight following that cave incident."

Dagan realized Yana had chosen her words with care, a response he deduced was a lie. "What else did Starla tell you? When?"

"The same *deega* you discarded me, she asked me to leave you alone because she loves you and had created a special bond with you."

"Starla told you she's in love with me?"

"Yes, and I believe her."

"Her treachery and connection to me could have gotten me killed. She didn't bother to confide in me or even warn me of my imminent peril, so she has a strange way of proving that love."

"Just as you failed to prove your trust and love to her by withholding the truth about yourself and why you really came to Noy. You endangered her life."

293

Dagan tensed, as the creature seemed to know secrets. "What 'truth' are you referring to, Yana?"

"That you're an *I-GAF* agent working to defeat Tochar and his band. That you're immune to *Thorin* and that's how you duped him during your tests."

"Where did you get such a reality-impaired idea? Who sent you here on such a ridiculous quest?"

"You can trust me completely, Dagan, or whatever your name is. If you wish to exchange facts on this matter, you must prove yourself to me."

"What are you trying to pull, Yana? Who sent you here? Why? I'm no *I-GAF* agent, nor a *Seki.*"

She fused her confident gaze to his cynical one. "Yes, Dagan Latu, you are. Before I tell you everything I've learned about Tochar, prove your identity to me, prove my positive assessment of you is correct."

"What do you mean?"

She lifted his right hand and said, "Show me your *I-GAF* badge and I can tell you facts which will help you carry out your mission. Perhaps we can work together to defeat Tochar, unless you prefer to work alone."

"Why would I want to crush Tochar?"

"Because he is evil and he must not obtain more moonbeams. With your help, perhaps we can shatter the white crystals in his *Destructoids* as I did with the others his *spacekis* stole during raids," she revealed to coax out the admission she needed. She knew she was exposing more than she had intended for Yana to relate this soon, but she felt he would have halted her probe by now if she was wrong about him.

Dagan took a few steps away from her, propped himself on the *seata's* back, and stared at her. "Who are you, Yana? What are you? Why did you really come here with this preposterous accusation?"

"First, earn my trust by confirming my theory is accurate. I have already told you more than is safe if I am mistaken about you. I can proceed no further until you verify your I-GAF identity."

Could Yana be the unknown factor instead of Starla, as he had decided this morning? "First," he countered in a sarcastic tone, "prove I should trust you by telling me how you seduced me so easily."

Without hesitation, she said, "With a spray which is a mixture of a heady aphrodisiacal fragrance and the ancient Kalfan mating pheromone. I know your species does not physically produce it anymore but your males are still susceptible to it. I know it is sold and used in mating problem cases."

Dagan frowned. "So, it was a trick as I suspected. You're lucky I don't strangle you for using me like a sex slave. I'll warn you now, woman, don't try it again. Now, tell me why you selected me to ensnare?"

"Because you aren't like the others here, riffraff of the Cosmos. I needed a means of obtaining information about Tochar and his raids, and possible protection if exposed. And I also found you irresistible."

Dagan ignored her last sentence and focused on her others. "You didn't learn anything useful from me, so you wasted your time and charms."

"No time spent with you is wasted; I enjoy you and your company." She noted his tense expression. "Relax, I'm not here to seduce you; that facet of our relationship is over by your insistence."

Despite her words, Dagan saw a gleam of desire in her blue gaze. "If I am an *I-GAF* agent, why did you wait until now to ask me to work with you?"

"I learned only *horas* ago there is an *I-GAF* agent on assignment here and surmised it is you; that is why I returned to speak with you. If I'm wrong, and I pray I am not, I'll have to slay you," she warned as she aimed the *lazette* at his heart. "Now that I have confided in you, I can't allow you to endanger me and my mission."

Dagan eyed the weapon and the way she held it, which told him she knew how to use it. But would she? The impassive expression in her blue eyes did not answer for him. He scolded himself for underestimating her prowess and placing himself at a disadvantage. "Why do you think it's me?"

"For many reasons, most of them impossible to explain, gut instinct I suppose. As a skilled and seasoned agent, you know we depend upon our intuition and perceptions as much as our training and experiences. Well, do we have a bargain? Do we make a profitable exchange? Do we work together, or separately if you prefer, to destroy Tochar?"

"You didn't tell me who and what you are, and what you know about Starla. Is she alive and unharmed?" He had so many questions to ask her. "Did Tochar tell the truth about her betraying him and what exactly did she do to provoke him? Does she work with you or for the same person? Where is she? Who and what is she?"

She was elated by his concern over Starla's fate. "I promise to reveal everything about me and all I know after I make certain you are what I hope and believe you are. My lips are sealed until you do."

"Didn't you overlook an enormous hazard?" he asked with a chuckle. "Computer, do not open the exit door except by my voice command, seal all windows, and respond to requests made only in my voice. If I don't cancel those orders within one *hora*, shut down the environmental control system." He focused a challenging gaze on Yana. "Now, answer my questions. If you shoot me, you can't get out of here alive."

Yana holstered her *lazette* and laughed softly. "Shall we see who runs out of air and relents first? I'm not afraid of you or of death; if I must sacrifice my life in the line of duty and for such a crucial goal, I will do so. There's nothing you can do or say to extract the truth from me until I see your badge, and I know how that procedure works so I can't be fooled. If you doubt my words and determination, let's sit down and wait until we can't breathe and you comprehend I am serious."

"Yes, Yana. I know you're serious."

"I'm your captive and can't leave without your help, so what harm can it do to reveal the truth? Unless you release me, who can I tell about you?"

"How do I know you're trustworthy, despite what you've revealed?"

"You certainly can't ask Koteas, Terin, or Syrkin. Phaedrig couldn't tell you who I am when you checked on me; that was sneaky stealing my fingerprints and voice pattern, though they failed to be useful. You also checked on Starla, and I know what you learned about her. I wonder what Tochar would do if he discovered how you passed his *Thorin* tests. *I-GAF* agents are protected against truth serum by *Rendelar* That's how you deceived him. I've had the *Rendelar* procedure, so neither you nor Tochar nor Phaedrig can extract anything from me, not even with torture. The only way you'll receive answers to your queries is by being worthy of them. Since I am your prisoner, you have nothing to lose by confiding in me, but there is much you can gain by trusting me."

Little by little, comprehension dawned on him. "So, you're the one who fed those clues into our computer network. How did you obtain our secret entry code, and gather so many facts about these beasts? How did you carry out those attacks on the crystals?"

Joy and relief flooded her as he half-admitted to her supposition. "I'll tell you everything you want to know. The insignia, Dagan," she reminded. When he remained silent and watchful, she added, "In case you think you can trick or frighten me, you're mistaken. I don't need you to release me from your chamber." With speed and nimble fingers, the weapon was in her hand, aimed at him. "This *lazette* is powered by a moonbeam that can cut through any material, including your walls."

"So, you tricked me again."

"I hoped thinking I was your captive would relax you into complying. I don't like deceiving you, but you are being stubborn. Can't you see I'm telling you the truth? Use those keen wits! This matter is grave, more important than either of our lives. Please relent."

Dagan studied her for a moment before he pulled a disk from his belt and held it over his right hand. His pressed the top surface to release the needed chemical. He set aside the disk and used his forefinger to spread a clear liquid from knuckles to wrist and from thumb to outside edge. He watched Yana's gaze remain fastened to his flesh as the symbol seemed to materialize as if by magic. He was befuddled when tears misted her blue eyes and an expression of delight claimed her face. He lifted his fist and held it before his chin. "Satisfied?" he asked as he watched her stare at the authoritative emblem he'd exposed.

Her softened gaze traveled from his hand to his blue eyes. "So, I was right about you all along; you are a good and trustworthy man."

"Am I?" Dagan retorted as he used a second chemical to conceal his badge. "If you trust me, turn over that *lazette* and tell me everything."

She saw his gaze widen in astonishment when she held the weapon out to him, smiled, and asked, "Can I wet

my throat first? Now that I've seen your *I-GAF* mark"—
she said for Cypher's benefit—"we have a long talk ahead
of us." When an astounded Dagan didn't take the
proffered weapon, she set it down on the counter as she
fetched a drink. "Want anything?"

"The truth will be nice," he quipped.

"Perhaps you should sit down before I shock you,"
she advised as she sipped the liquid from one of Yakir's
phials with her back to him.

"I am seated. I want to hear every detail. Get to
talking, woman, before I--"

"Keep silent and watch for a few *preons,* then you'll
understand." She observed Dagan as he gaped at her
during her transmutation into *Starla.* Twice during the
metamorphic process, he blinked many times and shook
his head as if he doubted his vision and sanity.

Afterward, she said, "My real name is Bree-Kayah
Saar, Bree to my family and friends. I was assigned by
Supreme Commander Thaine Sanger of Maffei Star Fleet
and *Raz* Yakir of Seri to defeat Tochar and to unmask the
traitors in Kalfa and Seri. If possible, to destroy his
crystals and weapons. I am an Elite Squad agent." She
halted to allow that information to be absorbed.

Dagan's gaze roamed her flushed face and he looked
into her pleading green eyes. She was alive and safe. She
was an agent, not a *villite.* She was within close
proximity, but he could not reach out to her yet, much as
he yearned to do so. She was... Yana. She had duped
him... He needed time to clear his wits, to get answers, to
ascertain her feelings about him. The name which
sounded like "Zar" was familiar to him, as were those of
Sanger and Yakir. "Are you related to Varian and Jana
Saar? To Galen and Amaya Saar?"

"I am their youngest daughter, a Star Fleet officer, a
member of our Elite and secret squad. Cypher-T is my

longtime partner. You could not access Bree-Kayah's file because the network computers were commanded to respond with my Starla Vedris identity. No record exists on Yana, and her voice print does not match mine. I have no fingerprints to expose me."

"How can you shapeshift into a woman so different from your real self?"

"Yakir provided the chemical for transformation; it lasts for twelve *horas* unless I use the antidote to return me to my form sooner. This is my true appearance," she told him as he studied her brown hair and green eyes and less voluptuous figure. "My image and voice pattern were programmed to respond only to queries about Starla Verdris in all data bases to prevent Tochar or his contacts from discovering who I am; at this time, all files on Bree-Kayah Saar are protected against retrieval by a special command cue. We didn't know a Maffeian traitor was working with him and would imperil me, After I reported my exposure to Thaine and Yakir and told them I would remain on the mission as Yana, Yakir told me an *I-GAF* agent had infiltrated Tochar's band, but he didn't know his chosen name or description. I took a chance—I hoped and prayed—it was you."

She was the daughter and sister of legends, not just in Maffei, but the past Tri-Galaxy, and now the entire UFG. "That's how Acharius recognized you."

"When Acharius saw me in the cave, he must have panicked because he tried to kill me. I dealt with him the only way left open to me. I tried to bluff it out with Tochar so I could save my mission, but he didn't believe my explanation." She related the cave episode in detail and how Acharius knew her. "I am not well-known as my family, so we didn't think I would be recognized this far from home. I wanted to disable Acharius, rather than slay him, but my weapon didn't have a setting to induce a coma to keep him silent about me. He was a traitor and criminal, and his sacrifice was necessary. I know his family and thought I knew him, so it was difficult."

"Is that what you did to Moig?"

"I did induce a coma after I questioned him with *Thorin;* that's how I learned about Syrkin and other things. But Tochar had Tochara's doctor murder him; I have the tape aboard my ship to prove it. Cypher-T logs everything I witness and he follows us on most of our treks to observe and record crimes."

"Since you didn't know who I was until last night, how did I fit into your plans? Why did you tempt me and use me as two different women?"

"I tried to ignore and resist you, Dagan, but you made that impossible by pursuing and tempting me. I'm sorry I was forced to deceive you. I wanted to confide in you, but I feared I was blinded by my feelings for you and couldn't make an accurate evaluation of you. How could I trust you when you kept passing Tochar's *Thorin* tests and you evoked raids on Sion and that medical supply ship and convinced me you were a *villite?* You also took me by surprise. I never expected to encounter a complication like you. I didn't know how to deal with that unfamiliar predicament. This is the first time I've allowed my emotions to sway me during a mission. After I got to know you, I was hoping to lure you away from your criminal life so we could share that future you offered. As Yana, I was appraising your true nature and character. I suppose, since you're an *I-GAF* agent on assignment, you were probably just using Starla to get close to Tochar and the others."

He smiled and shook his head. "You also caught me off-guard. I was wary about confiding in you, but I didn't lie to you about my feelings for Starla."

"You didn't?" she asked, afraid to trust her hearing or the look of honesty in his eyes.

"I was enduring the same agonizing dilemma you were because you were convincing as a *spaceki,* but I couldn't resist you. I kept trying to coax you away from Tochar and Noy so you'd be safe from incrimination and harm. Do you truly love me, Bree-Kayah Saar?"

"Yes, Dagan, with all my heart and soul. I was hoping there was a way I could save you so we could be together. I feared I couldn't entice Dagan Latu away from what I feared you were when you kept passing Tochar's tests and suggesting evil things. Yet, I sensed you were good inside and I could turn you."

Dagan pulled her into his arms. "I was right to pursue and tempt you because you are the perfect match for me. I love you with all my heart and soul, and we will have a future after this mission is over."

Their gazes locked and communicated feelings as they exchanged smiles and savored the wonder of their new relationship. Their eyes sparkled as if reflecting rays of moonbeams. They knew and accepted their fates and hearts were entwined, now and forever.

Dagan secured her in a cherished embrace, as if needing to convince himself Starla was alive and within his arms. His heart surged with love and relief. He brushed kisses over her forehead, the scent of her clean brown hair entering his nostrils. His lips traversed her exquisite cheekbones, the length of her slender nose, and the curve of her chin. He used a clean-shaved jawline to nuzzle her face, savoring the texture of her skin. He looked into her green eyes whose gaze was filled with undeniable emotions which matched his own potent ones. More talk could come later; for now, all he wanted to do was to hold her, to kiss her, to feel her heart beating next to his, to give thanks to the Supreme Being for the radical change in their destinies. *She's not out of your reach* kept racing through his head at lightning speed. Despite knowing that was true, he almost feared to believe it, as if accepting that reality would cause it to vanish.

"You can't imagine how scared I was about coming here to expose the truth to you. I don't know what I would have done if I'd been wrong about you." She laughed and jested, "I would have been forced to take you captive, transport you to my ship, and hold you prisoner. Naturally you would have been compelled to relent to my every whim." Her eyes brightened with radiant passion and everlasting love.

He cupped her beautiful face between his hands and noted the seductive gleam in her merry gaze. She was here, alive and safe. His responsive body flamed with desire. "With you as my captor, I would have made an excellent and obedient love slave."

"*Would* have made?" Bree-Kayah Saar echoed with a laugh and nibbled on his chin.

Dagan lifted her right hand and placed suckling kisses on each fingertip. He pressed its back to his lips for it to be covered; then swirled his tongue in her palm. His mouth trekked over her wrist, along her arm, past her shoulder, up her neck, and teased at her earlobe.

Bree swayed against him and mutely coaxed him to continue his sensuous course of action. Her fingers grazed his broad shoulders, the cords in his neck, and the bulges in his arms. His skin was cool to her touch, soft and supple flesh encased a rock-hard and strong frame. She closed her eyes and let her senses absorb every enthralling facet of him. She meshed her lips to his and clung to him. Victory was in sight.

Many times Dagan's tongue delved her mouth and savored her honeyed taste. His loins twitched with an earnest need to join with hers, but he didn't want to rush this heady reunion. His shaky hands untangled the tie at her waist. He removed the one-piece garment and cast it aside. They wriggled down her panties, exposing her every charm to his adoring gaze. He took off her sandals, then stood before her. He paused a moment to allow her to peel off his stretchy shirt before he brought their bare torsos into staggering contact. His mouth dropped kisses on her neck as it journeyed to one creamy breast to nibble there teasingly until his mouth fastened to the point and suckled it to taut attention.

Bree's hands roved his neck and stroked his black hair. Her insides quivered with anticipation and her body warmed with pleasure. She craved every sensation he evoked and enjoyed every emotion she experienced. She adored everything about him. Her senses were alive, yet, dazed. She was delighted, yet, tormented. *Pralu*, she loved him and craved him!

"If we don't lie down soon, Dagan, I'm going to melt into the floor," she gasped. "My legs are so weak and shaky I can hardly stand."

He chuckled and said, "I'm glad I'm not the only one who feels that way. Mercy, I love you and want you."

Dagan halted his loving siege to remove the rest of his garments and to relocate them to the *sleeper*. His provocative hand inched down her body and teased over her sleek thighs with sweeping and tantalizing strokes. He summoned everything he knew about lovemaking to give her supreme gratification. His mouth and hands explored her, evoking another hunger as soon as he fed the previous one.

Her stomach grew taut as his hands sought and found her secret haven and blissfully invaded it. She burned and yearned, using words and movements to plead for his deft caresses to continue. She reveled in the way his hands and lips made her feel primitive and rapacious. She relaxed and tensed simultaneously. His searing kisses and artful caresses sent all remnants of distracting reality fleeing. His adroit hand was clever and persistent as it pervaded her beckoning receptacle. Her hand captured his rigid manhood and stroked it from tip to base. The friction created enticed him to groan and squirm in need.

At her fervid encouragement, Dagan positioned himself between her thighs and entered her with one vital thrust. She was more beautiful than *Kimon,* the mythical Goddess of Love and Beauty. Her skin was as soft as *majee,* an expensive and luxurious material. Her taste was sweeter than *corvie,* an exotic and rare fruit. He had no doubt that he loved her.

Starla kneaded his firm buttocks. She lapped her ankles over his calves and held him in a snug grip. That marvelous and undeniable tension was building within her womanhood. Sheer rapture washed over her from head to feet. She felt weightless in space, as if spinning out of control. Never had she loved anyone more than this man. Never had she wanted anything more than she wanted this magnificent Kalfan. She surrendered totally to him and to the splendor of their new beginning, the sealing of their bond.

As her hands roved the rippling muscles of his back and he penetrated her over and over, she played havoc with his control, boldly and seductively threatening to steal it. As he entered her, she moved to receive him. As he retreated, she moaned at his loss and her uplifted hips quested for him. He was driven wild by the way her tongue danced with his and she rubbed her bosom against his chest, her nipples as hot as two tiny suns scorching his flesh. "Starla, my love, you're driving me crazy," he warned in delight, "shoving me dangerously close to the edge. *Kahala,* this is amazing."

Bree moaned and thrashed as she climbed the spiral. "Take me, Dagan, my beloved, now."

He increased his pace to a gentle savageness, his need and love for her so great and her responses so urgent he could barely restrain his ardor and prevent his release. "I love you, Starla. You're mine; at last you're truly mine, and I belong only to you."

His words and actions sent Bree falling over the crest of victory. Her cry of release was muffled by his mouth as she raided that delicious recess for countless kisses as ecstasy burst into full bloom.

Dagan's body shuddered from the force of a gigantic climax just as hers was ebbing. He labored with loving tenderness and waning stamina until their spasms ceased and they were slaked. Afterward, he could hardly catch his breath, and he noticed hers, too, was labored. He gazed into her flushed and damp face and saw wet strands of hair clinging to her forehead. He realized it was more than the glow of sated passion or the results of feverish exertions assailing them. The chamber was stuffy, oppressive, sultry. He was relieved they hadn't lost consciousness before he noticed the problem. "Computer, reactivate environmental control functions; bring them to normal as fast as possible. Sorry, my love," he said to Bree, "but in the excitement, I forgot about my previous order for the computer to shut them down in an *hora* unless I canceled it."

They took gulps of fresh and revitalizing air as it was sent flowing into the room and into their lungs. They relaxed as their bodies cooled and they reveled in the serene aftermath of the lofty experience.

"*Pralu,* Dagan, I thought you had shown me all of your skills but I was wrong. Your prowess is unlimited." She nestled against him in supreme contentment.

Their ardent lovemaking had surpassed all other encounters, and they knew it was because there were no secrets or hesitations or fears this time, only total surrender and complete trust. Their faith in each other was complete. Soon, they could make plans. For now, they relaxed and savored their commitment, and napped peacefully. They were blissfully unaware of what was happening beyond his chamber.

Chapter Sixteen

The next morning, the Kalfan left the cozy embrace of his lover with reluctance to respond to a signal from the *telecom*. He sat down and, to conceal the lower half of his naked body, slid the *seata* forward until his waist touched the table holding the unit. He pressed the initiation button. "Latu here."

"I wanted to know how you are doing."

"I'm with Yana," he said, and grinned at the *fiendal* whose image he viewed on the two-way visual system. Dagan knew his hair was mussed, his chest was bare, and his eyes revealed he'd just awakened. He knew his condition would evoke an advantageous assumption on the part of the *villite* leader. The Icarian would presume he had mentioned the female's presence to prevent Tochar from talking about Starla in Yana's presence and hopefully would presume, if he truly loved Starla and was aching over her betrayal, he would not be having sex with another female this soon. "Do you need me to dress and carry out a task?"

"Relax and enjoy yourself until tomorrow."

"Thanks, Tochar, but if you need me for anything, I'll come immediately."

"All is under control, Dagan, so do not worry."

"Have you resolved your annoying problem?" He decided it would be suspicious if he didn't make a query about Starla and thought himself clever to dupe Tochar by the way he worded it for alleged privacy.

"No, but I expect it to be eradicated soon. My men are working on it. I will inform you when that matter has been handled. Tochar out."

"Latu out." He fingercombed his hair as he pressed the termination button and chuckled.

"What is amusing? He's trying to hunt me down to slay me. Are you eager to be rid of me so soon?"

Dagan joined her on the *sleeper* and cuddled her in his embrace. "Never will I tire of you, my love, and he will never find you or harm you. Perhaps I forgot to tell you," he said amidst neck nibbles, "I am possessive and protective of my most precious treasure."

"You did, my handsome space pirate, as am I."

He rolled to his back, took a deep breath, and let it out slowly. "I'm the luckiest and happiest man alive now that I fully and forever have you."

She rested her head on his chest and listened to his heart beat faster as she said, "And I am the luckiest and happiest woman alive to have you forever."

Dagan stroked her tousled hair and basked in the radiance of their love. "We have a serious talk ahead of us, so why don't I get us some food from Radu before we begin? I have nothing to prepare and, yes, I know how to survive under primitive conditions. We missed our evening meal, and I'm ravenous. How about you?"

"Almost famished with hunger, but this time not for sex," she teased. "I need nourishment for strength."

"After we eat and talk, my tasty treat, I'll see what I can do about your lagging appetite in that area."

"Sounds perfect. Should we stay in Yana's dwelling where Cypher-T can send us food from my *servo* unit? That way we won't have to starve or go out for food."

"What I want is you aboard your cloaked ship and out of harm's reach. But," he added when she started to protest, "we'll discuss that later. I'll return soon." He took a quick shower, dressed, and left his chamber.

She retrieved her neck ring and spoke close to the *gem* with a transmitter inside. "I was right, Cypher; he is a man worthy of my trust and love. I'll contact you when I am ready to transport to the ship to make my report to

309

Thaine. First, Dagan and I must talk about us and our mission. We have much to learn about each other and many plans to make. Prepare him a disguised device for communicating with us aboard the *Liska* when we are separated. He must have a way to request a rescue from us if peril strikes. I love him and need him, my friend. Help me protect him, which will also safeguard our joint mission. Starla, out." She laughed and said, "I think we can use my real name now. Bree, out."

Energized by exquisite love, she was stimulated by suspenseful anticipation about teaming up with Dagan to defeat the *UFG's* worst enemy. She left the *sleeper* to bathe in a primitive shower which used running water and a bar of soap, unlike the automated cleansing unit aboard her ship and everywhere in her advanced world. She used an extra toothbrush and paste from a tube to refresh her mouth since she lacked a bottle of self-cleansing liquid. After she dried off, she donned her garments and neck ring and brushed her hair. She touched the pouch suspended from her belt to make certain she had another phial of transmutation chemical if needed. She decided she should contact Cypher and tell him to transport a container down with extra clothes, grooming aides, and another set of phials— the shapeshifting agent and its counteragent. But she didn't have time to carry out that task because Dagan returned with their food, and they sat down to eat.

After they finished their meal and disposed of its debris, they remained at the table. Their hands were clasped across its surface and their gazes fused. Dagan asked her to tell him everything about herself.

Necessary or not, so he would grasp her rank, she explained, "The Maffei Galaxy is comprised of thirteen planets and numerous planetoids. It's governed by the Supreme Council of three men: our ruler—the *Kadim*—and two other members, men who are all-powerful and who make our laws. An Alliance Assembly of sixteen men—the Supreme Council and thirteen *Avatars,* planetary leaders—carry out those laws. On each planet, *Zartiffs* supervise appointed regions. Our highest form of military is Star Fleet, based on the capital planet of Rigel. It is accountable to the Assembly, as are the ground units in the Alliance Force. The Elite Squad, a covert unit of special agents, of which I'm a member, answers to the Supreme Council and we work under the leadership of Thaine Sanger, who commands Star Fleet. Our most powerful weapons, drugs, and chemicals are creations of and produced by Trilabs, an inaccessible complex on the planetoid Darkar which orbits Caguas, where Acharius Faeroe's father is the *Avatar.* Trilabs is one of the prizes Tochar craves. Most of these facts you already know as an *I-GAF* agent. You are powerful men who roam the five allied galaxies. You are accountable first to your superior, then only to the rulers of the five galaxies in the United Federation."

Bree took a sip of liquid. "Just as I know, the Kalfa Galaxy consisted of ten planets and many planetoids. Gavas is your capital and Orr possesses moonbeam mines. Your galactic ruler is the *Autorie;* your space force is a unit of Rangers called *Sekis.* As with my world, Kalfa has planetary and regional leaders. You outrank me in every way with the badge you carry. I am proud and honored to share a mission with you."

Dagan smiled and squeezed her hands in gratitude and love. "Tell me everything about yourself, my love, about your personally," he stressed with great interest as he guided them to the *seata*. He settled himself beside her to listen and observe.

"I am Bree-Kayah Saar. I'm called Bree by family and friends. I'm twenty-two *yings* old by my father's timing but twenty-four years by my mother's. I'm sixty-nine *hapaxs* tall and I weigh one-thirty *pedis*. You can see that my hair is brown and my eyes are green. I'm the youngest child of Varian and Jana Saar. Both are retired and live on our family's private planetoid Altair which orbits Rigel. I have a brother and sister who are twins, forty-eight *yings* old. I was an unexpected and unplanned baby, so it is good Maffei no longer practices population control, as it once did."

She returned to where she left off before her humorous inclusions, "Galen is on the Supreme Council and is mated to Rayna who helps my sister run the research labs on Altair. They have three children, a boy and twin girls. My sister is bonded to Jason; he's in charge of Star Base Security on Rigel; he's a full-blooded Earthling like my mother. Amaya is a retired Elite Squad member; they have two children—twins. My mother is a renowned scientist; she's retired but still dabbles in research. She's a wonderful, strong, generous, beautiful woman who's done many important things for our world, including saving our people when a lethal alien virus attacked there before my birth. So has my father," Bree admitted without boasting.

Dagan saw her eyes glow with love, pride, and respect. Her stirring words caused him to miss and grieve over his lost parents and siblings.

"Father was a Star Fleet commander with his own starship for many *yings*. Later, he served as the Supreme Commander of Star Fleet, the Alliance Force, and Elite Squad—and was an ex-member of that unit. He saved our world many times from intergalactic and internal threats to Maffei and the TriGalaxy before the United Federation of Galaxies was created. He is a unique and special man. I am proud to be his daughter and to follow in his footsteps."

Dagan remarked, "Your great-grandfather was a past *Kadim*, a legendary ruler. I have read and heard much about him. I am curious: How did your parents meet, since she is from the distant Milky Way Galaxy and we have no contact with them?"

Bree knew the story of how her mother had been captured from her planet and brought to Maffei long ago to become a *charl*, a captive mate for reproductive purposes when most Maffeian females were sterile, a practice her parents helped eliminate. Her parents had fallen in love at first sight, but her father had been unable to bond with Jana Greyson for many reasons. That part of their story could remain withheld until after Dagan got to know them, so it would not affect his opinion of her father, a man entrapped by a cruel destiny which was altered later. "After my mother came to Maffei, she was tricked into uniting with Ryker Triloni, my father's half-brother, grandson of the past ruler of the Androas Galaxy, and a matchless genius in science. After his accidental death, she inherited Trilabs. Mother felt it was too powerful and important for one person to own and control so she turned it over to our government when she bonded with my father, almost forty-nine *yings* ago. My father was and is her only love. They taught me what true love is, and that is why I waited for the right man to enter my life."

She smiled, kissed his cheek, and continued, "My superior is Supreme Commander Thaine Sanger. He is also my brother's best friend since childhood, as were our fathers since their childhood and while serving in Star Fleet together. I went through training fast because my family had taught me so much before I entered the academy after being born and reared on Altair. After I scored so high in all areas, I was assigned to the Elite Squad where I trained in near seclusion with others. I've been a member for almost two *yings* and carried out two distant missions. Since the Squad works in secret and my face isn't well-known, *Raz* Yakir and Thaine selected me for this mission. They assumed a young female agent would be less suspicious than a male or older woman. *Raz* Yakir supplied the transmutation phials, my Starla Vedris record, and my means of making contact with Tochar. The crew of that pursuit craft were advanced androids that were programmed to look, act, and talk as if they were humans so Tochar would believe I possessed a dark heart and violent nature like him and his men."

She explained how she contacted her superior and the Serian ruler via an untraceable frequency, how she obtained needed data from network computers from them, how Yakir surreptitiously entered the clues and facts she gathered, and how she had received Cypher. She revealed Yakir's motives for sending her and for not telling Phaedrig about her presence. She reminded him Acharius was the son of the Cagaus *Avatar* and told him how they knew each other. "I hope my parents, friends, and his family will understand and forgive me for what I was forced to do to protect our galaxy and others."

He grasped her hand and gave it a comforting and gentle squeeze. "I'm certain they will, Starla. Or I should say, Bree-Kayah or Bree."

"We should not use our real names in private or we could make a slip when Dagan and Yana are in public. Now, tell me everything about you, my beloved. What is your real name?"

"I agree we should stick to Dagan and Yana even alone to avoid slips. I am Curran Thaiter. Born, reared and trained on the capital planet of Gavas in Kalfa. I am twenty-eight *yings* old. I am seventy-five *hapaxs* tall and weigh two-twenty *pedis*. My hair is the shade of our sun and moon. My eyes are kyanite. I normally have a small pit in each cheek and a cleft in the center of my chin." He watched her try to imagine how he looked in natural colorings of a perfect blend of blue and green eyes, light golden hair, and dimples when he smiled.

He found her study and expression so arousing, he hurried on with revelations before he was compelled to halt and make love to her. "My family was slain during a crime *yings* ago, but I'll relate that bitter story after I complete my history. I was a *Seki* for many *yings* before Phaedrig asked me to join *I-GAF*. I use many disguises and identities during my assignments. When I'm not on a particular mission, I partly live, work, and appear as Dagan Latu to keep that identity established for other missions. Dauld Phaedrig is my superior and I answer only to him and the five UFG rulers."

He wasn't sure of how much she knew about *I-GAF*, so he skimmed that subject to enlighten or refresh her. "Agents work alone, or in small teams, or in large units according to the crime we're solving or *nefariants* we're seeking. We can go anywhere in the *UFG* and no one can interfere with our methods. We cannot be questioned, reprimanded, or punished for them. Our assignments are requested by rulers or planetary leaders, but how we resolve the trouble is up to us. It's rare for an agent to have contact with rulers or leaders during a task. Phaedrig selects the agent or team to carry out a mission, and no agent has been disloyal, disobedient, or been terminated for a crime or incompetence. If one went bad, he would be hunted and eradicated by *I-GAF* alone. When an agent retires, crucial facts about *I-GAF* are erased from his memory. Although *Rendelar* prevents susceptibility to truth serum, elderly men with weakened bodies might not be able to resist revealing secrets during a torture session. As you know, *Rendelar* and *Thorin* are creations of Ryker Triloni and their formulas are known only by Trilabs. As with all Trilabs formulas, any attempt to analyze them results in initiating a self-destruct sequence. He was indeed a rare but evil genius. The chemicals and dyes used for our tattoos have similar self-destruct tags in them."

He turned his body sideways to face her as he continued, and she did the same to listen. "Phaedrig has access to all known computer networks and he inserts the data needed for mission identities. There is one system which cannot be used except by Phaedrig, *I-GAF* agents, and UFG rulers; that is the one which contains our assignment records, so they are safeguarded against traitor encroachment. All other networks have a cue inserted which alerts Phaedrig when one of his agents is investigated, but Yakir was too clever and fast to be traced when he checked on me. We carry no credentials to be found, and our hand insignias are made visible only by us when needed." He related the description of *I-GAF* headquarters and told her it was on a barren planetoid in Kalfa, but did not disclose its location.

"Back to my family," he said with a grimace. "I was on a *Seki* assignment *yings* ago when *villites* faked a chemical hazard in the area where my family lived on Gavas. Inhabitants were to gather their most valuable possessions and flee in supplied crafts, and told they couldn't return home until the contamination cleared away. During the evacuation procedure, *spacekis* attacked two rescue vessels carrying the wealthiest and most prominent citizens. Everyone was robbed and murdered, including my family and many of my friends. Those vicious *nefariants* took away my parents, my sister and her family, and my two brothers and one's family. Those monsters killed young and old, male and female, by blowing up the vessels after raiding them. When the *villites* proved to be elusive, I resigned as a *Seki* to work full-time to use my wits, skills, and energy to track down those responsible: Tochar and his band. The *fiendal* thought he had eliminated all witnesses and evidence, but he failed to notice a surveillance monitor at the boarding point. That's why he's adamant about their destruction during our raids."

"Tochar and his band murdered your family and others…" she repeated in horror. "He's worse than I imagined. You must hate him terribly."

He nodded. "I was able to capture or terminate all of them except for Tochar, Auken, Sach, and Moig; but their faces and names were seared into my memory. I realized I needed more power and a source of data, so I when back to being a Seki. For a strange reason, they always managed to evade me. I suspected my superior was involved in the *fiendal's* good luck; that would explain why the case was impeded, why clues I gathered were lost or ignored or dismissed, and why I was ordered to abandon my 'futile obsession' and assigned to another investigation. My suspicions compelled me to resign to work on my own. My prowess and persistence had seized the attention of *I-GAF*; that's why I was asked to join the Force. I needed distraction from my losses. I needed to have stimulating adventures and challenges to keep me going and to sharpen my wits and skills. I also believed it would get me within range of Tochar. My appearance was changed to conceal my identity, and Curran Thaiter was reported slain. Phaedrig inserted a fake record about Dagan Latu, and I created a dark reputation for him as an adventurer, *bijoni,* and dashing rogue who barely eluded arrest numerous times for shady incidents. Dagan is said to live for pleasure, money, and excitement, and is fiercely loyal to his leader. Perhaps you'll understand my suspicions about my past *Seki* superior when I tell you it was Syrkin." He noted her reaction and said, "That's right, the same Syrkin involved in this mission. He was probably Tochar's accomplice for *yings.* At least he's been dealt with by now and is off my mental list. When this trouble came up, Phaedrig assigned me, even knowing my past connections to the *fiendals* and my hunger for revenge, for justice. He was confident I wouldn't allow personal feelings to sway my judgment and behavior, and I couldn't be recognized as Curran."

She gave his hand a comforting squeeze. "That's horrible, Dagan. We'll punish them for slaying your family and prevent them from doing more evil."

"We'll do our best, my love. Now tell me, how did you destroy those stolen crystals? That is what you told me while you were Yana, right?"

She nodded, then explained what she had done and why that same procedure would not work against the *Destructoids,* how getting near them was impossible, lethal for one person to attempt. She listened as he related the reason for suggesting the raid at Sion, for coaxing Auken to attack the medical supply vessel, and for repairing Tochar's ship: tricks to evoke trust in him and to lure Tochar off Noy and into a trap. She revealed all she had learned and all she had done since starting her assignment. Curran told her what he planned to report to Phaedrig about her: the truth.

Bree reasoned, "He'll be angry with *Raz* Yakir, Thaine, and me for our secrecy."

"Miffed for a while perhaps. But he's intelligent, and victory is what matters. He'll understand and forgive their little deception."

"Will he resist Yana helping you defeat Tochar?" she asked. "Will he order me to leave? If he does, do I have to obey him?"

"How can he resist after all you've accomplished and with the skills you possess? You're as qualified on this matter as I am, more so, since you're the one who's gathered all the useful facts and thwarted Tochar in many ways. But if he did order you to leave, you would be forced to obey."

"Forced?" she echoed. "How so?"

"By insisting your superior recall you, and Sanger would have to comply."

"I'm not deserting you in the face of danger. If they attempt to order me away, I will resign and they'll have no authority over my actions."

Curran shook his head. "Even a private citizen must submit to *I-GAF* requests and commands; it is UFG law. Phaedrig would have your *Kadim* summon you home or you'd face arrest. Since your ruler is no longer a family member, he would honor Phaedrig's request."

"But my brother is on the Supreme Council; Galen would help me."

"Would you risk dishonoring yourself, the Saars, your superior, and your ruler for selfish reasons? If I'm left alone, I'll be fine; I promise."

"I know you're highly skilled and experienced, Dagan, but Tochar is evil incarnate. He is invincible at this point. You will be trapped here without me and my ship to supply an emergency escape if needed. I can provide safe communications and other things you might require in your task. If you're... slain, this mission will be defeated instead of Tochar. At least Yana can be here to take over, perhaps help another agent infiltrate his band. How is that being selfish? What will Yakir say if I am tossed off this assignment or arrested? He is one of the five leaders of UFG."

"Your reasoning is superior, my love, and I will repeat it to Phaedrig. After all you've done, I doubt he will ask you to leave. As for me, I wish you would depart, but I'm certain I cannot convince you to do so." He chuckled as he stood. "We have been doing so much talking, we need to wet our throats," he said, as he entered the other area to pour them a drink.

Bree watched him with an adoring gaze. She was elated that her lover was a man she could introduce to her family and friends. He deserved respect, admiration, and acceptance. There was no problem with him being Kalfan, a race compatible in biological and physiological areas, and comparable in appearances. It would not matter to them that her social status was higher than his, or that his authoritative rank was higher than hers. Though her family's wealth was enormous and her bloodline's achievements were legendary in the *UFG*, that would not make a difference to her or to her family or to a confident male like Curran Thaiter.

After he joined her on the *seata*, she told him, "The Saars will become your family. The only two things that will concern them are if you love me and are worthy of me; both are true, pirate of my heart. We'll have a wonderful future as mates. We can work together, or retire and do something new and different."

"We'll make our choices and plans later, after we defeat Tochar and get away from this awful place."

"What if we can't defeat him since he has those *Destructoids?*" The thought preyed on her mind.

"We'll eliminate him and those weapons. We have your ship for communications and escape if necessary, and Cypher for assistance and protection. With the three of us teamed up, how can we fail?"

"We'll make mission plans later. You'll be leaving soon with Auken and Sach and we'll be separated for a long time. Cypher and I will shadow you while cloaked to protect you and record evidence. He will make you a disk to wear on your belt so we can hear everything said and you can request help if needed. At least I'll be able to hear your voice and be there if needed. Right now," she murmured as she imagined his blond hair, kyanite eyes, dimples, and cleft chin, "I want you and need you to fill my storage bays for a long haul since you'll be unable to supply me with daily nourishment."

At that stimulating hint, flames of desire leapt through Curran's body and flickered brightly in his gaze. As Bree pressed close to him, it was as if he could detect a tangible matching blaze of fiery passion within her. He wanted, needed, and loved her so much that his potent emotions almost stole his breath. He followed her to the *sleeper* and paused beside it. He didn't assist when she undressed him first, then stripped off her garments. He was enspelled by the way her mouth made several sensuous and erotic treks over his face and chest. Her questing and experienced fingers and mouth had him squirming and moaning in exquisite delight as she tantalized, pleasured, and sated him in one way, only to reheat and cool him again in another.

He had not realized he could become aroused and slaked so many times in this period. He was enchanted by her provocative and generous actions. He pulled her body into place atop his so he could kiss her and reward her in like kind for the *hora* of rapture. His fingers kneaded her soft but firm buttocks. His mouth drifted down her neck, nibbled at her collarbone, and fastened to one of the smoldering peaks which dangled down and enticed him to capture and traverse it.

Bree was elated to be in his arms. Joy filled her as he heightened her hungers. She pushed aside thoughts and worries about the perils looming before them. All she wanted to know and feel was the effulgence of this occasion and this man. Musky scents teased at her nostrils, increasing her eagerness to have him. She was rolled to her back to give him freedom to roam her body from end to end, and to explore every beckoning region between those two locations. Tantalized into a near mindless state, she squiggled upon the firm surface beneath her as he drove her giddy with anticipation, then gave her sweet release in several ways.

Curran Thaiter received ineffable pleasure at each passionate encounter, whether he or she was the target of action. Although each union slaked him, he couldn't get enough of her. He always wanted, needed, craved more. His feelings and needs went beyond sexual ones. He loved her with all his heart and being. She filled his life in so many areas. She was unique, magical. She was his, now and beyond eternity.

Bree writhed and moaned as his titillating tongue caused colorful lights to dance before her closed eyes as ecstasy shook her to her core. She could not imagine her life without him, on and off a *sleeper*. He stirred her blood and wits and emotions. When he entered her welcoming body, her legs enclosed his hips and held him clamped against her. His kisses were pervasive, delicious, and ardent. Surely she would perish without him to give her love, passion, and happiness.

Curran relished the way she imprisoned him within her arms and legs, her mouth feverishly working upon his. When she reached the brink of release, he thrust rapidly to help push her over that precipice. Moments after she arched her back and sighed in transcendent fulfillment, his body erupted in a molten frenzy that resulted in his own transcendent appeasement.

With sweet triumph obtained, they cuddled and kissed, serene and exhausted. Yet, each worried about the other's safety and survival. Each knew within reach was the one person who could fulfill yearnings and a golden destiny. Beyond this cozy chamber was the one threat who could tear them apart forever, who could evoke dark chaos across the Universe.

Curran feared she wasn't safe without him or with him, as Tochar's unknown sources could track her down wherever she went and slay her. The *fiendal* he wanted to defeat was responsible for the deaths of his family and for many other innocents. If he wasn't cautious and smarter, that evil force could take from him his new-found love and joy. How could he protect her if she remained at his side, he fretted, even as Yana? Yet, where could he hide her from Tochar, who might have another contact in Kalfa and/or Maffei? What would he have to say and/or do to force her to leave if matters worsened when she was determined to stay?

Bree's troubled thoughts journeyed along a similar course: if Tochar discovered who Dagan was, her love would be tortured and killed, or torn to pieces and devoured by Skalds. She and Cypher must protect him, must help him carry out this vital mission. She wished there were no such things as Tochar, moonbeams, and perilous missions; but all three existed.

For the remainder of that *deega,* they talked, made love, ate a late meal, and fell asleep nestled together.

The following morning, "Dagan" was summoned by Tochar to do a task for him with Auken and Sach, saying only one *deega* was required and he would return to

Yana's side by dusk. Before he left his chamber, he insisted she shapeshift into Yana and remain there during his absence. He observed the transformation in amazement, and was relieved the process was not painful. As he embraced her and brushed his lips over hers, he murmured, "I feel deceitful kissing and hugging Yana, though it is you within her. This is a strange experience and it near dazes my wits."

She laughed as she viewed his playful expression and jested, "Perhaps I should welcome you back tonight with this sexy body. Yana is more endowed than I am," she said, as she rubbed her larger breasts against him. "With this magical secret, you can have two eager women as your love slaves."

Curran chuckled and caressed her cheek. "I only have enough stamina to sate one, as my prized treasure is most demanding and greedy."

"Your mating appetite will increase greatly if I splash on that irresistible scent," she murmured in a seductive tone and kissed his chin. She was eager to see him in his true form, and to call him *Cure'ran'*.

"As beautiful as you are as Yana, my Starla tempts, arouses, and sates me as no other female can. She is the one who captured my heart and enflames my body. If I don't leave fast, I may be compelled to overlook this Asisan image and be late meeting the others."

The disguised Bree watched her lover leave and stepped backward for the door to close. Earlier she had shared a long and sensuous shower with him and dressed when he did. She reminded herself she needed to signal Cypher to teleport items to her, including a meal so she would not have to leave his chamber. She started to retrieve her neck ring from the privacy room where she'd left it so sounds of passionate lovemaking would not singe the android's "ears," though she had forgotten about its presence earlier when fiery passion stole their wits in the bathing cubicle.

When the exterior door swished open, she halted and turned expecting to see her beloved returning to retrieve a forgotten item. Instead, two of Tochar's Enforcers entered. She tensed in alarm. "What do you want here? Dagan has left."

"Tochar wishes to speak with you," one said. "Come with us. Do not resist or refuse," he warned.

Yana stared at the black-clad men and tried to come up with a plan. "I do not understand. I—"

A low-energy beam stunned Yana into silence and darkness, too fast to defend herself.

When she awakened, she was strapped to the oblong table in the testing room at Tochar's dwelling and *the fiendal* was leaning over her imprisoned body. Without the transmitter in her neck ring, she could not alert Cypher to her peril, and—with it hanging in the bath chamber—he was ignorant of the wicked aspects of her abduction. She hoped Tochar did not keep her there for more than ten *horas,* as surely that was the span of time remaining in her transmutation scheduled...

Tochar stroked her hair and said, "Do not worry or be afraid, Yana; I only want to ask you a few questions; then I will release you."

"What questions do you wish to ask?" She watched Tochar place an *Airosyringe* to her arm and eject *Thorin* into her body. "What was that?"

Dark eyes locked on her expression, one that revealed confusion, not terror. "A harmless serum to entice you to speak only the truth."

She was prepared with a persuasive story, one records in Asisa would confirm if checked. Still, Yana must appear greatly distressed to dupe him. "You have no right to do this; my secrets are mine alone."

"This settlement belongs to me, Yana, so I have that right. Relax, let the serum take effect, and this will be over soon. If you lie or resist, pain will be excruciating, so please be honest and compliant."

"Does Dagan know you are doing this to me?"

"I will enlighten him at the proper time. Now, relax and sleep. Be honest and you are safe."

As she pretended to surrender to the *Thorin,* she fumed over her reckless capture. She had forgotten to ask Curran to enter her voice in the computer system so she could order the door sealed during his absence. It was apparent the Enforcers had gotten an entry card from Radu, who owned the rental abodes. She surmised that "Dagan Latu" had been lured away so Tochar could ensnare and interrogate Yana. Considering what her lover had revealed to her about this *fiendal,* she knew his evil far exceeded her previous beliefs. She could not imagine what the cruel and perverted Icarian might do to the ravishing Yana while she was unconscious or how she could prevent anything in her helpless condition.

Tochar could ravish, torture, slay, and dispose of her body without Curran's or Cypher's knowledge...

Chapter Seventeen

"Can you hear me, Yana?" Tochar asked later.

"Yes." When he parted her lids to check her eyes, she forced them to de-focus and appear glazed. She felt the heat of a flush on her cheeks, this time from anxiety instead of a chemical aide. With luck and training, she hoped she could dupe the *fiendal*. If he ever got his hands on Trilabs, he would have access to *Rendelar* and to the only chemical which could penetrate its power to resist *Thorin*. She must not let that happen or her world and others would be in grave peril. No UFG ruler or agent would be able to prevent mental probings. If Tochar got control of Trilabs, no secret would be safe from his discovery. As long as he didn't attack Darkar's defenses with a *Destructoid*, it was invincible.

The sadistic man asked, "Will you answer my questions with total honesty?"

"Yes," she said in a softened and slowed tone.

"Why do you spend time with Dagan Latu?"

"I desire him. He is handsome, virile, fun—"

"That is sufficient. Does Dagan love you?"

"I do not think so."

"Who does Dagan love and desire?"

Be careful and clever, Bree. Do not endanger this mission. "I fear it is Starla Vedris."

"How does Dagan feel about her treachery?"

"She betrayed and hurt him. Crushed his pride. She humiliated him. He is angry. He will not forgive her. He does not understand why she defied Tochar. He—"

"Did Dagan tell you those things?"

"No."

"Explain."

"I made conclusions from his expressions. He does not talk about her; it makes him angry."

"Will Dagan help Starla elude Tochar?"

"I do not think so. He is loyal to Tochar and angry with her. He trusts his leader."

"Why did Dagan turn to you for comfort so soon after Starla deserted him?"

"I think it is to appease his pain. To shove her from his heart and thoughts. For sex. For companionship. For—" She was pleased he interrupted her after she had given enough reasons to satisfy him.

"Has Dagan ever done or said anything to make you suspect he will betray Tochar in any circumstance?"

"No."

"Why were you afraid for me to question you?"

"I have secrets to protect. My life is in jeopardy."

"What secrets? Tell me who you are and why you are here. Explain in detail."

"I am Mayoleesee Bargivi of Crepal in the Asisa Galaxy. I was reported missing. The mate of my sister tried to slay me so she will inherit our family's wealth, power, and status which belong to me by birthright. I came to Tochara to hide until he is slain. I hired a *bijoni* to kill him, but he surrounds himself with guards and cannot be reached at this time. Until he is dead and his threat is gone, I cannot return home. I am certain he has hired men to search for me and slay me. They will not look on Noy. They will believe it is too distant and primitive and I had no way to get here."

"How did you travel to Noy?"

"I disguised myself and paid a trader to bring me here. I killed him after my arrival so he cannot reveal my location for payment."

He barraged her with questions. "How did you meet Dagan? Why did you couple with him? Where do you habitate? Who are your friends? How do you spend your time? Answer each and give details."

She related how and when Yana met Dagan, that he and Radu were her only friends in the settlement, how Yana allegedly spent her time, and the location of the unit she rented from Radu. "When I met Dagan Latu, I believed he is a man who can protect me if danger approaches. I seduced him to draw him close to me. He met Starla Vedris and discarded me. I pursued him again when I heard she is in trouble and missing. I am taking advantage of his anguish and loss. He is a good and generous lover. I will ask him to return to Crepal with me and become my mate, so he can protect me. I will offer him wealth, power, status, and safety."

"Will Dagan accept your enticing offer?"

"I do not think so. He is proud. He is an adventurer, a loner. He does not love me and will not desire to become a mate. I will use him until I depart."

"But you still intend to ask him?"

"Yes."

"Why?"

"It will give him comfort and restore his pride to know he is desired by another woman."

"Do you know Starla Vedris?"

"Only by sight and reputation. I observed her a few times when she was at the Skull's Den or walking in the settlement. I heard her speaking with Radu and others there. We have never talked or been introduced."

"Rest while I decide if I have more questions."

She heard him leave, and prayed he would believe her tale and release her soon. If not, she was in deep trouble when she transformed before his piercing black eyes or when he returned and found Starla Vedris strapped to the table. Curran would be imperiled by that incredible discovery. Perhaps Tochar had gone to seek verification of Yana's claims. She knew he would receive it, as the real Asisan beauty had been found injured and abandoned on a barren planetoid in the Serian Galaxy. Mayoleesee had revealed her heart-gripping story to *Raz* Yakir before she died. Yakir had told no one about the woman so he could use her tragic tale, and hoped that wasn't insensitive of him.

As the *horas* passed, Yana knew that Tochar was aware the *Thorin* had worn off long before this time. She couldn't imagine why the *fiendal* didn't return to check on her while he awaited a response to his query. It was strange that the reply was taking this long, if indeed it was. Surely Yakir had not confided the truth about Yana to the wrong person, to Tochar's accomplice!

She wondered if Curran had returned and found her missing. Even so, her beloved would think she had gone to her ship or to Yana's dwelling, and there was no way he could communicate with the *Liska*. And Cypher, if his program allowed it, he must be worried about not hearing from her by now. Then there was Thaine and Yakir, who had not received a report from her since she started her task as Yana; they must be concerned. The dark reality was that Tochar could get rid of her and no one would know what had happened to her.

At last, the door opened and two men entered the room: Tochar and "Dagan". The Kalfan approached the table and released her. With his back to the *fiendal,* Dagan gave her a wink to indicate everything was all right. For their target's ears, he said, "I'm sorry if this matter upset you or frightened you, Yana, but Tochar thought it was imperative to check you out since you're close to me and I'm close to him. You did fine, so we can leave now."

She caught his hints and played along with his ruse. "I was captive here for a long time, so I was afraid. I feared I might be sold to my enemy after my identity and problem were discovered."

"Do not worry, Yana, your secrets are safe with us," Tochar added. "Dagan will make certain no one and nothing harms you. If anyone threatens you, contact me or any of my Enforcers for help."

"That is very kind and generous," she murmured as she glanced at the now smiling Tochar.

"Dagan is a friend, so I must assist and protect those close to him."

"Thanks," the Kalfan said. "I appreciate it."

After they exchanged farewells, Dagan and Yana left the lofty location via the *trans-to.* While walking to their transportation unit, he whispered a warning for her to be cautious with her words in case a listening device was planted on her or in the vehicle, as he knew one was concealed in the lifter.

After they were seated in a landrover, she cuddled against his side, certain Tochar was watching them; the potent and evil gaze upon her surely must be his. For the *fiendal*'s ears, as she was positive he was listening to them, she said, "I was terrified when Tochar's men invaded your chamber and abducted me only a few *preons* after your departure. It is fortunate for me I was dressed, for they did not ask permission to enter. They stunned me with an energy beam. When I awoke, I was imprisoned to that table. I do not know what he asked me. Did he reveal my answers to you?"

Curran grasped her ploy and played along. "Yes, he told me who you are and why you're hiding here."

"I am sorry I duped you. Now that you know the truth, does it anger or disappoint you?"

"Of course not, Yana, but you should have confided in me. I can't help you if I don't know the truth."

"I'm sorry; I realize how strongly you must detest lies and tricks. I wanted to trust you, but I feared for my survival, and you turned from me for a while. I will be honest with you from this *deega* forth."

"Excellent, because I don't want contact with another deceitful woman. It's obvious that I picked the wrong female when I leaned toward Starla instead of you. She fooled all of us but forget about her; I will. If you don't mind, I'll continue to call you Yana. Your real name is long and hard to pronounce, and it could imperil you if overheard by the wrong ears."

"That is fine, and your caution is wise."

"Don't worry about Tochar endangering you. He knows we're close, so he won't sell you to your enemy. He's a good leader and he wants his men to be happy and satisfied."

"Do I give you joy and appeasement?"

"Any man would be lucky to have you."

"It pleases me to hear those comforting words. I will do anything for you."

"Thanks, Yana."

They kept quiet for the remainder of their ride.

As they entered Dagan's chamber, he gestured for caution until he checked the place for security with a concealed detection device. To mask their actions, he said, "After you refresh yourself, pour us a drink so we can relax before our meal."

When he was certain it was safe to speak and behave freely, Curran seized his lover almost roughly in his distress over her close call with exposure and death. He covered her face with kisses and embraced her with relief, joy, and love. "What if you had transmuted into Starla while he was holding you captive or if *Thorin* had an adverse effect on that shapeshifting chemical? I could have lost you, woman."

She clasped his handsome face between her hands and fused their gazes. "It was scary, but I'm fine. I have three *horas* to go before I alter."

"What if he had asked us to stay and eat with him or he had probed you longer? That was close; we can't allow it to happen again. I love you and need you, Bree, so I beg you to remove yourself from this peril."

"What do you mean?"

"You have to leave Tochara. Tonight."

"No. You will be alone, vulnerable."

"I'm in greater peril with you here because I worry about you and that's distracting. Besides, Tochar will become suspicious if I start acting crazy about Yana so soon after losing Starla. I might do so because I know it is you beneath her facade."

"I cannot leave you. If you ask your superior to force me away, I will feel betrayed and angry."

"You win, but stay where you're safe except when and if Yana has to make an appearance to continue our ruse. I have to concentrate on our enemy or I can endanger both of us and prolong this mission."

"I understand your dilemma, so I'll stay on the ship if you insist, but I'm not leaving orbit when you might need to escape fast."

He covered her mouth with his and kissed her tenderly, the compromise acceptable. "Now, tell me what happened this morning."

"Let me speak to Cypher and assuage his concerns about me. I've been out of touch too long."

She fetched her neck ring and contacted Cypher. She apologized and told him she would be returning to the ship later tonight and would update him on the events that had occurred. She told him to send down the communication device he had constructed for Dagan and another set of phials in case she needed them before her return.

After Cypher complied with her requests and she showed Curran how the device worked, she completed her revelations about this mornings' events.

Curran related his arrival at Tochar's and the shocking discovery he had made about Yana being there. "It was a struggle to conceal my panic and fear, but I told him it was fine with me to test you; however, he could have asked me to bring you in for questioning. He said it was done in secret so you wouldn't be alerted to his plans and attempt an escape if you had anything to hide. He said he needed to check you out for both our sakes and safety, but I'm certain he was concerned only about his. He played the recording of your session, and you were excellent, my love."

"Thanks." She disclosed that most of her tale about Mayoleesee was true. "I'm sure he checked it out and that's why he believed me and released me. Did he ask you how you feel about Yana?"

"I think I convinced him my only interest in you is sex. I joked I'm getting as much pleasure from you as I can before my next trek, but have no interest in leaving with you or becoming your mate. He appeared to be satisfied with my answers."

"Where did you go with Auken and Sach?"

"Into the wasteland to meet a *spaceki's* shuttle. It was a man named Koi from the Ceyxan galaxy. He had a load of high-tech chips and memory boards to sell to Tochar. We delivered the payment, collected the cargo, and stored it in that cave where you had trouble."

"If we decide to take that haul off Tochar's hands, I have the coordinates recorded in my ship's system."

"I don't think that's a wise idea. Tochar placed a heavy guard on all of his caves and the two defense sites. We can't risk getting caught around or inside any of them. He even had us install battery-operated motion detectors to sound an alarm if intruders encroached. I know how to bypass and disarm the sensors, but that would look suspicious since only Tochar, Auken, Sach, me, and the Enforcers know about them."

"You're right; it is too dangerous. We'll let him keep them for now."

He chuckled. "That's very kind of you. I'm sure Tochar will be appreciative of your generosity."

"What's next for us to do?"

"Tochar said the team might be leaving in two *deegas* for a raid, but he didn't reveal the target or destination. He said he'd know by tomorrow. That means we'll be parted soon for a long time."

Her gaze locked with his. She missed him already. "I need to feel you next to me. Life can end without warning if we aren't careful. Make love to me before I have to leave you."

"I feel the same. I need for our bodies to be united as one. Will you change into yourself? I need to fuse with the real you before you leave my side."

She smiled and nodded, then sipped from the appropriate phial. She watched him as he observed her transformation. He still was as amazed as she was about the astonishing procedure and their vast dissimilarities. She grasped his hand, and they walked to the *sleeper* where they undressed and lay down.

"I love you more than I can say with words or show you with actions, Bree-Kayah Saar. More than you can imagine. More than I ever thought possible. More than my own life and successes."

"The same is true for how I feel about you, Curran Thaiter, my one and only love."

With separation looming before them, they were compelled to make profound and earnest love. Even so, their feelings ran deeper and stronger than mere physical desire. They bonded on every level: emotional, carnal, and spiritual. They knew, if anything went wrong, this could be their last time to make love. Yet, even if everything went right, it would be *wegs* before they were together like this again, long and tormenting and lonely *wegs.*

Her fingertips brushed over his tanned face with its expression of intense concern and fervent longing for her. She inhaled his manly scent and stroked the raised muscles on his chest and arms. She moved her hands over his shoulders. His physique was splendid and virile. She opened herself to absorb pure and raw and magical sensations, the kinds only he could evoke.

Curran gave carefree abandonment to his hands, lips, and tongue as the magnitude of his hungers increased and he strove to heighten hers. Her brown hair spread around her shoulders and head. His fingers toyed in those wavy locks. He savored the silky texture of her bare skin, her creamy throat. His breathing became erratic as his eagerness escalated. He enjoyed kindling her to a combustible point and fanning those flames into a roaring blaze that licked magnificently over her luscious body.

He lifted his head and gazed into her green eyes, glowing with the same feelings that raced through his mind and body. He leaned forward and sealed their mouths once more. This woman had brought his deceased heart to life again. She had retrieved and given him a peace he had lost long ago. She was the one he wanted for his mate, to be the mother of his children. He knew he would sacrifice his life to save hers if such a grim occasion arose, and she would do the same for him. Yes, his joyful heart sang, they were as perfectly matched in numerous ways as identical twins.

Bree knew it would never have been this way with Antarus Hoy or any other male in existence. This man— Curran Thaiter—was the one she had waited, searched and longed for since coming of age as a woman. He was her destiny, her spiritual half. He was the owner of her heart, sharer of her future, forever.

They labored as one until they achieved an ultimate consummate culmination.

Each knew she would have to leave his side, arms, and chamber soon; but they nestled together for a while to savor the golden aftermath of the magnificent experience, their last one until it was safe to meet again; and both prayed that moment would come.

After Bree returned to the *Liska,* she related everything to Cypher that had taken place since she left her ship two *deegas* ago. She reported to Thaine, who would pass along the information to *Raz* Yakir. Thaine was delighted she was safe, was remaining aboard her cloaked ship, and was teaming up with the *I-GAF* agent. Thaine passed along words from her family. She gave him messages for her parents and her siblings and their families. She told her superior she would contact him again when she had something new to relate, which she hoped would be soon.

Before she left the bridge to retire for the night, she smiled at her android and said, "I love Curran so much, Cypher, and I don't want to lose him. Please help me protect him from harm."

"I will guard him as I guard you, Bree-Kayah. I will remain on alert and be prepared to rescue him from any peril that arises. I will record all he hears and sees via the unit you gave to him."

Bree was surprised she blushed and hesitated when she asked, "Did you record anything... private that happened between us?"

"My analysis of those situations indicated you would not want me to do so. Intimate meetings with him are not part of our mission's evidence."

She laughed and quipped, "You get smarter every *deega*, my friend. I shall sleep now, but awaken me if anything out of the ordinary happens."

On the evening after Bree's return to her ship, "Dagan" was summoned to Tochar's dwelling to be told he would leave at midmorning the next *deega* with Auken and Sach aboard the *Adika*. For the first time since he joined Tochar's band, he was informed of their target and destination: the planet Ulux in Seri for a load of moonbeams in his accomplice's possession.

As Bree and Cypher listened to and recorded the meeting via the disguised disk on his belt which was programed at a frequency which the *fiendal's* security system could not detect, they heard "Dagan" say he wasn't in the mood to visit Yana before his departure as she was getting clingy and he'd been feasting on her for two *deegas,* so he was exhausted and sated. Bree knew that was a hint for her to keep away from him tonight, which turned out to be a smart precaution.

Not long after her beloved returned to his chamber, he left again. She heard him order a meal from Radu, speak to others, enter the men's privacy cubicle, then contact her. She listened to his rush of words.

"I have to talk fast. I'm in the reliever at the Skull's Den. My place isn't secure; Tochar is testing me for loyalty following his disclosure. You heard what he told me. We leave at midmorning for Ulux to pick up crystals from his partner there. Don't come down as Yana because I can't remove the listening device in my chamber and he would hear everything we said and did. I've already given him an excuse for avoiding you. If I'm not seen with anyone and since my chamber is monitored, if anything goes wrong, he'll know I didn't betray him. Send a report to Phaedrig, but tell him not to take any action at Ulux. Cypher has the code to use. Follow me in your ship and record any evidence you hear. I love you. Take no risks."

She realized that before she shadowed his trek, she had to establish a plausible explanation to cover Yana's absence in case Tochar checked on her. She waited until her beloved left the Skull's Den before she entered it as Yana, as she had overheard something useful to her. As she sipped a drink, she told the owner she wanted and needed to shop for things unavailable in the settlement and to seek a diversion to alleviate boredom and stress, but she required safe passage. Radu provided the means for her to carry out her subterfuge; he persuaded a close and trusted friend—J'Ali—to give Yana a ride to another planet to which the alien was headed tomorrow, the news she had overheard between the Ceyxans as her beloved awaited his meal. By a stroke of good luck or the intervention by a Divine Hand, that location thanks to planetary alignments this time of *ying*—was in the same direction as Ulux, almost positioned between the two points of departure and final destination. She put her strategy into motion by smiling and accepting the "kindness" of J'Ali.

Afterward, she went to visit the near incompetent doctor who had been exiled for performing illegal procedures on patients. She said she needed a headache remedy, which he provided for a small payment for a friend of Radu and Dagan. The real reason she had gone to his office was to obtain its coordinates so she could make another visit during the night to retrieve two crucial items to aid future ruses.

The following morning, she entered the Ceyxan trader's vessel as Yana, confined herself to her quarters, and watched them leave orbit with the knowledge Cypher was following in her cloaked ship.

Her plan was to deboard J'Ali's vessel on the other planet, find a private spot, and have Cypher teleport her to the *Liska.* That necessary precaution would place her only *horas* behind Curran, a span which her faster craft could vanquish in a hurry. She deduced, if they could unmask the last traitor during this trek, that would leave only the *Destructoids*—an awesome task—to deal with after their return to Noy.

Suspense and anticipation surged through her as she reflected on a daring ruse which, if it worked, could resolve that one remaining obstacle and terminate its threat, leaving Tochara vulnerable to attack and defeat. She had put *Raz* Yakir on standby for assistance, as he concurred with her "clever" and astounding idea.

Now, she reasoned, all she had to do was protect Yana from discovery while on the Ceyxan's vessel, rejoin Cypher soon, catch up with Curran, and attempt her daring ploy—a scheme she had been unable to share with him since it entered her mind. Despite her cunning, there remained one problem to resolve: she must find a way to enlighten her lover without exposing either of them. That was where *Raz* Yakir's sly but hazardous suggestion would come in handy, if it succeeded. Yet, it didn't stand a chance if one or the other of them couldn't discover the identity of either the traitor on Ulux or his confederate on Kian. Yakir was working on both of those angles, and hopefully they would be given the facts they needed.

Bree settled herself against the *seata* and went over the entangled episodes many times to examine them for oversights and to work out the details. She hoped and prayed no threat would strike the Ceyxan *villite's* vessel while she was aboard, as *Raz* Yakir could not order Serian patrols from their path without it appearing suspicious to his traitor.

Either victory or defeat loomed ahead...

Chapter Eighteen

While en route to Ulux on the *Liska,* Bree and Cypher monitored an enlightening talk between "Dagan" and the two Icarians:

"Is the identity of our contact confidential? Will I be going with you two or staying aboard the ship?"

Auken laughed before saying, "We'll all go to meet with him after we dock at the space port and shuttle to the surface. You're one of us now, Dagan; Tochar trusts you completely. We'll be meeting with Iverk."

"Iverk? I'm not up to date with officials' names. I don't know who he is."

Bree's voice reflected her love and pride as she said to Cypher, "He's cunning, to pretend to be uninformed about Seri's leaders and politics so Auken will clarify and incriminate Iverk on our record."

"He's the Serian *Ysolte,* Head-of-Defense, third in their rulership line. He's powerful, wealthy, trusted, and clever. He visited the mine on Kian recently and had his hireling there give him a tour of the place; that's how he got the moonbeams we're going after."

"Tochar said the mines have tight security."

"That's why Eick couldn't smuggle them out. Eick concealed a stash in one of the chambers. Iverk wore his official garment on the tour, a long and flowing robe. He concealed the crystals in a pouch secured around his waist." Auken added between chuckles, "Security wouldn't dare search or question their *Ysolte.*"

"You're right; Iverk is sly and brave. Still, he risked a lot to take them. Any chance there's one of those big white ones among them? Tochar can use another one for a *Destructoid* aboard his ship or yours."

"It wouldn't do him any good without a weapon. Iverk told him no more had been constructed."

Bree and Cypher knew that wasn't accurate, as *Raz* Yakir had one made covertly and was awaiting a power source: a large clear moonbeam. She was elated that the ruler had kept his word about secrecy, even with the man who was only two steps below him in the line of rulership. If Iverk assassinated Step One and Two...

"How are we supposed to fly in and out of there alive? What if our images are checked, Auken, and we're exposed and attacked. Worse, trapped on Ulux? Do we have an escape plan if one's needed?"

"Don't worry, Dagan, we won't be caught, or even halted for a *preon*. Iverk is Head-of-Defense, so he deleted our records from their files. He gave us the correct passwords, and told us what kind of convincing papers to forge. We go in as legitimate traders."

Bree said to Cypher as the *Adika* crew chatted about unimportant topics, "*Raz* Yakir will be distressed to hear the traitor's identity. We must contact him with that information, thanks to my clever Curran. After we reach orbit in another *weg*, I'll teleport to meet with him and put his idea in motion. With the betrayer's name, Yakir's ruse is possible. It's a tricky ploy, and I'm leery about attempting it, Cypher, but we must."

"*Raz* Yakir would not allow you to use that tactic if he is not certain it will succeed. Do not be afraid or doubtful, Bree-Kayah. I will monitor your moves and be prepared to extract you at the first sign of peril."

"Keep a close watch on Curran for his safety. It's strange and contradictory that Tochar—if he trusts Dagan Latu—would have a listening device planted in his chamber, then allow Auken to expose such a valuable fact. We must be on alert for tricks, Cypher, but do not intrude on any situation until you are certain my life or

Curran's is in imminent danger. We're close to victory, so I don't want anything to impede it."

Bree was elated she had reached this point in her plan without trouble. If Tochar had checked on Yana since her departure, he should be convinced Yana is on another planet, taken there by Radu's trusted friend. Cypher had retrieved her where J'Ali dropped her off, and they had caught up with the *Adika* without problems. When the time came to return to Noy, if their impending plan failed and if she couldn't find a similar ride back, Yakir would arrange for a disguised craft to transport Yana to the colony to try another tactic.

"We must contact *Raz* Yakir and give him the bad and good news so he can finalize his part of our first cunning ruse." She looked uncertain, and turned to her android for encouragement. "Do you think it will succeed, Cypher? The hazards are many."

"If the episode is timed accurately and no unknown factors arise, it cannot fail. It is doubtful your next image and actions will evoke suspicions. It is believed that Yana is far away. We heard Auken reveal to Dagan that Tochar has been unable to retrieve any information about Starla's fate or location."

"That's true, but the *fiendal* is deceitful, a most untrustworthy leader to all hirelings except his two close friends. I believe Tochar doubts my guilt but will never admit he made an error. He entrapped himself by overreacting to the cave incident. Now he needs to slay me to prevent exposing his mistake, which he assumes others will view as a weakness."

"Your reasoning and conclusions are logical."

"Thanks, Cypher. Signal *Raz* Yakir for me."

As she spoke with the Serian ruler, Bree made a shocking and alarming discovery.

"Do not teleport down as Starla," Yakir warned her. "Someone has tampered with Starla's criminal record; perilous false acts were added to it, along with an order she is to be terminated on sight. If I delete the record or command, it will arouse the suspicion of my traitor. Come to me as Yana; that will be safe if you are seen, which I will try to prevent."

"The name of your traitor is Iverk, the *Ysolte,*" Bree revealed. "His hireling is a miner named Eick." She went on to relate everything Auken had told Dagan. She had anticipated the long silence that ensued her probably painful disclosure. She kept quiet as she gave Yakir the time he needed to digest that grim fact.

"I am astounded by his treachery. Yet, he is one of three I suspected and am having observed by my covert Cyborg unit. None of those men know they are being watched, as those units are highly advanced and have the ability to shapeshift at will; that prevents the same image from making too many appearances in close proximity to its target."

"I stole the blood sample you require and removed Starla's so it cannot be used to learn her identity. It is fortunate blood was taken from our enemies and stored for emergencies in that primitive location."

"I have my research team standing by to make cunning use of it. After you arrive, we will discuss our plans and finalize them. Rest and relax, Bree-Kayah; I will have everything prepared before we meet."

Cypher recorded the coordinates Yakir gave to him and a rendezvous time was set for one *hora* after they reached orbit in a *weg.*

While Starla prepared herself to teleport down as Yana, she reminisced on the quick and tender messages Curran had sent to her along his journey when he was alone. His voice and words had warmed her body and elated her heart. She wished she could have responded, but the device was a one-way transmitter. He knew she had heard him or Cypher would receive and relay his messages. She was eager to see her beloved. It would be soon, astonishingly sooner than he expected.

Later as she stood on the sensor pad, Cypher told her to be careful before he transported her into the presence of Yakir in his private chamber.

Bree—in her Yana form—and Yakir exchanged smiles as the ruler stepped forward to greet her, his eyes glowing with undeniable affection.

"It is good to see you again, Bree-Kayah Saar, safe and alive. I gave my word to your parents that I would protect you during your loan to me. You have done a superior job and I am forever grateful to you. I was certain of all your splendid qualities, but they have proved even greater than I imagined. I was wise to select you for this mission."

"Thank you, sir; your remarks are generous and appreciated. Here is the blood sample we need," she said, passing the valuable tube to him.

Yakir handled the item as a prized treasure. He walked to an alcove where a statue sat on a pedestal. He pressed a concealed button and a door opened. He handed the sample to a man and issued his orders.

As she observed him, the tall and slender man with a gentle brown gaze evoked her respect and admiration. His braincase was large and hairless; a deep indention traveled from his forehead to his nape, separating the two cranial hemispheres. Yet, no bulging veins or bumps were visible on his smooth pale-green flesh. His nose was thin; his eyes, round; and his mouth, small with narrow lips. Perhaps, she mused, the sizes and shapes of his bold features made his skull appear bigger than it was, particularly when added to his great height and slim build. She did not find the alien's appearance to be frightening or repulsive. On the contrary, Yakir possessed a calm expression and genial aura. He was extremely intelligent, educated to the highest degree. Almost everyone who met or heard of him held the cordial and wise ruler in high esteem.

After the door was sealed, Yakir said to her, "Come and sit while we talk. We have much to do and swift action to take before the *villites* reach Iverk and complete their task and elude us. They will dock at our space port within two *horas* and reach the surface one *hora* later, so our schedule is limited. It is fortuitous your ship is faster and you arrived before them."

She watched Yakir guide her to a comfortable sitting area. The elderly man—clad in a flowing black robe with gold braid trim and a gold Serian emblem to the left of his heart—moved slowly but gracefully, regally, across the enormous and beautiful room.

After they were seated facing each other, Yakir smiled at her. "Later," the aged and venerable ruler said, "you must tell me all you have seen, done, and learned. Reports-—of a necessity—have been swift and to the point. I am eager to hear details of your many successes. First, we have important work to do. Are you ready to put our clever ideas into motion?"

Her heart raced, but she replied, "Yes, *Raz* Yakir, I am ready, though I must confess I am nervous about the amazing angle you suggested. Still, I believe it can be done with your help and magic."

Yakir smiled, a mischievous twinkle in his eyes. "I have no doubt you can achieve our goal. You have proven to be smarter and braver than our enemies. We will not be interrupted unless there is an emergency. If one occurs, you will hide in my secret chamber."

She laughed and quipped, "It would be difficult to explain Yana's presence and how she came to be in here." She turned serious. "Although Iverk is occupied elsewhere, we would not want someone to mention Yana's strange visit to him."

"If our strategy is successful, Iverk will not be in a position to contact the evil *nefariant* and betray me. One of my cyborgs captured and hid the miner who aided Iverk's treachery. He is the one we will use to expose and snare our wicked *Ysolte.* Eick revealed the truth to me while in the grip of *Thorin,* so I possess the facts you need to trick Iverk. You will hear and learn them soon. Eick's blood was drawn and the transmutation chemical for your first trick has been prepared. Another cyborg is watching Iverk and will alert me the *preon* he meets with the *villites;* their images are programed into his memory for recognition. You—"

"He does know that Dagan Latu isn't to be harmed, correct? I'm sorry I interrupted you, sir," she gave a hasty apology for her impolite action. "I have told you about our love and bond and our decision to become mates, so I fear for his safety and survival since he is unaware of our risky scheme."

Yakir smiled and comforted her. "I understand your feelings and concerns. Do not worry or fear; the *I-GAF* agent will not be harmed. After their captures, you two will return to Noy to defeat Tochar in the manner you suggested. Auken and Sach will accompany you and do your bidding. There was sufficient time after you related your ruse to me for Trilabs to supply the drugs you require for it, and for my scientists to create your other needs. Now, we must go over every detail of our two deceptions to make certain nothing has become entangled or been omitted. I will explain my idea on how to enlighten Curran without exposing you two."

She was in awe as they hurriedly discussed the two daring ploys that could eradicate Tochar and his threat within a few *wegs*, if nothing went wrong. She knew timing was imperative, as was Curran's unquestioning trust and obedience. She hoped and prayed her beloved would believe her and cooperate instantly when she appeared before him in an unfamiliar guise, that of an enemy, a male whom he might suspect was only trying to trick and expose him.

"Eick! Why did you come here?" Iverk demanded, then yanked his hireling inside, glanced around the exterior, and closed the door. The tall Serian towered over the shorter alien from another planet.

In the transmuted form of Eick, she said in a rush in Eick's voice, "Iverk, we got trouble and somebody's going to catch *Karlee!* The Security Force at the mine is acting strange. Asking lotsa questions." She saw anger mingle with worry in Iverk's round gaze. The thin lips of his small mouth almost vanished as he tightened them. Anxiety was flowing through his body, as veins along the pale-green covering on his semi-divided braincase enlarged and protruded and fluttered.

"What questions? What did you tell them?"

The fake *Eick* glanced at Tochar's three men and asked, "Can we talk here?"

"Yes, tell me everything; these are trusted friends. What is wrong?"

"They said there should be more crystals. Said some are missing. I don't see how they could know how many and what colors we found. They questioned everybody several times. Asking the same stuff over and over. They strip-searched us and searched the mine twice. Even used a device to see inside us to make sure we hadn't swallowed any to smuggle out. They've been acting strange ever since your visit when I gave you them crystals to sneak out." She noticed that disclosure alarmed Iverk; the size of his round eyes increased and their shade darkened, veins on his cranium pulsated rapidly. He straightened to his full height and stiffened.

Eick gave a dramatic shiver. "I heard them whisper about using truth serum. I took my leave when it was time and came here. I made sure I wasn't followed. I can't return. I need the payments you've been holding for me. You have to get me somewhere safe to hide, maybe to Karteal or Maffei. Find somebody to alter my hair to blond and my eyes to kyanite. Since I'm not Uluxan like you, I can be disguised. I'll change my name, maybe to Galen or Raimi. But I don't want to escape on no weapon's transporter and have one of them spooky androids with silver eyes monitoring me. I want to go some place warm and pretty. I'm tired of dark caves; they're dangerous. You said if I helped you steal those crystals and put them signal boxes on the transport vessels, you would protect me and pay me good. I thought we had a future, but things have changed. I don't want no *I-GAF*er or no elite squader chasing me down. I don't want to be put in no coma or put down forever. It's over, Iverk; our plans have changed. This new one has to work for all our sakes."

"Calm yourself, Eick; you can go with my friends when they leave soon. They will take you to the haven where they live. You can find work there until it is safe for you to come back and return to Kian."

"Not me, never. Find somebody else to help you steal moonbeams for Tochar."

"Do not worry, Eick, I will protect you and help you. Auken," Iverk said as he faced the Icarian, "I want you to take good care of Eick for me. His loyalty and assistance deserve a reward and sanctuary from your leader."

"I'll take Eick where he needs to go."

The disguised Bree culled the unspoken message that passed between the two *villites:* Eick was to be taken away and disposed of en route to Noy. As Eick, she pretended to be duped and thanked Iverk and Auken, and hoped Dagan was intrigued by the many clues she was dropping for him.

"Sit down, Eick," Iverk said, "and relax while I finish speaking with my friends before they must depart. A long journey awaits you soon."

Eick took a seat, then leapt up. "Can I have a drink? Do you have any *mumfresia;* it's my favorite?"

"Yes, the refreshments are there," Iverk replied, motioning to a bar.

"Anybody else want one?" *Eick* asked. "How about you, space rogue?" she added as she neared where her lover was standing. The others said no.

Dagan requested a water. Why did Eick keep using words spoken between him and Starla? Was the man sending him clues? Had Eick's mind been programed by chemicals or the man been coerced into helping them ensnare Iverk? Yet, he reasoned, why wasn't the talk that had been taking place and being recorded by Cypher revealing enough to provide sufficient evidence? Why was Eick there?

Eick/Bree poured two liquids and handed one to Curran. "Look at my back," she mouthed to the baffled Kalfan, then presented it to him. She pressed a button on her belt which made a message appear, one hidden from the others' view by her position. She prayed her lover would believe what he saw. After she allowed him time to read it, she concealed it and gulped down the drink, a small one. "I'll have another," she murmured and went to get it, surreptitiously passing a special weapon to Curran as she did so. She filled the container, went to her seat again, and sipped it.

Curran held the weapon out of sight as he studied the situation. The astonishing message had said: *I'm Bree/Starla/Yana. Shapeshifted. Have a plan. Help me capture them. Trust me, love. Cypher-T on alert.* He glanced at the miner nearby as he took a swallow. Was it possible, he mused, that was his beloved Bree in Eick's form? He remembered how different Yana was from Starla. But, Eick was a male! Even so, only his cherished woman knew the things just revealed to him and related the clues "Eick" had spoken earlier. What strategy did Bree and Yakir have in mind? How could he credibly explain the captures of Iverk, Auken, Sach, and Eick and his sole escape when he reached Noy, when only by returning could he get close enough to Tochar to defeat him? He concluded that Bree and Yakir had come up with another way to destroy Tochar and his awesome weapons. Surely they would not jeopardize the crucial mission when victory was at long last within reach. He hoped they were right, because after they took action, it could not be changed. He bided his time as he awaited an attack signal from... "Eick."

Iverk handed Auken the container of moonbeams. "Without Eick's help in the mine, we cannot get more until I find a replacement. Tell Tochar not to worry, I will find another helper soon. Eick, it is time to leave. Go with Auken and the others. Here is your payment."

Eick took the bag and thanked Iverk, who nodded his large head. As the traitor and Icarians clasped wrists in a farewell gesture, she retrieved her special weapon, pressed it against Sach's back, and stunned him with haste. She was elated when Curran did the same to Auken without delay.

As both golden-haired men sank to the floor, Iverk gaped at the miner and Kalfan. "What are you two doing? This is treachery. Tochar will hunt you down and slay you both. These are his friends and crystals. There is no place in the Universe you can hide from him. You have slain yourselves."

"Tochar will be defeated and powerless soon," *Eick* said, "as you are defeated and powerless on this *deega,* Iverk, Traitor to Seri, *Raz* Yakir, and the *UFG.*"

Iverk looked at their weapons, then their faces. "Your brains have been destroyed, just as your bodies will be when Tochar finds you."

Eick walked to the door and opened it; *Raz* Yakir and four cyborgs were standing there. She watched the regal man approach Iverk and stare at him for a moment before shaking his head in revulsion.

When Iverk started accusing "Eick" and Dagan of breaking into his chamber and threatening his life, Yakir lifted his hand and said, "Silence! I know what you have done. The evidence of your greed and treason is recorded and it is undeniable. You are the first traitor Seri has known in over two hundred *yings.* You will die for your betrayal and dishonor."

"Your intelligence has left you, Yakir. I am the *Ysolte!* You cannot take me prisoner and terminate me. Our people will not allow such an evil deed."

Without raising his voice, Yakir refuted, "I am *Raz;* I am The Law. Your own mouth has sealed your dark fate. The incriminating words you spoke in your chamber to the *villites* who lay at your feet and the confession of Eick will be played for the High Council. No Serian will argue in your defense or protest your termination after the truth is heard. Have you no shame and remorse? You endangered your people, endangered all who live in the United Federation, and perhaps those beyond it? You knew the powers of the moonbeams and crystaline weapons. Yet, you gave or sold them to Tochar. That is unforgivable, high treason. You must die."

"No, Yakir, *you* must die!" Iverk shouted in a madness born of defeat and desperation as he drew a weapon and fired a lethal beam at the ruler.

Bree sensed the crazed man's reaction and flung herself in Eick's form between the two Serians as Curran sent a laser blast into Iverk's chest.

The witnesses stood stunned in place for a few moments as two lifeless bodies collapsed to the floor.

Chapter Nineteen

Bree gazed at the cyborg who had shoved *Eick* aside and taken a direct hit from Iverk's deadly blast. She realized the unit had saved her life, just as—from instinct and training—she had attempted to save Yakir's. She assumed the cyborg's advanced sensors had allowed it to scan Iverk's physiological functions, to analyze their meanings, to deduce the man's impending response, and to react to the threat much faster than she was able to do. As she had staggered backward, Curran had seized her arm and prevented a fall. She pressed herself against him, forgetting her strange image at the time.

Curran embraced her and held her for a *preon*, relieved and overjoyed he had not lost her forever. He leaned back his head, gazed into "Eick's" eyes, and chuckled. "Great stars, this is weird to be hugging and about to kiss a man. It is you, isn't it, my love?"

Eick laughed and said, "It's me, Curran, Bree-Kayah. I'm glad you believed that message and aided me, but we didn't anticipate Iverk's death."

Curran looked at the ruler. "Nor did I. I wasn't close enough to use the stunner she passed to me. Auken ordered me and Sach to set our weapons on the highest level to be ready for trouble. It was the only way I could disable him when he became reality-impaired."

"Do not worry, Curran Thaiter, you did the right thing. Iverk sealed his own fate."

Curran's gaze went from Yakir to *Eick*. "What's going on, Bree? Won't this obstruct our mission? How will I explain their losses to Tochar?" He motioned to the unconscious Icarians and the Serian's body.

"That will not be necessary," Yakir replied for her. "Sach and Auken will be returning to Noy with you."

Curran stared at the smiling ruler in confusion. "I don't understand. How is that possible? They won't turn against Tochar." His gaze brightened. "You're sending replacements transmuted into their forms?"

"No, they will go with you and do your bidding. We will discuss our next ruse in my chamber after this matter is tended." To the other cyborgs, he said, "Take the two prisoners to the holding room and Iverk's body to the cremation unit. Make certain no one sees them." He turned to Curran and *Eick*. "Come, we have much to prepare and do. After your departures, I will reveal Iverk's treason and assassination attempt to the High Council, but it will not be announced publicly until after Tochar's defeat."

Later in the *Raz's* chamber, *Eick* swallowed the reversal chemical to return to Starla's form.

As she did so, then changed clothes in an anteroom, Yakir explained to Curran the reason for using that tactic. "We obtained a sample of Eick's blood after he was seized. It is necessary to have a person's body code before it can be reproduced by another. Every race and person have their own unique colorings, features, and traits. Another chemical is added to complete a particular person's current image. That is how Bree-Kayah became Yana and Eick, using their blood codes and appearances. Perhaps she has already told you the tragic tale of Mayoleesee Bargivi of Asisa."

After Curran nodded, Yakir disclosed, "That same method is how you will trick and capture Tochar. You will appear to him as Iverk to lure him into your trap. Auken and Sach will be programmed by a mind-controlling drug from Trilabs to assist you. After all three are your prisoners, you will enter the defense sites as

Tochar and destroy the crystaline weapons; then the cloaked force standing by will attack the settlement. All *villites* will be caught for punishment. Other inhabitants will be ordered to evacuate before all colonies on Noy are razed. It will no longer be a haven for *nefariants.* Our assault in the Free-Zone will be justified because those who hide there invaded our sectors and provoked it. We have a right to protect our citizens and their possessions. Surely no other galaxy will protest our action."

"Even if they do, it will be too late to prevent it. But how will I get a transmutation phial made without Tochar's blood? Will your scientists be going with us and make it there after he's apprehended?"

"Bree stole a sample before she left the settlement to come here; the phial is ready for your use."

Curran looked at her in amazement. "It's a good thing Yana won't have to return and try to excuse her absence, but how did you pull off that feat?"

She explained how she had handled Yana's absence in case Yana's return had been necessary. "We couldn't attempt this ruse before because I didn't know about the blood storage until recently, when Auken told us to place ours there in case it was needed. Remember?" He nodded. "Also, I needed to gather enough knowledge about Tochar to dupe his men before he could be detained and substituted, if a way could be found to remove him from sight before he was replaced. Since I was never trusted with their secrets, I couldn't be certain whether or not a password existed for gaining entrance to the sites and for exposing an impostor. That's also why I never tried to become one of his Enforcers. Before we depart, you will review tapes of Iverk to help you play him convincingly. Auken and *Iverk* will lure Tochar to the *Adika* where you and I will take him prisoner."

She said with a grin, "This time, it will be Tochar who is subjected to *Thorin*. If there is a code word, you will have it before you leave the ship. Cypher and I will confine them and monitor you while you go to the surface as Tochar to destroy the weapons. Then we can join the final battle or allow the force to handle it." She was delighted when Curran praised her.

"Our mission would not be this close to victory without all you and Cypher have done, and with *Raz* Yakir's help," he added. "With success in reach and credited to you three, no one in the *UFG* or *I-GAF* can protest your secrecy and actions." He saw Bree and *Raz* Yakir smile in relief. "Will I use the same type of device Starla used to destroy the other crystals?

"Attach them near the crystals, set the timers, and put a safe distance between you and the explosions."

After plans were made, Curran remarked, "These are clever ideas and they should work."

"Using Iverk and Tochar's images were Bree-Kayah's suggestions," *Raz* Yakir revealed. "It was mine for her to use Eick's. I needed to have a recording of the dark bond between Eick and Iverk as evidence for the High Council. Our *Ysolte* was a leader of elite status; he was trusted, respected, admired. I am certain my accusations would have been believed, but having proof assures its acceptance by his friends and family."

"I think that's wise, sir," she concurred.

"So do I," Curran agreed with them. "Sometimes it's hard to believe somebody you love and trust can betray you." The Kalfan related how Syrkin had once been his superior and friend until Tochar darkened his heart and gained control of his mind and actions.

Bree explained to Curran that she hadn't related her ideas to him earlier because they had been out of contact when the schemes had occurred to her.

"I understand, and I'm glad you followed through with them. As I said, we're a perfect match, a perfect team; and my ego is intact."

"You and Bree-Kayah have done a superior job on this assignment. You have saved the United Federation of Galaxies and perhaps lives beyond it."

"First," Curran reminded the elderly man, "we have to defeat Tochar and destroy those weapons."

"You will succeed; I am certain of that fact. When your final deed is done, there will be a ceremony here to reward you two with our highest commendations and with gifts of gratitude. A celebration will follow it. Your family, friends, and superiors will be invited."

"That's kind and generous of you, sir, but we only did our duties."

"No, Bree-Kayah, you went far beyond your duties to achieve these glorious goals. I shall never forget how you offered your life to save mine. Your parents and family and people will be very proud of you."

Once more, she thanked the ruler for his kind and heartwarming words.

"Now, rest and visit with each other tonight and tomorrow while the preparations are being made."

Bree snuggled into Curran's embrace in the large and luxurious suite they had been supplied by Yakir, one guarded by a cyborg. They had feasted on a delicious meal with wine, laughed, talked, relaxed, and soaked for an *hora* in a sunken bathing pool with exotic flower petals floating on a bubbly surface. The room and water temperatures were perfect. The chamber's lighting was diffused. Soft and lovely music filled their ears. Heady fragrance wafted in the air. The setting was serene and romantic, and dark reality was far away. It was as if this was the first time they could totally be themselves, could feel safe and be assured of privacy, and could concentrate only on each other.

While in the soothing pool of silky water, they had kissed and caressed until they were compelled to make love in a feverish rush. They fed and extinguished fiery desires which had smoldered during their long span of denial but had been quickly fanned into urgent and blazing needs upon contact. Afterward, they had bathed, dried off, and moved to a spacious *sleeper.* They had talked and titillated each other for an *hora* until endless passions were rekindled.

Curran nibbled at her earlobe. "No one will disturb us tonight and tomorrow, so we have many splendid *horas* alone." He lifted his head and locked their gazes as he added, "But I'm glad that cyborg is standing guard since Yakir can't erase your fake record until Tochar is apprehended, in case he checks on Starla. He shouldn't, but the *fiendal* is unpredictable and dangerous. I don't want anybody reading that false file, then seeing you and harming you by error."

Bree kissed his chin and stroked his ebony hair. "Don't worry about me; I'm safe with you, my skilled parsec jumper."

"I hope so, but we aren't taking any risks. No showing this beautiful face and ravishing body outside this room or Yakir's meeting chamber."

"I'll be careful and alert; you do the same."

"I will." Curran drifted his fingertips over her bare skin. "Just out of curiosity, my love," he asked, "did you change completely into a man?"

Bree laughed merrily. "No, I was given only Eick's outward image. But," she added as she laughed again, "that would have been an interesting and enlightening experience." Her fingers slipped around his engorged manhood and moved up and down its sleek length. "Then, I would know how this feels."

"Wonderful," he responded in a husky tone as she stimulated him from tip to root.

"And how this feels," she added as her questing lips and tongue kissed and licked a path to her hand.

"Rapturous and breathtaking," he said in a now-ragged tone as his body burned and his craving for appeasement increased at a rapid pace. He moaned and writhed as she enthralled and pleasured him. When he began to teeter on the brink of release, he controlled that reaction, rolled Bree to her back, and rapturously assailed her body. He took her to the pinnacle of ecstasy many times with his roving hands, lips, and tongue before she cascaded over its beckoning edge.

Curran continued to stroke and kiss her, allowing that splendid and enchanting experience to mingle with the next, and then another as time seemingly ceased.

He looked at her radiant expression and glowing eyes. "You're the most beautiful and irresistible woman who's ever existed. I'm lucky you were unattached. I would have tried everything imaginable to win you away from him, even if I had to pursue you from one side of the Cosmos to the other. It's incredible I found someone so compatible and perfect for me. I can hardly wait until we are mates by law; then, you will be mine forever, Bree-Kayah Saar Thaiter."

Her fingers swept aside a stray lock of black hair, then looked into his adoring blue eyes. "I am yours, Curran, in every way except one, and that will be taken care of as soon as this mission is completed. I, too, would have done anything and everything to win you away from another woman, for I am greedy, selfish, and possessive when it comes to you. You stole my heart and wits with ease and speed, you cunning space pirate. I could never replace you if I lost you."

"You won't ever lose me, my love, never."

Their mouths meshed. Their hands roamed. Their spirits soared into passion's highest realm. They made beautiful, imaginative love until they were temporarily sated, fatigued, and contented.

Soon, they surrendered to peaceful slumber in each other's arms, to awaken the following morning to enjoy that *deega* and night in a similar manner...

Bree and Cypher left Ulux's orbit in the cloaked *Liska*. Dagan, Auken, Sach, and a cyborg guard departed in the *Adika*. Five ships of Serian patrol units followed close behind them, cloaked for secrecy. While en route, they would be joined by several *I-GAF* teams.

Curran stored the transmutation phials in a safe place. He was looking forward to the procedure and to the heady but dangerous adventure looming before them. The cyborg assigned to him was to guard the two prisoners and keep them drugged for their unknowing but willing participation. He was glad Bree would be staying out of the perilous action, as his concentration on the ruse would be better knowing she was out of harm's way, and *Yana's* presence at his side would be suspicious. At last, Tochar Galic would pay for his evil, including the murders of his family and friends, and would never be given another chance to imperil Bree-Kayah, the name soft and lovely on his tongue and in his head, perfect for the woman he loved.

In a few *wegs,* if all went as planned, this mission would be over and a new life would begin for Curran Thaiter and Bree-Kayah Saar, as mates. He wished they were taking this trek together, but this wasn't the time to indulge themselves or to appear unprofessional to the other team members while en route to a crucial event. Soon, they would have plenty of time to stimulate and sate their endless desires. They could enjoy a daily existence together with no secrets to guard, disguises to use, perils to confront and vanquish. At least they could communicate with each other during this journey, view images, and talk on occasion. But until they reached Noy, there was little to do but think.

Yet, Curran couldn't dismiss a twinge of worry. He hoped nothing had been overlooked and no mistakes were made. But with Iverk's unplanned death, they didn't know if the Serian traitor was supposed to contact Tochar after their rendezvous, nor did Auken or Sach when interrogated with *Thorin*. Tochar's standard order was that during raiding treks, there was to be no communication between him and the pirate ship to prevent any advanced technology from detecting their signals and locating their positions.

Yet, if Iverk had been told to contact Tochar and did not, Tochar's suspicions could be aroused to a hazardous level. The *fiendal* had the means to blast the *Adika* and all ships in their small fleet into oblivion. Even so, no weapon they possessed could match a *Destructoid* or be protected against its firepower. Or, Curran fretted, Tochar might refuse to come to the ship, even at Auken's and *Iverk's* urgings. Of course, *Iverk* could go to the *fiendal's* dwelling, but a nervous Tochar could have a unit of Enforcers with him or be heavily armed. If so, that would make the *fiendal's* capture difficult or impossible, and might create a situation where he—himself—was exposed. There was no way he knew everything the *villites* had said to each other, since a slain Iverk could not be interrogated. If Tochar caught him in a mistake, the game was over; and death was a strong probability.

There was a slim possibility that the shapeshifting chemical or process could fail. He certainly didn't want to remain as Iverk or Tochar for the rest of his life! There was a possibility, even if he reached the defense sites, the destruction devices wouldn't work. There was a chance he might encounter someone who suspected he wasn't the leader and challenged him. No plan, the *I-GAF* officer reasoned, was totally foolproof, but he hoped and prayed the impending ones were.

Aboard the *Liska*, Bree experienced similar thoughts, fears and feelings. "He'll be walking into this danger all alone, Cypher. There's no way I can go with him as a backup in any form. If I had thought about it sooner, I could have transmuted into Auken. I want to be with him; I want to guard him, to help him."

"Do not be afraid, Bree-Kayah. He will succeed."

She laughed and said, "That sounds like human confidence to me. Have you inserted a human traits chip I don't know about?" she teased.

"I have not been altered or upgraded since we began this mission. However, on future assignments, that would be a logical addition."

Bree did not tell the android this might be their last mission as a team, and she felt guilty about keeping that news from him. They had been together for a long time, and she would miss him if she retired. But, she and Curran might team up for a while until they were ready to settle down and have a family. Sharing adventures and meeting challenges together sounded exciting and tempting. Cypher would make an excellent protector and assistant for them. Could she persuade the *Kadim* to let her keep Cypher as a reward.

"He likes you," she murmured almost unknowingly to her companion.

Cypher's silver visual sensors locked on her. "That does not compute."

"Curran likes you," she clarified. "You heard what he said about you in *Raz* Yakir's chamber about how important you are to this mission and its success. As I do, Cypher, Curran views you as being alive, a friend, a teammate, a good and loyal companion."

The android analyzed her expressions, words, and tone. He deduced all were sincere and complimentary. "If I were human, your praise and feelings would be moving to my emotions. It is beneficial he views me in that manner since you have become close to him. He is a superior partner and mate for you. His personality and presence are acceptable to me."

Bree laughed at his use of "acceptable." "I am delighted you find Curran admissible and satisfactory for our tight unit. I wouldn't want you two conflicting at every turn when he joins us permanently."

"Will he resign *I-GAF* and work with us?"

"Yes. Do you have any objections?"

"I am programmed to protect, obey, and assist you. My chips do not allow me to defy your orders."

"But they allow you to have an opinion and to tell me if I am wrong."

"I do not locate a reason in my circuits to disagree with your decision this time."

"That's all I needed to hear, Cypher. Thanks."

***

After obtaining orbit at Noy, the mind-controlled Auken contacted his leader in the settlement. "We've returned, Tochar, but we have a problem: Iverk is with us and wants you to come speak with him."

Elsewhere on the *Adika,* Bree and the disguised Curran listened to the talk via a transmission device on Auken. Another one embedded in Auken's ear allowed Curran to pass messages to him which Auken relayed to his friend on the planet's surface. They had anticipated most of Tochar's questions and reactions, and they had prepared Auken for them.

"Bring him to my dwelling," Tochar said in an annoyed tone.

"He refuses to leave the ship," Auken replied.

"Let me talk to him via video-com."

"He's locked himself in my quarters."

"What is wrong with him? What happened on Ulux? Why is he here? This is foolish and rash."

"He's acting strange and secretive. He gave us the crystals, but he insisted on coming to Noy with us to speak privately with you."

"Put me through to him in your quarters." After Iverk's image appeared on his viewer screen, Tochar demanded, "Why are you here? This is reckless. You have probably exposed yourself. Come—"

In Iverk's voice and forcing the Serian's face to line with anger, he cut off *the fiendal.* "No, you come to me. We have matters to settle. I will not be surrounded by your guards when we talk. I will await you here."

"He disconnected our signal," a shocked Tochar said to Auken. "Where is Dagan?"

"He's preparing the shuttle for our return."

Tochar's fury mounted. "Tell him to come after me so I can deal with Iverk."

"Dagan is making a minor repair on the shuttle's engine. It will not be ready for use for another *hora* or two. Iverk is crazed. He's been acting this way during the entire voyage. Sach and I can't do anything with him. He won't tell us what's wrong. We're afraid he might harm himself or our equipment."

"You think I should not wait for the shuttle?"

"If you need Iverk back on Ulux, you should come settle him down. If there's trouble back there, you need to find out about it before he zones out completely. It will be faster and easier to teleport you here."

"You're right. Give me time to prepare myself."

Ten *preons* later, Tochar contacted Auken and said, "Lock on to my coordinates and bring me aboard."

"Sach, are you ready in the transporter?"

"Entering the coordinates, Auken. Transmission in progress. Stand ready to greet him."

After Tochar materialized on the sensor pad, his black gaze traveled from Auken to Sach to Dagan, who was standing behind Auken. "I thought you were working on the shuttle."

"Welcome aboard and into my trap," Curran sneered as he left the concealment of Auken's body, a weapon in his hand. He watched Tochar gape at him in confusion, which gradually altered to fury.

"What is the meaning of this treachery, Latu? Have you zoned out? Take him prisoner!"

Curran chuckled when the two men remained frozen to their spots, having been ordered not to respond to any of Tochar's orders. "They can't help you; no one can help you. By the authority of *I-GAF*, I arrest you for the many crimes you have carried out and instigated. Including the murders of my family."

Tochar gaped at the Kalfan, then at his fellow Icarians. "Are you two betraying me and siding with this fool? Explain your actions immediately!"

"Auken, Sach, return to your quarters and remain there," Curran said. He saw Tochar's dark gaze widen as he witnessed his men's defiance to his orders.

"What is wrong with them? What did you pay my friends to trick and betray me?"

"Nothing. They'll be sent to a termination unit just like you will after I get rid of those *Destructoids.*"

The door swished open. Starla/Bree and the cyborg joined Dagan/Curran.

"I see you have everything under control."

Tochar's gaze darkened, narrowed, and chilled. "You are both dead, food for the mutants. My Enforcers will never allow either of you to get near my weapons. I suspected something was wrong. I told Palesa if I had not returned within the *hora,* to alert them to danger. If I am not freed, she will have the weapon on my dwelling mounted to my ship. It will attack a different location on various planets until I am released."

"Don't worry, *Tochar* will return to the surface very soon. He will be the one to destroy your weapons."

"You are reality-impaired! What deception are you trying to pull? She will not believe you are me."

"By nightfall, your defenses will be destroyed and a large force of Serians and *I-GAF* agents will attack the colony. It will be razed, as will the other *villite* havens on this planet. Cloaked ships are standing by to carry out the assault when I give them a signal to begin."

"Where is Iverk? What has he told you?"

Curran was surprised by Tochar's response to the stunning revelation, as if the bad news hadn't registered in his mind. "Iverk is dead. He was exposed and tried to assassinate *Raz* Yakir. That was me you spoke to earlier. I presume I impersonated Iverk perfectly."

"How can you pretend to be Serian? No way."

"Let's just say I used a little magic and cunning." Despite his claims of deception, Tochar didn't look as if he believed him, but that didn't matter.

"What is wrong with Auken and Sach? What did you do to my friends? They are not themselves."

"You're right. We control their minds and actions with drugs." Curran saw panic and rage fill Tochar's gaze and stiffen his body. Obviously, grim reality was settling in on the ensnared *fiendal.*

"Why is Starla, here? Were you two working against me all the time?"

"Yes, separately at first. We teamed up after you tried to kill her. She's also an agent, but not for *I-GAF;* that's all you need to know before you die."

"How did you two pass my *Thorin* tests?"

"Let's just say we used another magical trick."

"*Rendelar,*" Tochar guessed. "Soon, I would have controlled that and all other potent chemicals. I would have exposed and slain you both."

"If you could have gotten your evil hands on Trilabs; you can't."

"Who are you, Dagan? A blood lust for me gleams in your eyes. You said I killed your family."

"Curran Thaiter. I was a *Seki* when you attacked Gavas with that faked chemical hazard and killed my family and friends." He watched Tochar's gaze brighten as the evil man recognized a name from the past.

"Thaiter was the one pursuing us with a vengeance, but he is long dead."

Curran glanced down at his body. "I don't think so. Do I look dead to you, my love?"

Her adoring gaze roamed his full length and she smiled at him. "Not to me, my beloved."

"What—"

"No more questions! Not by you. It's our turn to ask them, and you will tell us all we need to know."

"I will not tell you anything, Thaiter! If that is who you are. Show me an *I-GAF* badge."

"Oh, I think you will. Is the *Thorin* ready?" Curran asked the cyborg who nodded. "Put him under."

They watched Tochar try to back away from the cyborg's approach. He was unable to break its strong grip on his arms which were pinned to his sides. The *fiendal* thrashed and squirmed and cursed them as he was injected with the truth serum.

"You will regret this treachery!" Tochar shouted at the smiling couple.

"The only thing that feels better than defeating you, Tochar, is finding and winning this unique woman for my mate. I should be a little grateful to you since you're the one who brought us together."

Bree knew Curran was savoring these victories. At last, he had justice for his slain family, and the threat to their worlds would be over soon, and their bonding ceremony awaited them.

They listened and watched as Tochar used his remaining span of awareness to curse and threaten them with vows of horrible revenge, to which Curran chuckled. Then, Tochar's brief questioning began...

Bree stared at Curran in the transmuted form of their enemy. She asked, "How do you feel?"

He lifted his thick brows and took a deep breath. "Shapeshifting is a weird experience. You can feel your flesh crawling and itching as it alters. Even your bones and muscles change. It's amazing, stimulating, but a little scary. That isn't my voice I'm hearing or my body I'm seeing." Though he had taken on Iverk's vastly different form for a short time, assuming Tochar's more similar one seemed just as incredible to him.

"You look and sound like Tochar, my beloved. You'll dupe them. Soon, this mission will be finalized in a momentous victory. You have the password, so hurry before Palesa gets nervous and sounds an alarm."

"Tochar was probably deceiving us with that desperate threat, but I won't take a chance he wasn't telling the truth. I'll see you soon, my love."

"If not, I'll be coming down after you," she warned in a playful tone. "Please watch your back since I won't be there to do it. I love you, Curran."

He didn't kiss her or caress her cheek as a foe. "I'll be careful. I love you, woman. Now, send me down."

He stepped on the sensor pad and she teleported him to the *fiendal's* abode. She returned to the bridge and sat down, a device in her grasp to overhear the events taking place below her position. The drugged Tochar, Auken, and Sach were being guarded by the cyborg in Auken's quarters on the *Adika.* Cypher was at the helm of her ship, also monitoring Curran's progress. The mixed Serian and *I-GAF* force was on alert, ready to take action upon Curran's successful return.

Bree contacted her android and said, "Be prepared to rescue my love if anything goes wrong since I may lack time to signal you if that becomes necessary."

"Affirmative," Cypher responded.

Curran Thaiter masked his tension as he entered his transmuted form's lofty dwelling and immediately faced his first challenge: duping *the fiendal's* hermaphroditic lover. In public Palesa appeared to be and behaved as a woman—a ravishing creature with purple eyes, soft fair skin, and long silky red hair. She was *Binixe,* a race of androgynes whose bodies possessed male and female sex organs and were self-reproductive. They were a mysterious and private people who rarely intermingled with outsiders, so he didn't know how or when or why Palesa had coupled with Tochar; that meant he couldn't allow her time to ensnare him with a mistake. He should have asked the evil man those questions.

"What happened, Tochar? Where are the others? What is wrong?"

He had overheard Tochar's endearments for her and made clever use of them. "Only a minor problem, my beauty. It will be handled soon. Go to the Skull's Den and wait for me to join you to celebrate."

Palesa looped her sleek arms around his neck and pressed her sensual body to his. "First, we finish what we started before you were summoned. I will quickly arouse your appetite. Let me remove your—"

Tochar grasped her wrists and loosened her hold on him, smiling as he did so. "There is no time at the present to enjoy ourselves. I have guests coming. I will join you soon at Radu's after I speak to them."

"I will retire to my chamber and wait there, and we will go together."

He stroked her cheek as he asked in a mellow tone, "Why do you disobey me, my beauty? I have important matters on my mind, things to be settled. A man is arriving and he does not wish to be seen by anyone; that includes you, my precious treat. He is delivering a surprise for you," he tempted the epicene being.

"What is it? You must tell me or I shall be over-excited with curiosity."

He laughed and shook his head, flaxen hair swaying at his nape. "Do not spoil my pleasure by coaxing me to reveal it. You must leave now."

"If you insist, I will go, but join me soon or beckon my return. I will reward you in many wonderful ways for my surprise. I will—"

To silence her, he grasped her shoulders, turned her body toward the door, and said, "Go, quickly; my preparation time is limited. You can reward me later with those delicious treats."

Via a *transascreen,* the transmuted Curran watched the *Binixe* exit the *trans-to,* get into a landrover, and drive toward the settlement. He located Zarafa and had Tochar's abused slave teleported to one of the Serian ships for her safety and survival, disclosing to the astonished woman she was being freed and sent home. He didn't have to worry about Tochar's two robots, as the automatons remained in an inactive mode until the *fiendal* needed them to perform tasks.

He said to Bree, whom he knew was listening, "Palesa and Zarafa are gone. I'm going to plant the first device. I'll seal the door when I leave so no one can enter before the explosion."

After the device was in place and the timer was activated, *Tochar* took a landrover to the first defense structure. He gained entry with ease and speed using the password supplied by Auken and verified by the *spaceki* leader. He chatted with two men on duty while he surreptitiously planted the second device and started its timer. Afterward, he did the same with the third device at the second defense site.

At both locations, he ordered the guards to lock the structures and to check out the area for a possible intruder. He doubted their lives would be spared when the detonations occurred, but that could not be helped. Taking another action or assuming any other command would have been suspicious, even for their leader.

He rode to Yana's dwelling and entered it. "Bree, I'm ready to return. Everything is done here. Lock on to me and bring me aboard."

Bree was prepared to comply and did so. The moment he stepped from the sensor pad, she flung herself into his arms and said, "You're safe now, my beloved. Transmute to yourself so I can cover your face with kisses. We have fifteen *preons* until the blasts."

He cupped her face with his hands and fused their gazes. "I know you're a highly skilled and experienced officer, my love, but please stay aboard during the remainder of the action. There are a lot of *villites* down there who will fight their best to escape, and I don't want you injured."

It felt strange to be staring into Tochar's black eyes but speaking to Curran. "Do you have to go? Can't the others battle and capture them?"

"I'm an *I-GAF* officer, my love, and this is my assignment It's my duty to assist the others. You've taken more than your share of risks during this joint mission, and most of the accomplishments belong to you, so please stay here where you'll be safe. I'll be distracted with you in harm's path. It took me twenty-eight *yings* to find you; I don't want to lose you."

"What if you need my help as a backup?"

"I'll be fine, so don't worry about me. Besides, my friend Cypher will monitor and protect me."

She knew he had faith in her prowess. His concern was born from love for her. She must not distract and endanger him. She relented to his request.

"Thanks, my love," he said in relief and kissed her. "Now, I have to transmute. I don't want to go down there looking like this."

As soon as he was Dagan Latu again, they embraced and kissed. This time, their mouths meshed in a long and eager one. Arm in arm, they observed the three massive explosions on the viewer screen.

She hugged him. "Let's hope the devices worked and those *Destructoids* are gone."

"I'm sure they did. It's time for me to leave." Curran told the large force of men to prepare to start the action in ten *preons,* which would allow the dust and debris to settle. He checked his weapons, kissed her again, and teleported to another ship to join a unit of agents who were awaiting his arrival before departure.

"Stay safe, my beloved, and return to my side," Bree murmured to herself. She held a listening device close to her ear to catch every word Curran spoke, her heart pounding in apprehension as he again faced peril.

Chapter Twenty

Bree decided to teleport to her ship to observe the action with Cypher. She had the cyborg and prisoners sent to a Serian vessel for detainment. She set *Adika's* automatic pilot so it would circle Noy until its fuel was spent and its orbit decayed, if it wasn't confiscated for use by one of the other forces. If not, it would burn up upon entry into the planet's atmosphere. She gathered her things and left the craft for the last time—one in which she had spent many *deegas* and nights as an alleged *spaceki*, a notorious space pirate.

"How is the mission progressing?" she asked as she took a seat near Cypher on the *Liska's* bridge and locked her gaze to the monitor.

"The combined forces just shuttled or teleported to the planet's surface. The final battle has been initiated. The colony's inhabitants are fleeing in many directions. Some are hiding. Some are taking shuttles to their ships. Many are fighting or preparing to do so."

"So, sheer chaos is taking place. Those blasts must have terrified most of them. It must be clear to them the defense sites are destroyed; so is Tochar's dwelling. Perhaps they will assume he has been slain and they are helpless. With the advanced weapons we have and the skills of our combined force, the *villites* are sure to lose, but still they fight and attempt to escape."

"Many crimes will warrant termination."

"Others will require confinement to one of those penal colonies. Neither fate is an enticement to evoke surrenders. We're lucky we were born into good families and situations. I wouldn't want to be a real member of Tochar's band this dark *deega.*"

If it were possible, Cypher would have chuckled in amusement at her third sentence. Even so, he grasped her meaning and slip. It somehow pleased him to realize she thought of him as a person, a friend, family.

"Look," she said, "they're rounding up groups of people in several locations and scanning their records device to see who to apprehend. Those with criminal files are being taken aboard one of the vessels. Others are being sent into the Skull's Den and other structures to await evacuation. Curran said he will make certain Radu is given a chance to leave, unless the Ceyxan has charges against him which are unknown to us. I wonder what they will do with Palesa," she murmured, recalling how the *Binixe* had tried to seduce her beloved, though Palesa had thought it was her lover.

"*I-GAF* agents will decide the androgyne's and Mu's fates. Traders and visitors may be fined and released. Captive workers will return home or be relocated."

"Look there, Cypher," Bree said again, pointing to another screen. "Some of Tochar's Enforcers are taking refuge in the caves. Since I don't see any of our men in that area, I'll inform Curran of their hiding places."

Bree contacted him with the information, but did it fast to prevent distracting him longer than necessary. Any time a *villite* tried to sneak up on or lay a trap for Curran, Cypher warned the Kalfan and exposed the *nefariant's* location, giving Curran an advantage and a safeguard. Their advanced sensors and communication abilities also allowed Cypher to send Curran warnings for others who were fighting near him.

She saw a few of their men go down from lethal blasts, though her side was using stun-only settings for captures and interrogations. Their bodies were collected by fellow officers and teleported to their ships. Injured men were retrieved and treated aboard their vessels. She watched as some of the *villites* surrendered after their weapon's power was depleted. She saw visitors or noncriminal inhabitants turn themselves over to the assault team so they wouldn't be slain by mistake or accident.

She grasped why those who knew Dagan Latu as one of Tochar's men were attacking him: he had changed into *I-GAF* attire and made his hand insignia visible. *"Pralu,* Cypher, look at Curran! I just realized he's using his uniform and badge. I was so worried and distracted by his jeopardy, I didn't notice until now." Her green gaze roamed his striking image; he was so handsome, authoritative, confident in the dark-blue garment and while displaying his imposing emblem.

"It was a logical measure for self-defense."

Bree smiled and added, "And for intimidation. Even brave *villites* fear the awesome power and elite prowess of parsec jumpers. Isn't he magnificent, Cypher? So skilled and brave. My family and friends will love and respect him as much as I do. I can hardly wait for them to meet him. Mother, Amaya, and Rayna will be delighted to learn I'll have a mate soon. Such amazing *deegas* and exciting adventures await us, my friend. We three will become the most requested team for certain assignments. We'll travel the galaxies together until we're ready to settle down and have children. Of course you will come to live with us on Altair. Considering your many achievements, Father will appoint you leader of all the androids, in control of our security."

Cypher analyzed her remarks and emotions and deduced no response was required or expected. Yet, oddly and illogically, he found her words to have a pleasing effect upon him. Perhaps his emotions chip had begun to function better or he had gathered more data to assist his comprehension of certain human feelings and situations. He was amazed and confused that he *liked* and *was stimulated* by plans she had expressed.

Bree sat on the edge of her seat. With the use of laser instruments that were powered by moonbeams, no structure was impenetrable. She observed and waited in suspense as the confrontation continued until darkness and clouds partially obstructed her view. Night also compelled the combined forces to cease their assault until morning. She listened as secure areas were set up for the Serians and *I-GAF* agents so they could take shifts guarding, resting, eating, and sleeping. She was amused when Curran turned off his transmitter so she wouldn't overhear the men talking and joking, since he remained below with them.

"I shall eat, enter the cleansing unit, and sleep for a while, Cypher," she told her trusted android. "Summon me if I'm needed or peril strikes at my beloved." She doubted she would slumber well, but she wanted to be rested for what lay ahead of her.

Upon arising early the next morning, Bree dressed and hurried to the bridge. "Anything happening?" she inquired. "Is Dagan, I mean Curran, all right?"

"The one you love is safe from injury and death. He sleeps. *Villites* are being located and apprehended by our forces. Many have been taken aboard the other vessels. Some trader ships have been permitted to depart. Many who are not wanted for crimes were allowed to go with those leaving. Others are to be transported to new locations by the Serians."

She sat down and listened as the evacuation order was issued and the news was announced that the colony would be razed. Anyone in hiding was warned the event would take place in two *deegas*, allowing them time to surrender or depart. It was revealed that all other colonies on Noy would face the same fate, so it was foolish to take refuge in one of them.

"I wonder what the *Skalds* will eat after everyone is gone?" she mused aloud, the strange thought flashing across her mind like a comet.

"They will find nourishment on plants and animals or they will die," Cypher answered.

"We certainly don't want to rescue and relocate flesh-eating mutants. It's best and safest for others if they're left here to their natural fates."

"That is logical. They live, but they have the minds and traits of wild beasts. They must not be placed around other humans and endanger them."

"Good morning, my love," a mellow voice came over the transmitter.

"Good morning to you." His sound warmed her from head to feet. "When will you be joining us?"

"We have a few more pockets of *villites* to clean out, then I'll be coming aboard. I have to show our team where Tochar's caves are located so the stolen goods can be recovered. As soon as our reports are filed, we'll leave for Ulux. The rest of the team can finish up here and at the other settlements. They're smaller and less inhabited, so it won't take long. At least Noy won't be used as a stronghold or haven for more *villites* again. I-GAFers are taking charge of Tochar, Auken, Sach, his Enforcers, and a few others. The Serian patrols will take command of the other debris; they'll turn them over to whatever galaxy they're wanted in the most."

"That's good news. What about Radu and Palesa?"

"A Ceyxan trader gave them a ride to Mu where he's from. He was grateful to be spared. I don't know what either one plans to do later. They were warned to keep away from *villites* in the future or risk trouble."

"I hope Radu heeds those words; I liked him. He didn't seem to be the kind of person to live and work among such nefarious beings."

"He stopped by *yings* ago with a friend and won the Skull's Den in a *resi* game. That's why he stayed, or what he told us. Sorry, but I have to suspend transmission; I'm needed for those tasks I mentioned earlier. I know," he said with a chuckle, "I'll be careful and I'll see you soon. What can possibly happen to me with you and Cypher on guard? By the way, good morning to you, Cypher. Take care of Bree for me. Curran out."

"Affirmative. Cypher out."

"See, I told you he likes you."

"When my emotions chip is functioning at full capacity, I will like him, too," the android told an amused and delighted Bree.

As the *Liska* left orbit with Cypher in control of the bridge, Curran said to Bree in her quarters, "I just finished filing my last report with Phaedrig and turning in my resignation. As I told you, *I-GAF* agents must be single to prevent distractions. He said he hated to lose me, but he understands my decision and sends his congratulations and best wishes. He'll be on Ulux, so you can meet him there. I'm sure you'll like him. Phaedrig's planning to send the Thracians news about the crimes and fates of Koteas and Terin, and give them a slight warning about their acceptance and use of men like Tochar and the perils of dealing with them. After the Thracians learn how powerful the *UFG* is, which will be obvious from Tochar's stunning defeat, perhaps they'll join our Federation. The more galaxies that are included, the fewer to cause us problems later."

"That seems a wise precaution to me."

"I agree. I told him Tochar doesn't have any other accomplices, according to what he related during our brief questioning. I suppose with Iverk dead, we'll never know why he joined forces with Tochar. Phaedrig plans to question Tochar further to learn how and when he met Syrkin, Iverk, and Acharius and how he persuaded them to turn traitor to their people. It's helpful to learn *villite*'s motivations for use in future missions. After their final interrogations, Tochar and Syrkin will be terminated for their many crimes."

"They knew the laws when they broke them, so punishment shouldn't come as a surprise to any of them. This mission has been so long and hard and often frightening that it's amazing it's over. We shouldn't ever face this kind of threat again because *Raz* Yakir told me that all white and green crystals which are found in the future will be destroyed, and no weapons will be made from them again. Only moonbeams with good traits will be saved: you probably know red ones are useful in heating and lighting; yellow provide many medical purposes; and blue are excellent for superior surgical lasers. As Cypher said, it would be terrible to seal the mines forever, to destroy the good with the bad."

"He's right, as usual. Now, we have two things left to do, my love."

She nestled into his embrace. "What are they?"

"First, we attend the ceremony and celebration on Ulux, where I'll meet your family and get their approval. Second and most important, we must bond as mates and begin our new life and work together."

"I adore both ideas, particularly the last one. But you do not need my parents' approval, though you shall receive it, I am certain. They'll love, respect, and accept you as I do. Our good news will make them happy."

"Still, I want to speak with them before we bond. They're legendary and prestigious figures across the entire *UFG* and I'm eager to meet them. It will be an honor to join your family. Mine would be pleased and proud if they were alive to share in this happy event. Did you know that *I-GAF* agents study many of your father's past tactics for use in our missions?"

Bree realized he left the topic of his lost loved ones in a hurry, probably to avoid dampening their joy on this occasion. Yet, she knew he would relate his complete history soon, just as she knew he came from a family as wonderful as hers. Since his had been wealthy and prominent and involved in Kalfa's government, he would not feel out of place in her social rank. "No, I didn't," she answered his question, "but Father was and still is a man of superior intelligence, prowess, and statue. So is my mother, and my sister and brother. I'm not boasting, but their achievements are many and have been crucial to the survival of our people."

Curran stroked her brown hair and smiled. "I've read Maffeian history so I know you're telling the truth. It's normal to be proud of them, and I want to hear more about your family during our trek to Ulux."

"It's late now and we're exhausted, so we'll contact them on rising to let them know the final battle has taken place and we're safe and on our way. We can speak to them for a while, but you'll learn more after you meet them." Yes, she decided, during their journey she would tell him many awsome tales about her family's intergalactic adventures and seemingly star-crossed romances. All had been players in dangerous games of perilous intrigue and had surrendered to irresistible passions. They had challenged and defeated many enemies and powerful forces, and each had almost lost their chosen one during near-fatal battles. She wanted him to get acquainted with her family and for him to form his own opinion before she revealed dark episodes which her parents and siblings had confronted, endured, and conquered long ago.

"I'm looking forward to getting to know each of them. My parents, sister, and two brothers would have been delighted by my choice of mates. I never imagined I would be the son to carry on the Thaiter bloodline. We'll have a splendid time creating our own family after we retire from trekking. Have you told Cypher he'll be our teammate until we settle down in Maffei?"

"Yes, and he actually sounded and appeared to be pleased. I'm beginning to wonder if we aren't rubbing off on him; he talks and acts like a human more every *deega.*" She inclined her head toward him, changing the subject. "Tell me, my beloved, was it difficult to spurn Palesa's cravings for you?" she jested.

Curran chuckled and nestled her closer. "For a while there, I was afraid I couldn't get away from her grasping arms and lewd intentions."

"You did a superb job; she never suspected you for a moment. Of course," Bree said with a merry laugh, "I would have teleported down immediately if she had refused to stop tempting my property."

Curran rolled to his side and nibbled on her ear. "Possessive, are you?"

"When it comes to you, my dashing space rogue, I am. I adore your name, and I can hardly wait to see you as you truly are. I must confess, Cypher used one of our computer programs to display your image with sun-kissed hair and aqua eyes and the facial changes you mentioned. I should tell you, Curran Thaiter is far more handsome and appealing than Dagan Latu, which I never believed was possible for any man."

He warmed as her gaze roamed his face and her fingers trailed over his bare chest. "Thank you, my love. As soon as we reach Ulux, you can see for yourself if your assumption is correct. *Raz* Yakir said he would have a skilled medical team ready to restore me to myself. The procedure is quick and painless, especially with those new moonbeam laser scalpels. When I meet your family, it will be as Curran Thaiter. As for you," he murmured as he kissed her nose, "I much prefer Starla's image to Yana's." He chuckled. "I wonder how long it will require before Curran and Bree-Kayah roll off our tongues as easily as Dagan and Starla do now."

"I'm sure we'll make many slips since we've used those names for so long, but we have all the time we'll need to correct them. Right now, what we need is this." She kissed him and caressed his virile body, naked next to hers, their flesh in sensuous and stirring contact.

Curran sealed their mouths in a series of long, slow, and deep kisses which merged into intense, needy ones as their mutual desires heightened. His questing hands ventured over her responsive body.

Bree did the same, stimulating and enticing him upward on an intoxicating spiral to ecstasy. Curran had been right all along: they were a perfect match in every way. She kissed his lips. "I love you with all my heart and soul and we shall be so happy together."

He gazed into her glowing green eyes and radiant expression, and his heart overflowed with wonderful and potent emotions. "Yes, we will, Bree, for I love you with all my heart and soul."

Soon, their pleading bodies were joined in a blissful union and their spirits soared the heavens. The hearts and lives of Curran Thaiter and Bree-Kayah Saar—third child of Maffeian Varian Saar and Jana Greyson Saar of Earth—had been bound forever by generous destiny, just as those of Galen and Rayna, and Amaya and Jason had been forged long ago. Evil had been defeated, and now peace ruled the Federation.

As the *Liska* journeyed through the vast reaches of space with Cypher at the helm and recent perils left far behind, Bree-Kayah and Curran made rapturous love in a splendid setting which was ashimmer with starlight, moonbeams, and ever-present magic.

Two Hearts joined by Fate; Aliens no more.
Light conquered Darkness; Fiery passions soar.
On Wings of Splendor, these lovers wish to ride;
Trekking a Universe so perilous and wide.
Evil has settled; Treachery has fled;
Peace and Love now rule in their stead.
Moonbeams and Magic, though wonderous they be;
A glorious Destiny awaited Child Number Three.

Author's Note

It was a thrilling challenge to create Book #4 in the "Moondust Series", a saga that stands on its own for those of you who haven't read the first three books, but I hope you will. I am grateful for the letters so many of you sent to me and to my publisher Kensington Books requesting its continuation. I originally planned three books in the series After writing #3, Starla and Dagan leapt into my head and heart and begged me to share their romance and adventures. Naturally I was hooked immediately and helpless to resist their pleas.

If you missed sagas #1-3 the revised, re-edited, new editions are available from Amazon/Georgia Girl Books or through your local bookstore. These new editions feature amazing new covers and interiors by Ashley Fontainne of *One of a Kind Covers*. If you buy a print or ebook without the new cover, you will not be getting the updated and revised edition.

Ebook revised editions with new covers are being released by Kensington Publishing Company, available via all electronic sources.

Audio books of new editions are in the works.

In book #1, *Moondust And Madness,* Commander Varian Saar (Zar) of Maffei abducts Earthling research scientist Jana Greyson to take her to his galaxy as a captive mate, as most of the Maffeian females were rendered sterile years ago by an enemy's treachery. Jana finds herself a pawn in an intergalactic struggle with foes determined to destroy Varian and to conquer his world. Jana seeks her fate and freedom with an alien starship commander whose looks, fame, power, status, wealth, and prowess are enormous. Yet, his secrets are many and hazardous.

Under their law and from enemy threats, Jana is out of Varian's reach as a mate. Or is she...

In book #2, *Stardust And Shadows,* is a sequel to #1. Jana, after winning Varian's love and acceptance, believes she went to sleep in his arms and aboard his vessel, a bright future in store for them. But she awakens on Darkar—weakened and dazed from a near-lethal illness—to find herself with Varian's treacherous half-brother, legally bound forever to Ryker Triloni, a scientific genius, owner of Trilabs, one of the most powerful and invincible forces in existence. Worse, Varian is about to wed another woman, Jana's arch-rival and the bitter enemy who had placed her in Ryker's clutches. She is forced to accept the truth that she loved and trusted the wrong brother. But Ryker seems to be changing for the better and he promises to save Earth from certain doom, as he possesses the only weapons and knowledge that can do so. Yet, there is a price she must pay for his aid: she must surrender willingly to him and produce him an heir to his holdings and to the rulership of the Androas Galaxy, for which Ryker is next in line. As a gigantic meteor heads for Earth and the Tri-Galaxy heads for war, Ryker pursues her heart and commitment with a sincerity she cannot deny.

In book #3, *Starlight And Splendor,* twenty-six years have passed since Ryker's death and the marriage between Jana and Varian, who are still very much in love and savoring blissful passions. Now, their twins face perils and bittersweet romances. Galen seeks his destiny in the arms of a beautiful and deceitful seductress who might be his doom and a destroyer of his world. During what was to be a short visit to Earth with the Sangers to study her mother's world, Amaya's wits, courage, and skills are tested to the fullest when she meets an irresistible but forbidden Earthling and is taken captive by evil scientists. All Saars join forces to battle their sadistic enemies and to thwart certain destruction of their galaxy when an alien virus—one without a cure that spreads and kills rapidly and against which the Maffeians have no immunity—is unleashed on their planets, along with vicious criminals who wreak havoc on all planets before they mysteriously vanish until a next attack, forewarned by an unknown traitor. Three romances and many adventures are entwined in this story as the Saars battle for survival and to win the hearts of those they love.

Many of you have requested more books in this series. If Fate and time allow, I will write #5 about the grandchildren of Varian and Jana. Many notes are done with a working title of *Moondust Rapture*.

Check me out at www.janelletaylor.com, and on my author page at Amazon.

Reading is fun and educational, so do it often. Until next time, best wishes from *Janelle Taylor*.

About the Author

JANELLE TAYLOR has won multiple awards for her writing and books, and has nine *New York Times* bestsellers. The University of Georgia Library houses a collection of her books, manuscripts and papers, including the hand-written manuscripts of the first two books in this series. She writes in many genres for various publishers with Kensington as her first and longtime publisher. She also publishes with Amazon/KDP under her Georgia Girl Press imprint. She has over 65+ million books in print, plus ebooks and audio books. She has 57 books in print, three 3/bk collections, and has contributed to other authors' works. She is published worldwide, in many languages, and Braille. She is listed in the Top 100 Most Famous Georgians, RWA Hall of Fame, RWA Honor Roll, Legends of Romance, Pioneers of the Romance Industry, and has been featured in and on the covers of numerous magazines and newspapers, including *New York Times Business Week*. She has appeared on/in numerous TV shows, radio programs, and newspapers across the USA. She co-hosted a book show on QVC.

Janelle has been married to Michael for 54 years, has two married daughters and four grandchildren. Before becoming an author, she worked as a Medical Research Technologist IV at Medical College of Georgia.

Made in the USA
Monee, IL
01 September 2022